SENTINEL
EVENT

ALSO BY E.A. PADILLA

Rule One Twenty

Michaso

Tunnels

Gamers

SENTINEL

EVENT

E.A. PADILLA

EAP Publishing

Sentinel Event

E.A. Padilla

EAP Publishing

eappublishing.com

Copyright 2022 E.A. Padilla

ISBN 978-0-9664818-4-7 (paperback)

Second Edition 2022

Copy edited by Gordi Moeller

Back cover photograph provided by
grafixbygordi.
from the heart

PUBLISHER'S NOTE

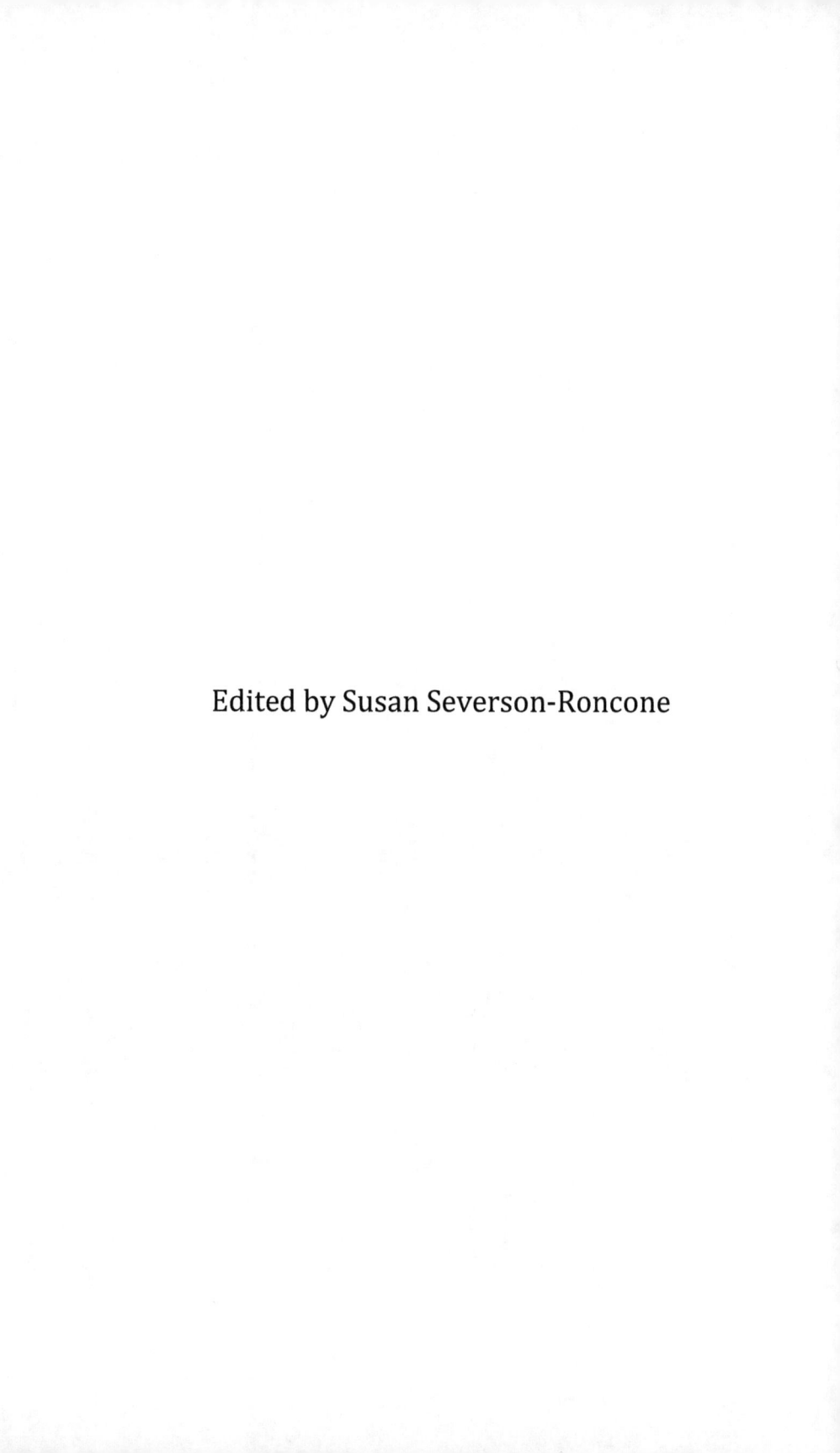

Edited by Susan Severson-Roncone

Dedication

I want to extend a shout out of gratitude to my friends, loyal readers, and family. Thanks to those who volunteered the use of their names for newly introduced characters in this book: My friends Peter Katzmark, Cathy Chapin, Julie Walters, LaRae (Winstead) Pfeffen, Marty & Jean Sweet, Joyce Kaiser, Bessie Sinor-Gebien, Martin Schmid, Theresa Gall, Roberta Finchum, and Brianna Van Aelst Johnson. Also, a special thanks to Yvonne Berkenkotter-Ick for introducing me to the term "Sentinel Event".

In Memory of Robert J. Neebling

1

He was down to his last case file. His thirty-six-year career in law enforcement flew by. For the last eighteen years, he was a homicide detective in the San Jose Police Department. Peter Katzmark was born and raised in downtown Chicago. A smoker since graduating college, a habit that worsened after entering the U.S. Marine Corp. He had that typical scratchy smoker's voice. His face was stern, projecting a serious demeanor. Those that knew the "real" Katzmark saw through the façade.

Katzmark was determined to close his rediscovered case before retiring. It involved a male patient admitted into the hospital without any identification, no next of kin or any one capable of identifying him. Once these types of patients enter the hospital, the hospital is required to contact local law enforcement. Until the person is identified, there are specific rules and guidelines to follow. This protocol was called a "Sentinel Event."

In most cases, Sentinel Events end quickly. A family member, friend or by-stander provides information to help law enforcement identify the person. In cases where no one comes forward, many patients wake and self-confirm who they are. On some rare occasions, no one steps forward, and no new information is obtained and exacerbated if the patient never regains consciousness. Or does but is unable to speak and communicate. This oddity is most frequent in brain trauma cases. For the safety of the patient and surviving next of kin, law enforcement is required to investigate to determine the person's identity.

"Joan?"

"Yes detective."

"I'm heading down to O'Conner Hospital. This is it. I'm down to my last case file," Katzmark said with a hopeful smile. "Where's the portable Blue Check ID Scanner?"

"It's in the spare Crown Vic. Car eleven," she replied. She raised her eyes and looked away from her paper covered desk and pointed at the clipboard hanging on the wall. Detective Katzmark sauntered over and grabbed the keys. He slid the clipboard under his arm and practically skipped out of the area heading toward the station parking lot.

Katzmark was the most senior homicide detective and worked some of the more high-profile homicides in the Bay Area. He even worked the strange, apparent heart attack that Drakeson, the eccentric weapons contractor, succumbed to. Drakeson's hobby was buying and racing horses. During one of his horse races at the new Bay Meadow Race Track, he suffered a sudden heart attack in front of the crowded track restaurant. During the mayhem, his body was somehow lost while in transit. Katzmark worked that case.

Now, on the door steps to retirement, down to his last few days, there was no need for a partner. Katzmark would fly solo.

"Hey Pedro! Where are you going?" asked the Police Captain who paused in the hallway leading to the parking lot.

"Heading to O'Conner Hospital. Trying to clear my last case before I hit the road Cap!" Katzmark's case load had been reduced from the high-water mark of one-hundred-and-twelve to this final straggler. The captain opened the door for Peter.

"Sounds good Katzmark."

As the door closed, the captain felt a slight twinge of envy. At the end of the month, Katzmark was out of there with ninety percent of his normal pay as his pension. Katzmark's wife had passed several years before. He still had family in Chicago and back in Germany. He had already renewed his passport and purchased a round-trip first-class ticket to Berlin. He would be there three months to travel throughout Europe. He couldn't wait to start his retirement. His cubicle was covered with brochures of every country he planned on visiting.

As detective Katzmark climbed into the dark brown *Ford Crown Victoria*, he turned on the air conditioning full blast. He glanced around the parking lot before he lit a cigarette. He made sure to crack his window before he climbed in and reminded himself to exhale the smoke out the open window. For years, the captain rode him about smoking in the cars. Now, it was useless; he was a short timer.

Katzmark opened the thin folder and read the summary. A Caucasian male, approximately thirty years old, no tattoos, five-foot-ten, one hundred and eighty pounds. The patient was admitted into *O'Conner Hospital's* ER. He cringed when he noticed the admission date; almost three years ago. Katzmark failed to notify the hospital administrator, who should have called weekly in search of the patient's relatives. That had not happened.

Katzmark turned the page and reacquainted himself with this John Doe's injuries. The patient was found at the site of a gas leak explosion that leveled a house. It was assumed the patient was the owner or from the neighborhood. But upon further investigation, the homeowner died in a commercial plane accident from Los Angeles to Hawaii. The home was on the market to be sold.

The assumption was that this unfortunate John Doe was just somebody out for a walk and had the misfortune of being next to the empty house when it blew up. No one came forward and a "Sentinel Event" was called by the hospital. They needed help locating the next of kin.

Katzmark was embarrassed that nothing was done for the last three years. These types of cases almost always ended with either the patient dying or a family member coming forward. Upon death, a more pressing protocol is required which expedites the matter. The morgue housing the corpse elevates the urgency until the issue is resolved. In this case, because the person had regained consciousness, combined with a next of kin coming forward and paying the hospital bill, there was no constant follow up initiated by the hospital. Given that many of these types of cases result in the death of the patient, it made sense to assign these cases to a homicide detective from the onset given they would become involved in most cases anyway.

As Katzmark pulled out of the parking lot and guessed that this John Doe either died or regained consciousness. It was the only thing that made any sense. If the patient was still considered a John Doe, the hospital would be doing everything it could to locate the next of kin and recover from all the expenses. Based on an indigent patient health directive reimbursement protocol, Katzmark hoped the hospital had secured the release from the morgue and submitted the paperwork to recover their expenses. In their haste, they probably neglected to notify him. Three years was too long for them not to have resolved the issue by now. Before retiring, Katzmark's goal was to close this last file.

As the traffic light turned green, Detective Katzmark tapped his cigarette and exhaled a thick billow of smoke. With the air conditioning blasting, that smoke escaped outside through the cracked window. The breeze knocked cigarette ash sending flakes toward the back-seat area. Katzmark made a mental note to pick up some air freshener before turning in the car. What were they going to do, write him up?

*   *   *   *   *

Curt recuperated in Germany. After being whisked away from the Agency, he had a brief stay in the Las Vegas Burn Center. After regaining consciousness there and stabilizing, he was transferred. For the rest of his life, he would need to deal with the scars covering most of his body. Since that accident, when he was not focused or preoccupied by something, his mind would replay what had happened.

Curt remembered smelling the strong odor of natural gas. By the time he recognized the danger, it was too late. He was lucky to have survived at all. After reviewing his medical records, he learned that he had almost died enroute to the hospital and had flat-lined while in surgery. He was lucky. It must not have been his time.

Diane Klein had saved his life. If he had not been rescued, the Agency would have finished him off. He would never have regained consciousness. She was motivated to save Curt to learn the truth about her niece. She had to be careful. She was acting on her own without the knowledge or consent of her employer. After learning the truth, she was confused about her loyalties. How could she betray the Agency, her country? She felt overwhelmed by the discovery that Curt Anderson had, somehow, escaped the plane before it crashed. It made no sense. Why did the Agency act so reckless?

Curt was shocked to learn that the Agency had murdered hundreds of innocent Americans, including Diane's niece, to hide the evidence. What he knew could never be made public. It was something that the Agency could not resolve by reprimanding a few select employees. What Curt knew would prove the widespread involvement and coordinated efforts by a sophisticated network. It went well beyond a few rogue agents. It would implicate the entire US intelligence community.

During Curt's recovery, Diane used him as a sounding board. During those talks, therapy sessions really, he focused on her every word, every fact, every idea, every theory she had on the matter. Through those conversations, a sense of trust, a bond was established that strengthened with each visit. He believed, for now anyway, that she could be trusted. Without her help, he would have died. During that time, Curt awoke to find Diane at his side.

Each weekend she traveled to Las Vegas. She took the first flight from San Jose on Friday night and returned on the Sunday evening flight. When she arrived, she used a device and scanned Curt's room, making sure there were no listening devices.

At first, Curt thought Diane was over thinking the Agency's desire to pursue him. He was certain that the Agency still thought he'd died on the plane. When Diane shared that the Agency entered his hospital room, after his transfer to Las Vegas, and killed another burn victim by mistake, that all changed. He realized that the Agency knew he had somehow escaped the plane. Hearing about this second attempt on his life, Curt formulated his own plan. Recovering from his gross disfigurement became secondary to his bigger concern. He was confident he would survive his injuries. His biggest concern now was to keep moving.

Curt knew his days were numbered. He had no idea how long he had until the Agency found out. It was inevitable. There were too many loose ends, a literal paper trail. With the resources available to the Agency, they would learn the truth. Then, it would not take long to track him down. He needed to continue to transfer to new hospitals and reduce the paper trail, while creating misdirected leads to nowhere.

For the time being, Curt's saving grace was that the Agency thought he was dead. The facts surrounding his murder were hidden inside the Director's file, locked away inside Director Gamboa's safe. For now, the case was still closed.

Curt turned to his only living relative, his biological grandfather. While still attending college, Curt's mother passed away. At her funeral, Curt reconnected with his grandfather. For his age, he was in excellent health and in great physical shape; thin, standing six feet four inches tall, and weighing no more than 180 pounds. He had short-cropped hair with side burns. Surprisingly, there were no facial wrinkles to speak of. His most distinguishing trait was his piercing bright blue eyes. He had an intense stare and an air of sophistication, power, and authority. Just by looking at him, he evoked a man that demanded respect. At his mother's funeral, his grandfather convinced him to spend a year abroad to study in Germany.

Confined to a bed in the Las Vegas Burn Center hospital, he had to trust Diane with another favor. He had no choice. There was no one else to turn to. He asked her to call his grandfather. Curt recited a telephone number that his grandfather made him memorize. He recited it as soon as he awoke in the morning, with every meal, and before he went to bed. It had become a daily ritual. His last week in Germany, he was forced to recite the number each time he drank or ate anything. It was a number that only a select few knew existed. This number could never be written down. It was to be used only under dire circumstances.

Curt instructed her to explain everything. He would learn soon enough. Curt listed his grandfather as the sole heir to his estate. The house, life insurance, and remaining money from both of his parents' life insurance policies. He had a sizeable net worth.

"Diane. I have a favor to ask."

"What is it?"

"I need you to purchase a pre-paid cell phone. It needs to be able to make international calls."

"To which country?"

"Germany."

Curt watched as Diane's face tightened. Confusion and concern washed over her face. The request added to her suspicions causing her to question his innocence. Understanding her concerns, he needed to keep her informed, full disclosure. The last thing he needed was to create suspicion and make her question his intentions. It was inevitable that she considered the possibility that he was a spy, justifying her employer's attention.

"I promise that together, we will make the call. I will place the call on speaker phone. I will let you hear every word that is spoken."

"Who will you call?"

"My grandfather. He lives in Berlin, Germany. I spent a year living with him as a foreign exchange student. He is listed as my sole beneficiary. He is my only living relative. I have no one else. He will have the means to help me get out of the U.S."

Diane studied Curt's eyes. She listened to each word, each phrase, and every inflection of his voice. She knew he was telling the truth.

"Okay. I'll do it. I'll be right back."

*   *   *   *   *

Curt stared out across the Spree River. His modest apartment looked out over the water front. The river traveled 255 miles through Berlin to the Czech Republic toward the North Sea. It was an area during the Cold War where many people died trying to cross the Berlin Wall. But that had been decades earlier. Now, it offered a beautiful, picturesque setting, where the Bode Museum and the Oberbaum Bridge hid its macabre past.

Curt escaped the U.S., putting as much distance between him and the Agency as possible. He turned to the only living relative he had; his biological grandfather, Cornelius Van Aelst. He remembered making the call with Diane from his Las Vegas hospital room. She heard the entire conversation and even spoke with his grandfather. She was instrumental in orchestrating several other intermediate transfers that were orchestrated by his grandfather. Diane finally met him during his final transfer from New Jersey. All the transfers between each hospital took several months. His grandfather was patient. He knew that initiating the transfers too close together would draw unwanted attention.

He made it appear that each transfer was based on Curt's progress. Each time they moved him, it was deemed a signal, a step forward into Curt's medical recovery. Each new hospital represented another rehabilitative milestone. His grandfather's handlers explained to each departing and receiving facility that the transfer was based on the receiving facility's specialized area needed to further Curt's recovery. From skin grafts, burn specific cosmetic enhancements, counseling developed specifically for burn victims, and so forth. Van Aelst held telephone conference calls with Curt and Diane detailing and then rehearsing the storyline behind each move. With precise planning, each transfer went smooth without any of the facilities being the wiser. None of these reasons mattered. Van Aelst's primary goal was to continue to hop around the continental United States transferring Curt from facility to facility, creating new names, new background stories describing how he was injured, where he came from, and where he was headed.

With each transfer, Curt's name was changed. Different birthdates, driver's license numbers, social security card numbers, home addresses and parents' names. It was all fabricated and weaved into his new temporary life. With each transfer, Curt slipped farther and farther away from the grasp of the Agency. His grandfather made sure that Diane was informed during each transfer. He kept her in the loop. She had proven her worth and could be trusted. Van Aelst learned years ago, that understanding a person's motivation was not the key. The key was to witness a person's actions. Loyalty was demonstrated not verbalized.

Before leaving for Germany, Van Aelst devised a plan where Curt and Diane would remain in contact using a simple yet effective means of communication through a public email system. On the thirteenth of each month, she would compose and save an email. It would be held in the out-folder. The next day, Curt would open, read, and then delete the message. He would follow the same process to reply. The following day, Diane would retrieve the composed message, read then delete the entire message. Using a specialized program, she would permanently erase that section of computer memory so that no address, password, or connection histories could be found.

From his second-floor window, Curt stared down at the clean brick lined roadway below, and watched his grandfather exit the train. Like most everything in Germany, the train was right on schedule. For a man in his late eighties, Curt's grandfather looked great. His mind was sharp as a tack. He was in good physical condition and visited a gym three times a week. His workout included cycling machine for an hour, swimming ten laps in the indoor pool and lifting free weight dumbbells. Upon waking, he performed 50 perfect military push-ups followed by 50 sit ups. It was like an old Jack Lalanne regimen, old school physical fitness. The cliché of "use it or lose it". Still donning a full head of silver-gray hair, he kept it meticulous, seeing his barber each week. In the states, you were hard pressed to find a man in his early 60's in such good physical and mental condition.

Curt watched his grandfather pause along the street corner. Van Aelst wore dark sunglasses and a knee-high trench coat. Curt could just make out his grandfather's face behind the rolled-up fur collar. With each breath, a billow of steam rose up distorting the image of his hidden face. Van Aelst never looked up. His grandfather knew Curt was hidden behind the drawn curtains watching him below. Curt learned that his grandfather had worked as a Field Agent for the Stasi, the German Democratic Republic State Security Police. Through that experience, Van Aelst gained a special set of skills that he never lost and had only slightly diminished. Van Aelst told Curt that he was now retired and maintained a non-active status within the now defunct Stasi organization.

During the Cold War, his grandfather had been captain in the hated and feared GDR's (German Democratic People Aka East Germany) State Secret Police. Having ties to the original Nazi Party as a youth, it was natural for him to be recruited into the Stasi following World War II. Having studied in London and traveled inside the United States, he spoke perfect English with only a slight German accent. In his later years, he was a recruiter tasked with planting covert GDR Stasi Agents abroad. He was responsible for developing sleeper agents in hopes of utilizing them for some unknown reason in the future. He was known as a "gardener".

Following the death of Curt's mother, Van Aelst considered recruiting Curt. It was an informal project. Van Aelst kept Curt's training off the books. No one in the Stasi organization knew about this association. Because of the circumstances surrounding Curt's adoption, no one in Europe knew of their blood relationship. During those college years, Curt had become Van Aelst's hobby project. It kept them in contact without drawing unnecessary attention. No one in the old GDR knew Curt even existed. The official records showed that his daughter had passed away while delivering her first child.

When the GDR learned about the child's adoption, everyone assumed that Van Aelst had no interest in raising the child on his own. By this time, Van Aelst had been a widow for years. The GDR assumed Van Aelst favored the adoption to avoid being burdened by familial responsibilities. In the dark world of espionage, being a widower without any family was a plus. There would be no distractions. It was a common factor when selecting covert agents. Being alone, allowed the agent to be more focused, and less susceptible to coercion. There were no loved ones to leverage. No one to protect from being kidnapped; no other lives to threaten to control the agent. No family reunions or weddings to attend. No double lives to lead simply to protect others. There were literally no distractions. Van Aelst liked it that way. He earned the nickname of "The Lone Wolf". It fit.

Peeking through the curtains, Curt watched his grandfather step off the curb and stride across the boulevard. With a slight tilt of his head, and a brief smirk, Curt saw his grandfather glance up toward the covered curtain window. With a smile, Curt suspected, even though it was impossible for his grandfather to see him, he somehow knew Curt was watching. If anything was wrong, Curt was instructed to leave the curtains open. This was their signal. It warned his grandfather not to come up.

Van Aelst continued through the crosswalk passing in front of the apartment. He then cut across the street and hailed a cab. He instructed the driver to take him across town and wait for him outside of a coffee shop while he ordered an espresso and pastries to go. After scanning the area, certain he was not being followed, he exited the café. After scanning the streets, he glanced up in the sky for a plane or drone. It took some effort before he knew he was in the clear. Carrying the pastry bag and his espresso back to the cab, he instructed the driver to take him to the ferry terminal. After being dropped off, Van Aelst waited for the taxi to drive out of view before he hailed another cab from another taxi company and instructed this new driver to take him in the opposite direction.

For the next hour, Van Aelst darted across the city. He switched from the cab, then walked a short distance to the city bus. Each conveyance, he paid for the services with cash. These bills were wiped clean prior to the trip and were only touched with his gloved fingers. He never over tipped and avoided doing anything that would draw attention and could be recalled later. He avoided conversations, animated expressions, or unusual comments. Van Aelst did everything in his power to be ordinary and unremarkable. He tried to blend in and remain forgotten. It worked. Over the decades, he mastered the ability to blend in. It was second nature.

Van Aelst checked his watch. His training was engrained to the point that the entire "cat and mouse" charade was part of his normal everyday process. He did it unconsciously. It was something he automatically factored in when he met his contacts. He was never caught and remained hidden in plain view. He walked the last five blocks meandering through the back alley and cutting through businesses. He avoided using the same business locations more than once every year. He never wanted to be predictable.

Finally, he arrived at the downstairs common laundry room of Curt's apartment. Van Aelst used the restroom making a point of flushing the toilet. This was an older building. The plumbing was loud, and the noise of the downstairs lavatory could be heard from Curt's apartment. It was his signal to Curt. He was inside the building and prepared to enter the second-floor landing.

Curt felt a slight vibration along the water pipe that ran through his bedroom wall, to the downstairs lavatory. His grandfather was the one that heard it first. If he had not pointed it out, it would have gone unnoticed. Hearing the signal, Curt shuffled across the wooden floor toward the back bedroom.

Curt's legs were still stiff from the skin grafts taken from his thighs. What little hair Curt still had on his head he chose to keep his head shaved; at least until his hair began to grow back evenly. His facial scars healed without discoloration. Only from a close examination, could one see the scar tissue. Otherwise, his face looked normal. His doctors were certain that his face would heal, improving to the point that no one would guess he had been severely burned. Other than his hair growth issues and the loss of hearing in his right ear, he was in rather good health.

Everything was fine. While his grandfather bounced around the city to shake any tail that may be following, Curt watched the ten remote wireless cameras. During the late evenings, he installed them. He felt the best he had in years. As an electrician, installing the cameras gave him something to do. Up until that point, it had been the only time he went outside. He avoided contact with anyone in the building.

Curt enjoyed these visits. They were his only real connection to the outside world. His grandfather still brought food and supplies. They had agreed. It was best to avoid home deliveries. All their efforts were to enhance the charade that Curt no longer existed. He was forced to hide, isolated alone inside this apartment.

The ten monitor screens reminded Curt of his previous hidden surveillance room. The room that no longer existed. Destroyed along with his house in the explosion. Unlike in San Jose, California, these cameras did not need to be hidden in a secret closet. Only Curt and his grandfather would ever see the equipment. If someone from the Agency discovered his location, they would not be concentrating on the monitors.

Curt heard the creaking stairway. It was his grandfather making his way up to his third story apartment unit. Since everything was clear, Curt kept the doormat facing the doorway. It was another signal. If the words "Willkommen" were facing opposite, upside down toward the unit, it would warn his grandfather to keep walking. They also used a back-up signal involving the hallway camera. If there was a problem, he would switch the LED light to red. Utilizing either of these signals required Curt to have enough time. They each understood that it was still possible to be caught off-guard, unable to leave any warning.

Curt heard someone approaching the doorway. The distinct echo of footsteps on the old wooden stairway was another reason his grandfather chose this location. As agreed, Curt retreated to the deep corner of the apartment and hid behind the bedroom door. Curt ducked inside and left enough of the door open to peek through. Closing one eye, Curt squinted through the opening and waited.

*   *   *   *   *

Diane was adjusting to her new reality. Since the death of her niece Gina, Diane's life had forever changed. The Agency, once the source of her life's work, transformed into a perverse corrupt institution that no longer held her respect. After returning from a two week break from work, she found herself dwelling over the clandestine missions she had participated in. She began counting the number of recruits she evaluated, how many lives she had ruined all for the sake of the greater good.

Her niece's death was the sole cause of her change of heart. It was a human reaction. As people age, things that were once important, become less meaningful. Age has a way of mellowing a person. The burning desire to pursue a promotion, achieve some form of recognition, diminishes. The sudden and unexpected loss of her niece, a person whom Diane helped raise, expedited this process. Diane felt a deep sense of guilt for encouraging Gina to pursue a career in the Agency. Diane breached protocol asking the Director to give her niece extra attention. Diane wondered if she had not been so persistent, maybe Gina would not have pursued the Agency? Maybe she would not have been selected? None of that mattered. She was picked.

To Diane's shock, she began contemplating the absolute arrogance and total disregard the Agency showed toward others. For the first time, Diane was impacted by one of the Agency's decisions. A decision that tossed away the lives of everyone on board the airplane, including her niece. Diane could not stop thinking about it. The sadness, loss, and betrayal replayed over and over in her mind on a continuous loop. She became fixated on what happened.

As each week passed, Diane's attitude worsened. She began fantasizing about paying back the Agency and those involved. She reasoned that those in charge knew that Gina was her niece. How could they have let that happen? Why not consider all the years of dedicated service she showed the Agency? Had that loyalty warranted their consideration for her loved one? Especially from the Director. It would have been his call. He should have protected Gina. Diane's mind replayed this betrayal. Her feelings and the well-being of her family was disregarded. She was thrown away like a used paper cup tossed into the trash can.

Without realizing it, Diane sat frozen in a deep trance, staring out into the empty lobby. The noise from her tapping toe drummed out in a steady cadence. The sharp staccato snap of her heel echoed off the lobby walls. The very same room Gina entered for her interview months before.

"Lt. Colonel Klein?" asked the guard.

Diane turned her head and stared up into the guard's face. After exhaling a deep sigh, she recognized his blank confused expression. She allowed her shoe a finale slap against the tile floor before responding.

"Yes."

"That was our last interview. No one else is scheduled for the day. Are you waiting for someone?" he asked. "We're getting ready to secure the lobby and transfer the surveillance tapes to archive."

"Oh right." She forgot. She glanced up at the wall mounted clock. It was almost 5:00pm. "Sorry about that. I was thinking we had one more"

With a soft self-conscious smile, Diane turned and walked through the double doors. The guard held the doors open. then closed them behind her. After she passed through heading toward her office, there she saw Director Gamboa leaving. He paused, glanced up the hallway, and waved. Diane raised her hand and waved back. She turned and walked down the hallway. With her back to the Director, she whispered "bastard."

*   *   *   *   *

Director Gamboa was finishing up a file review with Agent Cathy Chapin. Chapin was a rising star from Northern California. She spent a lot of time in the State Capitol, Sacramento. After graduating with a master's degree in Criminal Justice, she had hopes of pursuing a career in law enforcement. She interned as the CSI (Crime Scene Investigator) for the Sacramento Sheriffs. Those plans changed. During a career recruitment day on campus, she was approached. She had no way of knowing that he was an Agency recruiter. He was one of her professors.

Throughout the year, while teaching, he included a few Agency recruiting questions in tests and quizzes. They were dropped inside mid-terms and final exams. At the end of the term, the professor used the answers to these questions to create a candidate-profile. Based on these results, the Agency identified the top candidates and placed them under the microscope. Chapin had no clue she was under constant evaluation throughout her entire undergraduate studies. The Agency funneled their top candidate through certain professors. The University had no clue these classes were filmed and later dissected by Agency recruiters. For candidates that continued toward an advanced degree, more test questions were hidden in more quizzes and exams. The Agency went so far as to hack the University system making sure that each semester, their professors taught at least one of the courses for each potential agent. Over time, the candidates were whittled down until they arrived at their top two candidates.

Chapin was a rarity. The Agency had monitored Chapin's entire college career. Most candidates transferred in from a Junior College. In Chapin's case, they monitored four years of undergraduate and then two more years in her master's Program. By the end of the six years, the Agency knew everything. During the initial phases of her evaluation, the level of surveillance and screening increased. Before the Job Fair, the Agency had bugged her cell phone, internet connection and laptop. Each device was duplicated and mirrored so that the Agency could monitor all her communication activities. Her apartment and intern's desk at the Sheriff's Department were bugged for both video and audio. All her financial records, credit card statements, student loans, and housing records were reviewed.

Until she willingly applied for the job, a full background and security clearance interview would not be done. To encourage her, the Agency made sure to spoon feed her favorable news articles and stories, recommending books, anything that would reinforce the benefits and joys of working for the government. Although the Agency name was not displayed, her *YouTube* account and *iPod* playlist were tampered to provide subliminal suggestions. She had been bombarded non-stop for six years. Every video she streamed, every *Google* search she ran, every song she played on her *iPod*, the Agency was there working its magic.

Cathy was an avid reader. She was also one of the few students who took German as her foreign language. Upon entering the Agency, she was sent to an advanced language training and immersed into both German and Russian languages. Like most other agents, she spent her personal time watching *CSI*, *Bones* and *Dexter*. It was something about these people that gravitated her toward this occupation. This predisposition was in their DNA.

"Good work on that case Chapin," said Director Gamboa. It was one of those rare moments when he truly meant it. She just cleared a "Snap Shot" case (a spur of the moment decision) that required an entire family to disappear. It was another file that would be locked away in the Director's Only safe.

"Thank you, Director," replied Chapin. With down cast eyes, she stood and stretched her right hand out to shake his hand.

"Any plans?" he asked.

"Just heading home. Just got the final season of *Dexter* on DVD. Gonna binge watch it this weekend," she said with a big smile.

"Oh man! I love that series," Director Gamboa replied.

*   *   *   *   *

Everything was different. A new name, a new identity, and now working overseas. Previously she had spent a little time in Europe. The most difficult part of this new assignment was breaking all her ties. No more contact with family and friends. Just before she took the plunge, she created a fictitious *Facebook* profile and "friended" herself. She knew that it was the only way she could safely troll her friends without anyone, even the Agency, knowing. She thought to herself "who would it hurt?" She had no plans of posting, commenting, or liking anything. Even though she could never re-establish contact, she just wanted a means to follow their lives from afar.

After disappearing, she waited several months before sneaking into the library to check her accounts. Seeing the tributes discussing her sudden death, made her feel guilty to cause so much pain. She recognized that this was what happened. What she did was not unique. All deep cover agents went through it.

The Agency relocated her to France. This location was geographically placed at the center of Europe; the UK to the north; Spain, Italy, and Africa south; and Germany and the old Eastern Bloc countries to the east. The Paris office was a great training ground where the Agency broke in their newest international recruits. There were only a select few of these types of agents. By design, these agents were separated from their comfort zones, forced to assimilate into another country. This isolation helped the newbies remain focused. Until these green horn rookies cut their teeth, they would be stationed in Paris for the next 36 months.

The newbies could tag along during active cases, playing only back up roles. After graduating from this training period, many would be sent abroad to begin the creation of yet another new cover story for a life that the Agency would conjure up to fit the needs and circumstances of the situation. This lifestyle required these agents to be, for the most part, self-sufficient. If their cover was blown, even inside of an allied nation, depending on the circumstances, it could result in the agent being imprisoned as a spy. In some extreme cases, even executed.

Valued agents are classified as a persona non-grata and are granted diplomatic cover as a low-level duty attaché. If discovered, the agent would face being expelled from the country. Although such situations did not result in physical harm to the agent, their career as a clandestine agent would be over. Depending on the circumstances of the outing, the agent might be allowed to finish their career in some other domestic capacity. Many senior analysts arrived at their current positions down this path.

Assignments abroad are like a double-edged sword. Agents are recognized as important assets and allowed to prove their value abroad. However, if their assignments are deemed intrusive enough, even an ally nation would be forced to disavow the agent within twelve hours. The result is one of abandonment by the Agency and its allies. Abandonment, in most cases, would result in a death sentence.

Roberta Finchum was cleared. This name was her new Agency name. All prior associations under her original birth identity were scrubbed. That person no longer existed, legally dead. Roberta was now who she was. Until she completed her 36 month trainee agent tour, she was assigned as a low-level attaché with diplomatic immunity. Roberta was someone the Agency held with high regard.

"Hey Finchum!" yelled her new Supervisor Sinor. Sinor was another American Agency transplant. Originally assigned to the Berlin Office, Sinor was stationed in Europe for the last fifteen years. After concluding her deep cover assignment in Germany, the Agency kept her in Europe. She was a key player for the Agency and acted as the primary field trainer.

"Yes ma'am?" replied Finchum. It was getting easier for Roberta to recognize Finchum as her name. It was not an immediate response. There was still a slight delay. A trained field agent would have noticed, just from the pause, that something was off.

Supervisor Sinor paused flashing a slight frown toward Finchum. She could not hide her dissatisfaction at her delayed response. Without speaking, her expression said it all.

"We've got a little drop taking place tomorrow. It's local and I want you to get your feet wet. Just a little."

Roberta flashed an eager grin, trying to suppress the flutter of internal excitement. Finchum's eyes widened as she stared back at Supervisor Sinor.

"Are you up for it?"

"Yes ma'am. In any capacity. Whatever role you have for me. I'm ready."

Supervisor Sinor held her stern gaze before glancing and staring out the window. Atop the 27th floor office, only the Director of Paris had a better view. She worried about her agents proud yet to lose one. She knew maintaining a perfect record was unrealistic. It was a mathematical certainty. She turned her head away from the glass window and stared down her newest trainee agent Finchum. She thought to herself "Would Finchum be my first?"

"The lead agent will be LaRae Dubois. I'll introduce you to her this afternoon. We'll go over your role during the briefing."

Sinor stood and shoved her right hand out. The meeting was over. Finchum stood and exchanged a firm handshake before bolting for the door. Finchum's blood was pumping. It was natural. Regardless of her role, it was happening. She just received her first assignment. She could not wait.

As Roberta closed the Supervisor's door, she made a beeline to the indoor shooting range. The Agency had a special basement area deep inside protected by ten-foot-thick concrete reinforced walls. Shooting her *9mm Barretta* always kept her focused. Just a quick three clips to calm her nerves. There was something about the pungent smell of nitroglycerin after firing. It was calming.

*   *   *   *   *

Director Gamboa pulled out his encoded red ink blot stamp and saturated the stamp in the ink. With a loud thump, the Director forced his stamped impression on the cover of the thick case folder. After placing his thumb into the ink, he pressed down transferring his print onto the cover, then signed, dated, and time stamped the file. It was one of those special folders destined to be locked away inside the Director's safe.

He opened the safe. As he slid this file inside, he saw the corner of the last file that he stored inside peeking out. That other file was much thicker and stowed in the maximum storage capacity of two legal sized boxes. It was years since he thought about that file and represented the most complicated case of his career. There were so many deaths associated with it. At least "We got the bastard", Gamboa thought to himself. As he placed the new file on top, he felt a sense of satisfaction. The new file covered the top of the Curt Anderson file. Gamboa had no desire to relive that matter again.

After setting the alarm code and securing his room, the Director locked the safe and exited his office.

"Good night, Sandy."

"Good night, Director."

If Gamboa could have predicted what was coming in the weeks to follow, he would have taken his wife out to a nice dinner and a movie. But he had no way of knowing what was in store. His most difficult case, the Curt Anderson file, was about to raise its ugly head.

*　　*　　*　　*　　*

Detective Katzmark waited in the hospital administrator's lobby. He was unusually happy; more so than he could remember feeling since he had been promoted to homicide. Today was the day. His final case. A basic sentinel event case. It was six months since he unwittingly glanced at the upper corner of the hidden file. The case involved a John Doe that had somehow been injured in an explosion and structural fire. Katzmark assumed that it was some homeless person. A case of being in the wrong place at the wrong time. There was no indication of wrongdoing. As such, Katzmark had no pressure to jump right on it. In his mind, it was more a missing persons case unworthy of his time as a homicide detective.

Over the years, Katzmark learned that most of these cases ended in simple misidentifications. Given that the hospital had not been following up on the matter, the guy probably passed away. If the hospital had not spent too much time and a nominal bill had been generated, it would not be something they were motivated to track down. Either way, Katzmark assumed that the actual disposition of the patient had long sense been resolved. The John Doe case had simply slipped through the cracks of both the hospital and law enforcement systems. Katzmark had already started his paperwork. He just needed copies of the hospital discharge papers to close the case.

As he entered the hospital administration receptionist area, a woman's nasally high-pitched voice interrupted his train of thought.

"The administrator will see you now detective Katzmark."

Katzmark stood, practically bouncing across the lobby as he walked. Even if he tried, he could not wipe the silly grin off his face. His excitement was contagious. Without thinking, the receptionist returned the detective's pleasant smile with one of her own. His positive energy flowed through him. She held the door open allowing the detective to walk into the administrator's office without breaking his stride.

"Peter. Long time no see. What brings you down here?" asked the hospital administrator. Looking over his paper covered desk and overflowing in-basket, the administrator noticed that the detective looked different. Typically, Katzmark's deep wrinkled faced held a perpetual scowl. Today the detective flashed the grin of someone who may have just won the lottery. Like the Cheshire cat, he held an expression that he had just gotten away with something.

"Boy, you certainly look happy detective."

Katzmark flopped down in a stiff metal chair placed in front of the administrator's desk. Holding a thin manila folder, he waved it in front of his face.

"It's my last case. Ever. I retire at the end of the month."

"Good for you. Congratulations! No wonder you're so happy. Any plans?"

"Already bought my first-class tickets to Europe. I'll be staying there for three months. Plan on seeing everything. I'll be visiting my family in Germany before heading back," Katzmark replied. His smile was ear to ear.

"I'm jealous." After a brief pause, the administrator sighed as he surveyed the mountain of paper covering his desk. Eager to get going, he pressed on. "So detective, which case are you interested in? Must be one of the sentinel events, yes?" The administrator seemed distracted as he lifted piles of papers looking for any open files. With a final shrug, he looked up at the detective before continuing. "It looks like we closed all of them. I don't have any open files."

Those words were music to his ears. "I thought so," Katzmark replied. "It was an older case. It must have slipped through the cracks. Normally, I would have followed up before now. But since I hadn't heard from you guys either, I figured it must have resolved itself. Anyway."

"When was it?" asked the administrator.

"It was about three years ago. There was a Caucasian male, in his late twenties or early thirties. He was found in a sub-division house explosion. The fire department confirmed the explosion was caused by a natural gas leak. The entire house blew up. The John Doe was brought here. No ID and no next of kin came forward. His injuries were so serious that the ambulance transport didn't think he would survive the trip to the hospital. After he was admitted, I came down to the hospital and checked him out. He was in very bad condition. His burns were so bad that there was no sense in attempting to get fingerprints." After catching his breath, Katzmark looked up from his notes.

"Oh yeah! I remember hearing about that patient. He survived. As I recall, a relative came forward and identified him. His bill was paid, and he was transported out. Let me pull his file. I'll have the discharge documents copied." The administrator said with a smile and was surprised thinking it was not possible for the detective's attitude to improve any more. As the administrator stood and left the room, Katzmark stood and thrust his arm punching his fist into the air in celebration.

Detective Katzmark could imagine the feel of the plush reclining oversized first-class seat. As he waited for the administrator's return, Katzmark tapped his right foot. Turning his head and watching the administrator return carrying his own folder. He paused in front of his desk and began reading the contents.

"Here we go. Yes, the patient's relative identified him. No insurance information was provided. However, she ended up paying the bill in full. There's a copy of the final bill and her cashier's check. She also arranged for his transfer to another burn center." After he leafed through more paperwork, he looked up from the folder and continued. "His transfer was authorized by the Feds." The administrator punched a button on the intercom sitting on his desk.

"Yes Doctor?"

"Could you please come inside? I need you to copy the discharge papers for the detective."

"Right away."

Detective Katzmark was right. There must have been some mix-up or miscommunication. Anticipating as much, he had already prepared the form. It was ready for the administrator's signature. With a quick flick of his wrist, the detective checked the box with his ink pen to confirm that the patient was identified and discharged. Katzmark placed the pre-completed form on top of the paper stacked on the administrator's desk.

"If you could be so kind as to sign and date this form, I would appreciate it."

As the administrator scribbled his signature, the detective continued. "With the copies of the formal discharge and federal transfer documents, I'm good to go."

With great expectations, Katzmark watched the administrator sign and date the form. Without realizing it, the detective exhaled a deep sigh. For a brief second, Katzmark was startled. He was surprised as an unexpected sadness crept into his thoughts like a slow soft wave permeating inside his chest. This was it. He was done. His life's work was over.

"Detective, are you okay?"

The voice interrupted his train of thought. "No, I'm fine. It just hit me. I'm done. This was my last case, ever. I never really thought about the finality of it all until just now."

"I have a quick remedy for your sudden melancholy feeling detective. Just think about your first-class seat aboard that airplane on its way to Europe, the vacation of your lifetime. Most people only dream of such a thing. You're actually going to do it," he said in an upbeat and envious tone.

Katzmark stared into the administrator's eyes absorbing his words. He was right. The next chapter of his life was about to begin. The administrator stood and reached out to shake his hand.

"Congratulations, detective. You've earned your retirement."

The receptionist entered the room and handed Katzmark the copies. Flashing another ear-to-ear smile, he turned and left the small office. He walked down the corridor. Out of nowhere, a tune came to his mind. The detective, under his breath, began singing, "Zip-a-dee-doo-dah, zip-a-dee-ay," as he practically skipped down the hall. He slid the copy of the discharge papers inside the folder and punched the elevator button. The doors slid open. It was empty. Katzmark entered, punched the button to the downstairs lobby and began searching his pockets for a cigarette.

Once the elevator doors opened, Katzmark made a beeline to the exit doors. As he pushed the heavy double doors open, he flipped a cigarette into his waiting mouth and thumbed his butane lighter. Before his first step landed on the concrete walkway, he inhaled and took a full hit. As he approached the police car, he debated whether to finish his smoke outside of the vehicle. With a quick smirk, he laughed to himself. His entire career, he never followed their stupid rules about smoking in the car and was certainly not going to start now. Taking an extra-large drag, Katzmark opened the door and made a point of exhaling the smoke into the interior of the cab. This small rebellious action brought another smile to his wrinkle lined face. He was going to miss antagonizing his fellow detectives and his captain. He derived a sick kind of pleasure from it all.

Finishing his cigarette, he opened the folder and reviewed the discharge photocopies. Almost immediately, the happy go lucky, higher than a kite emotional high began to wane. Katzmark leaned forward and studied the first page of the federal discharge document. Something did not look right.

Katzmark stopped. Frozen in his seat, he grabbed the paperwork and raised it up close to his face. He pulled down his glasses. He wiped the lenses on his shirt making sure he had a clear unobstructed view. The form. It was an older version. But what struck him as most unusual was the seal.

After 911, all the national law enforcement agencies were required to undergo an extensive all-day training session. The Feds came down, face to face. No videoconference. They wanted to be certain that every branch of law enforcement received the training. The threat of increased domestic attacks, from San Bernardino,

Orlando Night Club shooting, to the Brussels bombing, a greater emphasis was placed on these types of sentinel events. There was a belief that terrorists might attempt more isolated small-scale missions on a local basis. Consequently, should any national law enforcement agency become involved in any capacity, a new universal form would be used.

Implementing a new form was more than symbolic. It marked the beginning of a greater widespread mutual interagency cooperation. A new logo was created. It was a circle divided into equal quadrants depicting a portion of each agencies' emblem. The discharge form copy had no logo seal.

As Katzmark continued to study the form, he considered the possibility that it was an old form. Maybe the agent who authorized the transport of the John Doe had forgotten to stock up with the new form? It was a possibility, he thought.

The detective spent his entire career working inside this bureaucratic system. He had filed countless thousands of forms, log notes and statements. He had reviewed autopsies, receipts, tickets and over time, these form numbers were revised. As Katzmark stared down at the bottom corner of the form, it hit him.

The immediate change in his attitude was like Marlin in the *Disney* Animated movie *Finding Nemo.* At that instant, Katzmark's "good feelings were gone". The huge, ear-to-ear grin evaporated and melted away. His face was now dominated by deep lines and a serious scowl. Even his forehead scrunched up forming a pulsing roll of flesh on his forehead. Any pleasant thoughts about his European vacation vanished. The euphoria from closing his last case evaporated.

Katzmark stared at the numbers. It was a small matter, but significant, nonetheless. The form number ended in 2001. There was no way that an active agent would still be using forms that were over a decade old. It was impossible. During his annual file reviews, such an oversight would have been detected and he would have been forced to retrieve and destroy all his old forms.

Before going into homicide, Katzmark had spent time in VICE. He had some time dealing with forgery and counterfeiting. Many cases were blown wide open for the smallest of such mistakes. It was always the small details that tripped people up. Katzmark's mind started to spin, working through the problem. He deduced that the person who created the document was probably in a hurry. He had to whip up something on the spot. He had no time for in-depth analysis. Creating something that was good enough. If the forger did not have an in-depth understanding about the bureaucratic forms, it could easily be overlooked. A simple oversight. He probably knew the significance of the numbers, but in his haste, he just missed it. He made a mistake.

Katzmark's eyes lifted from the document. He thought about what the administrator said. The relative had paid the bills in full. There was no insurance. As he thought about this information, Katzmark nodded his head up and down. Smart. The prospect of a full reimbursement without any reduction in fees that had been pre-negotiated with the health insurer would have clouded their judgement. It made sense. Katzmark bit down on the cigarette filter. He asked himself the next logical question. But why? Who was this guy? Who was helping him?

The interior of the vehicle was thick with smoke. In Katzmark's distracted state, he failed to turn on the air conditioning or open windows. In a disgusted and frustrated manner, Katzmark jabbed his finger and depressed the console button turning on the AC. He glanced down to the door and depressed the buttons on the door to drop the windows. As the smoke inside the car cleared, Katzmark chastised himself for getting ahead of himself and considered the possibility that the form had not been forged. Maybe there was some other reasonable explanation? Something that he was not thinking about. He closed the folder and slid it onto the passenger's seat. He was going to make a stop before returning to the station.

He started the car and drove north toward the city. Katzmark had a friend in the FBI. Something about the San Francisco FBI office gave him the creeps. It was probably because it was located on the 13th. Like most law enforcement officers, Katzmark was superstitious.

Katzmark jammed the *Crown Victoria's* accelerator down and drove toward Highway 101. He wanted to get in the city before rush-hour traffic got crazy. He adjusted the rearview mirror and grumbled out loud to an otherwise empty car. "So much for a closed case."

*   *   *   *   *

Curt remained hidden behind the bedroom door. He heard the metallic sound of a key slide into the deadbolt lock. His grandfather urged him to stick to protocol and wait behind the door holding his loaded *Lugar* pistol. Curt felt this precaution was a waste of time. If the Agency located him, he would need more than a World War II pistol. Besides, Curt was certain. If the Agency found him, they would come under the cover of darkness avoiding daylight.

Curt stared through the crack between the door and the frame. Holding his breath, he watched his grandfather step through and close the door. Before opening the bedroom door, Curt waited until he removed his jacket.

"Hello Opa (grandfather)," Curt whispered as he stepped out from hiding behind the door.

Van Aelst flashed a confident smile while he removed and offered Curt a pastry from his paper bag. "Would you care for a pastry Herr Pfeffen?"

Curt smirked. "I'm still getting used to that name Opa."

"It will take some getting used to," Van Aelst replied.

They sat at the dining room table. The only significant furniture in the room.

"Something's happened," Van Aelst said. His grandfather's intense stare got Curt's attention.

"Have they found me?"

Van Aelst remained calm and in control. "Not yet. But an investigator has been nosing around the hospital." After a pause, he continued. "It was inevitable. The Agency still doesn't know. We both knew it was a matter of time."

Staring across the sparse apartment, while his mind wandered, Curt bit into the fresh croissant.

2

"Agent Gall."

"Yes?"

"You have a visitor," explained her secretary. Theresa looked up in surprise.

"I'm not expecting anyone?" she replied in a questioning manner. "Who is it?"

"A Detective Katzmark from the San Jose Homicide Unit. He has a missing person that he needs to speak to you about."

"Oh. It's Peter! I haven't seen him for years. Sure. Send him in."

As Detective Katzmark entered Agent Gall's office, she stood, and they shook hands.

"Detective Katzmark. It's been a long time. How have you been?"

"Hello you! Thanks for seeing me on such short notice. The good news is I retire next month," Katzmark explained with a subdued smile. "I've already planned a vacation. I'm heading to Europe for three months. See the sights and catch up with my relatives." His ear-to-ear grin reappeared enhancing his deep facial lines.

"That's great. I'm jealous. So, what's up? My secretary says you have a missing persons case?"

"That's right. It's a Sentinel Event out of *O'Conner Hospital*," he replied. He placed a thin folder on her desk and sat in one of the chairs in front of her desk. He handed her the discharge paperwork from the folder. "The reason I'm here is this document. It has me confused."

Agent Gall studied the form. Until she saw the form number at the bottom, it looked legitimate. Katzmark continued.

"At first, I thought it was just an old form. The form revision date is more than ten years old."

Agent Gall returned his puzzled stare. "Where'd you get this?"

"From the Hospital Administrator. I just left there. Then, I came straight to you."

Very seldom are agents blindsided. For the most part, being an FBI agent was predictable and uneventful. Unlike the movies, most of the agents did not work in the field. They handled mundane cases that required reviewing a lot of documents. Only a select few ever handled high profile cases. Agent Gall broke the silence.

"If I didn't know any better, I'd venture to guess that this document was forged." She paused thinking it through. "However, before we get too excited, let's contact some of the other agencies. It could be one of their cases. Have you shown this to anyone other than me?"

"No."

"Let's keep it that way. Until we get clarity, I'm placing you on notice that this is now considered an FBI matter. If we turn up anything, that we can share, we'll let you know. Sorry Peter. These days, things have gotten complicated. In any case, I absolutely appreciate you bringing this to us."

Agent Gall opened the thin folder and removed all of the documents. She took her pen and scribbled a note on the inside. Before handing it back to Detective Katzmark, she dated and signed the note. She handed him one of her business cards and pressed the intercom button on her desk.

"Yes, Agent Gall", a voice replied.

"Could you please come to my office?"

Detective Katzmark sat in the chair staring back in shock. It happened so quick. As the secretary entered the office, Agent Gall stood and extended her right hand to Katzmark.

"I'm sorry Peter. I have to get on this right away. You understand you cannot mention this to anyone, right?"

"But what about my report? What do I tell the captain?"

"Just show him your folder. He'll understand."

With that, their meeting was over. Agent Gall extended her arm and shook Detective Katzmark's hand. After a quick pump, Agent Gall left the room carrying his paperwork. Without turning back, she spoke over her shoulder.

"Please show the Detective to the lobby."

With a puzzled look of confusion, Katzmark opened the otherwise empty folder and read what she wrote.

Case reassigned to the FBI," with her signature and today's date underneath. Peter raised his head and saw the secretary staring back with a polite yet stern expression. It was time for him to go. Katzmark followed her as she escorted him to the front door of the office. When he reached his car, speaking out to an otherwise empty car, "I guess it's closed after all."

*　　*　　*　　*　　*

James Winstead worked for the FBI for the last nine years. He was a research assistant. One of the few who maintained *Top Secret Clearance*. During the research phase of most high-profile cases, it was this group of unsung heroes that did the tedious work. Like all intelligence agencies across the globe, the easiest means of infiltration was through the lower ranking positions. Hidden from the attention of most of the international community, still existed the old Stasi connection and networks. After the fall of the Berlin Wall, many of those old relationships and contacts remained intact.

It took much effort and cost many lives to infiltrate the FBI. The newly formed Federal Republic of Germany (FRG) chose not to dismantle their intelligence networks. Nor did they choose to share these resources with the new regime. Over time, the FRG fought for international validation and established new resources, agencies, and personnel. The new guard understood the importance of supporting, through indirect means, using unique untraceable assets and resources. The old guard had no formal official part in the new intelligence world, yet those fringe connections made it a point to protect their identity. And, from time to time, it benefited by tapping into this hidden clandestine network. James Winstead was one of the last of these loose connections. His handler, a senior ex-Stasi agent recruited him and placed him inside the FBI.

Winstead was on his coffee break when he overheard a conversation between two agents. It was not against the rules to openly discuss cases. But only those involved in the active investigation were privy to the details. Everything was on a need-to-know basis. Unlike the Americans, Winstead was trained by the Eastern Bloc old school KGB. The KGB had no tolerance for agents discussing sensitive information, even amongst other agents who had the proper security clearance. Winstead thought it was careless for these FBI agents to discuss the case in the open breakroom.

He could tell that, for many low-level agents inside the FBI, the boredom and monotony had set in. His supposed colleagues viewed their assignments as just a job. They viewed their position as a low-level research assistant focusing only on their pay grade and not appreciating their importance to the overall organization. Over the years, he saw first-hand their animosity and jealousy toward the higher position analysts and management. It was human nature.

"I'm working on a wild goose chase assignment this time," said one of the men as he stirred the coffee inside a ceramic mug with the letters "FBI" inscribed on its side.

"Oh yeah? What's going on?"

"I'm researching a John Doe case. This guy was injured in a random gas leak explosion in a sub-division. He was severely burned and buried in the rubble. He was found with no ID and almost died several times on the way to the hospital."

"So, who cares? Why all the interest in this guy?"

"That's just it. After he stabilized in the hospital, he was transferred. The hospital assumed that we or witness protection had facilitated the transfer. Discharge and transfer documents were provided. From the hospital's perspective, it looked on the up and up."

"So, what's the problem?"

"When the local LEO (law enforcement officer) came to the hospital to clear his John Doe case, he questioned the validity of the discharge form."

Both men paused raising their eyebrows. Their interests were peaked.

"Pretty observant to notice something like that," offered one of the agents.

"That's what I thought. It was an old, experienced Homicide detective that caught the discrepancies. He brought it over here," said Agent Gall before taking the sheet.

"And?"

"He was right. The documents were forged."

"Really?" After a brief pause, the agent continued. "Who the hell would have been motivated and connected enough to pull something like that off?"

"Exactly."

"You should do an internal Bureau scene location search. The John Doe case might have some connection to another active case. If it does, you'll get a cross-referenced file that you can refer to. Stranger things have happened. He could have been one of our guys, or one of the other agencies. Ten-to-one the guys a spook like us."

"Like us?" the other research analyst replied in a questioning sarcastic manner.

"Well, you know, an intelligence agent, but a field agent."

They both sighed contemplating that important distinction between research analyst and field agent. The only similarity these two positions had was they were both paid by the same agency. From there, all similarities ended. Inside their world, each job required much different skill sets, pay-grades, and autonomy. Analysts and Field Agents have nothing in common. It was night and day.

"Have you ever considered testing for the Field?"

"It sounds exciting. But, if I'm being honest with myself, I'd be scared to death. What they do is the real deal. It's not for me." After a brief pause, he nodded then stood. "My break's over. Keep me posted."

"You bet. Unless it turns into a *Need-To-Know* situation."

"From what you've told me, it probably will."

The other analyst stood and followed him out. After the breakroom door closed, Winstead shook his head in disbelief. In his presence, without a care in the world, they discussed the case. The professionalism of his FBI colleagues disappointed him. They treated the information they possessed as fodder to be shared like idle gossip. With a shake of his head, the only saving grace was the ease at which he secured sensitive information.

Winstead closed his paperback novel and placed it inside of his lunch pail. These props became his main means of getting information. The little table inside the breakroom had become his favorite hang-out. It was all part of his charade. As he finished his break, he almost wished extracting information was more of a challenge...almost.

This information needed to be passed to his contact-The Lone Wolf. As Winstead walked down the hall, he wondered what his handler looked like. They had never met him. During all these years, he only received indirect communications through other State Side ex-Stasi Agents. A few years ago, he was warned to be on the lookout for anyone researching the case associated with Curt Anderson. Based on what they were discussing, without naming him, it sounded like the parameters surrounding that case.

*   *   *   *   *

Agent Chapin was one of the Agency's rising stars. Each field agent selected into the elite Alpha-Team (A for Assassin Qualified) had an unusual rotating assignment. It was a tradition that started back in the day when pagers were still considered new and cutting-edge high technology. Certain Top-Secret cases that originated in their jurisdiction, were constantly monitored. They had long life spans.

Years after these high-profile cases closed, certain key words and phrases, locations, and facts specific to that case were monitored throughout every law enforcement agency throughout the United States. A huge amount of computer resources was dedicated to the monitoring and tracking of any searches performed that appeared to be specific to those select few *Director-Only Closed* cases.

If the Agency computer detected anyone searching a combination of key words, the IP address of the computer initiating the search was flagged and all future searches performed were monitored. An entire 50 analyst department worked around the clock sifting through the mountain of hits that the computer generated from all these potential searches.

Once these search hits came through, the data was printed, electronically stored, and then routed to this unit. The department was divided into smaller units that specialized in the key words associated with a specific case. Each Agency location was responsible for monitoring their own searches. Although these analysts were familiar with the name of every "Director-Only Closed" cases and all the key words that were being tracked, they had no idea what the case involved or the specifics surrounding the case. It was like an intellectual puzzle. Their responsibility was to be proactive and identify anyone that may be nosing around one of their files. These cases were beyond *Top Secret*, where all contents associated to the file had been reduced to no more than two legal sized boxes. Only one file was maintained. All other information was purged and destroyed in Agency burn bags. These files were locked inside the Director's office, secure in the Director's safe. No other person in the Agency, other than each Director, had access to their closed files.

Each unit was tasked with reducing the huge mountain of data. They focused on identifying those pieces of information that warranted follow up by an Alpha-Team Field Agent. Given the top-secret nature of these files, only an Alpha-Team member had the authority to investigate and delve deeper into the actions of others. In every case, each Director's file involved the use of lethal discretion.

Agent Chapin stared down at her belt loop. It was so strange for the Agency to still use a pager system. This antiquated technology was simple and straight forward. It did not require Wi-Fi access, or constant system upgrades. It served its purpose. Each week, the black plastic pager was handed off to another A-Team Agent. During that week, each agent on duty was responsible for following up on any new leads that the Scrub Team uncovered. The term was something the field agents had created. On most occasions, the follow up efforts turned out to be a waste of time.

On rare occasions, if the field agent was convinced, depending on the location, concentration and frequency of the searches performed, the assigned agent would look more closely into the data uncovered. The duty agent had standing orders, should something of importance be found, they needed to immediately contact the Director. There were no exceptions, even if the Director was on vacation, or it was a national holiday. In the five years that Agent Chapin was assigned to the Alpha-Team, over the countless weeks she was scheduled as the agent on duty for the Scrub Team, nothing of any significance had ever warranted contacting the Director. That was about to change.

As Chapin stretched her sore back against her ergonomically adjustable chair the buzzing from the black pager got her attention. Chapin was surprised by the vibration and almost fell forward out of her chair. She reached down and read the message: "Unit G."

"Great."

With an obligatory expression, Agent Chapin stood and made her way back to the research area searching for Unit G. As she rounded the corner, it was impossible to miss the commotion. There seemed to be a mass of conversation and shuffling of papers coming from this area of the building. As she continued down the aisle, the Scrubbers saw her approaching. In unison, five sets of wide-eyed analysts looked up.

She recalled how, on prior occasions, the Scrubbers' expressions were identical. Their faces were lit up, full of excitement, like a group of kids on Christmas morning waiting for their parents to arrive to give permission to unwrap the presents.

Unable to contain his excitement, the most senior Scrubber spoke first. He was practically shaking trying to suppress his excitement.

"Agent Chapin, this one is the real deal," announced Jean Sweet.

With a weak smile, Chapin met Jean's intense stare. Trying her best to show appreciation for their efforts, Chapin suppressed her thoughts. She came to expect, like each prior occasion, this would be a monumental waste of time. Suppressing the sarcasm, she forced a smile before sitting in the chair the Scrubbers strategically placed in front of their workstations. She could not miss a pile of printouts stacked on top.

"So, what have you guys got for me?"

As soon as she finished speaking, Jean dove right in, speaking fast barely taking a breath.

"We knew we had something right away. I mean, bam! The top-level search criteria came in ten for ten."

The other Scrubbers nodded in unison as if choreographed and practiced to perfection. Their eyes were wide open each staring at Agent Chapin analyzing her reaction.

"But then, right away, the lower-level search came back twenty for twenty. Twenty for twenty!" Jean blurted out with bulging eyes trying her best to control her excitement. "So, of course, we begin to search for the location of the searches, and" Jean paused to catch her breath pausing longer than normal as if trying to create an affect.

Chapin widened her eyes urging Jean to continue. Unable to wait longer, Chapin interjected "...and."

"Right. The location comes back from the Bureau in the San Francisco Office. We were even able to isolate the computer that initiated the searches. It's only one. There is no doubt, 100 percent, those guys are nosing around one of our closed *Director-Only Files.* The area went quiet as all members inside Unit G stared at Agent Chapin studying her reaction.

"Really?"

"Really!" replied all five members in unison.

Agent Chapin leafed through the reports. She reviewed the key search terms and confirmed the matches. "Gas, leak, explosion, John Doe, Wild Flower Way, *United Airlines*, crash, *O'Conner Hospital*, burn victim, San Jose California, Caucasian and male." She studied each term. She never had a Scrubbers report come back ten for ten. With a tilted head, she smiled and stared up at the team.

"Good job people! I will definitely need to bring this to the Director's attention."

As she stood, the members of Unit G exchanged high-fives. For these research analysts, it was like winning the Super Bowl. It was the first time that a Scrubber Unit had such a complete single search match. Wasting no time, Chapin scurried toward the elevator and took it up to the Director's floor. As she exited the elevator, she made eye contact with his secretary.

"Sandy. Is Director Gamboa available?"

"Yes, he is. Can I let him know what it's about?"

"The Scrubbers found something."

"Oh?"

"Ten for ten, twenty for twenty and location specific, all within a single search query."

"I'll let him know right away." Sandy stood and left Agent Chapin waiting in his outer lobby. A voice coming from Sandy's desk intercom got Chapin's attention.

"Agent Chapin. Come on back," said Director Gamboa through the intercom.

As Chapin entered the Director's office, Sandy held the double doors open before returning to her desk.

"Wow. A ten-for-ten and a twenty-for-twenty hit," replied the Director.

"Plus, a location match."

"Is it the Bureau?"

"It is. From San Francisco."

"Hum. Let's look," replied the Director as he reached out and took the folder. Chapin sat in one of the plush oversized chairs located in front of his large cherry wood desk. While he read the data printouts, his facial features changed. Unable to control his emotions, the Director spoke.

"I want you up in San Francisco right away. This takes priority over all your other cases. How many are you working?"

"Just four active. I'm closing one later today," replied Chapin. By his reaction, she knew that something big was happening.

"Depending on what you uncover, I may be reassigning all of your cases. I need you to find out what's going on over there."

"What are my parameters?"

"Keep it tight. Don't let them know it's one of our files yet."

"You're sure it's one of ours?"

"100 percent. It's one of mine."

"What pretext should I lead with?" Chapin asked.

Director Gamboa paused. He rolled his eyes up as his brain went into overdrive. He had an idea.

"Do you know the Agent assigned to the computer terminal?" The Director glanced down and found the name. "A T. Gall?"

"I think so. I think its Theresa Gall. She's a Field Agent."

"How well do you know her?"

"Not very."

"You're about to." The Director reached inside his desk and pulled out a pair of *San Francisco Giants* baseball tickets. As he handed them to Chapin, he knew his wife would be disappointed. "Here's some tickets. I want you down there to make all chummy with Gall. I'll call over there before you arrive." He paused as he thought through his plan. "I'll pitch the idea to her boss." With a wry smile, the Director continued. "I think we need some inter-departmental training, a Homeland Security type national intelligence cooperation angle. Some pre-planning relationship building."

"What's the reason we're reaching out to Agent Gall?" asked Chapin playing devil's advocate.

"I'll tell her supervisor we're considering bringing her over to the Agency. I'm certain she would perceive it as a promotion. It comes with higher pay."

They stared at each other considering this impromptu plan. Agent Chapin tilted her head back and forth lost in thought. After some consideration, she replied.

"It actually sounds plausible."

With a smile, the Director replied. "I think so too." With a gentle nod, he stood. Agent Chapin stood to leave his office. On her way out, the Director spoke up. "As soon as you get back, let me know what you found out."

"Yes sir," she replied. She pushed open his heavy door and left.

*　　*　　*　　*　　*

James Winstead made a point of leaving late. It increased his odds of seeing some activity stirring. Without knowing the particulars of an ongoing investigation, by watching the players who stayed late, and by paying attention to the agents who appeared to be distracted, frantic and otherwise pre-occupied, he could get a sense if something was happening. For years, he was a solid fixture in the department. He knew the inner workings and the typical behaviors. By being observant, he could take a pulse and make some solid inferences. Winstead could get a general idea if something big were happening.

Tonight, it seemed like the Fraud Division was busier than normal. Winstead peered over his cubicle and watched one of the Fraud secretaries shuffle by with her arms full of paperwork. Close behind, chased Agent Gall. They were focused on a time line and found no need to exchange any pleasant chitchat as they raced back to Gall's office. To get a better feel, Winstead loitered outside the breakroom, before doubling back to his cubicle. Taking the long way back, he paused outside the Fraud Unit, pretending to leaf through a useless folder that he brought along just for this purpose. Standing out of sight, but close enough to hear, he began to eavesdrop.

"Agent Gall?"

"Yes," she replied without taking her eyes off the papers in front of her.

"The boss needs to see you. Someone from the Homeland Security Task Force will be stopping by to see you."

"Me?" Gall asked with a curious look. "What for?"

"I don't know, but the boss wants to see you."

Annoyed, Agent Gall stood up and carried the folder with her as she walked to his office.

"Boss. Did you need me?"

"Yes, Theresa. A Homeland Security liaison is heading down to see you. She should be here any moment."

"Not a good time boss. I'm working that Fraud Case from *O'Connell Hospital*. Remember, that weird form?"

"Right. Well, that's gonna have to wait. Do you know a Catherine Chapin?"

"The name sounds familiar. Why?"

"She's apparently part of some modified Homeland Security detail. That group must have some weight," he said with a twinkle in his eye and a tilt of his head. "They're actually considering you for a different position."

"In the Bureau?"

"Nope. But still a Federal Government position. It comes with a bump in pay, same seniority. I've heard they have a sweet heart of a retirement deal, no mandatory time periods. It's based on the total number of international assignments. You would do great in that environment. Regardless of your time over there, once you're accepted into the program, you become fully vested. 100 percent. "

"Really? And you said international?"

"That's what I've heard."

They stared at each other. There was a brief pause as they let it all sink in. The muffled chirp from his desk intercom broke the silence.

"A Ms. Chapin is here sir."

"Send her in."

Winstead was listening just outside his open door behind the first row of cubicles. Hidden behind a tall wall divider, he glanced around the corner to get a look at the Homeland Security Liaison. He heard a set of footsteps padding down the carpeted hallway. As the footsteps approached, Winstead stepped out and walked back toward his area. He exited just in time to see the secretary leading the liaison. Without being obvious, Winstead feigned interest in the contents of his only folder and continued walking while avoiding direct eye-contact. As she walked by, using his peripheral vision, he got a good look.

Winstead went straight back to his cubicle, locked the folder in his desk before heading down to his personal car and waited for the liaison to come back out. From there, he would follow her. Once he was inside his car, he scribbled as much detail as he could recall about the conversation he overheard about the liaison and Agent Gall's potential new assignment with the Homeland Security Task Force. He was certain that something was up.

*   *   *   *   *

After entering Agent Gall's boss' office, Agent Chapin shut the door and sat next to Gall.

"Did Director Gamboa call ahead?"

"Yes. He called me earlier. So, what can we do for you Agent Chapin?" he asked.

During her drive over, she thought through what to say.

"With the increase in global terrorism landing on our doorstep, my people feel it makes sense to consider joining forces to create a single unified team approach. This cooperation would be in spirit only and no formal intent to consolidate the Bureau and the Agency. The Bureau has jurisdiction over domestic issues, while the Agency looks internationally. These jurisdictional restraints are like having blinders on. We each tend to miss things. If we had access to more information, things that are considered jurisdictionally out of bounds, we could be more efficient. We wouldn't be wasting time and energy trying to avoid stepping over the line and onto each other's toes."

"Is it a new department all together?" Gall asked

"It wouldn't be a department at all. Rather, it would be a team concept. It wouldn't be under the direct control by either the Bureau or the Agency. It would be an autonomous stand-alone self-sufficient team," Chapin elaborated.

Gall glanced at her boss. Chapin was thinking that her little story was sounding pretty good. When their eyes turned facing Chapin, she continued speaking.

"Nothing official has been decided. They're just kicking the tires. The final decision will come from way on high. For now, my people believe the idea has some serious momentum. Rather than get blindsided, the Director wanted to get ahead of the curve. In case the higher ups want to proceed, he wanted us to get the wheels in motion. He's donated these two *Giants* tickets as an opportunity for us to chat. Give us a chance to get to know each other. Do you have any plans for tonight?"

Agent Gall stared at the tickets. "Field level. Nice." With a smile, she looked at her boss.

"Just above the *Giants'* dug-out," Chapin elaborated. "Is there a Mr. Gall you'll need to check with first?"

"Nope. Haven't found the time or inclination to acquire one of those just yet," replied Gall.

"Me either," said Chapin.

*   *   *   *   *

Winstead pulled his older *Toyota Corolla* out of the Bureau's secure parking lot. It was one of the most popular cars in America and blended in with traffic. There was only one exit. He pulled across the street, grabbed his binoculars, and scanned the parking lot. Until he studied the visitor parking spaces, he worried about locating Chapin's vehicle. There was only one car, a new black *Ford Crown Victoria*, parked in the designated visitors' parking spots. He zoomed in on the plate and saw the exempt status. It was definitely an Agency vehicle.

Winstead watched as both agents approached the car. He watched the vehicle exit the parking area and drive by his spot in front of the gas station before he slid in behind. Because of the *Giants'* game, traffic was heavier than usual. As they approached *AT&T* Park, the sedan turned down Willie Mays Plaza. Staying several cars back, Winstead followed them toward the stadium.

He saw Chapin maneuver the vehicle toward the valet parking area. Cutting across several lanes, he repositioned his vehicle careful to keep several cars between him and the black sedan. As they stopped at the Valet area, Winstead reached into his center console and depressed a false bottom compartment. Inside, he extracted a compact magnetic tracking device. While these trackers were not in use, they were connected to an adapter. Using the vehicle's electrical system, it was kept fully charged, ready to use at a moment's notice. Just one of the many devices that covert agents kept in their arsenal of gadgets. To his advantage, the valet line began backing up. As Winstead watched both women begin walking toward the stadium, he depressed his hazard lights and exited his car.

Working fast, he approached the awaiting black sedan. The parking attendants were distracted, busy handing patrons a ticket, then driving their vehicle toward the designated valet parking area. Winstead made certain that one of the drivers saw him drop his keys as he approached the back end of the black sedan. The keys slid next to the back tire. Just in case someone was watching, Winstead spoke up.

"Oh man! I dropped my keys!"

Catching one of the valet worker's attention, the attendant watched as Winstead bent down. The vehicle blocked the attendant's view. Using his other free hand, Winstead placed the magnetic tracker underneath the vehicle's chassis. He felt the tracker snap into place as the magnet was drawn away out from his grip and adhere to the metal. As Winstead rose from between the parked vehicles, he raised his keys and dangled them pointing toward the on-looking attendant. To the attendant's surprise, he watched Winstead make an about face and return to his parked *Toyota Corolla.*

After entering his car, Winstead turned off the hazard lights. After checking his rearview mirror, he flipped a U-turn and maneuvered around the waiting cars heading in the opposite direction. With a shrug of his shoulders, the on looking Valet had seen it many times before. He assumed that the driver must have forgotten something. It was not unusual. It happened all the time.

Winstead drove to a nearby *McDonalds.* He parked and began calibrating the tracker. After activating the device, he confirmed that it was transmitting and receiving a strong signal. After Winstead was certain everything was working correctly, he drove the car through the drive-thru. After ordering his dinner, he re-parked the car. He turned on the radio and located the AM channel *680 KNBR* and began listening to the *San Francisco Giants'* game. He was prepared to wait the entire evening if necessary. He kept glancing back at the tracking monitor. After the sedan was parked by the valet, it had not moved. The GPS and map overlay confirmed that the vehicle was motionless parked along Willie Mays Plaza. This tracker came with movement notification that repeated an electronic chirp whenever the vehicle began moving.

The tracker had a 5-mile following radius from Winstead's car. If he somehow lost contact, he could resort to a satellite hookup that would extend his search area to a 20 x 20-mile area. After that, it would require a desktop computer to engage a different program. He was certain that would not be necessary.

With everything in place, Winstead adjusted the seat backward into its full reclined position, turned the volume up on the radio and waited. With a quick glance at his gas gauge, he was certain that everything was in order. With a deep sigh, he got comfortable. It was going to be a long night.

*   *   *   *   *

Van Aelst set his cell phone on the kitchen table. Curt was eager to hear what his grandfather had to report.

"Today, I received a message. One of my contacts confirms that an investigation into your disappearance has begun. Your former name has been mentioned. It's possible that they may be onto something."

As Curt's facial expression froze, the lines in his forehead deepened. Having now recovered from his burn injuries, the Agency was starting to search for him again. Being hidden away on the other side of the globe gave him some comfort. Curt was leery knowing the Agency's power. The Agency utilized the resources at their disposal, they could locate him. It was only a matter of time.

"What happened? What did they find out?" asked Curt.

"A local law enforcement official, a bean counter really," explained Van Aelst, "has uncovered the forged discharge papers. Something wasn't in order. He took the document to the FBI. Your name isn't being used. For now, they are asking themselves who the John Doe was and who was helping him."

Neither man spoke. In a daze, Curt stared at his grandfather's cell phone. He wondered how long it would take before the Agency discovered his grandfather and placed him under a microscope. Van Aelst was Curt's only living relative. The recipient of his considerable estate. If they suspected he was still alive, regardless of how well they had covered their tracks, they would eventually place his grandfather under surveillance. Their only hope was that the Agency did not believe that Curt was still alive.

With a worried expression, "What are we going to do?" Curt asked.

Van Aelst, although technically retired, still had contacts including several loyal moles inside the US government. Much of his vast global network was still intact and available. Because of Curt's situation, Van Aelst maintained contact with key covert operatives. In order to protect Curt, he knew he needed access to their information. For that purpose, Van Aelst kept his status as semi-retired. He had not earned the nickname of "The Lone Wolf" for nothing.

"This is nothing new. I've lived my entire life dealing with this kind of situation. For the next few months, until I can guarantee that everything is clear, I will not be coming to see you. It's too dangerous."

"How will we communicate?"

"We'll use the same technique you and the American woman use." Van Aelst handed Curt a piece of paper. It had an email address. The password was "lonewolf". The system he and Diane used was brilliant. For now, their communications were limited to monthly contacts. However, if either person wanted to change the frequency, the only limitation was the change would have to be made during the next monthly communication exchange. This initial delay was a limitation. Until now, it had worked fine.

Using a shared email server, one that both Diane and Curt could access, they could view composed emails. A drafted message would remain in the folder without being sent. At the pre-determined interval, each person would check the email account and access the drafted email. After reading the message, information and requests could be made. The emails were never sent. No electronic trace or message trails were created. The only information one could obtain was the IP addresses giving the physical location where the account was accessed. But by using a VPN (virtual private network), hunting down the IP locations would be useless. At his grandfather's suggestion, they had selected Korea and Israel as their VPN routing locations.

"There will be one change. I will be using a pre-formatted letter head document. If you open the leader head, I will store another document within my message. By editing the letter head, my message will be hidden under the logo. There, you will find my information."

While Van Aelst explained, he opened the email account and showed Curt how to access and edit the hidden text document. As he watched his grandfather manipulate the document, he was impressed by how easily he navigated around editing and hiding the icon. As he listened to his grandfather explain the process, he began to appreciate the spy stories that he shared with him. From what he saw, he no longer thought those tales were embellished. If anything, they were toned down to hide the depth of his skill and involvement. It was becoming clear that his grandfather was a real player.

*   *   *   *   *

Director Gamboa waited for Agent Chapin to leave his office. Once she shut his door, he opened the Director's safe. As he peered inside, he could not miss the Curt Anderson file. It was a huge file that was purged down to the maximum allowable size-two boxes. Gamboa supervised this case. A case that would not stay closed.

After sliding the two boxes out, he shut the heavy safe door. The first thing Gamboa pulled out of the file was the activity sheet. He stared at his red inked thumbprint impression. Without seeing the date etched on the deep red color stamped impression, he would have thought that the file was only recently closed. He stared at his signature, a perfect match. Glancing at the file contents, Gamboa hoped that he never had to open this file again. It felt like his mind was playing tricks on him. It seemed like he had just put the file into the safe. When, in reality, it was three years ago almost to the day.

Gamboa paused and glanced at a picture of his family. Sitting on his desk, the picture was inside a crystal frame. Gamboa racked his brain. Why was the Bureau looking into the case? A voice blared through his intercom and broke him from his trance.

"Director. John is here as you requested."

The last time Gamboa and John were in his office with this file open lying on his desk was the day he authorized a "snap shot" decision. A decision to murder someone, presumably Curt Anderson, lying asleep in the *O'Connell Hospital's* ICU.

*   *   *   *   *

Agent Walters had just transferred from the New Jersey Office. She was a computer forensic analyst and had no aspirations of joining the Alpha-Team. She already had ten-years in the Agency and established herself as a top-notch computer technician able to hack through the highest commercial grade fire walls used to protect corporations and governments around the globe. It was a feather in her cap to be asked to transfer to the West Coast South Division. With her information technology experience, being placed inside the famous Silicon Valley validated her place inside the Agency.

She was smart, quick witted, and kept her opinions close to her vest. However, once she had all her ducks in a row, all the pieces in place, she was not afraid to lay it all out there subject to criticism or second guesses. Walters never backed down from an intellectual challenge. She loved her job and it showed. Those that underestimated her, paid the price. Unlike an over-confident flamboyant cocky stereotypical Type-A personality agent, Walters epitomized a thoughtful, analytical, and articulate analyst. She rarely jumped to premature conclusions.

Agent Walters stared at the painting she just hung inside her modest sized office. She relished the fact that it had its own door. It was not just a cubicle in a common area. She cracked a slight smile of satisfaction. Getting this assignment allowed her to reflect at the road she had traveled; to take stock in what she had achieved. She was not one that needed constant praise from her superiors, nor formal awards and plaques. She was self-motivated and remained brutally honest to herself and others. Clicking off her mental checklist of career goals was what kept her satisfied. This assignment represented one of those boxes that she mentally checked off as goal achieved. Next!

A knock on her closed door got her attention. "Yes, come in."

"Hey, Agent Walters. All situated?" smiled Director Gamboa as he glanced around her room. "Place looks great."

"Thank you, sir. As a matter of fact, I am situated. Can I help you with anything?" she asked.

"Perfect," replied Director Gamboa. "Something just came up. Nothing too crazy, but I need you to check into something." After a brief pause, he explained, "Something the Bureau is sneaking around in one of our closed files."

"The Bureau?" Agent Walters asked. "As in the FBI?"

"Yes. Those guys," with a straight face replied Gamboa.

"Do I have the clearance for the case?" she asked. She wanted to make sure they did not accidentally stumble out of bounds right out of the gate.

"You're cleared. As a matter of fact, because of times like this one, is why I wanted you here. I've got a meeting in my office scheduled with the Alpha Team Supervisor John at 1:30 today. I want you there. It will just be us three," explained Gamboa "...for now."

"A-Team?" Walter asked in an elevated voice. "Sir, I am only an analyst. I'm not trained for the field. To date, I've been excluded from A-Team involvement." Walters wanted to be certain that she should be included in the discussion.

"Oh, right," Gamboa responded with a broadened smile. "There are a few offices that extend A-Team classifications to Analysts. Don't worry Agent Walters. I won't be sending you out into the field with a list of civilian names. Not yet anyway," he joked with a slight chuckle.

Agent Walters cracked a forced tight-lipped smile attempting to project a team-player attitude. But deep inside, she had reservations about flying too close to the sun. She had no desire to walk on the wild side of the Agency.

"Out of curiosity," she asked, "where are the other locations where this happens?"

"Seoul, South Korea and Berlin, Germany," he replied.

Director Gamboa opened a thin folder that he was holding. He pulled out her introductory welcome form letter and handed it to her. Before she could read it, he spoke.

"Welcome to our little part of the world Agent Walters," and he stuck out his right hand. Walters reached out. After they exchanged firm confident handshakes, Gamboa pivoted and exited her office. Just before closing her door, he leaned back and stuck his head inside. "Oh, by the way, your position here comes with a pay bump. You'll be dealing with more critical cases, plus, a cost-of-living adjustment to help with the relocation differential," he blurted out as he shut the door and left.

Shocked by everything she just learned, she plopped down behind her aluminum desk and leaned back in her ergonomically adjustable chair. She glanced down at the paperwork and read her new title "Team Alpha Analyst 3". As her eyes scanned the paper, she saw her new pay. It stopped her cold. She was now earning six-figures. With an unexpected sense of achievement, she marked off another box in her mental checklist. This time, she spoke out loud as she said "Check!"

*   *   *   *   *

Diane waited until after dinner before driving to the internet café. She chose an isolated strategically located workstation. From there, no one could look over her shoulder and none of the interior security cameras got clear direct views of her face. Part of her routine involved altering her appearance; large dark non-prescription glasses, layered clothes to appear heavier, a constant rotation of head covers from beanies, caps, and sports specific ball caps. She even rotated her shoes. She looked like anything but an intelligence professional. Rather, she fit the image of a local Berkeley intellectual. The final touch required covering her finger tips with a thin acrylic covering her finger print ridges.

Diane sat down, inserted a flash drive, and started the computer. She used a special program that used a random IP address scrambler to boot up the computer masking her Internet connection. Once connected, she ran a test confirming her Internet connection appeared to be coming through Florida. Only then, did she open her email server.

Once inside, she composed the email by copying and pasting a message from the flash drive, one she saved from another computer. Diane wanted to reduce the amount of typing while exposed at the Internet café. She pasted her pre-composed message onto the top of the page. Then, she slid the preformatted letter head and covered the encrypted message. Before saving it, she password protected the document. It was never sent. With everything complete, Diane closed the email program, accessed a special program that wiped away temporary passwords and the site visited from the computer's temporary memory. Finally, it overlayed an MPEG file of Whitney Houston singing the national anthem from her 1991 Super Bowl performance over the memory areas used during the session. It was a standard process used by the Agency hackers. She could not help herself. It was an inside joke that very few people understood.

Looking around the café, Diane finished her decaffeinated coffee and waited for that computer to restart. Certain the computer was re-sequenced leaving no trace of her activities, she stood and left. This was one of the dozens of cafes she visited. She rotated to a new location every month, certain never to visit any one café more than once a year. She kept track making sure she used different disguises with each visit. Over the last three years, once she deviated from her routine. An unexpected café was undergoing renovations. Without missing a beat, she moved this location to the bottom of the list and continued through the rotation.

Until now, Diane had no reason to increase her communications. Tucked away in Europe, Curt was safe still recovering from his burns. Curt's last transfer was handled by his biological grandfather. They all agreed that keeping in contact made sense. Still working for the Agency, Diane could alert them should the matter be re-opened. And likewise, should they uncover any unusual activity suggesting that someone was snooping about, they could put her on alert. This cooperation prevented them from being caught off-guard. They promised to keep the other informed. Their shared secret forced them into this unique pact. For better or worse, they needed to trust each other.

Diane saved Curt's life. Other than his grandfather, Diane was as close to a friend that he had. The rest of the world assumed he was dead. As Diane returned home, she doubled back, making sure she was not followed.

Like all prior communications sent to Curt, her route to and from the cafes were random. She used varying modes of transportation, buses, taxis, and subways but never her own personal vehicle. This trip, she was going to use the subway *BART* (Bay Area Rapid Transit) and travel under the San Francisco Bay. As the train barreled underground, the interior lights blinked off and on. Her ears popped from the pressure change as they continued deeper under the bay. Based on the conversations she heard over the cubicles, she had a suspicion that her communications would need to increase. She prayed Curt's case never re-opened. She was in this business long enough to understand that the Agency had a way of uncovering things. She hoped that just this one time, this case could fly under the radar. Unfortunately, that was not in the cards. It was just a matter of time.

3

Curt and Diane agreed to exchange their emails starting on the thirteenth of each month. Choosing that day as it was supposed to be a lucky number; lucky thirteen. Due to his physical condition and limited mobility, Curt agreed to use a specialized laptop computer. As his health improved, Curt convinced his grandfather to allow him to venture outside the apartment. Like Diane, he used Internet cafes. It was a tried and tested method. His grandfather made certain that Curt's excursions included escorts from his Stasi and KGB network of retirees and hi-tech experts. His grandfather appreciated the side benefit; an increase in his physical activities would help his recovery.

His grandfather lied and told him that the escorts did not know what happened. It was not necessary. For all Curt knew, the escorts thought he was in hiding from a drug-dealer. When, in fact, the retirees knew every detail.

Curt was curious about his grandfather's background and past dealings. He knew he was very influential inside Germany. Until now, he had no reason to know the details of his past. At a very early age, his grandfather was burdened with a huge responsibility. During World War II, he was one of the few Hitler Youth members not sent to the front. He was one of the lucky ones assigned to the underground railway to assist with the Fuhrer's escape. After their evacuation, a trusted few were granted access to the hidden treasures that the Third Reich pirated away. They were responsible for distributing these hidden resources. The sole agenda was to assure the continuation and provide financial guarantees for the future post-war Germany.

Curt waited for a reply. He used the same email process as Diane. It was essential that the drafted message be read and deleted as soon as possible. The goal was within 24 hours. They did not want to give anyone the opportunity to hack the account and review their conversations. As Curt made his way to the cafés and libraries, he never saw his tails. Having lived in the U.S. for most of his life, Curt felt very uncomfortable walking amongst the other Germans.

After much effort, Curt located a desktop computer inside the library. He scouted the spot on his last visit a year ago. Tucked away on the second floor, he found the perfect computer to use. There were no obvious surveillance cameras in the area, and no other cubicles or approaching foot traffic created by the aisles of books. He was confident that no one would be looking over his shoulder.

In a quick motion, Curt slid his arm down and inserted a flash-drive. He accessed the program and booted the program. He also cleared the RAM and the hard drive making certain that some hacker had not installed malware to copy his keystrokes aimed at infiltrating some unsuspecting German's financial information. With everything clear, Curt activated the IP address generating program which routed his Internet connection through Atlanta, Georgia. After verifying that the connection was masked, Curt accessed the email account.

After accessing the message, Curt saved a screen shot of the message to the flash-drive and would read it later off-line. He then, double clicked the file from the flash drive and accessed the message he had composed earlier and typed "R E A D" in the otherwise blank page. After dragging the letter head back over the blank message document, Curt closed the email program. Following protocol, he activated the program and re-wiped the RAM and hard-drive data and began saving another MPEG of Whitney Houston's national anthem performance. After the computer rebooted, Curt removed the flash-drive from the USB port and stood. The entire process took less than five minutes.

With his flash-drive tucked away inside his goose down jacket pocket, Curt made his way back down the escalator and then out the library's front doors.

*   *   *   *   *

"We've got him back in view. He's exiting the location."

"Copy that," replied Herr Van Aelst.

"The tail just exited the location. I have a thumbs up. All clear," reported the Stasi retiree. Following Curt had become a well-orchestrated maneuver involving several groups of retirees.

"Track him all the way back to make sure he gets home safe," ordered Van Aelst.

"Copy that."

"Keep me posted. Give me five minutes advance warning before he enters the building," ordered Van Aelst.

"Copy that. I'll report back before his arrival. Out."

The radio went silent. Van Aelst knew his team would protect Curt. They were all professionals. They had all proven themselves. Their prior missions were far more dangerous and involved. Having this simple task babysitting his grandson walking the safe streets of Berlin seemed like a cruel joke compared to the countless life and death missions each member accomplished during their prior lives as active Stasi agents. The least experienced agent had five kills, while the most senior one tallied over thirty.

To a novice, this detail would be considered boring. But for these seasoned veterans, it was different. They knew that the game Van Aelst's grandson played was beyond dangerous. The Americans played for keeps. They knew it was only a matter of time and a lot of time had passed. This was the calm before the storm. Surviving so long inside the brutal East Bloc Communist and Nazi regimes, being pessimistic was an ingrained mindset; something one developed over decades. For his miscalculations and stupidity, no one in the team had any fantasies that Curt would go unscathed.

Their leader, Van Aelst, aka The Lone Wolf, took everything in life seriously. Nothing was taken for granted. It was just how he worked. He knew that he did not have too many years left. But until then, he would not relax. He had no desire to retire. If he remained in good health, he was going to stay involved and continue his command.

While Curt walked down the concrete stairway to catch the next train at the U-Bahn subway, two discreet retirees followed. They watched Curt enter the subway doors before following him inside. They chose separate seats well away from Curt, careful to keep their distance. With their experience and older appearances, they blended in. As the subway doors closed, above ground, four other retirees in two separate cars followed. Everyone in the group read the texts being sent between the retirees inside the train. Using GPS tracking, everyone in the group knew each person's location.

Feeling the constant vibration from the rolling steel wheels along the tracks, combined with the staccato clacking and low hum reverberating inside the train, Curt relaxed. With a deep sigh, he thought about the transportation changes ahead; bus, taxi then a walk around before cutting through the common laundry room of his apartment building.

The surveillance team knew his routine. Although they never knew which transportation mode he would take, based on his prior runs, they were prepared for them all. Two agents inside the train and the other four above ground in two cars waited. After each switch, a group text was sent. The above ground tracking vehicles would stop, while a fresh agent exited the car and picked up Curt's trail. The driver rotated to the passenger seat and let the agent exiting the train drive until the next switch point. The drill repeated each time Curt switched transportation modes. This rotation kept the team fresh and alert.

Over the last few years, Curt was known to make as few as three switches and as many as nine. It was all up to him and depended on his mood and the weather. Like a grown-up game of follow the leader, the retirees followed Curt and kept him out of danger. The retirees took every stage of this dance seriously. Unlike Monopoly, this game had no get out of jail cards. There were no game pieces available and came with lethal consequences. There were no do-overs and no second chances.

Curt walked up the concrete stairwell preparing to connect with a taxi above ground. All he thought about was reading Diane's message. He wondered if this message was the one that would change everything.

*   *   *   *   *

Van Aelst waited curbside at the San Francisco International arrival terminal. He flew a non-stop flight from Berlin-Tegel. His appearance was best suited for Business Class. Besides, he preferred the larger spacious seating. It accommodated his tall frame. With the modern conveniences of international flights and a premium rate, he was well rested having slept in the fully reclined seat with its expanded bulkhead spacing.

The message Diane sent Curt was troubling. It was time to check in with his FBI mole. There was only so much back and forth that could be accomplished using encrypted email communications. The Lone Wolf was old school. There was nothing like a face-to-face conversation. He needed too much information that would require too many days of back and forth using email. It was faster and safer going in person.

Winstead was nervous. It was his first face-to-face meeting with the infamous "Lone Wolf," a living legend inside the Stasi and KGB. He had his other car, a black *GMC* SUV detailed and waxed and wore his favorite charcoal pinstripe two-piece suit, heavy starched and pressed white long-sleeve fitted cotton shirt and a bright red power tie. As Winstead drove on around the loop inside *SFO's* International arrival area, waiting curbside, was a tall elderly gentleman.

As he drove the car up to the curb, Van Aelst stepped forward and grabbed the door handle. Without waiting, Van Aelst opened the passenger front door. With bright blue steely eyes, the Lone Wolf stepped into the SUV, and slammed the door closed. He had no luggage and no carry-on items.

"Guten Tag Herr Van Aelst," said Winstead.

Winstead had lived in the US too long. He forgot that introductions are initiated by those in authority. In a disgusted stare, Van Aelst turned his face toward Winstead. In a forced reply, Van Aelst replied.

"Sehr angenehm (nice to meet you)."

Turning back and facing forward staring out through the front windshield, Van Aelst continued speaking. "To avoid attention, we should speak only English".

"Yes. Right. Of course. My apologies," sputtered Winstead.

Van Aelst exhaled as if frustrated. He could not escape his notoriety which affected how others treated him. Like other introductions, Winstead seemed abnormally nervous sitting in his presence.

"Since this is our first face-to-face meeting Winstead, why are you so certain I am who you think I am?" Val Aelst asked in a condescending manner.

Hearing the words, Winstead froze. He had been so distracted by meeting the "Lone Wolf" that he forgot protocol. Gripping the steering wheel tighter, his knuckles turned white. His mind went into overdrive deciding how to resolve this dilemma. How was Winstead going to verify this gentleman's identity? Turning the steering wheel and maneuvering the vehicle away from the curb, he regained his composer and replied.

As he studied the old man's face, Winstead said. "I can ask you the same thing. How are you so certain I am who you think I am?" As he waited for a reply, he questioned the wisdom of playing this type of game with "The Lone Wolf".

In a confident arrogant manner, Van Aelst reached into his coat pocket and removed his phone. He tapped its screen and tilted it so Winstead could see before he replied.

"I have been watching you from a satellite tasked overhead. I tracked you from your parking lot space at the Bureau, to the auto detailer. From there, you entered a gas station. I presume that you purchased gasoline. You left the station on Montgomery before leaving the city. At least you drove in the opposite direction across the Bay Bridge through Oakland and doubled back on Interstate 80 before you got onto Highway 101. I will give you some credit for taking that side detour through Daly City near the *Cow Palace*. You at least tried to avoid being tailed and aren't a complete imbecile."

After hearing Van Aelst, Winstead felt aghast at his shortcomings. After a brief silence, they turned facing each other. After a brief pause, Van Aelst flipped his index finger against his smart phone's glass screen and swiped away the live satellite view from above. With unexpected quickness, Winstead watched Van Aelst locate something on his phone. After finding what he was looking for, he tilted the screen toward Winstead and continued speaking.

"And I have a recent picture of your face...see," explained Van Aelst as he stuck the screen into to Winstead's face.

Trying to keep an eye on the freeway, Winstead glanced at the phone screen. Without a doubt, it was his face. Stymied, Winstead's mind raced trying to decide what to do next. How was he going to extract himself from this precarious situation? The first thing he needed to do, was verify the man's identity. Recognizing the area, Winstead took the Millbrae Avenue exit and swung the vehicle onto the off ramp. In a split-second decision, he drove to the only spot he could think of. Accelerating off the freeway, Winstead maneuvered the vehicle to a frontage road that led into the Bayside Manor Park. It was a small local residential park on the outskirts of Millbrae. He reasoned that at this time of day, it should be void of any parents and children.

Winstead scoured the area and drove toward the small parking lot near the playground. This location gave him a view of all traffic in and out of the park. He needed to be certain that this man, was in fact, Van Aelst. If not, he had no choice and was prepared to put a bullet between the old man's eyes. With the awestruck adoration he held for the "Lone Wolf", Winstead forced those feelings from his mind. In one fluid motion, he pulled out his *Berretta M9* pistol, flipped off the safety and aimed it at the man's forehead. After taking a deep breath, Winstead steadied his eyes. With an intense glare, he spoke.

"When did you and I first make direct contact? I warn you to answer carefully. You will not be given a second chance."

The old man tilted his head down. With a slight smirk, he replied.

"I initiated the telephone call. It took place nine years ago, before you were accepted into the Bureau."

The two men remained motionless waiting for the next set of questions. As he concentrated, Winstead's eyes rolled back into his head trying to recall the answer. Regaining his composure, he recognized the need to slow everything down. He needed to ask another question; one he knew 100 percent the answer before he asked the question.

After a brief pause, Winstead formulated the next question. A question that only "The Lone Wolf" would know. A question so obscure, one that required a specific detailed piece of information.

"When we discussed my first assignment, why did you repeat yourself? What happened?"

Winstead held his breath. He concentrated and studied Van Aelst's expression. He watched Van Aelst's eyes rotate upward and to the right as he accessed his left brain. His face appeared calm. Other than his pursed lips, his face was expressionless.

During the awkward pause, Winstead considered his options. *What if he doesn't remember? Is it too specific? If he doesn't know, should he ask another question?* Waiting, Winstead adjusted his shoulders to offset the weight of his heavy gun.

Van Aelst smiled. "The noise from the sea gulls and a ferry horn blaring. You were at the *Fisherman's Warf* pier," said Van Aelst breaking the awkward silence. "I asked you to repeat your response."

Winstead sighed and relaxed. He lowered the pistol and returned it inside his concealed shoulder holster, relieved that he averted an unnecessary disaster.

"Ok. I'm certain you are Herr Van Aelst. Are we good?"

"Yes. Also…" Van Aelst paused and turned toward Winstead. With a stern expression and intense unblinking blue eyes, Van Aelst leaned forward. In almost a whisper, he said, "This is the only time I will allow you to point a loaded gun at me. Ever. Do you understand?"

Winstead was surprised at his intensity. Van Aelst had to be well in his eighties. But the unwavering confidence he exuded, the way he spoke, regardless of their age differences, Winstead found himself intimidated, despite outweighing Van Aelst by at least 50 pounds.

"Yes. I understand," Winstead replied in a hushed voice.

"Good. Now drive me to the *Hyatt Regency*. I have a meeting scheduled in my suite."

"Yes sir," replied Winstead. Taking the SUV out of park, he maneuvered the vehicle back toward Highway 101 and drove back to the city.

*   *   *   *   *

Agent Gall stared across her desk. She did not know how she felt about being considered for a transfer to the Agency. The Bureau handled domestic issues. The Agency, on the other hand, was a global affair. She avoided long-term relationship, a sacrifice required to pursue advancements. Taking the Agency position would prolong the prospect of having a love life. She questioned the wisdom knowing it could jeopardize her chances of ever having children.

Agent Chapin could see Gall's internal wheels spinning. She needed to redirect their conversation back to the forged discharge papers.

"The other day at the *Giants* game, you mentioned that case about the homicide detective. What was that all about again?"

Flattered that an Agency Agent would show interest in her domestic case, Gall elaborated.

"Right. That's a weird one. Who had the means to get that guy out of the hospital under false pretenses?"

"What are you thinking?" asked Chapin.

"The guy is either a spook or has some friends in some very high places. Who else could put on this kind of dog and pony show? Maybe he was at the wrong place at the wrong time."

"Cartel?"

"I don't think so. He doesn't seem to fit the profile. No tattoos. He was allegedly walking a dog at the time, so the report speculates."

"What was the cause of the explosion?"

"The Fire and Arson Cause and Origin report confirmed it was a gas leak from the kitchen area. There were also no signs of foul play in terms of the explosion."

"What about the homeowners?" Chapin asked.

"Place was vacant. Property was for sale. Apparently, the owner died in a commercial plane crash earlier. No other injuries or victims from the blast. Just our John Doe."

"So, this John Doe has an extreme case of bad luck. He's walking in front of a house that just happens to get blown up. Then, he somehow survives the ordeal and is later whisked away by a phantom relative who pays the outstanding medical bills and uses bogus discharge documents. The only reason we catch wind of anything 'hinkey' is our local law enforcement, while trying to clear his Sentinel Event investigation, notices something strange about the discharge document. Interesting..." explained Chapin. "Were you able to track down the transfer?"

"Not yet. We're still working on it though."

"It's got to be a spook," countered Chapin.

"That's what we thought too. But nothing is coming up on an inter-agency search. It's like this guy fell off the face of the planet," Gall said.

"What about the hospital surveillance tapes?"

"A dead end. Unless the hospital suspects foul play, the hard drive is re-used and written over. In the past, their main concerns center on unauthorized use of their prescription drugs and a few sexual harassment cases. Unless they locate something out of the ordinary like missing drugs inside the pharmacy supplies, or some other unusual event..."

"Such as?" asked Chapin.

"Like an altercation between patient and or between the hospital staff, or any alleged sexual harassment between any hospital staff and patients, the hospital would have no reason to save and archive the surveillance tapes."

"So, no tapes?"

"Nope. No tapes."

"What about the discharge papers? Any fingerprints?"

"Just the nurse that filed the paperwork and the hospital administrator. Nothing from the alleged Agent. The agent must have been wearing some prosthetics to cover his fingerprints."

"Wow. They're definitely pros. What about the payment for the hospital bill?"

"It was not copied. Which is strange. The Hospital administrator says that standard operating procedures requires that these types of payments be copied. Needless to say, no copy was found," explained Gall.

"Inside help?"

"We're looking into it."

"What about the transaction as it cleared the bank? You might get lucky there and get an image of the payment."

"We were able to locate the financial confirmation from the records. Unfortunately, the payment processed through a now defunct *Washington Mutual Bank* which was absorbed by *Chase*. Nothing is available from those transactions. We're still looking, but a dead end."

"Gall, that is one strange puppy," added Chapin as she shook her head in disbelief. Having extracted a lot of information, she started thinking of a way to bow out of the conversation. She wanted to get back and fill in the Director. As if on cue, Chapin's cell phone buzzed. Glancing down, she could tell that it was just an email notification. Normally, she would have been annoyed. This time, she used it to her advantage. She looked up at Agent Gall who was staring back with an inquisitive expression.

"Something important?" Gall asked.

"It's the Director. I'd better head back," Chapin added. With a quick smile, Chapin stood and stuck out her right hand. While exchanging handshakes, Chapin suggested coming back the following week to discuss the Agency position.

Agent Gall watched Chapin leave her office and watched her image disappear around the doorframe. Agent Gall could not help but be impressed. Chapin had good instincts. Her questions were dead on bull's-eye in terms of her investigative skills and verbal rapid-fire questions. Gall contemplated whether she had what it took to work for the Agency. She redirected her attention to her paper covered desk, with her thoughts turning back toward her newest case and the vanishing John Doe.

* * * * *

Agent Walters waited outside Director Gamboa's office. Arriving early, she sat rigid, staring forward outside the Director's intimidating large double doors. She did not want to disturb his secretary and was prepared to wait as long as it took. She was in no hurry.

At precisely one thirty, the Director's doors swung open. Out walked a female agent. Without making eye-contact with the secretary or Walters, the woman walked by without saying a word heading toward the Alpha Team wing. The Director's voice erupted from the secretary's intercom.

"Send Walters in now please."

"Yes Director," replied Sandy his secretary.

Without waiting, Walters stood and walked through the double doors. Once inside, she nodded and flashed a calm controlled smile.

"Agent Walters. This is John, the A-Team Supervisor."

After exchanging firm handshakes, Walters sat in the only available chair next to the Supervisor.

"Agent Walters, I have a computer in the Bureau that I need to get a look at. Can you do it?" Director Gamboa asked.

"Do we have the IP location and terminal location information?" she asked.

"Yes," replied the Supervisor.

"No problem," she replied. Glancing between the Director and the Supervisor. "Is there anything specific you're trying to obtain? I might be able to isolate your search."

The Supervisor glanced at the Director. Without speaking, they were trying to decide how much they wanted to share. Walters was still a newbie. After a brief pause, Gamboa faced Walters.

"We need to know why they're peeking around one of our closed files. It's been closed for the last three years."

Agent Walters expected more details. But that was it. Director Gamboa and Supervisor John stared back with blank looks on their faces.

"Ok. Fine. What specifics about their searches do we have?

"John held a thin folder containing a list of the key search terms that the Scrubbers found. He handed the entire folder to Walters.

"Here you go. It has all the key terms that were found. Are you familiar with Scrubbers detail Agent Walters?" the Supervisor asked.

"Yes. It's kind of like a hazing ritual, a rite of passage in the New Jersey office anyway," she replied.

"Same here," explained the Director. "We need you to copy everything they're looking at and how long they've been at it. If we give you a week, will that be enough time?"

Walters examined the Director's and Supervisor's expressionless faces. She knew this was all the information she was going to get from them. She did not need the back story. Her job was to extract the facts and uncover any and all potential evidentiary items. She was perceptive enough to recognize that she was on a need-to-know basis. And by their expressions and lack of additional details, neither of the men felt she needed to know anything else.

"That should be enough time. I'll get to work on it right away. You'll have my report no later than next week. Earlier if I'm done sooner."

"That's great Walters. I'll be in touch," said the Director. He stood and stuck out his right hand. It was obvious their meeting was over. She stood, exchanged handshakes, and left. When Walters reached for the door handle, the Director spoke up. "Oh, be sure to store all your research in your secure safe."

"Safe, sir?"

"Ever use one in New Jersey?" asked the Director.

"No sir."

"John, can you escort Walters back to her office and explain how her safe works?"

"Sure," replied the Supervisor.

John followed Agent Walters to her small office. Once inside, he approached her metal desk and pointed underneath. She had not noticed it. It was a small, metal safe about the size of a portable folder bin, hidden in the corner tucked under her desk.

"Is there a combination?" she asked.

"No. It's biometric. It's triggered by your thumbprint."

She stared back at the Supervisor in curious wonder.

"It's open now, so before you close the door, reach down and press your right thumb down on the small square plate."

Tilting her head, she stared down. The safe was floor mounted. To reach it, she bent down, like a football player, took a knee. It felt soft, like a rubber surface. While pressing her thumb, a bright green light blinked on and off followed by a loud electronic chirp.

"There you go. It's set. Now, only 'you' can open it."

"Really? What happens later when I leave? Can't anyone else open it or change the recognition impression to use it for someone else?"

"Nope. Not unless they cut off your right thumb and tried opening it that way."

She smiled and almost laughed. As she stared into the Supervisor's face, she could tell he was not joking. Her smile turned into a disturbed expression.

"Are you serious?" she asked.

"Yes. Serious. But it's only theoretical. It's never happened to an inside analyst before. So, I wouldn't worry," he said while raising his eyebrows trying to convey his sincerity. She could not miss his emphasis placed on "inside" analyst.

"What about field agents?" she pressed.

The Supervisor paused. As he thought of a reply, the office seemed to shrink in size. It was obvious he was struggling to find the right words hoping not to create any unnecessary stress for this new agent. He detected her discomfort. With a blank expression, she appeared shocked and uncertain. Having reached her limit, she decided she did not need to hear any more details.

"It's different with field agents. They aren't issued floor safes. They're worried about more than just their thumbs." Realizing too late that this explanation was making Walters even more uncomfortable, John decided to cut the conversation short. He still had one last obligation to fulfill.

"One last thing. Look into your top tray inside the safe. There is a device you need to keep on your person, so I would suggest placing it on your key chain. There is a procedural memo with it. It's self-explanatory."

The Supervisor paused, reluctant to go any further. He got the impression that Walters was fixated on this part of her new position. He dealt more with Alpha Team field agents and realized he needed more practice addressing analysts and forensic specialists. He never thought much about how analysts would react to these things. Agent Walters made no effort at hiding her discomfort. With a forced smile, the Supervisor turned to leave her office.

"Anyway, be sure to read the procedure memo before locking all your work material inside. All notes, outlines, printouts, everything. No exceptions. Got it?" he asked as he paused at her doorway.

"Yes sir. I'll read the memo and attach the device to my keychain right away," she said trying to sound confident.

The Supervisor nodded before disappearing out her open door. Walters sighed and glanced around the room. In a soft whisper, she said to her otherwise empty room "I'm not in Kansas anymore am I Toto?" Walters walked across her office floor and shut the door. She fought the urge to peek outside to look around. Making a beeline to the safe, she reached inside and located the instructions he mentioned. The outside label read "Thumb Scrape".

She ripped open the sealed envelope and found a small metal disc with a detachable face plate, similar to a necklace locket. She located and read the procedural memo the Supervisor mentioned. It read:

"To prevent unauthorized use of your thumb print, use the attached scraper. Open the metallic disc and place it on a hard surface. With as much force as possible, press your right thumb down onto the metal scraper and turn your wrist clockwise."

Located on the same piece of paper, along with the written instructions, there was a diagram explaining the process through simple sketches. Under the sketches, there was a paragraph providing more detail. The disc contained a dense pack of metallic razor edges. They were coated with hydrogen peroxide to prevent infection and to enhance the healing process. The scrape was guaranteed to provide enough thumb damage scarring the thumb print patterns so that even after healing, the thumb print pattern would be forever altered. Thus, preventing the biometric safe from being opened. The sensor was sensitive to one one-thousandth of an inch accuracy and included a temperature gauge to make sure the thumb was healthy and theoretically still attached to a living person.

The Agency recognized that other more sophisticated means could be used to access the safe. However, this small somewhat theatrical use of the biometrical safe had another purpose; to indoctrinate analysts and set a proper mindset. The psychological process forcing analysts to become personally accountable for their work product combined with the importance of security breaches was the first step down the rabbit hole. Even analysts needed to appreciate that this career was fraught with lethal consequences.

After reading the entire memo, Walters fastened the disc onto her key chain. As she returned her car keys to her purse, she sat in her adjustable chair and read through the folder the Supervisor gave her.

Finding it difficult to concentrate, she re-read the first page twice All she could think about was having to use the thumb scraper. *What had she gotten herself into?* Now, her new title and pay raise was not sounding like such a good deal after all. Her mind kept flashing back to one of her favorite childhood cartoons. In her mind's eye, she saw the small clownfish, Marlin discovering that the light that made him so happy was not a light after all. She kept hearing his words: "Good feelings gone."

*   *   *   *   *

Winstead sat at the dining room table inside Van Aelst's Suite. He waited for the Lone Wolf to return. He was a little shook up over their first face-to-face meeting. He attribute his lapse in judgement to spending too many years working inside the FBI doing mundane analysis. His skills had deteriorated. He was an expendable asset.

Winstead thought he was forgotten. It was only three years ago that he was re-contacted by his handler. Up until that point, he was just another legitimate civil servant having broken zero rules and yet to steal any classified information.

He was warned. His colleagues told him that this job involved absolute boredom, with flashes of insanity sprinkled with life and death decisions. As quick as it started, it could be followed by more boredom. Living a lie, residing inside enemy territory, abandoned by his country, and facing the prospect of being executed as a spy. It created a constant stress that could drive the most stable person crazy. Every recruit new their place and recognized their expendability. The profile of a mole attracted introverts and loners. Moles were driven by a different form of internal motivation.

The front suite door opened. As the magnetic key card slid through the locking mechanism, a faint electronic tone echoed in the otherwise empty living room. The noise snapped Winstead from his thoughts. Seeing Herr Van Aelst walk across the living room, Winstead sighed and waited for his instructions.

"Is the room clear of any listening devices?"

"Yes Herr Van Aelst."

"The room charges?"

"Everything booked on-line. I obtained the keys last night before your arrival, through another associate. A prepaid credit card and a forged out of state driver license was used. No passports are required in the States. Everything is in order. I've reserved the room for four nights and instructed the front desk no room service is needed the entire stay. The do not disturb sign is already hung outside. I was about to install the interior cameras but wanted to wait to proceed with their installation upon your orders" replied Winstead in a robotic voice as if he were reading off a checklist.

Working alone, Winstead did not have the benefit of other resources. Any associate he secured he had recruited on his own. Any additional funds or resources he needed, he secured himself. Moles were trained to be self-reliant, a jack of all trades. It was like floating alone without the benefit of a deserted island trying his best to avoid the sharks.

Van Aelst was impressed. Other than Winstead's initial lapse in protocol, he had everything in order.

"Very good. You've done well Winstead."

It was the first praise he had received in years. Winstead was surprised at the effect these few words had on his attitude. Words from none other than "The Lone Wolf". His confidence grew.

"What have you found out?" Van Aelst asked.

"A local law enforcement officer, a Mr. Peter Katzmark, homicide detective from San Jose, started everything. Apparently, these types of John Doe cases require law enforcement involvement. Unaware of the forgery, the hospital assumed that everything was in order and closed the case.

"However, Katzmark, following procedures, came around looking into the matter. He noticed the inconsistency in the paperwork right away. He contacted the FBI and showed them the document. The FBI agent verified the forgery and took over the matter. Katzmark closed his file based on a jurisdictional transfer."

Van Aelst listened to every detail. He knew his grandson's life depended on it. "You've had time to think things through. Where is the biggest loose end?" Van Aelst asked.

With a deep sigh, Winstead turned away cradling his chin in his hand. He wanted to think it through. After a few brief moments, he turned back and looked Van Aelst in the eye.

"I've hacked into the FBI Agent's file. I've had a look at everything they have. All hard evidence leads nowhere. No access to the original cashier's check used to pay the hospital. The bank became insolvent. All prior records, physical and electronic, were destroyed and are no longer available. No surveillance video was archived. All they have are the medical records. However," Winstead stopped speaking, unsure if he should bring it up.

"Yes, what is it?" Van Aelst asked.

"The only hospital personnel still working there who worked back then is an ICU nurse. Everyone else has moved on. She was there the entire time the John Doe was being treated. In fact, she was the only one who spoke to the relative and participated in his transfer to Las Vegas."

"Has the FBI interviewed her yet?"

"It's scheduled for tomorrow afternoon."

"Have they considered looking into the ambulance transfer yet?"

"They will. It's the next logical step. It's all they can do. They need to determine who the John Doe was, and I'm sure the discovery of the forged discharge document raised the biggest red flag."

"Red Flag?"

"Oh. It's an American euphemism. It refers to something out of place; something that draws one's attention to an inconsistency."

"I see. Yes, I would think the document would have that reaction." Van Aelst paused thinking about the nurse before continuing. "Does eliminating the nurse make sense? What else could she add to the investigation?"

"I don't think it's necessary. The discharge document confirms the John Doe's and alleged relative's names. However, the document indicates the relative was the John Doe's sister. So, the FBI is aware the relative was a woman."

"The document did not state the real name?"

"That's the odd thing. I read the document three times. The document only referred to the John Doe as 'patient'. It never mentions a name."

"That's interesting. I wonder why no one demanded a name be provided. They probably included another document to initiate the transfer and switched the paperwork before leaving," offered Van Aelst. "The move was almost like a snatch and grab. I bet the entire transfer took place within hours of him regaining consciousness and being stable. The hospital administrator was most likely distracted by the big check being offered to pay the entire bill. With the relative present, combined with the presence of what appeared to be Federal involvement, the hospital personnel were led to assume that John Doe was in the witness protection, and didn't feel it necessary to pry. "

"That makes sense," Winstead replied.

"I'm still concerned about the nurse. She may recall something not on the documents. It's possible. What if the nurse mentions something about the transfer, about Diane, and Curt, without even realizing it?"

Winstead watched Van Aelst's face. In a calm calculating manner, the Lone Wolf seemed to crunch the probabilities utilizing his vast years of experience. It was Van Aelst's call. After a moment of contemplation, Van Aelst made his decision.

"I'll take care of the nurse."

*　*　*　*　*

Diane carried a small grocery bag into her condo. She lived alone and stuck to her routine, her schedule. There was no need to coordinate anything with anyone else. She could get most of her food for the week in one shopping trip. She was single and never entertained. She never purchased things in bulk. There was no boyfriend or close friends, and no need for a *Costco* Card. Everything was purchased in single small quantities; one steak, one small pack of chicken, one tomato, and one head of lettuce.

After struggling through the front door, Diane carried her weeks' worth of groceries to the kitchen. Distracted, she did not notice a tall thin elderly man sitting on her sofa. Had she seen his bright clear blue eyes, she would have known it was Curt's grandfather, Cornelius Van Aelst.

The last time she saw him, was during the final transfer from New Jersey. Van Aelst thanked her for all she did for Curt. She was relieved to hear him say he "would take it from here." He exhibited zero fear and exuded absolute confidence during Curt's third transfer from Chicago.

There was something about Van Aelst. His cadence. The way he spoke. He had a slight German accent. And his smile. He was much more than just Curt's grandfather. After retelling the entire story, recounting how she came to be involved with Curt, she was taken aback. Van Aelst was calm and remained unfazed. He was polite and remained in complete control of his emotions. She was beyond shocked when he offered to reimburse her for all her expenses. She refused his offer. After returning home, she regretted turning down his offer to finance Curt's escape. She pulled most of her retirement account. At the time, knowing everything she could about her niece's accident, she never questioned doing whatever it took to make that happen. Curt was her only available resource to give her accurate, unfiltered and nonmanipulated information. She knew the Agency's routine and understood the futility of searching for truths there. Besides, prying inside the Agency was a certain death wish. For now, she was in search of answers and would do anything to protect that source.

A month following Van Aelst's intervention, Diane received a surprise. A letter from her bank approving her request for an oversized safety deposit box. The letter included her new box number and explained that her old key would still work. After a little digging, she learned that the request was processed from a small branch in the Chicago suburbs- the Midland Branch Office.

Since she was not the person that made the request, she guessed that it was Curt's grandfather. What was he up to? After re-reading the letter, she went to her bank. She presented her key and asked to access her new safety deposit box. After taking her key and verifying her identification, Diane signed the visitation log. After the teller verified Diane's signature, she released the security latch and buzzed Diane inside behind the counter. Following the teller inside the vault, Diane watched the woman insert a key into the oversized box. It looked about 12 inches wide and 18 inches tall. She had to wait to pull out the box to see how deep it was. After inserting the master key, the teller glanced back at Diane. With raised eyebrows, the teller watched Diane insert her key in the empty bottom key slot.

"I will leave you alone now," the teller said. She extracted the master key, pivoted, and turned away exiting the vault. Diane waited until she no longer heard the snap of the teller's heels against the tile floor. Then, she lifted the heavy metal box out from its slot. The box had thin metal sidings and was surprisingly sturdy. While sliding the box all the way out of its slot, she noticed its substantial weight. She bent her knees to gain more leverage and hoisted the box onto the only table located inside.

Looked over her shoulder, Diane checked both directions. Certain she was alone, Diane opened the box. Inside she found stacks of crisp $100-dollar bills, still wrapped in the bank's $10,000 bands stacked in neat rows. She removed the money, placing it on the table, and counted out 50 bundles. With her hands on her hips, she contemplated where the $500,000 cash came from. The exact amount she withdrew from her 401(K). How did Van Aelst know how much she spent? She took ten bills from separate bundles before returning all the money back into the box.

Wrestling it back into the slot, she pushed her palm against the cold metal and pushed the box until she heard the box snap into place. Closing the door caused a high-pitched metallic snap. The noise reverberated in the otherwise empty vault room. Taking the randomly selected bills with her, she left the room, then waited outside a Plexiglas wall for the teller to buzz her back outside. The same teller approached.

"Did you need anything else?"

Diane asked the teller a question. "I'm curious, is your Midland Chicago Office still open?"

"Midland in Chicago? In Illinois?"

"Yes."

With a tilt of her head, the teller clicked away on the computer. While waiting for the teller searching through a list of offices, Diane glanced around the safety deposit box area. After scrolling through several pages, the teller looked at Diane.

"The only offices we have in Midland Chicago are small ATM sites. They're technically shared ATM access points. They're not ours." Explained the teller. With raised eyebrows, the teller waited as if asking Diane if she needed anything else.

Diane blinked, surprised at the teller's answer.

"I must be confused. My memory isn't as good as it used to be. My mistake," Diane said before flashing a forced smile.

In return, the teller exchanged an equally forced insincere smile before depressing a button under the counter, causing a loud buzzer to sound near the Plexiglas door. As Diane left, the teller wished her a nice day and scurried back to her normal duties. Diane walked out the front doors and never looked back.

*   *   *   *   *

Diane continued to the kitchen placing her items in the refrigerator and pantry. Finished she walked back to the living room. Seeing Van Aelst sitting on her sofa, she raise her hand to her mouth gasping in shock. After recomposing herself, she closed her eyes and exhaled before speaking.

"You startled me. Is something the matter? Is Curt okay?"

With steely unblinking crystal-clear blue eyes, Van Aelst replied. "We have a problem."

4

Sitting in her cubicle, the only thing she thought about was Van Aelst's unexpected visit. She was still recovering from hearing there was a low-level inquiry surrounding a routine hospital procedural. During that process, they uncovered the forged discharge paperwork. Standard operating procedures required local law enforcement's involvement. The investigating officer was suspicious about the form and contacted the FBI, who was now looking into the matter. Van Aelst expressed his belief that the Agency would reopen the case. It was inevitable. Soon, they would learn Curt did not die on the plane. She needed to increase her email communications to every other day. If things heated up, maybe daily.

She knew the questions he asked were too pointed, too direct. She was too far into this cat and mouse game to turn back. She helped Curt escape. Over the last three years, she retraced her actions, thought through everything that happened. Every time she relived those events, she came back to the single fact that the Agency had killed her niece. Knowing what she now knew, she would do it all over again. But now, things had changed. It was clear. Van Aelst's questions we designed to acquire names. As a trained professional, Diane understood the consequences. It was essential that her name not appear. The Agency's long reach, when directed at any one person or organization, came with dire consequences.

With closed eyes and deep exhale, Diane tried calming her nerves and recalled her conversation with Van Aelst.

"Diane, do you remember the name of the supervising Agent?"

"It was John. He is still a supervisor in the A-Team."

"Would any other team be involved?"

There are three other teams Alpha, Bravo and Charlie. But at the time of the accident, it was John's team running lead."

"Who was the Director?"

"It was still Gamboa."

"Is there a chance this operation was off the books?" Van Aelst asked.

"What do you mean? Unsanctioned?"

"Yes. A decision isolated to Gamboa and the A-Team. Is it possible that there were other priorities, other concerns, other forces in play here?"

"I don't know. I've never been part of the decision-making process. I was a field agent thirty years ago. It was a different time. A different place. I never really thought about who makes those types of decisions. I was a soldier. One of the moving pieces on the board." *Diane raised her hand to her mouth. She paused thinking through his questions.*

It hit her like a kick to the stomach. All those years. All those missions. During all that time, she had not thought about it. Not about the decision makers. She always assumed that a great deal of effort went into these types of decisions. She assumed the orders underwent great consideration. She had never taken an in depth look at the entire process. Killing a human being was such an important decision.

She was not naïve. She recognized that, in some cases, under certain circumstances, a snap decision was necessary. But certainly, with most of her missions, great effort must have gone into those decisions. They had to be. As her mind considered her answer, Van Aelst studied Diane watching her struggle formulating an answer.

Van Aelst came from a different country, a different era. He witnessed first-hand the brutal nature of those in power. His parents shared their stories and the stories of his grandparents. His early years were dominated by the struggle within Europe and then the USSR. The Russian revolution, World War One, the fall of France, Italy siding with Germany, the Nazi Regime, World War Two, the Jewish Holocaust, the Cold war between the East and West, the building of the Berlin Wall, even the Korean Conflict.

Those battles occurred front and center, where millions of humans lost their lives. Throughout Europe, murder became common place, witnessed first-hand, were survivors' memories were forever etched in their realities and molded their world perspectives. Van Aelst considered this uncensored unfiltered experience the differentiating factor when understanding the idealistic Americans. Back when the ordinary U.S. citizens witnessed atrocities of war, it came at a time when ideals of freedom from Great Britain and the emancipation of slavery justified the carnage and loss of life. The injustice of the circumstances justified the extreme sacrifices required. Relatively speaking, those wars took place over a short period of time. America's lack of experience, not having experienced extended global conflicts kept them somewhat naïve.

Van Aelst watched Diane struggle to understand the reality of human nature, coming to grips with the reality. The fact that, most of the time, those in power are free to abuse the weak; those unable to protect themselves. But unlike most of the world, the United States goes to great effort to convince their populous and perpetuate the notion that everyone has an inalienable right to be protected from tyranny. That the US was created with the concept that the government in all its power, if allowed to run unchecked, would naturally become corrupt dominating and abusing its citizens. Van Aelst was convinced that it was this concept of individual value, freedoms and rights which blinded most Americans from the terrible, selfish nature of most other humans on the planet. It was this cultural indoctrination by the Americans that made it difficult for most Americans to believe or consider the argument that all humans possess a bias, a primal tendency to yield power over others.

Van Aelst waited for Diane to respond. He was amazed how often he saw this response from Americans. It was as if they were mentally hard-wired to believe that at the root of human nature, regardless of one's upbringing or biases, humans were naturally good. A deep-

seated belief that although a small minority of people were bad, most were good. From Van Aelst's perspective, outside the US, that was not the case. In his experience, from what life showed him, given the choice, when a person is in power over others, that power ultimately leads to the elite abusing their power to dominate and exploit others. Unfortunately, most other people, like most other countries, will resort to murder to achieve that end.

Diane raised her head awaking from her thoughts. Her movements caught Van Aelst's attention. Hearing Diane's voice broke the silence and jarred Van Aelst away from his thoughts.

"It's possible. The Director along with the supervisor could have acted on their own." She focused on Van Aelst. After a brief pause, she continued. "As hard as I find it to believe, it's possible. But to what end?"

"I have had an advantage. I've been contemplating what happened for the last three years, trying to conclude the rationale. The fact of the matter is I have a 100 percent certainty that my grandson was not working in concert with anyone else. He acted alone. He was not instructed to spy on the Americans."

With reservations, Diane listened to Van Aelst. Something always bugged her. When he woke from his coma, why did Curt speak German? In addition, it was obvious that his grandfather was affiliated; his ability to open the safety deposit box in her bank without her assistance, the money, his ability to secure resources and contacts to help transfer Curt to Europe and keep him under the Agency's radar away for all these years. And today, at this very moment, breaking into her condo without any fear to explain things that only a spy could know.

Diane forced herself to remain calm. By helping save his grandson, she earned his trust. Unfortunately, her involvement was a spur of the moment decision, a knee-jerk reaction. She unwittingly jumped into the deep end of the pool unprepared for what lay ahead. With a deep sigh, she leaned forward and listened to Van Aelst.

"So, the question is, why go to all of the trouble to destroy a full commercial passenger plane? They could have eliminated him with less collateral damage. Why do it? What was the urgency? Why involve so many innocent victims?" asked Van Aelst.

Diane considered his questions. He knew this line of questioning hit a sensitive nerve. He knew her niece's death was the sole impetuous causing Diane to become involved. He watched her facial expressions transform into a scowl. As her facial features tightened, her anxiety manifested into a physical response. Unable to wait for her answers, Van Aelst provided a possible answer.

"I'll tell you why Ms. Klein. It's because they could." Van Aelst paused allowing her to absorb his words. "It was a poor decision. Too much chaos. Too many lost lives. It was arrogant. It was something only a tyrant would do. It was an unnecessary waste of human lives, especially for an American Agency operation. I'm certain that decisions were made to influence and tamper with others."

"It's possible," whispered Diane. Yet, she was unconvinced of Curt's innocence. Why did he copy the file? Why did he go to all the trouble to get hired by the photocopy firm? It was obvious- he wanted to infiltrate the Agency. If he was not affiliated, why would he do that? for what purpose?

"Ms. Klein. We need to plan ahead. It is inevitable. Your Agency will reopen the case. We need to increase our email communications

to every other day. I also suggest you create a reason to take an extended vacation. I want you to come to Europe. You'll need to create a situation where your decision to travel abroad will not appear unusual."

Diane listened to Van Aelst. She had no idea how she could make that happen. Van Aelst's next question interrupted her thoughts.

"Is it true that you play golf?" asked Van Aelst.

She tried not to look shocked. She wondered how he knew that little bit of information. Without hesitation, she replied. "Yes, but it's been a while. How will that help us?"

"What was your handicap?"

"It was around 14. Why?"

"If you started taking a renewed interest in golf to relax, a way to distract you from the loss of your niece, to reduce the guilt of recruiting her to the Agency, it would make sense why you turned back to golf as a hobby. It would make sense that you started watching golf on television or started attending professional events in person," said Van Aelst. He turned away from Diane. His cadence was fast and clinical as if he was developing an impromptu alibi. Satisfied, he returned his gaze to Diane. "To watch the LPGA (Lady's Professional Golf Association) match in Berlin this coming year."

Diane started to see where Van Aelst was going. "I could see that. That seems plausible," she replied.

"I've already looked into where the women's play in California. The men and women have annual visits to Pebble Beach in Monterey. The women go to the Kia Classic in Carlsbad, near San Diego and a

National Tournament is held in the LPGA in Rancho Mirage, both in Southern California."

"But how does that translate to getting me to Europe?"

"Once you show an avid desire to go to these events in person, it would be understandable why you would go to the British Open and attend the international competition between US and the European nations."

Diane listened to Van Aelst's plan which required her to re-engage her passion for golf.

"You see Diane, this year, the LPGA's international competition, The Solheim Cup, will be held in Germany."

"Why don't I just go on vacation there?" Diane countered.

"It would be seen as unusual, out of place. When was the last time you were in Europe? Van Aelst asked.

"It's been a long time. I was on a mission for the Agency."

"Exactly. If, for no reason, out of the blue as you Americans say, you started traveling abroad, it would look unusual, suspicious. During your annual polygraph, the questions would center on these new trips. The golf angle makes sense. Avid golf fans tend to travel to new courses. A good start would be to start requesting vacation time to attend West Coast golfing events. Start putting up golf paraphernalia in your cubicle. Bring a putter to work. Keep your golf clubs in the trunk of your car. Post your golf scores from your Agency computer. Although it would be considered a minor infraction, it would speak to your new-found passion. Do golf searches of all types from your office computer."

Then it hit her. She stopped cold. Frozen in fear. "You think the Agency will start to look at me?" she asked staring into Van Aelst's deep blue eyes.

"They might. We need to develop an exit strategy. Just in case."

"Do you really think that will be necessary? That it will come to that?"

"It only takes one mistake," replied Van Aelst.

*   *   *   *   *

U.S. Senator Anthony successfully won his bid for re-election. He was excited about another six years. The last few years had been a whirlwind. He was still the Chairman of the U.S. Intelligence Oversight Committee. This position gave him the highest Congressional security clearance available outside of the Presidential succession positions; POTUS, Vice President, Speaker of the House and then the President pro tempore of the Senate, followed by the Cabinet. The longer Anthony remained in Congress, he became even more seduced by the power his privileged position yielded.

Besides, being a Senator gave him celebrity status. His name was the answer to several questions posed to every immigrant on the naturalization test in California. Likewise, his name required learning inside the educational systems across the state to be tested in civic and political science questions. The lifestyle of a U.S. Senator required him to maintain offices in several large California cities and of course in Washington D.C. It was not unusual for Anthony to make cross country flights several times a week. It was as if he commuted to his job by plane.

The government provided Congress members with allowances necessary to accomplish their jobs. Although most of Congress avoided the bad publicity that resulted from chartering a plane or flying first class, Senator Anthony took no umbrage in maximizing the allowance options made available to him. As he stared out the first-class window, he could not remember the last time he flew coach.

After drinking his third complementary bloody Mary, Anthony turned his attention to his favorite staff member.

"That was a landslide victory Senator."

"Thanks. You and the staff have been a great help with everything," replied Anthony. He was so conditioned to flash what appeared to be a sincere politician's smile that he forgot what it was like to have a real one. His frozen insincere fake smile faded after hearing what his assistant said next.

"What a stroke of bad luck. If the State Assemblyman hadn't died in that plane crash several years back, who knows?"

Senator Anthony peered over the rim of his spectacles and studied his staff assistant. With a slight nod, the Senator wondered what he would think if he knew the truth. With a final sideways glance, Anthony watched the assistant open a folder and begin to read its contents. Hoping they were finished idle chit chat, Anthony concentrated on his drink, before reclining the oversized first-class seat. Closing his eyes for good, he wondered if anyone inside the Agency would ever question the decision to down the *United Airlines* flight to Hawaii.

He yearned for sleep. He needed to clear his mind. It was a while since he thought about it. *Why did he bring it up anyway?* Senator Anthony tried to push all thoughts about the "supposed" up-and-coming Assemblyman out of his mind. What choice did he have? He gathered so much momentum that his name was all he heard about in Washington. *"How is the kid doing? Better be careful Senator, he looks to be in a position to steal your seat."* They had said. *"He sure knows how to campaign. His fund raisers and contacts make him a serious contender,"* they warned.

With a final sigh, Senator Anthony welcomed the numbing buzz that the alcohol created and started to relax. He was certain that the Assemblyman's airline tickets were off the books. The Senator used one of his special loyal aids, who paid cash. The Senator accumulated so much dirt on these guys, they had no choice. The only regret he had was the Assemblyman's. It was not until the news stories about the crash started running, that the Senator found out. After hearing the Assemblyman's wife and two children were onboard, the Senator started making inquiries. His special contacts confirmed initially, one ticket was purchased. After some quick digging, he learned that the Assemblyman exchanged the first-class ticket for coach using the price difference to purchase tickets for the rest of his family. The fund-raiser would double as a family vacation.

As Senator Anthony drifted to sleep, he pushed back the guilt justifying their deaths as collateral damage. The opportunity to rid himself of two problems at the same time was too good to pass up. Why had the Assemblyman involved his family? The Senator complained blaming them for never being to Hawaii before. It was their first visit. With a deep sigh, the Senator wondered *"Who lives in California and has never been to Hawaii?"* before drifting off to sleep.

*   *   *   *   *

The Burn Unit ICU nurse felt fine all day. She had just returned from her afternoon break at *Starbucks* in the lobby. It was her afternoon ritual. She ordered a Venti coffee latte with chocolate powder flakes and cinnamon. It was her personal concoction.

She relaxed at her favorite table. On her smartphone, she checked her *Facebook* feed. Other than an older gentleman with bright blue eyes wearing a dark pinstriped suit and tie asking for directions to the ICU, her break was uninterrupted. After finishing her drink, the nurse hurried to the elevator taking it back to the ICU. As the elevator doors closed, she felt a sudden tiredness wash over her body. By the time she left the elevator and walked across the tile floor to her nurses' station, she could barely keep her eyes open and her head up.

Feeling dizzy, she laid her head on her desk. When the other nurses returned, they thought it was unusual for her to sleep at her work station. Taking a closer look, they were shocked to discover she was not breathing. A rush of medical personnel and doctors administered emergency medical procedures, trying to resuscitate the fallen nurse. Nothing worked. 15 minutes later, at 36 years old, she was pronounced dead. The stress from working in the ICU and learning about her father's prior heart attack, the medical examiner attributed her family's heart issues as the cause of her sudden death. An autopsy was ordered but nothing unusual would be found.

*   *   *   *   *

As Agent Gall entered the ICU, she noticed everyone was distracted. After approaching the receptionist area, she saw several nurses talking in whispered voices. They were rattled. Their faces were stern, with blank shocked expressions. Gall waited for someone to acknowledge her presence. After several minutes waiting, she spoke up.

"Excuse me. I have an appointment to speak with ICU nurse Franklin. Is she available?"

The nurses stopped talking and turned her direction with blank expressionless faces. With a slight irritated glare, one nurse broke the silence.

"I'm sorry. What's your name?"

"I'm Agent Gall from the San Francisco FBI office."

Hearing her title, they stepped forward. Leaning against the receptionist counter, one nurse stretched out her hand, took and stared at Gall's business card.

"I'm sorry, but Nurse Franklin passed away."

"I'm sorry," replied Agent Gall. "I didn't know, otherwise I would have rescheduled the appointment. Was it recent? How did it happen?" she asked.

Neither nurse returned Gall's stare nor was prepared to reply. After an awkward silence, the same nurse finally spoke up.

"It just happened. Maybe twenty minutes ago." The nurse paused. Turning away from Agent Gall, she pointed at the now empty work station behind the receptionist counter. In a dazed manner, she continued. "She just returned from her afternoon break. No one saw what happened. When we came back, her head was lying on the desk. We all thought she was taking a nap."

They stared at the vacant cubicle. There were several open folders and a pen laying on the desk. They stood around like witnesses loitering at a crime scene. With a deep sigh, the same nurse spoke. "Is there anything we can help you with Agent Gall?"

Gall blinked and flashed a blank expression. She had studied the *O'Conner Hospital* ICU staff and knew the names of everyone present during John Doe's transfer. Nurse Franklin was the only one still working here. Everyone else either transferred, retired, or passed away. There seemed to be a pattern. During Gall's investigation, she noticed that the *O'Conner* ICU had an inordinate number of deaths.

Out of the 20 ICU personnel present during the transfer, only six people had direct physical interactions with either the John Doe patient, the alleged relative, or the bogus Federal Agent. Nurse Franklin was the only surviving person who came into direct contact with them. The other five all passed away. One doctor was involved in a solo car accident on Highway 17 through the Santa Cruz Mountain pass. Another doctor drowned while surfing on Ocean Beach. He was an avid surfer and good swimmer. The other surfers did not see what happened. One nurse was diagnosed with a rare blood cancer and another nurse developed a brain tumor. The hospital administrator, during an apparent random carjacking, was shot twice. The car was recovered along a dead-end street in downtown Oakland off San Pablo Blvd. Nurse Franklin was Agent Gall's last opportunity to speak to anyone who had direct face-to-face contact with any of the suspects.

Agent Gall stood with a blank expression frozen on her face. No one paid attention to the other. Gall got the impression the nurses were caught up in their own superstitious disbelief, as if somehow, one of them would be next. From their defeated expressions, Agent Gall recognized the synchronicity and irony of the situation. As if the mathematical improbability that all six co-workers were now dead. The nurses may not have made the connection and assumed that working at this hospital's ICU was simply bad luck- a coincidence. Gall could almost hear the nurses counting their days wondering which one of them would be next.

"No, that won't be necessary. I needed to speak to Nurse Franklin. I'm sorry for your loss." With nothing left to say, Agent Gall made a hasty exit. Upon entering the elevator, Gall glanced back and saw the nurses standing with perplexed expressions. They were not speaking to one another and appeared trapped in their own thoughts.

* * * * *

Unable to interview the nurse, Agent Gall searched through the ambulance services trying to locate the company that transported her John Doe. After her second time reviewing the list, she came up empty without any new leads. She was biased by her years of experience focusing on the physical evidence; the paper trails; surveillance from nearby video cameras; un-interviewed witnesses. In this case, Agent Gall's experience worked against her. She was unable to look outside the box, trapped by the things she learned before. If she could only consider other options. Without a clear game plan, Gall started from the beginning looking for something that she might have missed.

With her head down, FBI Agent Gall read her case file and notes. Computer Forensic Specialist Agent Walters watched Gall. She had hacked into Gall's system and was spying on her. Using multiple monitors, Agent Walters kept an eye on Agent Gall while simultaneously scanning Gall's computer hard drive. To prevent being detected by the FBI, Agent Walters did not download anything. Rather, she resorted to taking screen shots and saving those images. Although this process was tedious, it was the safest way to get the information without being detected. Masking her actions with a customized software program, Agent Walters was able to breach the Bureau's system without being detected.

After saving the entire case file through screen shots, Agent Walters spent the next two days categorizing the data and preparing her report. When finished, she created three separate folders: one for her, her Supervisor John and Director Gamboa. Sitting inside the Director's office, Agent Walters walked Gamboa and John through what she uncovered.

"The FBI is at a standstill. All the paper trails lead them to nothing but dead ends. They're following all the available physical evidence; the forged transfer documents, interior video surveillance, ICU employee interviews of those who had physical interactions with the John Doe. Everything goes nowhere."

"How?" asked Director Gamboa. "There are too many loose ends. They had to leave some sort of trail?" he said out of frustration.

"Oh, there's a trail all right. It's just that the FBI doesn't see it. They're simply missing it," explained Walters.

"You mean the physical evidence?" asked John.

E.A. PADILLA

"No. The traditional physical evidence is a bust. The forged documents show the Administrator's and nurses' fingerprints. The hospital surveillance tape wasn't archived and was recorded over. It's impossible to pull anything off that hard drive once it has been written over. This event took place three years ago. The hard drives have been written over at least thirty-six times since.

"As for the interviews, there is no-one left alive that had any physical dealings with any of the suspects." Walters paused and glanced up over the top of her prescription eye glasses. She studied their faces trying to detect any reaction about this last piece of information.

"Wait a minute," interrupted Director Gamboa. "Why no interviews? There has to be several personnel that had direct contact with the relative or bogus agent. What happened to them? They couldn't all have transferred away. Even if they did move to another facility, it would be worth our time to follow up with them, right?" Gamboa asked.

As Walters looked back at the Director's and Supervisor's faces, their expressions were clear and unambiguous. They expected her to clarify this point. Until that moment, Agent Walters had assumed that the Agency must have had something to do with the disappearance of these witnesses. Now, based on their reactions, she realized she was wrong.

"That's just it. The six hospital personnel with direct physical interactions with the suspects have been identified. Agent Gall was about to interview the last surviving hospital personnel. The others all died. One by car-jacking incident, one by a rare blood cancer, another with a brain tumor, another drowns, and one in a freak solo car accident on Highway 17 through the mountain pass."

As they listened to her reading the list, the Director looked at the Supervisor with a look of disbelief. It was obvious to Walters that neither man expected that.

"What about the last remaining witness?" the Supervisor asked.

"Literally minutes before she was to be interviewed by FBI Agent Gall, nurse Franklin passed out on her work station desk and died a few moments later. She never regained consciousness. Her autopsy is scheduled for tomorrow. By all indications, she died of a heart attack."

After hearing the last piece of information, Gamboa knew that someone was eliminating these witnesses. Although it was mathematically possible, it was highly improbable. Gamboa exchanged a stern look with the Supervisor before directing his remarks to Agent Walters.

"A little too coincidental for me. So, Walters, you say there's a way to track them down without using the physical evidence. How so?" asked Gamboa.

Walters contemplated citing a scene from one of her favorite *Star Trek* movies, *Wrath of Khan*, but dismissed the idea as a little too nerdy for the A-Team Supervisor and Agency Director. During her prior assignment in New Jersey, as one of their satellite surveillance analysts, all her co-workers, including management, would have understood its reference. But not here.

"The FBI agent is thinking two-dimensionally. She is limited in her ability to consider outside resources. She is blinded by her jurisdictional capacity and limited access to all available tools. As I know you are aware, the Bureau handles only domestic issues. As such, they are limited in terms of expanding their evidentiary collecting resources through permissible and admissible factors."

"Two-dimensional?" asked the Supervisor.

As if a light turned on in Director Gamboa's brain, he began speaking in a rapid excited manner. He seemed to understand what Agent Walters was alluding to.

"Right! I get it Walters. The satellites. Located inside the US Boundaries, we rarely utilize this option. quite frankly, until now, it really wasn't necessary. A counterpart of mine overseeing Mexico City explained how they use satellite images to document and backtrack apparent Cartel activity. After an incident takes place, they can utilize the after-the-fact information to pinpoint the location and then backtrack the vehicles leaving the scene of the crime. It worked in Juarez and in other districts," explained the Director.

"Exactly," replied Agent Walters. "In this case, we have the location and exact time of the ambulance transfer. All we need to do is back track the ambulance transport from when it left the hospital. It will require a lot of man hours to scan the tapes. If the ambulance doesn't drive coast to coast, we should be able to Frankenstein each transport from this hospital to its next stop."

With a confident smile, Agent Walters placed her clasped hands-on top of the desk and allowed a slight exhale of satisfaction. "It's theoretically possible."

The Director and Supervisor stared at Walters with a sense of admiration. With a shrug, the Supervisor spoke next. "Very impressive Walters. So, the question of the day. Do such videos exist? If so, who has access, and how do we get them?"

"Well sirs, that's above my Analyst 3 pay grade," replied Walters. "But off the record, I know it's possible. After 9/11, and being from the New Jersey Office, I cut my teeth on those types of tapes."

"That makes sense that the New York Metro area would have dedicated satellite imagery. But what about the area surrounding the hospital. San Jose isn't necessarily the biggest financial district?" asked the Supervisor.

With a shrug, Walters looked at the Director before replying. "I'm guessing that the San Francisco Bay Area in general is also watched. San Francisco is the home to the Pacific Exchange. The Alameda Naval station and Travis Air Force Base combined with landmarks, the Golden Gate Bridge, UC Berkeley, and Stanford, that were all nationally recognized. Also, with Levi's Stadium in Santa Clara, I'm certain that satellites were deployed for the Super Bowl held in 2016."

"When you factor in the high-tech Silicon Valley, I would guess that Walters is right," offered Gamboa.

"Do we have access to satellite data?" asked the Supervisor.

"The Agency enterprise has access to this kind of information. However, for political reasons, all agencies located inside the United States do not have direct access. Directors assigned domestically cannot supervise any of these specialized heavy surveillance satellites. The temptation would be too great. I'll need to contact another Director located internationally.

"Where are they?" the Supervisor asked.

The Director paused. He was not breaking protocol by disclosing the locations. It was not prohibited. It just was not something that was openly discussed. He decided to answer using vague references to regional territories. It narrowed their guesses down, but they would only be guessing as to the exact locations.

"The agencies located in Europe, the Middle East, Mexico, South America and Asia have specialized satellite teams. I'll contact one of the Directors and see if they can lend me a hand. I'll let you know tomorrow what our next move will be," said the Director as he stood. The meeting was over.

*   *   *   *   *

Glancing over Diane's shoulder, Agent Chapin watched Diane tack a new wall calendar up in her cubicle. It was an oversized *LPGA* calendar. Chapin saw several dates in March circled with a thick black sharpie pen.

"Nice calendar," said Chapin flashing a supportive smile.

"Oh thanks. I've been getting into golf these days," replied Diane as she pointed at her putter leaning against the cubicle partition. Lying on top of the carpet next to the putter were three new golf balls fresh from its sleeve.

"Wow! You've brought your putter to the office. Now that's dedication. I used to golf in college," added Chapin. "So, I have to ask, what's your handicap?"

"It used to be about fourteen. I'm trying to get it into single digits." With a shrug of, Diane continued "We'll see."

Chapin nodded. Compared to Diane, she was a hacker. "So, why are the weekends in March circled?"

Diane glanced at her new wall calendar. "It's the *LPGA*. They make a West Coast swing through San Diego and the Palms Springs area. I was thinking I'd go down there for the weekend and watch Saturday and Sunday. Something I always wanted to do, but never made the time. I'm thinking that time is slipping by. I'd better stop thinking about it and just make it happen."

Without effort, Diane finished speaking. She spoke in an honest and sincere manner. Without realizing it, a sense of sadness washed over her face. As she thought about embellishing her cover story, the principal motivation for all her actions surrounded the guilt and sadness she felt over the loss of her niece. Hearing her words, Diane felt the pain associated with her loss. Without trying, a sense of dread and misery settled over her demeanor. During an awkward silence, Chapin felt Diane's pain.. It was obvious that she was struggling trying to adjust to her loss.

Everyone in the Alpha-Team knew what happened to Diane's niece. They knew how proud she was when her niece was accepted into the elite A-Team. After the plane crash, and Diane's subsequent transfer out of the recruitment division, there was a sense that she was winding down her Agency career preparing for retirement. She had earned it.

Diane caught herself drifting off into her thoughts and forced herself to lift her head and make eye-contact with Agent Chapin. Recognizing Diane's emotional state, Chapin flashed a sincere smile.

As if to say, "I feel your pain. Everything will be all right." Without speaking, she projected a knowing look of concern and empathy. It was an unspoken moment.

"A couple of weekends down south sound wonderful Diane. Like a mini vacation. It sounds great. A change of scenery never hurt anyone," offered Chapin.

"Exactly. A change. It's long overdue," replied Diane.

*   *   *   *   *

Roberta Finchum's training in France was coming along. Her Supervisor Marie Sinor was tough, tough on everyone, including herself. She had to. A single mistake out here could cost people's lives. For the first six months, Roberta participated in ten outside field work training sessions. Each mission, she was assigned as the look out. For her part, each live mission lasted less than two hours. Finchum was frustrated being the lowest agent on the totem pole. If anything happened, she could only help extract other agents. Yet, her roles did not include making the drops or making the meet. For now, her sole responsibility was to memorize a long list of mug shots.

She needed to be able to identify any number of faces from a sea of pedestrians that passed by. If that happened, she would use her hidden microphone alerting the other team members that a bad guy was present. Finchum had yet to see anyone suspicious. For this mission, Finchum was positioned at the corner café to be drinking a coffee and reading a newspaper. She felt like dead weight.

While waiting, she thought back to her first mission. She was so excited. She was nervous and had studied deep into the night memorizing all 252 various mug shots. Many of them modified versions of the same person with varying hair lengths and colors, while others depicted the face clean shaven.

The only original contribution Roberta would make to that mission was her attire. She was not required to wear anything specific. She was given a general instruction to "wear something casual." It was typical for a lookout to wear pants, a baggy jacket, and flat shoes. A jacket hid her pistol. The pants in case she needed to run.

Roberta focused on remaining positive. She recognized that every trainee agent started this way. Although her assignment was not glamorous, she represented the first line of defense. Her role was not only important but vital.

In contrast, today's mission offered some excitement. An informant was being moved from France and transported to the Berlin Agency. He was promised immunity and new credentials in the country of his choice, in exchange for vital intellectual cooperation. The espionage vernacular for this mission was a "hand off".

Roberta settled into her role. It was her longest and most important mission to date. As each minute passed, she seemed to acclimate. It was a new experience. The sound coming through her ear piece caught her attention.

"Our contact is in site," whispered the senior field agent Briana Moreau. Roberta could not help but think how intriguing Briana's heavy French accent added to the mission.

"Roger that," replied Supervisor Sinor from the safety of their headquarters. Although she was not present on the scene, she watched everything unfold from two different satellite images hovering above. "All clear on the backside," whispered Roberta. Glancing over her newspaper, she studied each passing person's face. Her eyes darted back and forth behind her sunglasses making sure to check the bicyclists too. So far, no one matched any of the mug shots she memorized. As the other lookouts checked in, Roberta continued surveying her assigned area. Everything was clear.

Briana saw her "musician", the slang term for clandestine radio operator. He was her package and would escort him to the safe house. He looked jumpy and on edge. He was walking way too quick making jerky unnatural movements. His head kept turning from side to side as he rushed down the sidewalk. Seeing his behavior, Briana knew that this guy was certainly a technician or analyst, too nervous to be a field agent. A field agent would never exhibit this type of behavior. She was afraid his inexperience and nervousness would attract unwanted attention. Eager to get control of the situation, Briana stepped in front of the man. Seeing his face, she knew this was her guy.

"Calm down. Relax. You are attracting too much attention," said Briana under her breath.

The man's eyes opened wide, as he froze in his footsteps. The shock on his face was too exaggerated. He seemed to be more than just surprised by her sudden appearance. His excitement level was over the top even for an inexperienced analyst. Briana's frustration became a distraction. Rather than continuing to scan the area, she was too focused on her contact.

Like sharks drawn to blood in the water, several men closed in. They must have followed him. Their sudden appearance took the advance team by surprise. In an orchestrated attack, two Agency lookouts were hit with tranquilizer darts. The dosage was not lethal. Just powerful enough to drop both 200-pound men, immobilizing them for the next five minutes. The attackers hoped to get them alive to interrogate them later. Otherwise, they would have just been killed.

As the Agency men collapsed, the attackers reached down. With a swift motion, the attackers grabbed something from each man. From the satellite views above, Supervisor Sinor guessed what was happening. The only noise coming through sounded like the microphones were being ripped away from their necks. Afterward, nothing but silence transmitted over the communication network.

"Briana! Both forward lookouts were just dropped," shouted Supervisor Sinor over the shared communication link.

Briana reached out to steady the contact's hands. Unable to move, the contact stood frozen in his tracks. His inexperience and fear started the snowball chain reaction of circumstances. Without any warning, another attacker stepped up behind Briana. When the contact's eyes bulged out in fear, she assumed someone was approaching from behind.

Without warning, she felt an oversized calloused hand encircle her neck muffling her microphone. With a quick flick of his wrist, the microphone was disconnected, thrown to the ground, and smashed under his boot. Briana was taken aback by the sensation of his hand. The skin felt like rough sand paper. It happened so fast.

Only after the hard metal end of his *Gsh-18* Russian made 9mm pistol was stuck into the small of her back that she realized what happened.

"So, my little Frenchie," grunted her attacker spoke with a thick Russian accent. "You didn't expect to see us now did you?"

Briana's arm was twisted away and yanked behind her back preventing her from recovering her *M9 Berretta*. While the large man put Briana's weapon into his jacket pocket, the other two attackers grabbed the contact by his shirt and corralled him close. Glancing around, the men led Briana and the contact in the opposite direction.

Unable to see what was happening, Roberta broke radio silence.

"Briana?" whispered Roberta over the network. Still no response. She knew something was wrong. The sound of Supervisor Sinor's voice got her attention.

"Finchum, something went wrong. The contact and Briana have been detained. They're being led your way," explained Sinor. Just then, Roberta saw two men practically carrying their contact pushing him forward. She studied their faces and recognized them both from the images she memorized. The attackers were unaware of Roberta.

Finchum glanced up and down the walkway. She saw another large man coming up behind them. Briana Moreau was being pushed forward by a huge barrel-chested man. He stood at least 6 feet 7 inches tall with a tight grip around Briana's arm. There was no sign of the other two look out agents. From that moment, everything slowed down.

It was as if everything she learned, every hypothetical scenario, every practice shot taken at the shooting range had prepared her for this moment. It was not her first battle field experience, nor her first shoot-out. But at that moment, she was posing as another person all together. She had a new identity, new appearance, and was technically fighting on foreign soil, assigned to the French Agency. Without any fear, without complicating the situation by overthinking, she did what came naturally.

Roberta slid her pistol out from under her oversized jacket. With her other hand, she retrieved her silenced pistol then released the safety. Like the voice of a fighter pilot speaking in a robotic monotone manner, Roberta whispered into the neck mounted microphone.

"I see the contact. He is surrounded by two bad guys. No sign of our two backups. Lead is being man handled with a gun at her back," relayed Roberta.

Back at the headquarters, sitting in silence, Supervisor Sinor listened and watched the overhead satellite images. She did not want to distract Roberta. Everything had gone wrong. It was supposed to be a simple escort mission. Their little charade was uncovered, and their contact was blown. It was too late to send in additional backups. They would arrive too late. She had no choice but to leave it up to the newbie. Before Sinor could give any instructions, Roberta reacted.

"If I don't act, we'll lose our contact and Agent Moreau. I'm taking them out."

Peeking out from behind her raised newspaper, Roberta watched the huge man herding Briana come around the light pole.

127

Holding the paper up in front of her face, using her other hand, Roberta gripped the silenced M9 up just out to the side of the paper. With smooth confidence, she aimed her pistol at his forehead. He was so tall his head towered well above Briana's head. It was a clear shot. She hoped the bullet would drop him without causing his hand to spasm involuntarily discharging his weapon. It was all she had. Squeezing her index finger, the pistol kicked back causing her wrist to recoil back.

The silencer suppressed the gun fire. Very little was heard over the normal sounds of the plaza. Some birds, unaccustomed to the high-pitched spitting sound that echoed across the open space, flew away. As Briana continued forward, she felt the pressure from the huge man's pistol ease and disappear. Without warning, Briana heard a thud as the huge man's body fell forward collapsing to his knees before his face slammed against the asphalt walkway.

The unusual noise sounded like a watermelon falling onto the ground and caught the other attackers' attention. Holding the contact between them, they turned back glancing over their outside shoulders. Seeing their comrade splayed out face first, they looked around trying to locate the shooter. Frantic, Briana turned around, and dove on-top of the fallen Russian. Looking for her weapon, she searched his jacket. Recognizing the danger, one attacker released the contact and pulled out his pistol ready to stop Briana.

The two attackers were so distracted by Briana neither noticed Roberta sitting at the table behind the newspaper. Without warning, another suppressed muzzle shot slammed another bullet into the center of the attacker's sternum. Roberta stood ready to take her final shot. Seeing the newspaper fall forward, the final attacker saw Roberta. With pieces of the newspaper cascading about, like falling confetti during a New Year's Eve party, the last attacker tried using the contact as a shield. Reacting too slowly, he felt the bullet impact slap against his forehead. The bullet entered his skull between his wide unsuspecting eyes. There was no time to react. He was dead before his body crumbled onto the asphalt walkway.

Not missing a beat, Roberta stood and grabbed the contact. He was in shock staring down at the three dead men. Roberta shoved the contact back in the direction they came from. Before following Roberta, Briana recovered her gun from inside the dead Russian's jacket.

"Attackers eliminated," whispered Roberta into her neck mounted microphone. "We're returning to our downed agents. Pick us up at the corner by the train station," she instructed Sinor. Roberta spoke in a calm controlled voice, as if she did this sort of thing hundreds of times before. "I have Briana and the contact."

Supervisor Sinor listened. Any covert mission had the potential to turn on a dime. It was a fluid game of cat and mouse. It was times like this that tested a person's salt. There was no substitution for a real on-going operation. Simulations went only so far. As Supervisor Sinor processed Roberta's words, she raised her hand and waved over two other agents across the room.

"Roger that. I have two agents enroute to you now. They'll be there in five minutes," said Sinor as two agents hurried up next to Sinor waiting for their orders.

"Copy that," replied Roberta.

Sinor turned her attention to the men. "The switch went bad. They're naked down there. Take the van and wait for them at the corner near the train stop."

Both men nodded before sprinting for the elevator. Sinor waved over another set of agents.

"We've been burned. You two get down with our Agency ambulance. It sounds like we've got three kills. If the city beats you there, video document the scene. I really want a look at the attackers though. We need to know their affiliations."

"Yes ma'am," they replied in unison. They glanced at each other and started for the elevator. Sinor yelled at them as they crossed the floor.

"Put your siren and lights on. If I hear that a real ambulance gets dispatched, I'll let you know."

"Roger that!" one yelled back over his shoulder.

Sinor turned her attention back to Roberta.

"Roberta, I need an update," asked Sinor.

"I can see our two field agents struggling to their feet. They seem to be okay. No local law enforcement present. Several bystanders standing about. Otherwise, still clear."

"Can our two guys walk?" said Sinor while watching the satellite monitor images from above and listening to the background noise coming from Roberta's microphone heard Briana say something about the two agents. Other than Roberta's, the other three's microphone were gone taken by the attackers.

"They look okay. We'll rag tag it to the corner. We should be there in five minutes," replied Roberta.

"By the time you guys get there, you should see our van at the corner," explained Sinor.

"Copy that."

The agents still feeling the effects from the tranquilizers, Briana helped steady them, while Roberta kept a firm grip on the contact. The last thing she wanted was for this guy to go rabbit on her. With an intense stare, she glared at the frightened contact.

"Don't even think about running off," Roberta warned.

The contact's eyes bulged. He saw what she did to the others. Any ideas of taking off had vanished. She had his full and complete attention. With a quick forceful nod, she shoved the contact forward.

Glancing about, Roberta saw no new attackers or police, and followed Briana with the two other field agents. Briana turned back toward Roberta.

"Thanks."

With a tight-lipped smile, Roberta nodded in acknowledgement. Seeing the two other field agents following, Briana turned her attention forward. With everyone grouped together, they fought the urge to run. With steady confident strides, they made their way to the corner and saw a large white van with dark tinted windows pull up and park. The engine idled while the driver tapped his hands on the steering wheel.

"We're almost to the van. Everyone is present with the package in tow," relayed Roberta through her neck mounted microphone.

"Instruct the driver to take you to the safe house," ordered Sinor. "I'll meet you there."

Briana was the first to arrive. With a quick jerk on the handle, she opened the door. Roberta pushed the contact through the open door and helped the other two get inside.

"Package inside and secure," explained Roberta. Looking through the van's open side door, she spoke to the driver. "Cuff the package to the seat. He's way too jumpy." Speaking to Sinor again, "We're all inside. Heading to the safe house," explained Roberta before slamming the van door shut.

"Good job. I'll see you there."

"Copy that," Roberta replied.

"Out."

"Out," confirmed Roberta.

As Sinor sat back, she exhaled a deep sigh of relief. Thinking to herself "*that could have gone badly.*" As the rush of adrenaline from the situation subsided, Sinor regained her composure. With everything returning to normal, a smile appeared on her face. With a shake of her head, she looked up speaking out loud to an otherwise empty room. "That Roberta is something else."

5

Gamboa sent an encrypted email to his counterpart, the Director in Korea. She just completed a mission along the DMZ (Demilitarized Zone) that separated Korea. Korea was a powder keg of international concern. Gamboa knew she managed one of the Agency's SAT-INT (Satellite Intelligence Units). He assumed most of the wrap up was concluded but opted to send an email first. The matter to reopen the Anderson case was not urgent. He would wait for her to find free time to contact him.

With a 16-hour time difference between California and Korea, Gamboa sent his message at precisely 1700 hours PST. Given her location in Korea and being across the International Date Line, he figured it would be about nine in the morning over there. Minutes after sending his message, his direct line rang through. The caller ID listed the area code as 01182. He knew it was an international call from Korea. It had to be her.

He broke protocol as he knew who was calling. "Wow, I just sent that email. How have you been Nena?" said Director Gamboa into his encrypted and secure back line.

"Hello '*Director*' Gamboa," she replied in a calm smooth manner. Sharing the same title, she pronounced the word director in a sarcastic self-deprecating way.

"Right...I've heard, unofficially of course, that you and your team have been quite busy these days," countered Gamboa.

"Let's put it this way, the old triple jump never gets old," she replied in an upbeat positive manner.

Gamboa knew she was referring to her express flight from Seoul to Washington DC. Although he was not fond of those cross-country flights, he felt a slight sense of envy knowing she got to ride backseat in a fighter jet for part of her trip, before being transferred to an Agency modified Concorde jet for the remainder of the way.

"So, it's safe to say that our nemesis to the north didn't escalate things?" Gamboa asked in a joking manner.

"They did send a squad across the DMZ. A couple ROK (Republic of Korea aka South Korea) escort vehicles got hit. We were concerned that they were going to take out a civilian bus transporting people from a border town village. It could have been really ugly," Director Valdez replied. Cutting through the gossip, Nena said "So Gamboa, what's up?"

"I have a situation. There was a downed commercial passenger plane traveling from LA to Hawaii. It happened about three years ago. You may have heard about it?" asked Gamboa.

"Vaguely."

"Anyway, we may have tracked down a key player involved. He was never identified and remains a John Doe in a local hospital. If it's our guy, he had to have some outside help. We uncovered some forged hospital discharge documents."

"Gutsy," she replied. "And connected. That's no easy feat."

"So far, our investigation is a dead end. All we have left is to back track the ambulance transport and need dated satellite images. That's your area of expertise ma'am. So that's why I sent you the email." Gamboa paused thinking that he needed to provide Nena with some additional clarification. "Also, we're only interested in this John Doe. We don't need or want any information on U.S. Citizens."

Nena thought about Gamboa's request. She knew that Agency locations inside the US and its territories were legally bound and prohibited from utilizing this new form of surveillance, except under a narrow set of parameters, most notably, terrorist situations. Due to constitutional restrictions, many stateside Agency Directors had to be careful when utilizing this technology.

Nena had no such concerns. She was in Korea and had no constitutional restrictions to consider. Other than little Guam, her birds were free to fly and survey to her teams' hearts content.

"Understood. How long do you need to go back? We only started archiving areas after 2010."

"That's perfect. What areas do you have archived?" asked Gamboa.

"Because of the Super Bowls being obvious terrorist targets, we began tracking along all major interstates throughout the US. In California, the main corridors being Interstate 50 and 80 to the north and 8, 10 and 15 in the south, as well as Interstate 5 dissecting the State."

"That many?"

"Well, Sacramento being the Capitol of California, and that State being so large, it requires a stepped-up surveillance. Since 9/11, an emphasis on terrorism has become a serious threat."

"Since we don't have regular access or use for this type of surveillance, I haven't stayed up on our satellite advancements," said Gamboa in an apologetic manner.

"You'd be surprised. We have most of California blanketed with coverage. The high population, presence of high-tech industries, the large number of national monuments, combined with the number of military installations, California keeps us pretty busy. San Diego County is ridiculous. With the Marines at Camp Pendleton, the Navy and proximity to the Mexican border, not to mention the presence of cartel activity, we run a virtual freeway of satellite surveillance there.

"That many satellites?"

"We actually use drones there. They can hover in one spot for 24 straight hours. Only down side is it creates a lot of work for local law enforcement."

"What do you mean?"

"The lights on the drone make people think that they're seeing a UFO."

"Seriously?"

"Tons. Next time you get a clear night sky, look up. You'll see them in Northern California too. If you look close, they have white, green, and red lights. This way, if the ground team is in real time chase, they can determine which side of the drone they're on."

Listening to Nena's detailed explanation was impressive.

"So, you know, as protocol dictates, only my team can access these images. How pressing is it for you to analyze the data?" asked Nena.

"There is no rush at all. Our Scrub Team got a hit and I had to re-open a Director Only File. So, we're just now determining whether we should formally assign any hard assets to delve into the issue again. We just can't ignore it. We need to follow up on what the evidence warrants and exhaust our resources to determine if anything else needs to be done."

"Understood. Well, under those circumstances, I have two guys riding on the *George HW Bush* for a few months. I can put them on it during their transport over. Will that work?"

"When could you get started?" Gamboa asked.

"Email me the event date and approximate time line with the GPS coordinates and description of what we're looking for. Once we get that information, we'll find it. It's just a matter of time."

"Really. That easy?"

"We almost always succeed. Using this backtracking process, combined with our superior satellite data, it's rock solid. The only way to avoid detection is if the "purps" anticipate what we'll do. If that's the case, it becomes a shell game. And that's only happened one time before."

"Where?"

"In Berlin. Those old school Stasi and KGB guys," said Nena as she rolled her eyes in disbelief. "They don't miss a thing."

*   *   *   *   *

Lt. Kyle Benjamin sat down on the deck just below the *CV-77 George H.W. Bush's* flight deck. He stared out over the Pacific Ocean while his legs were dangling over the ledge. Without realizing, he rubbed the back of his neck. He still had random head aches and a puffy feeling in the back of his head. He knew he was lucky not to have sustained a full blow-out orbital fracture from the fall he took inside the tunnel under the DMZ.

Kyle contemplated how his life changed. For the longest time, his life centered around flying fighter jets. After developing an unexplained intolerance to G-forces, that all changed. The disappointment came late during his flight school. He was only weeks from receiving his wings, jet type, and squadron assignment. Facing the disappointment, Kyle opted out of aviation all together.

With little effort, Kyle transitioned into the Marines as none other than a sharp shooter. After a brief, yet successful career there, he was approached with the opportunity to enter the covert intelligence world inside the Agency.

Kyle's first mission was a solo invasion into a tunnel labyrinth of the DMZ between North and South Korea. Having survived the mission *Hummingbird,* Director Nena Valdez sent him along with newly promoted Field Analyst-3 Lt. Doug Elliott, aka Moon Dog, with the Carrier Strike Group 2 to get some much-needed R&R. Lt. Elliott's recent success using UVA (Unmanned Vehicle Aircraft), was a perfect match. The *USS George H.W. Bush* was the first carrier to deploy UVAs in combat situations. It was mutually beneficial and a good use of everyone's time. The Carrier Strike Group was on its way to its Garrison Head Quarters and home port of Norfolk, Virginia by way of the Mediterranean Sea through the Suez Canal. Lt. Elliott could babysit the newbie of the group Kyle while pulling double duty with the UAV combat operators on the carrier.

Kyle stared down at the massive wake created by the aircraft carrier. The otherwise calm sea was disrupted by a virtual floating city traveling in excess of 35 knots. The sound of rhythmic footsteps echoing through the cave-like area announced the approach of someone. Looking over his shoulder, Kyle saw Moon Dog.

"I thought I'd find you here," said Moon Dog.

The loud roar from a F/A 18F Super Hornet being slung off the deck above echoed in the background. The unmistakable thud from the hydraulic catapult tossing the jet off the deck vibrated throughout the ship. Neither man was accustomed to the constant jet roars and unusual sounds and smells. They waited for the noise to subside before uncovering their ears and resuming their conversation.

'I wonder if the new digital catapults will create less of a vibration?" asked Moon Dog.

"I don't know, but the guys up top told me the *USS Gerald Ford* is having some issues. It may be a while before they iron out all of the kinks," Kyle replied. Moon Dog detected a sense of envy in Kyle's voice. Knowing Kyle's background, Moon Dog was not surprised. Unable to pilot jets would take a long time to get over, if ever.

"These ships are amazing. It's like a floating city," Moon Dog said with an ear-to-ear grin. With a deep sigh, Moon Dog changed the subject. "Well, so much for our little relaxing cruise to the Med?"

"What's up?" asked Kyle.

"I just got word from the Director. She needs us to do some tedious satellite tape reviews," replied Moon Dog. It was obvious from his scrunched up facial expression that he was not excited.

"What?" replied Kyle displaying a similar expression making sure Moon Dog got his meaning. "Isn't that just for Analysts? I thought I was a field agent," offered Kyle.

"Easy there mister. It wasn't too long ago when that's all I did. But this one involves some high-level clearance. It's stateside Director's-Only closed file. It must be some serious shit," Moon Dog replied. "The Agency has its own designated room on all of these new Nimitz-Class Super-carriers. It's totally off limits to all other naval personnel. The area is sealed off and only opened under the direct orders by an Agency Director. "Lucky us," said Moon Dog in a sarcastic manner. "The order's been given."

*   *   *   *   *

Winstead was meticulous. His assignment kept him on his toes. His work at the Bureau was impeccable. His analysis and reports were clean and to the point. All his recommendations included ample supporting documentation. Over his time as the mole, he was the least likely person inside the San Francisco office to be suspected as a spy. Working both sides of the fence gave Winstead a different perspective. He was motivated by much deeper factors.

Success at his job meant much more than receiving a plaque or some promotion. Doing a good job kept him safe and avoided being sentenced to death. Unlike his co-workers, Winstead maintained a much higher motivation level that persisted throughout everything he did. His life and freedom depended on it.

As Winstead waited for Van Aelst to return from his meeting with Diane Klein, he stared out the *Hyatt Regency's* suite window. The night lights radiated across the city. In the distance, he watched the cars pass over the Golden Gate and Bay Bridges. His view was breathtaking. With nothing to do but wait, Winstead relaxed. His emotional state was much different than before. Interacting face-to-face with the infamous "Lone Wolf" had its affect. His assignment, being trusted to obtain valuable personal information, information that was vital to protect Van Aelst's grandson. This mission held much more personal meaning than some unknown contact, switch, or infiltration. Winstead viewed this mission as an honor and privilege. It was something that would, without doubt, advance his career, elevating him to bigger and better things. He was still hopeful being reassigned outside the states and back to Europe, preferably inside Berlin.

The sound of the electronic tone echoing on the other side of the closed door, announced the "Lone Wolf's" return. Winstead turned away from the window view and waited for instructions. As the door opened, he heard Van Aelst's distinct voice call out.

"A beautiful city, yes?"

Winstead watched Herr Van Aelst approach the window. Standing side by side, with their hands stuffed into their pants pockets, they stared out the large window looking at the city lights and the bridges over the bay.

"It's almost as beautiful as Berlin. The Spree River. The shining lights. My favorite time of the day is after sunset," whispered Van Aelst.

Winstead leaned closer to the Lone Wolf. He wanted to hear every word. It was an intimate moment. Smiling, Winstead nodded. Van Aelst's deep blue eyes pierced through the darkness.

"After this matter is resolved Winsted, I will be recalling you to Germany. You must first complete this last assignment." Van Aelst paused, making sure Winstead understood its importance. "Afterward, it will be too dangerous for you to stay."

Hearing these words, Winstead's eyes dilated. With a new rush of adrenaline, he could not restrain his curiosity. "What do you need me to do?"

The Lone Wolf dropped his gaze and gathered his thoughts. He took his time to reply. He wanted to deliver the instructions with clarity, untainted by his emotions, without exposing the danger that he placed Winstead in. In a controlled, confident manner, Van Aelst spoke.

"I need you to eliminate FBI Agent Gall and a Supervisor inside the Agency, and..." said Van Aelst.

Winstead's eyes remained focused. Unblinking and unfazed returning Herr Van Aelst's gaze. "Someone else?" asked Winstead.

"Yes. One more person," replied Van Aelst.

"Who?"

"US Senator Anthony."

*   *   *   *   *

Agent Gall lived in the East Bay in the Oakland Hills. In the 1990's, the area was destroyed by a raging fire. After the ashes settled, the area looked like a war zone. A brick chimney standing on the scorched hillside represented the only proof that a home was located there. Underneath the dirt, concrete foundations crumbled having been incinerated turning a pinkish hue from the intense heat.

The insurance industry rebuilt the neighborhoods. Gall purchased one of these refurbished homes located inside the Hiller Highlands Community. Agent Gall's morning commute took her through a steep narrow winding road. There was one way in and one way out of her subdivision.

Winstead studied the area and located a dangerous section of road. It was perfect. Based on the warning signs and newer reinforced guardrails, it was clear accidents took place there. The locals referred to that section of roadway as hamburger hill.

During the evening, Winstead rigged Agent Gall's vehicle tampering with the brakes and planting metal shards inside the airbag system. With a synchronized explosion, the airbag would send metal projectiles. It would have the same effect as a shot gun pointed at her face. When Gall approached the hairpin turn, using a remote trigger, Winstead planned to detonate the explosion.

Waiting along a vacant section of the road, Winstead stared into his rear-view mirror. On cue, he watched Gall's white convertible soft top *BMW* coupe speeding down the road. It was her favorite part of the commute. Over the years, she enjoyed pushing her car around that turn. Today was no exception.

Depressing the accelerator, Gall smiled pushing her vehicle faster. She concentrated timing her braking around each turn. It became a personal challenge. Over the years, she tried to see how fast she traversed the turn. Her best effort so far resulted in 58 miles per hour. Today, the street was clear in both directions. The road was dry. Without having to worry about oncoming traffic, she felt that this was the day. With the car just having its 30,000-mile check-up, combined with a new set of tires, Gall was poised to break her personal best.

As Gall accelerated approaching 63 miles per hour, her eyes widened with excitement. With a sense of satisfaction, she moved her foot to brake. Her adrenaline spiked. She felt the powerful natural endorphins kick in and rode the mental rush.

Without warning, something exploded underneath the car. At first, she thought she ran over something. At the same time, the brake discs shattered like thin window glass. The jolt reverberated upward shaking the entire car. The shock wave ricocheted off the roadway sending the vehicle upward causing the tires to lose contact with the asphalt road.

Gall felt the brake pedal go soft as it sunk to the floor. Without any resistance, the vehicle increased velocity and sped down the road. Without thinking, Gall sensed the danger. Her time as an MP (Military Police), included protective detail training for VIP's and foreign dignitaries. That training included staged driving scenarios placing a limousine into a spin. The goal was to evade and maneuver the vehicle out of danger all while driving in reverse. Another scenario dealt with high-speed evasive maneuvers while being chased. That training culminated in the use of live gunshot rounds and explosions to enhance the situation. Every effort was made to make the training as realistic as possible. After training hundreds of hours, the drivers could handle most driving situations.

As if on autopilot, Gall's instincts knew she lost her brakes. Without thinking, she grabbed the hand brake pulling back with all her strength. The emergency brakes are run off a separate caliper that grips onto the rear wheel rotors. It was designed as a stand-alone system precisely for this type of situation.

The rear tires locked up. If the explosive forces had not forced the tires upward causing the rubber tires to lose contact with the road, Gall's *BMW* may have slowed enough. Unfortunately, the handbrake required contact with the roadway. Once the tires came back into contact with the road, the new tires gripped down onto the asphalt surface causing a plume of grayish smoke into the air.

With the unmistakable sound of screeching tires, a pungent odor of melting rubber filled the sky.

The convertible crossed over the yellow dotted lines heading straight into the metal guardrail. Seeing the railing, her instincts kicked in. She steered the vehicle away from the railing. She wanted to avoid overcorrecting. She knew the car could flip. Everything happened so fast. Each decision was sub-conscious as her training took over. The reduction in speed combined with the slight turn of the wheel prevented her from hitting the guard rail head-on in a perpendicular 90-degree angle.

As the *BMW* hit the railing, sparks flew. When the quarter panel pulled away from the car's frame, the screeching metal on metal sound reverberated. The air bags deployed sending shards of metal shavings toward Agent Gall. Her thick sunglasses provided enough protection deflecting the metal away from her eyes. The remainder of her upper body did not fare so well. As other metal shards continued along their trajectory, they sliced through her checks, neck, shoulders, and upper arms. Several larger metal pieces penetrated through the glasses and became imbedded across her forehead.

The impact with the guard rail, combined with the injuries knocked Gall unconscious. Before coming to a stop, the *BMW* continued forward sliding along the guard rail another 200 feet. Had the vehicle hit the guard rail perpendicularly, the railing would have failed sending the vehicle and Gall over the cliff falling to the bottom of the ravine hundreds of feet below. The momentum from the accident rolled the vehicle onto its side then came to a rest. The contrast in sounds was abrupt. From the sudden onset of screeching tires and metal on metal, followed by absolute silence was surreal.

Taken aback by the destruction, Winstead stared out his front windshield. Two sets of tire tread skid marks lay behind the crumpled heap of metal on the side of the road. With a deep sigh, Winstead looked up and down the road. With nothing approaching in either direction, he drove up for a closer look.

He rolled down the window and stopped next to the overturned *BMW*. Glancing inside, Agent Gall was lying against the spent airbag hanging upside down, held in place by her seatbelt. Leaning closer, he saw a lot of blood. She was not moving. He considered getting out but decided against it. He was too exposed parked next to the wrecked vehicle. Any moment, he expected to see a commuter make their way down this busy roadway. Glancing at the guardrail Winstead was surprised the vehicle did not plunge over the edge.

Winstead heard the distinct sounds from an engine motor and unique hum from rubber tires gripping the asphalt. He had no choice. He sped away down the twisting road. Glancing at the reflection in his rearview mirror, Winstead was desperate trying to maneuver beyond the next roadway bend before the oncoming vehicle came into view. Accelerating down the road, he was certain he was not seen. With a deep sigh of relief, he hoped everything worked out as planned. He would have to wait and see.

* * * * *

Diane Klein booked a flight for her weekend golf trip to San Diego for the *LPGA* Kia Classic in Carlsbad. She made a point to leave her computer screen open to the airline website. If the Agency was monitoring her actions, she wanted to be certain, with no doubt of her plans. While entering her credit card information, Agent Chapin walked into the A-Team area. Diane thought Chapin looked distracted lost in her thoughts. She did not acknowledge the other team members working inside the other cubicles. Diane watched Chapin slumped shoulders as she sat in her chair.

Diane waited for Chapin to look her way and make eye-contact before speaking.

"What's up Cathy? You seem distracted," asked Diane.

"Just weird that's all. Agent Gall, the FBI agent, she missed our meeting this morning. I spoke to her last night to confirm." Agent Chapin said with a puzzled confused expression.

"Did you try her office?"

"Yeah. I thought maybe she got distracted and spaced it. But she didn't make it to the office either." After a pause, Chapin continued. "No one knows where she is."

With a concerned expression on her face, Diane replied. "I hope she's all right."

"That's just it. Last night, she told me she needed to tell me something. She didn't want to talk about it on the phone or send anything over email," said Chapin while exchanging a cryptic look with Diane. "It was like she was afraid. As if she suspected she was being watched."

*   *   *   *   *

As Van Aelst instructed, Winstead took a round-about route back to the office making sure to enter several different multi-levels parking garages, entering and exiting from a different one each time. After crisscrossing back and forth over the Golden Gate and Bay Area bridges, he returned to the Bureau parking lot. Upon arriving, he requested a pool car and went east on Interstate 580 before cutting across to connect with Interstate 5 south. Once on Interstate 5, he enjoyed the benefits of driving with exempt federal license plates and set the cruise control to 85 mph. As his black *Crown Victoria* barreled down the freeways, seeing his plates, the other vehicles moved over giving him a wide berth and free access even through somewhat thicker traffic. Most drivers, thinking it was an unmarked California Highway Patrol vehicle gave Winstead a clear unobstructed run along Interstate 5 South.

Winstead made great time. In no time, he was climbing the Grapevine Pass and entered Los Angeles County. Here, even his federal exempt license plates went only so far. The traffic was so thick that eventually, he had to take the vehicle off cruise control and reduce his speed. Following Van Aelst's instructions, Winstead scheduled a meeting in Koreatown on Wilshire Blvd. The Lone Wolf was specific, insisting that Winstead use only his old DPRK (Democratic People of Korea aka North Korea) contact in LA. It was essential that only Koreans be used in this part of his plan. There could be no deviations.

Winstead approached eastbound highway 101 interchange just as the afternoon commute traffic began. Fighting his way through the log jam of cars, his *Crown Victoria* crawled along the highway. Seeing the Vermont exit, Winstead looked forward to surface streets escaping the congested highway. After passing several streets, he turned onto Wilshire Blvd continued driving until he heard *"You have reached your destination on the right,"* from his navigation program.

Winstead pulled inside the underground structure and parked. Before getting out, he sent a text and waited for a reply. Within seconds, he received it.

"Go into the restaurant on the top floor. The receptionist will meet you there and walk you back to my booth."

Winstead exited the car and took the ground level parking lot elevator. Glancing about he saw only high-end new *Mercedes, Lexus, Land Rovers* and *BMW's*. No *Toyota's, Kia's* or American made cars for that matter, anywhere. Winstead was taken aback. The place was spotless. Not a single discarded cigarette butt, nor hint of graffiti spray paint. The flooring was immaculate shiny white marble. With a puzzled expression, Winstead stepped inside the oversized elevator and pushed the button for the top floor.

As the elevator opened to the top floor restaurant, he saw two counters: one for take-out and the other for in-dining. A young Korean woman glanced up and met Winstead's gaze. She was calm and exuded confidence. Her hair was cropped just above her shoulders and was dyed a dark reddish brown. Winstead approached and read her name tag- Angelie. Without any hint of an accent, she spoke in perfect English.

"May I help you?"

"I have an appointment with a Mr. Hong," replied Winstead.

With a quick glance up and down, Angelie sized him up. Although he spoke English, she detected a slight accent. For some reason, she got the impression he was educated in Europe, probably in Germany. Angelie stepped around the counter and led him to the seating area. Without turning around, she called over her shoulder.

"Follow me please."

Winstead followed and scanned the area. There were several families already seated beginning to eat. He heard soft Korean music piped through the ceiling speakers and admired the oversized wall paintings. The place projected a relaxed calm atmosphere. Nothing was like what he expected. Winstead followed her around the corner and through an alcove opening. Inside, were larger banquet rooms. In this back area, there was no music. The only noise was the echo from their footsteps. They continued to the last room. Peering through the doorway there were no lights. The room was dark. A few candles provided the only illumination. Peeking inside, he saw two tables separated by tall bamboo partitions.

"Back here," instructed Angelie and pointed her index finger toward the dark room. Winstead paused. As he approached the table, it was so dark, he could not see the ground. While leading him inside, to avoid stumbling, Winstead walked on her heels staying as close as possible. Holding the curtain area open, she finally looked back.

"Mr. Hong is waiting inside."

Winstead paused. For a fleeting second, he froze in place wondering how to proceed. Unfazed, Angelie held the curtain fabric open. From inside, he heard a man's voice.

'Please. Mr. Winstead, come inside."

With a forced tight-lipped smile, Winstead stepped through the opened curtain.

"Have a seat, please," Mr. Hong said in a cold expressionless tone.

As Winstead slid inside, he felt a cold metal pistol barrel jab into his ribs from behind. In an awkward bent position, Winstead froze. The man sitting inside raised a cell phone. With a quick flip of his wrist, an unexpected camera flash stunned Winstead. Having his picture taken, was the last thing he expected.

"We must be careful you see, Mr. Winstead," said the man holding the smart phone. After texting the picture, the Korean raised his head and stared back into Winstead's face. "Now, we wait," he explained.

"For what?" asked Winstead.

At that very moment, Winstead's cell phone rang. Surprised, with raised his eyebrows, Winstead made eye-contact before speaking. "Should I answer my phone?"

"Yes. It should be our mutual acquaintance," replied the Korean man.

Winstead reached into his back pants pocket and retrieved his phone.

"Place the phone on the table and put it on speaker," instructed the Korean. Doing as he was told, Winstead avoided speaking resorting to sign language afraid of upsetting him. Winstead reached out and touched his smart phone screen to answer the call.

"You're on speaker," explained Winstead as the call came through.

"To be expected," replied Van Aelst in a calm and controlled manner. "Mr. Hong," continued Van Aelst. "The man standing before you works for me. His ID will show that he works for the FBI. We need a favor."

"And who are you?" asked the Korean leaning forward to speak directly into the phone.

"You know me as my code name, The Lone Wolf."

There was a long pause before the Korean spoke again. "Where did you and I first meet?" he asked trying to verify the authenticity of the caller's identity.

Without any pause, Van Aelst replied. "In Moscow. We helped you out with a sensitive airline downing issue over South Korea."

"And after that, the next time. Where did we meet again?"

"There was no next time. I was supposed to meet you in Beijing, but our meeting was cancelled."

With a slight nod, Mr. Hong seemed satisfied that he was speaking to The Lone Wolf. Speaking in Korean, Mr. Hong glanced up at Angelie. "Ka ja (go)."

Angelie removed her pistol from against Winstead's ribcage and backed out of the area then closed the curtain. Keeping the call on speaker, Mr. Hong continued the conversation.

"It's been a long time Mr. Van Aelst. After all of these years, what can we do for you?"

"We need some of your regional powder to eliminate a few Americans. I also need some Korean muscle to make some noise," replied Van Aelst.

"Why not go to your European contacts?" Hong asked.

"This situation is personal. I cannot involve my normal channels. I'm using only my contacts, personal contacts. I need comrades that I trust beyond a shadow of doubt."

"It has been a long time Mr. Van Aelst. How do we know with any certainty that we can still trust each other?" asked Hong.

"You still have contact with the old woman in Seoul, yes?"

"Yes."

"She told me to contact you. She asked me to remind you about the debt you still have with her. Until it's paid, she'll be sure to keep your family safe inside the DPRK."

With a deep sigh, Mr. Hong turned away from the cell phone looking into the darkness. Nothing else needed to be said. After a moment, Mr. Hong stared into the light coming from the cell phone. "You must want some Country Jasmine. That will not be a problem. How many men?

"At least five."

"I'm guessing, with all of your contacts, you've searched us out again, hoping to capitalize on the recent events inside our country.

154

If my suspicions are correct, you also want my men's involvement to be loud and obvious, out in the open?"

"Yes, that's correct. In fact, the louder the better," replied Van Aelst.

Mr. Hong thought as much. He recognized Van Aelst's plan taking advantage of the incident along the DMZ. The Lone Wolf wanted the Imperialists to believe that whatever came next involved North Koreans and not Germans. Hong was concerned that his involvement could cost him some of his men. It was a struggle that Korea seemed helpless to avoid. Just another superpower, another country taking advantage of their size and relative weakness. With a sense of helplessness, Mr. Hong nodded in submission.

"I'll get Winstead what you need," said Mr. Hong. Without waiting for a response, Hong raised his index finger and abruptly ended the call.

*   *   *   *   *

Supervisor Sinor stared across her desk. She knew it was time. Roberta was ready. Without fanfare, Sinor upgraded Finchum from trainee to active deep cover agent status. And with this promotion, it was time. She had proved to be more than capable, ready to be assigned as the lead agent on some smaller cases.

*   *   *   *   *

"Kyle how are you doing?" asked Moon Dog.

"Pretty good. I've tracked them to five different locations. Finding the first one was a bitch. I had to watch over 80-hours of surveillance time and track 71 outbound ambulance transports before we got them. Once you know what you're looking for, it's not too bad," replied Kyle.

"Matching up the surveillance video with the discharge paperwork helped too. We just track all ambulance transport departures from each hospital and match it up with the arriving transport vehicles. If the names don't match up, bam, that's it. The challenge becomes a matching game. Finding the names and verifying the paperwork, that's the key," replied Moon Dog.

"It's boring as hell though," complained Kyle with a disappointed expression as he stared across the paper covered table. "It's not at all what I expected," Kyle added.

"Well, this is what analysts do. Keep in mind Kyle, you're more suited for Field Work. You know, guns, bombs, running around," smiled Moon Dog while pointing at Kyle's injured right eye. "But then again, analysts rarely get injured," joked Moon Dog.

Kyle smiled back. He still had some time before his eye-orbit would heal. Until then, he would get a lot of experience as a "temp-analyst". Staring back at his notes, Kyle noticed a pattern.

"If nothing else, this guy is consistent," he said.

"What do you mean?" asked Moon Dog.

"He keeps moving east."

Moon Dog's mouth gaped open. How could he have missed that? They had tracked him to the *Lions Burn Care Center* in Las Vegas, then to *North Colorado Medical Center* in Greeley, Colorado. After a month there, he moved to *Loyola University Medical Center* in

Chicago, then transferred again to *West Penn Hospital* in Pittsburgh. Moon Dog was so caught up in the minutia linking the paper trail with the video evidence, then verifying the dates, times and names used, that he missed the obvious.

Moon Dog glanced over at Kyle. He was too tired and distracted by the surveillance feed, to notice Moon Dog's stare. With a silent smirk, and slight tilted head, Moon Dog reminded himself never to under estimate a person. For a jar head field agent, Kyle was much more observant than he gave him credit for.

Moon Dog grabbed a United States wall-map and tacked it up on the cork board above the oversized conference table. Using colored push pins, he plotted the location where each ambulance transfer took place. With their hands on their hips, Kyle and Moon Dog studied the map. It seemed obvious now. With a confident nod, Moon Dog turned to Kyle.

"He's gott'a be heading to the East Coast, right?"

"That's my guess too," replied Kyle.

As if preparing to start a daunting task, Kyle released a deep sigh and rolled his eyes. "Are you ready to tackle another exciting 40 plus hours of examining and backtracking images from multiple archived satellites? God knows how many transports will be leaving Pittsburgh?"

Moon Dog studied the transport data and dropped his head in despair. With slumped shoulders, Moon Dog replied. "Based on the numbers we obtained from that particular hospital, there are 68 transports that came and went from that location."

"That's all?" asked Kyle in a sarcastic manner.

"The sooner we get started, the sooner we can get off this detail," explained Moon Dog. "Ready?"

"Fire it up," said Kyle.

Moon Dog started the archived overhead surveillance tape and fast forwarded to the time frame for the first one. Based on the prior tapes, most ambulances arrived through the ER Lobby. After locating the hospital schematics, they isolated close-up views around those areas grateful this hospital had a circular driveway providing a perfect over-head view of the ER traffic. There was only one way in and one way out.

From the experience they gained so far, they were proficient at differentiating between the overhead images of ambulances and police cars. The former being much wider with red and white fringe markings. On occasion, a private passenger vehicle turned the wrong way and entered the ER parking area. For the most part, 99 percent of the vehicle tops were ambulances.

"And there's our first customer," announced Kyle in a forced sarcastic manner as he studied the overhead tape images and pointed his index finger at the image on the large projection screen image on the wall.

"Time stamp?" asked Moon Dog.

"7:12 am. An early riser," smiled Kyle.

"That would be a Mr. Silva," said Moon Dog as he cross referenced the time with the first name on the three-page list. With a dramatic stroke of his wrist, Moon Dog checked off the name from the list.

"Remind me again why we caught this detail Moon Dog?"

"It's all about security clearance and availability. Plus, our location is one of a few locations that specializes in this type of satellite surveillance capabilities. Our ride along on the *George H.W. Bush* carrier was something extra, a way to get you and me out of Korea until things cool down. Unfortunately, we have a much more flexible schedule as opposed to the regular duties inside INT-SAT (Intelligence Satellite Division)."

"So, you're telling me we're special," replied Kyle.

"Something like that."

After a long pause, Moon Dog glanced up waiting for the next ambulance departure images to come into view. In a frustrated edgy voice, Moon Dog said "Next!"

Kyle sighed again before leaning forward and continued to scroll through the images. Under his breath, speaking in a whisper, just low enough to prevent Moon Dog from hearing what he said. *"This is going to be another long day."*

* * * * *

Winstead glanced out his window driving northbound along Interstate 5. Mr. Hong provided him with a large powder filled vial. Encased with several plastic wrap layers, and then placed inside multiple zip lock bags making sure the top opening was placed at the bottom of the proceeding bag. He did not need to be reminded about the poisonous powder's lethal strength.

Just outside Bakersfield, Winstead took the next exit. Paying cash, he purchased some beef jerky and an extra-large iced cup of root beer. The last thing he needed was an artificial bump of caffeine. After topping off the gas tank, he drove back onto Interstate 5 heading north looking for the Bay Area connection, grateful to see the 680/880 signs through Los Gatos. With clear traffic, he reverted to his prior tactic setting the *Crown Victoria's* cruise control at a comfortable 85 mph. In no time, he merged back onto the 101.

Winstead glanced down at the paper he received from Mr. Hong in LA sitting on the passenger's seat. The Korean crew's telephone number was scribbled on the paper. The crew would handle some unpleasant disinformation-based maneuvers. They only needed a day's advance notice and the location. They would do the rest.

With clear sailing, Winstead sped along the Bay. When he arrived in San Francisco, it was almost 1:00am in the morning. After returning, Van Aelst instructed him to go straight back to his hotel. He would be waiting.

*   *   *   *   *

Van Aelst's arrangements were made. He knew that, for now, neither the FBI nor the Agency made the connection. His only blind spot was inside the Agency. He assumed that the FBI was doing the lead. For now, it was a domestic issue. The only reason the Agency was involved was because their Scrub Unit picked up on the Bureau sniffing around their "Director-Only Closed" case.

Van Aelst was certain, if the Agency came up empty on the ambulance transport unable to track Curt back to Europe, they would eventually give up interest. Besides, no information copied by Curt had ever made its way to the media or general public. Regardless, the Agency had a way of following leads. It is what they did. Van Aelst's only hope was the ambulance chase came up as a dead end. Without any leads to follow, combined with the inability to verify the identity of their John Doe, the need to continue their investigation became moot.

Being from counter-intelligence, Van Aelst's mind worked backwards. His plans assumed that the Agency would eventually discover everything. He wanted to create events, that when analyzed in their totality, could be related to their investigation. Hopefully, the Agency would divert resources away from Curt. Van Aelst hoped that these new issues, the Korean angle, would lead the Americans in a different direction. Maybe, their interest in Curt would wane.

While Winstead was in LA, Van Aelst received an update from one of his other resources. Van Aelst needed clarification before moving forward with his plans. The sound of the electronic card reader announced Winstead's arrival.

As Winstead entered the room, he saw the Lone Wolf sitting at the dining room table. Still wearing his same dark pinned striped suit, he saw Van Aelst's piercing blues eyes.

"Do you have the vial?"

"Right here," replied Winstead. Still wrapped inside the zip locked bags, he handed it to Van Aelst.

"And the telephone number and contact's information?"

Winstead searched his jacket pocket, retrieved, and handed the piece of paper to Van Aelst. Van Aelst read it before slipping it into his outer breast pocket. Deep in thought, he paused, as if trying to determine if all the pieces were now in place.

"The woman. The FBI Agent Gall."

"Yes," replied Winstead.

"She survived. She's recovering at the *Kaiser Hospital* in Oakland." Van Aelst made a point to maintain an unblinking glare as if staring him down. This face-to-face scrutiny multiplied his failure until he turned away. As the Lone Wolf, Van Aelst played this game of flinch for decades, long before Winstead was born. Knowing when to back off, Van Aelst turned his gaze away from Winstead and focused on a random spot on the carpet. Unsure how to respond, Winstead offered a pathetic whispered reply.

"I'd hoped her vehicle would have crashed through the metal rail guard. I watched everything as it unfolded. Her unexpected reaction was commendable. It saved her life."

"Yes. It would seem so," was all Van Aelst said. After a long awkward pause. "You must be tired from your trip. Take a seat while I use the restroom."

Remained standing, Winstead watched Van Aelst walk across the carpeted floor. As Van Aelst closed the bathroom door, Winstead peered about the dark suite making certain they were alone. After retrieving a bottled water from the kitchenette refrigerator, he sat on a chair choosing the one facing the restroom. As he waited for Van Aelst to return, he wanted a wall to his back.

Until the bathroom door opened, Winstead focused on the light coming under the closed door. After opening the door, Van Aelst turned off the light. In the darkness, Winstead could just make out Van Aelst's silhouette and hear his footsteps padding across the carpet. Van Aelst paused near the coffee table, bent down, grabbed the television remote control, and reduced the volume. Winstead, distracted by the sudden silence failed to notice Van Aelst deposit a blue envelope on the coffee table.

From the darkened living room, Van Aelst's voice cut through the blackness. "There's a change in plans."

Interested, Winstead squinted listening to Van Aelst's every word. Unsure what to do, Winstead found himself searching Van Aelst, his hands, his waist. There was nothing out of place. Even still, Winstead felt a sudden urge to protect himself. His sixth sense was on high alert. His years of training, the skills, and intuitive feelings he acquired, everything he learned to survive as a Stasi Agent, working as a mole inside the FBI. All this accumulated experience was screaming from inside his being, demanding to be heard and acted upon. With his eyes pried wide-open and his senses on edge, Winstead waited for Van Aelst to make the first move.

Out of nowhere, Van Aelst reached across the coffee table and turned on the lamp. The sudden presence of light distracted Winstead. With what appeared to be a sincere carefree heartfelt smile, Van Aelst reached out his right hand.

"There's no longer a need for you to stay. You've done your job. The Koreans will take it from here. It's time for you to return to Germany."

Taken aback, Winstead rose and crossed the room. He reached out his right hand and exchanged a firm handshake. Still holding his hand, Van Aelst kept his steely blue eyes locked on Winstead's.

"While you were in LA, I made the arrangements. I've booked you a first-class ticket. Tomorrow night, together, we'll take the red-eye flight, non-stop from SFO to Berlin."

Winstead was relieved. This last week, he took too many chances. To get the information Van Aelst wanted, he was reckless. It was bound to catch the attention of others. His luck would catch up to him. With a tired expression, Winstead's shoulders drooped. With a deep sigh, he looked up into Van Aelst's face. This assignment took its toll. His nerves were frazzled. Over the years, deep creases now covered his once youthful face. The dark rings under his eyes were now more pronounced. He had aged well beyond his years.

"It's over?" asked Winstead.

"Yes Winstead. It's over. You've earned it."

With a soft sincere smile, the Lone Wolf patted Winstead's back with a soft open hand.

"Let's get you home. You need to pack only a precious few items. Today will be your last day as James Winstead."

Hearing these words, Winstead glanced up. The news seemed to drain his energy reserve. The decade long adrenaline rush was ending. Like a long overdue sleep, Winstead yawned. His eye lids seemed heavier than normal.

"Who will I be now? I can't go back to my real name. That identity has long since been retired. I even have a grave stone, so I've heard." Winstead's voice continued to soften, speaking just above a whisper.

"How does Schmid Sound? Martin Schmid."

As Winstead contemplated his new identity, the only other sound came from the television. With a soft nod, Winstead smiled.

"Sure. That sounds perfect."

Van Aelst grabbed the remote control and turned off the television. He grabbed the blue *American Airlines* envelope off the coffee table and handed it to Winstead.

"We have one more thing to do tonight," said Van Aelst. Winstead paused as he contemplated what was left to do. With a smirk, Van Aelst's voice broke the silence.

"I have one more meeting tonight," Van Aelst said as he raised the plastic bags protecting the vial. "You trust me, right?"

6

"Chapin, how's our progress with the satellite surveillance tracking the ambulance transport?" asked Director Gamboa.

Agent Chapin sat slouched forward in one of the wooden chairs in front of Gamboa's oversized desk. With a stern tight expression, Chapin gathered her thoughts. She felt frustrated waiting for others to give her the next clue. She understood the politics and legal constitutional issues surrounding the use of this type of data. Even still, feeling out of the loop, being relegated to sitting on her thumbs was playing havoc with her psyche. She needed a mental adjustment. Opening her folder, she updated Director Gamboa on the investigation.

"The two men, Lt. Benjamin, and Lt. Elliott have been scouring over hours of surveillance videos. They're tracking the John Doe going due east; Las Vegas, to Greeley, Colorado, then Chicago to

Pittsburgh, Pennsylvania. That's as far as they've been able to trace the transports."

"What names were used in terms of the transfers?"

"The same m.o. (modes operendi) a few weeks stay, cashier's check for services rendered, and then he's moved under the feigned assistance of the Federal government agent. One common element is the person posing as the federal agent seemed to be much older than expected. That's all we've been able to uncover at each of these locations."

"So, no more ploy about some long-lost sister or relative was used?"

"Nope. That only happened on the first transfer out of San Jose. Other than that, it looks like they're making it look like a witness protection situation. They're even posting plain clothes protection detail," explained Chapin.

She glanced up at the Director. With a scrunched face, she continued. "It's almost like they're going out of their way to be obvious about the protection detail."

Nodding, Gamboa turned to face the panel of surveillance cameras behind his desk.

"Pretty smart. They transfer him as a WITSEC (Witness Security Program), pay the bill without insurance, transport him away using forged documents, all while he's still listed as a John Doe. They roll in anonymous and leave unannounced."

Agent Chapin sat listening. She had been around the Agency a long time. This was the first time she heard anything like this case.

She waited for the Director to finish his thoughts and look her way before speaking.

"Strange. Why don't they just transport him out of the country straight away? Why all the hop scotching around?" Chapin asked.

"What type of medical treatment did he receive?"

"It looks like he was undergoing a lot. He had serious deep burns. It looks like he was having difficulty stabilizing from the shock. His recovery was stinted from being moved too soon. In each case, the doctors expressed their reservations and made sure to document those concerns in the medical notes. They were probably fearful of some medical malpractice lawsuit should the John Doe die as a result of being relocated." Looking up from her notes, Chapin continued. "So why move him in the first place?"

After a pause, the Director shrugged and offered a hypothesis. "Maybe they needed to make sure he was going to survive before they made up their mind how to proceed."

"It's like their primary goal is to keep him away from whoever is looking for him. If I had to guess, this guy is unaffiliated. It's like amateur hour," John explained.

"What do you mean?"

"If this guy was a player, his sponsoring government would have swooped in and pulled him out without making any unnecessary stateside jumps," the supervisor said. "If he was affiliated, they would worry about his medical treatments once they got him home."

Chapin and Gamboa nodded in agreement. After a brief pause, Chapin spoke up.

"What about the payments? That's some serious money to be dropping. Pretty sophisticated ground game too." Asked Chapin.

"Still, a lot of unnecessary steps. Too many risks involved. Definitely not the work of professionals," added the supervisor.

"Cartel?" offered Gamboa.

"It's possible, but doubtful. They wouldn't show so much empathy and concern for his well-being. Rather than go through all this effort, the cartel would more than likely just have him wacked," offered the Supervisor.

In frustration, the Director looked up at the ceiling. "Please tell me we've checked with WITSEC and confirmed he's not one of theirs."

"Affirmative. That's the first place we looked," replied Chapin. "They've got no one fitting this description from any of those locations."

"Well, I guess we'll have to wait and see where Benjamin and Elliott track him to. That will be our best clue. It may not be politically correct, but if this guy ends up being transported to the Middle East, we're shipping this file to the Military Intelligence. If he goes to Mexico, we ship it to the DEA (Drug Enforcement Agency). If it stays stateside or goes to Europe, we keep it," said the Director.

With disappointed looks on their faces, agent Chapin and John nodded in agreement. They needed to wait and see what Kyle and Moon Dog dug up.

*   *   *   *   *

Winstead and Van Aelst pulled into his apartment complex. Looking up, Winstead noticed his apartment lights were on and thought he saw shadows moving about inside. With a quick sideways glance, Winstead glared at Van Aelst.

"Is there something I should know?" asked Winstead.

"We need to say good bye to James Winstead remember?" replied Van Aelst.

"Right," replied Winstead. With a worried look, he continued driving into the underground parking garage. What choice did he have? If Van Aelst wanted him dead, he could have done it already. With a forced smile, Winstead parked his SUV in his assigned spot. As he was about to get out of the vehicle, Van Aelst spoke.

"If you want something out of your vehicle, take it now. This will be your last time inside."

Winstead paused and reached up to the visor. Turning it down, he searched through the CD organizer and pulled out two CDs -*Billy Joel's* greatest hits. Reaching into the center console he removed a circle shaped CD carrying case. "It might be difficult to get this in Germany," smiled Winstead. "I'm guessing, there will be some down time, yes?"

Van Aelst smiled and nodded. "Nothing else?" he asked.

"No. That's all I want."

As they made their way to the elevator, Winstead squeezed his car key remote. The SUV's doors locked, the lights blinked, followed by a high-pitched electronic chirp. Winstead thought *he would miss this place, his SUV, and even his job at the FBI.* It was surreal. Until the last few weeks, he had never been called to do much of anything. He was just a hard-working FBI agent. During his career there, he received only exemplary reviews and was on track to be promoted to the field. It was all a charade. Even still, he took pride in his work. And in some respect, he felt as if he was part of that team. The entire time, he waited for that inevitable call to duty to betray his co-workers and the U.S.

As they exited the elevator, Van Aelst spoke.

"Inside your apartment, a crew is waiting. It's being staged. We'll be leaving behind a scene that will explain your disappearance. I realize you've never played an active role in your disappearance. So, this will be your first experience. We'll send James Winstead off in style. He has served us well," smiled Van Aelst.

Winstead stopped in front of his door. With a deep sigh, he reached for his door key.

"They're expecting us. The door is unlocked," explained Van Aelst.

Winstead paused. Everything in his mind told him to run. The hair on his neck stood up. His nerves were like live wires trying to extract any information about what lay behind the door. His senses were raised on high alert fighting the urge to bolt and run away.

But where would he go? They would catch him no matter where he went. His only hope was to trust Van Aelst- The Lone Wolf.

"Don't be afraid. You'll be fine."

Winstead's feet were heavy, as if glued to the ground. He turned his head and faced Van Aelst. "I don't even know your first name."

"It's Cornelius. My first name is Cornelius. You trust me, right?"

"I do," replied Winstead.

"You should. Everything will be fine. We're just going to stage your apartment. Relax," urged Van Aelst.

Before reaching out and turning the door knob, Winstead took a deep breath then walked inside. Just before the door behind him closed, he heard what sounded like plastic tarp being unwrapped followed by the distinct sound of the deadbolt lock sliding into place. Entering the living room, the curtains were drawn. He saw several shadowy figures moving about. In a soft voice, he heard Van Aelst's say, "You're almost there. Just step into the hallway, in front of the bathroom."

As Winstead walked around the corner, he saw three Asian men. One was holding a video camera, while another man screwed a silencer on the end of a pistol. In front of the bathroom floor, lay a thick black plastic tarp. He heard others down the hallway but out of view. During those last few seconds, Winstead heard shuffling feet and people breathing. Everything appeared in slow motion. As the video camera's bright light activated, Winstead thought he smelled something. It had a distinct metallic aroma. Then it hit him.

It was human blood. Winstead squinted blinded by the bright light. He raised his hand to shade his eyes, then felt something hit him in the center of his chest.

From behind, he felt several sharp metal barbs pierce his back, followed by a surge of electrical current. It all happened quick and without warning. The last thing Winstead saw was the reflection off the shiny plastic as he fell and collapsed on the plastic tarp.

*   *   *   *   *

"What the...?"

Moon Dog was making his way back from the coffee pot when he heard Kyle's voice.

"What's up? You find something?"

"I just lost the transport vehicle. It went into the Lincoln Tunnel," replied Kyle in a confused manner. "Now right here, watch this," continued Kyle as he pointed to the screen. "Now get ready, it's about here," he urged Moon Dog to watch as he fast forwarded the surveillance tape.

"What are you doing? Why are you fast forwarding the tape?" Moon Dog asked.

"I've been staring at this section of tape for the last twenty minutes. The ambulance transport is going through the tunnel here. I've checked the distance. From this point, it runs one and half miles long. At 60 mph, it would take him about 90 seconds to enter and then exit the tunnel."

"Okay?" replied Moon Dog in a questioning manner.

"So here it comes. Are you ready?" Kyle stopped fast forwarding and let the tape play at normal speed. They both stared at the screen in anticipation. Kyle leaned forward.

Right on cue, an ambulance came out the other side of the tunnel. Moon Dog was prepared to make a snide remark when he saw another identical vehicle exit, followed by another, and then another. As each ambulance exited, Kyle stood up and counted off its corresponding number while raising his fingers on his hand.

"Two...three...four...," continued Kyle.

"What?" asked Moon Dog.

"Exactly!" replied Kyle as he continued counting. "...five, six, seven..." Kyle went on counting and resorted to using the digits on his other hand. With the presence of each ambulance that entered the screen, Kyle's voice became louder and louder, "...eight, nine, ten!"

Moon Dog turned away from the screen. Kyle had all his fingers stretched out and his eyes bulged to their maximum capacity almost yelling at Moon Dog. "Ten! What the hell?"

They both stared at each other in disbelief.

"Where did they come from?" asked Moon Dog.

"Thin air," Kyle replied in a sarcastic tone.

"No. Really?"

"I'm serious."

"Is there another converging tunnel from another direction?" Moon Dog asked.

"Not that I'm aware of," explained Kyle. "I even rewound the tape thinking that they drove in earlier. I was thinking maybe they were delayed inside and just so happened to come out now. Other than that, I have no idea. Nothing?"

"Weird?"

"Yup. I've been looking at this too long. I need a break."

As Kyle walked outside, before the door closed behind him, the noise from another jet taking off roared above. Wasting no time, Moon Dog started from where Kyle left off. He wanted to look for himself. There had to be an explanation.

*   *   *   *   *

While Van Aelst waited for the Koreans to finish staging Winstead's apartment, he thought about his earlier meeting with his old friend. Three years prior, while trying to move Curt across the country, Van Aelst activated one of his ex-Stasi retirees. He explained it as more of an extended vacation really. A way for the retiree to supplement his retirement.

Van Aelst instructed the retiree to relocate to the San Francisco Bay Area. He was to lay low and wait acting as a hidden resource available at a moment's notice. He could be a tourist, pick up a hobby like golf or, badminton, whatever floated his boat. The only stipulation was the retiree must continue to withdraw his monthly retirement stipend. He would not need the funds to survive but needed to give the appearance that he was traveling abroad. Van

Aelst provided him with an open-ended debit card. He had an endless available credit limit. The retiree knew better than to abuse the privilege.

It was a dream assignment. Van Aelst required the retiree to take two three-week breaks each year to return to Europe and renew his visa and maintain contact with his family and friends back home. This retiree was not experienced as a deep cover agent. His biggest bargaining chip was that he was hand-picked by the Lone Wolf. It was more as a personal favor. The retiree's presence gave Van Aelst another set of trusted eyes and ears.

Tonight, Van Aelst called in his chips. He knew that, someday, his friend would pay dividends. Earlier that night, after speaking to Winstead at his hotel suite, Van Aelst took the poison-filled vial with him.

Peering over his drink, the ex-Stasi retiree watched Van Aelst enter the bar. The retiree knew the drill. He waited for Van Aelst to signal. This location was perfect and chosen long before tonight. It was a quiet, high-end night club tailored to the elite. The music selection was modern and set at just the right volume to prevent conversations from being overheard. There was no cover charge. Yet, the exorbitant drink prices catered to the eclectic and kept the local blue-collar workers and infrequent tourists away. One look at the menu, where a single mixed drink started at $45, usually did the trick. The patrons that frequented here were motivated by their need for discretion. Although California laws prohibited smoking inside, this high-end clientele appreciated the customized exhaust systems that complemented the spacious and well-appointed booths. It was a customized feature installed well after the city inspectors signed off and issued the permits.

Anticipating Van Aelst's arrival, the ex-Stasi retiree depressed the button on the booth console. Seeing the green neon LED light appear, he knew the ventilation system was working. Returning his gaze across the room, he saw a bright flame illuminating Van Aelst's face as he lighted a cigarette. That was the signal.

Glancing around, certain the area was clear, the retiree stood and waited for Van Aelst to approach the booth. Without any unnecessary introductions, Van Aelst slid into the plush booth. They each searched for curious glances. There were none.

Van Aelst reached inside the breast jacket pocket, removed, and placed a small metallic device on the center of the table. It was an electronic jamming device. The retiree waited for Van Aelst to confirm the area was clear before speaking.

"Comrade, it's been a long time since we've shared a drink."

"Too long Herr Van Aelst."

"Please...it's Cornelius. We've been through so much over all the years," replied Van Aelst. "It's time we drop the formalities. Besides, this little operation no longer involves orders from the GDR (German Democratic Republic) or our friends at the KGB. No, it's just me. A personal issue, receiving help from my personal associates on a personal family matter," said Van Aelst as he shrugged and flashed a whimsical smile.

"Even so, Herr Van Aelst, I mean Cornelius, even our...hobbies involve the great imperialist American capitalist pigs. Not such an easy feat, not such a simple matter, even still," replied the retiree with a slight tilt of his head before pausing for another glance around the room. He finished the remainder of his martini before returning the empty glass to the table. With a tattered toothpick lodged in the side of his mouth, the only remnant of the olive long since consumed, he gulped down his drink. The deep creased lines along his wrinkled forehead complimented his confident capable features.

Each man, well past their physical prime, through their espionage underworld, accumulated decades of experience in the art of warfare. Upon a closer examination, an observant person would detect a skill set that warranted a wide berth. Those that avoided interacting with these elderly statesmen would be well rewarded and allowed to see another day.

"What did you have in mind?" the retiree asked.

Van Aelst reached under the table. After recovering something, he returned his hand from underneath and placed a glass vial, double sealed inside of two zip locked bags. For additional precautions, Van Aelst taped it shut. Examining the object, whatever was contained inside, the retiree knew it demanded respect. If the Lone Wolf went to so much trouble to encase its contents, it must be extremely lethal. The retiree assumed the contents would advance some unsuspecting person's life to a premature end. He examined the vial and wondered why it appeared one third full.

"Is there a reason you want me to use this specific compound?" asked the retiree.

"I need to make sure a specific trail of evidence can be identified. Bread crumbs if you will," smiled Van Aelst.

"Like Hansel and Gretel, eh?"

"Exactly like Hansel and Gretel my friend," replied Van Aelst as he flashed a broad toothed smile finding it humorous that his friend referenced this German fairytale.

"And our target?"

"An Agent," Van Aelst paused. With an intense stare, his deep blue eyes cut through the dark lit booth before he continued. "An active American Agent."

"Which branch?"

"The Agency. And he's a Supervisor," replied Van Aelst as he slid a piece of paper across the table toward the retiree's outstretched hand. Without looking, the retiree took the paper and wrapped it around the plastic encased vial before placing them both in his coat pocket.

"When?"

"As soon as possible. Preferably, within the next few days."

"Do your plans require a particular location?"

"None."

After a final glance around the area, they were certain no one was watching.

"My friend," said Van Aelst. "This will be our last job. I will no longer require your services to be specific to California. I am in your debt."

With that, Van Aelst slid an envelope across the table. Inside, were first-class tickets for the same flight he was taking, along with a new unused passport.

"If you conclude your business in time, I hope you can join us on that non-stop flight to Berlin. The flight leaves tomorrow. Otherwise, using your debit card, you can make other arrangements.

"We're heading home together?"

"Yes, old friend. It's time. It's long overdue."

"It's the perfect assignment to end on. Us, a bunch of old Stasi bastards, sticking it to the Capitalists. I know this one isn't for the Motherland. Nonetheless, it still feels good."

Van Aelst smiled. Before standing, he leaned forward and whispered one last set of instructions into the retiree's ear.

"Be sure to leave some residue for the investigators to find. However, be extremely careful. Do not get any of that stuff on you. Do not breathe even a morsel. Ingesting even a minute amount would be your end," warned Van Aelst.

The retiree nodded and watched the Lone Wolf, his old friend Cornelius Van Aelst, slide out from the booth and made his way to the door. Feeling a sense of nostalgia, he remembered them working together. It was the end of World War II. They were so young, only fourteen years old at the time, worried fearing they would be charged with war crimes. At Van Aelst's recommendation, he was recruited into the GDR's Secret Police. After the fall of the Berlin wall, a few old timers were kept on the books. They both made the cut. Over the years, Herr Van Aelst looked out for him. In the underworld of clandestine covert operations, he was his only constant comrade. His only surviving true friend.

As he watched the Lone Wolf push open the front door, a group of young men, seemingly overdressed, trying to impress others, scowled at the presence of unwelcomed elderly men. With a condescending glance, they brushed him aside assuming he was out of his element. With a straight back and confident stride, Van Aelst returned their arrogant youthful gazes with a "look". The kind that communicates an aura. Like a man suppressing a controlled rage. It was impossible to miss. A sense of imminent danger. Exuding an aura that this person demands respect. As if some unseen energy field projected from Van Aelst, like a beacon warning others to steer clear. With one final glare, Van Aelst almost snarled. Without saying a word, he projected the clear unmistakable belief that they were inferior. Fearless, Herr Van Aelst proceeded forward pushing his way through the group. The men back stepped and cleared a way. The Lone Wolf continued forward never looking back as he entered the dark street beyond.

The retiree smiled. That was his friend, the pride of Germany. Like the predator he was, in a moment's notice, he could transform from Herr Van Aelst to the Lone Wolf.

*   *   *   *   *

Since his decision to down the airliner, Senator Anthony continued down the rabbit hole, becoming more cavalier. Being the chairman on the Oversight Committee for Foreign Affairs, he was considered part of the clique, a senior statesman. He felt untouchable. Being the Senator for the most populous state, with an economy that not only represented 20 percent of the national GDP, but also rivaled the prosperity of many developed countries inflamed his ego. Senator Anthony let his privileged position with the alluring fringe benefits go to his head. It was his fatal error.

The power and fame muddied his perspective. In his mind, being a Senator became more than a necessary part of the checks and balances within the huge bureaucratic machine. The large number of districts and electoral votes that came from California, combined with the specialized commercial industries, ranging from agriculture, fossil fuel, medical research and development, entertainment, information computer technologies, and even the military industrial complex, it was no wonder the special interest groups treated him with an elevated status, higher than other Congressional members. Being singled out amongst an already egocentric group of individuals, who, in their eyes, deserved celebrity status, was his undoing.

Before taking the position, each elected official is warned of the danger of becoming corrupted and seduced by its power. In hopes of staying clear of such pitfalls, each member voluntarily surrounds themselves with advisors and trusted colleagues, hoping to keep their egos at bay. Being exposed to the extra privileges, getting a glimpse behind the curtain, having intermittent access to unregulated, unrestricted, budget-less projects, and understanding secret dealings was intoxicating. Like the *Skunk Works*, shrouded in secrecy inside *Lockheed Martin's* Advanced Development Programs (ADP). Or *Boeing's Phantom Works*. Each project performing research and development for the defense department and receiving untold trillions of dollars in annual funding free from oversight committees.

Even Senator Anthony's committee had no influence over any of these projects. In fact, these groups remain unaccounted for and classified, so even Congress and the Executive Branch were excluded. This unfettered power created an arrogance where even POTUS (President of the United States) is considered a mere temporary employee and does not always meet the strict guidelines that warrant their involvement. The only governing body and enforcer for these projects lies within the framework of the Agency.

The single "watch-dog" inside the government, representing the only entity possessing the authority and ability to wield a big enough stick to curb abuses, was the Agency. As the last guardian to champion the ideals of the nation, only those that need to know are brought into the mind trust. In most cases, even POTUS is excluded. In most cases, POTUS has no legitimate need to be involved. Without a congressional mandate, POTUS has no authority to compel the Agency to do anything. As a professional courtesy, the National Agency Director may choose to provide the Executive Branch intel, with the understanding that it does so at its own discretion.

For political reasons, and under a rare set of circumstances, infrequent few individuals are allowed inside the Agency's secret society. In most cases, only specific projects warrant such access, a very narrow and limited amount of access. Over time, the Agency realized, from time to time, to foster goodwill and a sense of unity, they needed to grant such access. Otherwise, constant, and complete isolation could create enough pushback whereby the legislature could grow tired of perceived abuses. If ignored, growing dissatisfaction could result in a congressional change uncloaking everything as a matter of law. In order to maintain national security, it is widely believed that this clandestine approach is a necessary evil. The general public, its allies and enemies could not appreciate or justify many decisions made behind the Agency's closed doors. To achieve this goal, as much as 25 percent of the annual budget is diverted to the Agency and these other black projects. They are always hidden behind a veil of secrecy.

It takes a special person, one with great character, one who possesses the will-power necessary to avoid such pitfalls. Unfortunately, over time, it became clear that Senator Anthony lacked such self-control. In fact, he perverted his primary responsibility as an objective monitor placed strategically in the position to advocate for the needs of the public and to balance decisions keeping these secret projects in-line. Rather than acting as the champion for the system, he abused it. Senator Anthony became an exploiter and deceiver. Like a corrupt judge or policeman, a person that abuses one's authority taking advantage of the very thing he was sent to protect.

This unchecked greed for wealth and power caught the attention of Agency internal affairs. Unlike normal departments, the Agency was not conducive to be a system of self-monitoring. Rather, it is a system obsessed with keeping secrets and detecting breaches in security systems. Having a secret, all-powerful organization comes with a price; being ill-equipped to police itself in matters that do not jeopardize national security. With a laser focus designed on achieving espionage goals, the Agency instills a culture directed on those issues, not ethical ones. Consequently, the Agency promotes leaders and tacticians, not necessarily human resource specialists or compliance officers.

The Agency recognized the dilemma. Corruption was a mathematical certainty; a human behavior; something unavoidable. Each Agency Director knew and appreciated the realization that humans were unpredictable. A person with unimpeachable character could, under the right set of circumstances, be coerced to abandon their moral truths and personal principles. A line had to be drawn somewhere.

Therefore, if a Director uncovers one of its members, regardless of tenure or position, who has acted in any manner a Director deems inappropriate, he is authorized to deal with the matter in the way he sees fit. Each Director is granted the authority as the final judge and jury in the matter. A Director's jurisdiction is boundless. There are no personnel committees or some other authority in which Directors defer to. A Director's judgment is deemed supreme and unquestioned. A Director answers to no other authority and cannot be compelled to divulge anything whatsoever to anyone other than the National Agency Director. An Agency Director is all powerful and untouchable.

"Director Gamboa?" replied Director Nena Valdez as she heard her telephone make the overseas connection.

"Yes Nena."

"I wanted to give you a heads up. Given we're assisting you with the satellite images on your John Doe situation, I thought it was prudent to back-track on any issues peripheral to the main case," she explained.

"Understood. Text book. I would have done the same thing. Fresh set of eyes are always welcomed. Did you find something unusual?"

"I'm not sure. It's about the knock-list. The one Curt Anderson, copied."

"Yes, what about it?" Gamboa asked in a concerned voice. *Had he missed something?*

"It goes without saying that every Director, myself included, handles these matters at their own discretion. Our decisions are never second guessed. By providing my assistance and some of my agents, and because your Agent Chapin was brought into the case, I asked her to double check something. I asked to see if she found anything unusual about anyone on that list," explained Nena.

Gamboa appreciated how she was handling this matter. He was in her shoes a time or two. He felt the same and approached it in a similar fashion. They both appreciated that Directors were human and could feel a little taken aback when another Director appeared to be criticizing the handling of one of their missions. Directors did not like being second guessed. At the same time, he had nothing to hide. He felt confident in his decision-making process then and now.

"How do you feel about Senator Anthony?" asked Nena.

"How so?"

"He's the assigned legislative watchdog. It seems too coincidental that his biggest challenger for his upcoming Senate seat so happened to also be on board the downed plane," said Nena raising her eyebrows waiting for Gamboa's response. There was a brief silence on the other end as he processed the information.

"I wasn't aware of that."

"I didn't think so," Nena replied. "Who vetted the passenger manifest?"

"The Senator's team."

The line went quiet as each Director processed the information. Nena realized that Gamboa's decision to drop the plane was beyond dramatic. But she also recognized that, from his chair, he needed to protect the Agency's actions. The knock-list Anderson copied was a PR nightmare. If the notes were made public, with all the information scribbled in the margins, it could have devastating ramifications. Such a revelation could jeopardize the Agency's ability to maintain its favor in Congress. Nena understood why Gamboa could never allow that information to go public. Such a public outing would bring unwanted attention and scrutiny down on the Agency and its clandestine operations. Although Gamboa would not face any formal disciplinary action or be subject to criminal charges, he would be retired with a not-so-subtle golden kick in the backside as opposed to the golden parachutes that corporate executives are given in the private sector.

The very concept of "don't ask don't tell" started inside the Agency. Not having all the information, no one would second guess him. There was another unwritten rule-quid pro quo, which meant to grant an advantage in exchange for something in return later. In this case, it might become necessary to turn a blind eye.

"It's still your call. It's your "Director Only-Closed" file. It was your mission. I just thought you should know that Chapin was looking into the matter on my orders. Furthermore, I've yet to talk to her about any of this."

"I appreciate the heads up and discretion Nena. I'll talk to Chapin as soon as I hang up with you," confirmed Gamboa.

"We good Gamboa?" asked Nena.

He knew she was not snooping around. He was the one who asked her for help. Her people were burning up hours and allocated two satellite analysts to look deeper into the matter. He would have done the same thing.

"We're more than good Nena. I owe you one." After a pause, he continued. "I'll get back to you tomorrow," and ended the call. Before he punched the intercom to summon Agent Chapin, Gamboa thought to himself "*what the hell was the Senator up to?*"

*   *   *   *   *

Winstead's eyelids were heavy, and he struggled opening them. As his vision cleared, he realized he was lying on his back staring up at his bedroom ceiling fan spinning above. He glanced around the room. Men were still walking in and out of the bathroom and down the hallway. As he lurched forward trying to get into a seated position, he felt a deep bruise on the center of his chest. Unable to sit up all the way, he extended his elbow out like a kickstand to hold up his weight. He noticed a cotton ball taped to the crook of his arm. He was naked with a bloody towel draped across his lap.

"Mr. Van Aelst, Winstead is coming around," said the man who earlier aimed and shot the silenced pistol into Winstead's chest.

Van Aelst returned to the bedroom. He entered the room and looked down at Winstead. With a tilted head, and a sincere smile, he spoke.

"You look a little groggy. How's your chest feel? It looks like you'll have a deep bruise for a while," he said almost laughing.

Winstead raised his eyes with his chin still propped up on his chest. "What happened?"

"We need to make sure no one comes looking for James Winstead ever again," Van Aelst said while raising a computer memory stick and waved it in the air. "We filmed it all, one uninterrupted shot, and no edits. It looks authentic."

Van Aelst knew it was time. Winstead needed to get moving.

"Get dressed," Van Aelst ordered. You can shower up at my place. You can't shower here. The bathtub has been staged just the way we wanted. We also took the liberty and extracted enough of your blood and sprinkled a little bit of it here and there. We even yanked out of few strands of your hair, roots and all, and placed them inside the drain," Van Aelst explained. "I hope you like being a blonde," he added.

Hearing about his hair, he raised his hand up and felt his head. Only to find, his hair had been clipped. It was decades since he had a crew-cut. Winstead ran his fingers through his short cropped stubby hair, barely an inch long.

"Blonde?" Winstead asked.

"Be sure to check yourself out in the mirror before we go," chuckled Van Aelst. He handed Winstead a cold glass of ginger ale. "Here, drink this. You're probably very thirsty."

Winstead reached for the glass. The drugs were still wearing off. He had to concentrate in order to grab the cold drink. As he drank, he watched Herr Van Aelst walk back into the hallway. Looking around the bedroom, he noticed a stack of new attire. Everything he needed, shirt, underwear, socks, and shoes. Tossing the towel off his lap, Winstead grabbed the new shirt and started dressing. He noticed what looked like a long black plastic body bag lying in the corner crumpled up on the carpet. He tilted his head to one side and read the writing on the outside. *"San Francisco Morgue."*

*   *   *   *   *

Agent Chapin needed to see her newest friend. Agent Gall's family members cleared out for the evening. Chapin flashed her Agency ID and was granted access to Gall's protected ICU private room. Sitting beside the bed, Chapin waited for Gall to awake. Gall was lucky. If she had hit the railing any harder, she would have pierced the guardrail and plunged over the steep embankment falling several hundred feet below.

After hearing what had happened to Gall, on a hunch, Agent Chapin located the vehicle. It was towed to a local salvage yard awaiting the insurance adjustor to inspect the damages. It was an obvious total loss. The timing of the accident seemed too coincidental. The night before the accident, Gall mentioned wanting to speak in private about something. Less than 24 hours later, yet to have that conversation, Gall had almost died in a freak auto accident.

Chapin studied Gall's sleeping face. Several deep lacerations covered her face and neck. Apparently, when the airbags deployed, metal shards flew out. It was a known issue that resulted in many manufacturers recalls. Her neck and head were frozen in place from the neck brace. The left side of her body was thrown against the inside of the driver's side door as the car slammed into the railing. Her left shoulder took the brunt of the damage. With only a broken clavicle and three cracked ribs, she was fortunate. It could have been much worse. The depth and location of her facial lacerations made it look worse than it really was. The doctors' biggest concern was her concussion. The nurses would monitor her throughout the night. For the most part, she slept off and on all day.

Agent Chapin looked up from her folder. Gall seemed to be stirring and coming to. She began moving her arms. After a few attempts, she opened her eyes. It took a few moments before Gall realized Agent Chapin was sitting next to the bed. In a scratchy weak voice, Theresa Gall spoke.

"You're the last person I expected to see," Gall said with a weak attempt at a smile.

"Hey, you can't get rid of me that easy," joked Chapin. "How are you feeling?"

Gall yawned before replying. "Mostly tired. Must be the pain pills. My shoulder still hurts like hell though. I guess I broke my shoulder and a few ribs," shrugged Gall then winced in pain.

"Hey there. Better relax and take it easy for a while Theresa," chuckled Chapin. "What do you remember? Anything?"

"It's all my fault," Theresa explained. "It's stupid really. From time to time, I push my little Beamer hard down that hill. The road was clear in both directions. I actually thought I could set a new all-time personal best speeding through that corner," said Theresa with a sideways glance at Chapin. After a brief pause, she continued.

E.A. PADILLA

"But I'm not gonna mention any of that to the insurance company," she said with a smirk.

"So, you lost control?"

Theresa paused and thought back before replying. "That's the weird part. Everything was going great! Then, just as I entered the corner, it was like I hit something in the road. I heard a loud thud, almost like an explosion, like a blown tire or something. The car seemed to bounce up a little and I felt like I lost contact with the road. When I applied the brakes, the pedal went to the floor. Good thing I grabbed the hand brake. Otherwise, I would have gone over the guard rail."

Gall's voice softened. Avoiding eye-contact, she added "Pretty stupid."

Agent Chapin leaned in close listening as Theresa explained everything. She wondered if she should bring up everything she had uncovered. Chapin deduced that Gall was coherent and only exhibited a little pain. Otherwise, aside from a few broken bones and the concussion, she seemed fine. Her speech was clear. She did not seem to have any deeper cognitive issues. Based on her assessment, Chapin chose to push ahead.

"Are you working on any abnormal cases?"

Theresa shifted her eyes toward Agent Chapin.

"No. Nothing comes to mind," replied Gall with a curious expression.

"How about any recently closed cases. Can you think of any one you may have pissed off? Give someone reason to take something personal and seek retribution?"

Theresa's expression became more rigid. Her eyes moved from side to side as she thought. "Nope. It's been a few years since I had any direct one-on-one cases. Most of my cases have been task force stuff. Forgery and RICO (Racketeer Influenced and Corrupt Organizations). Why? Did you find something?"

Chapin paused and leaned back in her chair. She concentrated as she chose her words. "I had your car checked out."

Agent Gall's facial expression changed. Gone was the wounded woman just injured in a random car accident. With a flip of a switch, she was on the job. She focused her eyes. Her mind began processing everything Chapin was saying.

"And?"

"I had the salvage yard raise your *BMW* on their lift. I also brought in our C&O (Cause and Origin) experts from the Agency forensics team to take a look."

"What did they find?"

"Somebody tampered with your brakes. It was pretty uptown shit too. Looks like a remote detonation was used."

At first, Agent Gall remained silent trying to understand the information. With a stern face, she glanced up to meet Chapin's stare. "Anything else?" Gall asked.

"The air bag was also tampered with."

That last piece took things to a whole new level. It was obvious that someone wanted her taken out of the picture. *"But who? And for what reasons?"* thought Agent Gall.

"What were you going to tell me yesterday? It seemed important. You said you didn't want to talk about it over the phone or through email."

"Right. With the accident, I forgot about that. Someone has been peeking into my computer?"

"What do you mean? How do you know?"

"Over the last week, I noticed that as the day progressed, my computer seemed to slow down. I asked one of the IT (Information Technology) guys to check it out. He confirmed that it wasn't being caused by any system upgrades or anything that they were doing. I was thinking that maybe the short-term memory card was messed up or something.

"But, then the other day, I came back to my office. Everyone was gone as it was well into the evening. When I opened my office door, I could have sworn that my screen was on. But after I turned on my light, the monitor seemed to blink off. Just before the screen went blank, I thought I saw an open file with my notes displayed."

Curious about Theresa's story, Chapin squinted and tilted her head to the side. Chapin's mind went into overdrive working through what it all meant. Before Chapin could interject, Theresa continued her story.

"So, you know what I did?"

Without speaking, Chapin raised her eyebrows and opened her eyes in an exaggerated manner as if, through sign language, urging her to explain.

"I went old school. Without looking directly at my cell phone, and while pretending to be concentrating on a stack of papers on my desk, I set my cell phone on airplane mode to prevent any calls from being received. I then, turned on the camera and started filming. Just before I left the desk, I purposely turned away from the monitor keeping my actions hidden behind my body and slid my cell phone against the back of my credenza angling it so it could film my monitor."

After a brief pause, Theresa continued speaking. "In all honesty, I thought it was a test."

"A test?" asked Chapin.

"Yeah. I figured it was you guys at the Agency testing me; seeing how I would respond or even if I would notice." Based on Chapin's lack of reaction and blank expression, Theresa knew that it was not the Agency. Someone else must be tampering with her computer.

"When I got into the office the next morning, my phone was still filming. I rarely use the camera feature and have a scant few pictures or film clips. I was grateful that my phone had enough internal memory to keep filming. Still wanting to prevent from being detected, I waited until I sat in the chair, before turning around and placing my purse in front of my phone. I booted up my computer. As it came up, I kept to my normal routine and set off to the break room for my morning coffee. As I grabbed my purse, I retrieved my phone with my other hand," smiled Theresa feeling proud at how she handled the situation and flashed Chapin an ear-to-ear grin.

"So, what did you get on the tape?" asked Chapin.

"Just what I thought. About five minutes after I left the room the night before, my desktop monitor magically came out of hibernation. The curser was moving around the screen. Whoever was snooping around went straight for the John Doe file I told you about. The person had to have been sneaking around my computer a long time by then because the person seemed very familiar with the location of everything. The video clip showed the mouse movements and files opening very quickly. The person knew exactly what pathway to go to in order to access the files. There were no pauses, just click, click, click.

"That's why I thought it was you guys. I figured it was some kind of test."

The room seemed to get quiet. Other than the electronic tones coming from her life-support monitor, one could have heard a pin drop. Chapin's mind was spinning through the revelation, thinking through all possibilities. Lost in thought, Chapin glanced up at several plants with bright bows sitting on the bed-stand. One of the plants, seemed overly large and out of place. After considering everything; the tampering of Theresa's car; someone hacking into her computer; and now, this oversized plant. For some reason, Chapin found herself focusing on the plant. Under the circumstances, it now seemed very relevant. "What's up with the huge plant?"

Theresa glanced over and studied the large plant with its equally large pink ribbon with the words "Get Well Soon" inscribed on the bow. The base of the plant was at least two feet across in diameter.

"Oh, it's from the guys at the office."

They both stared at the potted plant and other flowers arranged on the end-table. After a brief pause, Chapin continued speaking. "Can I take a look at your cell phone? I want to see the video clip."

"I figured you'd want one. I copied the file to a flash drive. I was planning on giving it to you when I saw you this morning," said Theresa while craning her head searching for her purse. "There's my purse, on the floor. The flash drive is inside. Go ahead and grab it."

Chapin walked around the bed. On the floor, next to the table, she noticed Agent Gall's personal belongings stuffed inside a see-through plastic bag. When her mother left, she forgot to take it with her. Chapin grabbed and opened the plastic bag. She extracted the purse and handed it to Theresa. As she returned to her chair, Chapin could not help but notice the plant again. Gall rummaged through her purse and found the flash drive and handed it to Chapin.

"Here."

*   *   *   *   *

Diane spent all her free time doing something golf related. She took two consecutive weekends down to Southern California and attended two *LPGA* events: one in Carlsbad and other at Rancho Mirage. Every evening since returning, she stopped by the driving range, followed by some chipping and then the putting green. On the weekends, if she was not attending either an *LPGA* or *PGA* event, she was playing a round of golf at her local course. As the summer days stretched out, during the week, she even started playing nine holes after work.

She even signed up for an on-line golf handicap service making a point to post her scores from her work computer. During any conversations with her co-workers, she found a way to interject and share her increased involvement and commitment toward her new hobby. Her efforts were paying off. Everyone in the office noticed her new-found excitement with golf. It was hard to miss the oversized golf calendar, autographed hats and other golfing paraphernalia that decorated her cubicle area. It was a subtle change and had grown to the point that her co-workers forgot when Diane was not obsessed with golf. No one would have fathomed that Diane was strategically placing them to maximize their exposure to anyone passing by her desk. Her apparent obsession manifested into a practical shrine for a golf enthusiast.

Diane's email exchanges with Curt increased. After playing a round of golf, she entered an Internet café to post her golf score, then read Curt's drafted message. It was the perfect cover. No one at the Agency had any reason to suspect Diane of any wrong doing. That was all about to change.

7

At the end of the day, John was leaving the office and saw Diane at her desk. Seeing her golf items, he stopped to chat.

"Wow, you have certainly caught the golf bug" he said with a smile. He glanced around her cubicle admiring the golf paraphernalia.

"Yeah, it keeps me busy," shrugged Diane. "I'm actually heading across the pond next month. I've always wanted to watch the men's British Open in person. The *LPGA* is also having an international event the following week. I'm gonna spread my time between both events," Diane explained for the tenth time this week.

John studied Diane as she spoke. It was the way she avoided eye-contact. He assumed, like everyone else, she was just searching for a distraction, anything to keep her mind off the loss of her niece. He noticed her nieces' picture posing with her bright red Corvette was missing. He assumed that Diane removed it and guessed it was difficult not thinking about her all the time.

John sensed Diane's pain. As her long-time co-worker and friend, he wished he could somehow help relieve her pain. But he could not. What he knew, the secret he kept, was above her grade and against protocol. That decision had to be made by someone else, not him. It was up to Director Gamboa to share that kind of information.

"That sounds like a great vacation Diane. Well-deserved too. How long will you be gone?

With a slightly bowed head, Diane peeked out from under her bangs and replied, "Two weeks."

"Good for you," replied John.

He waved goodnight and started walking toward the exit. He could not help but feel bad for Diane. She had dedicated her entire life to the Agency. The loss of her niece was devastating. He made a mental note to talk to Director Gamboa. Maybe he could do something. It was against protocol. Maybe an exception could be made.

Diane watched John walk away. She felt terrible. Everything about the Agency seemed to be coming unglued. The guilt she felt about recruiting Gina was now compounded by all the other changes. She asked to be reassigned from the Recruitment Unit and felt like an outsider.

Three years ago, she felt a burning need to understand what really happened. It outweighed everything else. Diane always appreciated the ease in which the Agency used personal relationships: children, spouses, and even parents. They were a means to coerce agents into cooperating. There were other reasons, but principally, for that reason, Diane avoided marriage. Marriage was more than just a distraction to her career. The presence of a spouse created a weakness, a vulnerability. One that could be exploited. Diane had not counted on the love bond created with her niece. At the beginning, Diane had her parents and sister. Then, after the passing of all three, Gina became her only living relative. Her loss had a profound effect.

Saving Curt, the surrogate victim, the sole survivor from that plane. In her mind, she reasoned that if she could not save Gina, she could at least save Curt. By transporting Curt out of the Agency's grasp, even if only temporarily, she felt empowered and free from some of her guilt.

Initially, her shock grew into resentment. She could not imagine why the Agency chose to throw away her niece's life. It was too much to contemplate. Diane concluded that all her years of service, loyalty, and sacrifice in support of the Agency was for nothing. After the downing of that passenger jet, Diane reeled in search of meaning, desperate to find an answer and to place blame.

Over time, Diane's anger and sense of betrayal subsided. It still flared. But for the most part, she came to peace with what happened. However, her intervention to help Curt, placed her in serious peril. Her decision to assist a known fugitive was inexcusable. The copied material was never passed to the media. Even still, Curt's version of events was too fantastic to imagine. What he uncovered created a public relations nightmare.

If the public knew about the Agency's unlimited resources, without any form of accountability, the outcry would be immediate. It could jeopardize its legitimate place inside the government. The cogs of the U.S. bureaucracy appreciated the need for the Agency and understood that maintaining its existence was a balancing act. Those in power recognized that their covert activities needed to remain hidden from view. An underlying fear throughout the entire government became almost a philosophical and moral quandary. *How would the Agency respond if Congress absolved or even drastically changed the way the Agency was run? Would the Agency voluntarily relinquish its authority? Or would the Agency be forced to crawl underground to continue its operation?*

Diane understood the Agency. She knew the Agency could never walk away. They would keep pursuing Curt. His very existence and the evidence possessed, made the situation worse.

The sound of the heavy double security doors leading through the lobby broke Diane's train of thought. With a sad feeling, she tried to smile. Her impulsive decision to help Curt led her to this place. She could not turn back the clock. She depressed the button turning off her desktop computer. Preparing to leave the office, she obsessed over her hasty decision. That decision set her down a path that jeopardized everything, her future, her freedom, and her peace of mind. In a daze, she stood and walked away from her cubicle. With a methodical stride, she marched past her co-workers heading toward the back unaware of their waves wishing her a great time in Europe. With a forced hypnotic smile, she passed through the aisles, and out the door. She found herself sitting inside her car not knowing how she got there. She had no way of knowing that this would be her last time inside the Agency walls.

She started her car and received a friendly wave from the guard as she exited the parking lot. Her decision to help Curt came full circle. Her life was about to forever change. She just did not know it.

*   *   *   *   *

The retiree Stasi Agent waited outside of Supervisor John's house. Certain no one was watching, he snuck up to the front door. He slid a mini-drone the size of a thin quarter, under the front door before returning to his vehicle. From the safety of his car, he activated the device. Using a remote controller's monitor, he maneuvered the mini-drone inside the living room. The images transmitted were clear and full color.

The retiree studied the view searching for any alarm key pad and surface mounted motion detectors. As the drone maneuvered around the living room, he found them. A typical commercial alarm key pad and several monitors. When activated, the drone was the size of a large bumble bee, small enough to defeat the motion detectors programmed to ignore small flying insects.

The retiree weighed his options and decided against tampering with the security system. He did not want to leave an electronic signature of any kind. He thought about humans being creatures of habit. He knew these people. He was one of them. This Supervisor's job was tedious and created paranoia. He probably set the perimeter alarm system before he went to bed and reset it when he left. The retiree hoped John liked to shower after work. If he did, the time it took to shower, provided more than enough time. He desperately wanted to get this job done now and make that flight back to Germany with Herr Van Aelst.

From inside his vehicle, the retiree studied the small monitor as he maneuvered the mini-drone through every room. John left each door open. It made sense. As a covert operative, the Supervisor was concerned with an intruder hiding behind a closed door. The retiree continued his survey of the entire house and could not locate any wall mounted cameras but found three motion sensors located outside each doorway opening.

There were no family photos mounted on the walls and no pictures on his night stand. Like most agents, his life was "the job." As the drone went through the laundry room, the retiree noticed an oversized rubberized garbage can. As the mini-drone hovered above, looking inside, he found countless empty aluminum cans. Based on the number of cans, he was certain John had a drinking problem.

The mini-drone flew into the kitchen. Next to the refrigerator, he found several full beverage containers sitting on the counter-top. Angling the drone's camera, he landed near the containers. A supersized close-up of the label dominated his view; "100% Lemonade." He counted four full containers, lined up in a neat row, one behind the other. Based on what he saw, even with the refrigerator door closed, he was certain, inside he would find beer and an open lemonade container.

Fearing the Supervisor would return, the retiree maneuvered the mini-drone back to the living room landing it on the coffee table, aiming the camera at the front door. He wanted to catch the Supervisor entering and deactivating the alarm system. This sophisticated device came equipped with a motion sensor and infrared. The retiree placed the drone in hibernation and waited.

He glanced at the dash mounted clock. It was approaching 5:30pm. Assuming normal traffic conditions, John should arrive in the next hour. Stretching his arms, the retiree reached down for the side adjustment handle and reclined the seat. After adjusting the drone's surveillance monitor, he raised the volume, reached inside his jacket pocket, and pulled out a pair of syringes. They were pre-mixed, saline solution and the poison from the vial. Wearing a surgical mask and latex gloves, he smoothed the lumps out with a spoon before pouring the poison solution inside. These syringes were stronger than normal designed specifically for this purpose. They had no model number, nor manufacturer information of any kind. The complete absence of markings was a dead giveaway. The goal was to avoid leaving any physical evidence.

Real life was not always neat and orderly. Humans were not infallible. Mistakes were always a possibility. It was the nature of the business. Hopefully, tonight things would go as planned.

*   *   *   *   *

Agent Chapin waited inside Director Gamboa's office sitting in one of the rigid chairs. She came straight to his office arriving early. She wanted to catch him before his normal day started. What she learned from Agent Gall had to be related to the Curt Anderson file. She just knew it.

"So, the tape confirms that the hacker, whoever it is, did not actually download anything?" asked Gamboa.

"I've had our IT (Information Technology) guys check it out. They even snuck into their systems certain that they won't alert the Bureau. If there's a mole inside the Bureau, by sticking to our surveillance protocol, we'll tip him off. But from what our guys see, someone was only accessing the files. Nothing was altered or downloaded. It's as if the hacker just studied Gall's investigation, eaves dropping on her progress," Chapin elaborated.

"And the hacker hasn't accessed any of her other files?"

"Negative. Nothing else, just the John Doe file."

"When did the hack start nosing around?"

Agent Chapin raised her eyebrows, as if to accentuate the unusual timing. "The day following Gall's receipt of the forged transfer papers."

Director Gamboa turned away from Chapin's notes. They exchanged blank stares, followed by a brief silence as they processed everything. A knock at the door, interrupted their thoughts.

"Yes?"

From the other side, they heard John's voice as the door opened.

"I got your message Director and came straight here. What's up?" the Supervisor asked.

"Somebody's hacking into the Bureau's computer. The only thing they're looking at is the file related to the John Doe case. And, today, the assigned agent was involved in a staged accident. Agent Chapin confirmed with our C&O guys that the brakes were sabotaged. No prints," explained Gamboa.

While the Supervisor processed the information, Chapin added, "A few nights before the accident, Agent Gall came into the office late at night and noticed her desk monitor blink off. Just before it went blank, she was certain an open file was displayed. And it wasn't some screen saver image."

The Supervisor's face scrunched into an inquisitive manner before he responded. "Hinky? (law enforcement slang term for strange)"

"We're all in agreement," said the Director.

"Now what?" asked Agent Chapin.

"Let's get the new girl Walters on this right away. Let her do her thing and see if she can turn up something else. This is right up her alley. She's pretty damn smart," said the Director.

"I'm on it," replied Chapin as she gathered her things and left.

"Boss, this case just won't die," said the Supervisor.

"Contact Nena's guys on the *USS George H.W. Bush.* I want to know who was helping the John Doe. If we find that out it might make it easier to figure out who's been hacking into the Bureau."

"I'll get right on it, Director."

As the Supervisor was about to leave the office, he paused.

"Hey boss, a sidebar issue, but I've been watching Diane Klein. She looks pretty bummed out still, way out of sorts. She's been a trooper for all these years. I just thought you should know. Ever since the downing of the jet, she just hasn't been the same. She transferred out of Recruitment and is now assigned with the A-team."

The Director knew they were longtime friends. He knew John wanted to avoid stepping over his authority. Gamboa agreed. He had noticed her demeanor. She still seemed devastated.

"I was thinking you could brief her in on 'that' mission. I realize this would be way out of bounds and against everything in the book and then some. But shit boss, Klein's one of us, she's earned it, right?"

Director Gamboa nodded in agreement. He should have done it sooner.

"When she gets back from her vacation, I'll let her know. As much as I can," agreed Director Gamboa. "No one else knows, right? Just me and you," he added.

"That's right boss. Just the two of us."

*   *   *   *   *

"So, what do we know?' asked Moon Dog in a frustrated and exhausted manner.

"Ten identical hospital ambulance transports come out of the Lincoln tunnel. They all came out at the same time," replied Kyle. "But we never see them enter the front end of the tunnel."

"Which we know is impossible. We confirmed that there are no other side tunnels, so they couldn't have entered from another direction. The tunnel is designed for cars only. Its height is only thirteen feet tall. It can't even handle a semi-truck."

"What else?" asked Moon Dog.

"Technically, there are three tubes, with a total of six lanes. The center lanes are for buses only. During peak times, the authorities convert the center lane to accommodate the flow of traffic either way. Other than that, only normal passenger cars and motorcycles use the tunnel."

"It's like a shell game," explained Moon Dog.

Kyle and Moon Dog stared at the screen. They pulled the overhead satellite tapes 30 minutes before and after the appearance of the ten transport ambulances. It was running on a loop so they could study the tape without having to rewind it. They ordered copies of the surveillance video from inside the tunnel. Given that the event took place three years prior, the tapes had to be manually retrieved from the New York Port Authority that oversaw all such surveillance videos for New York and New Jersey. It was going to take some time. Since Hurricane Sandy, much of the Authority's non-essential documents were damaged. The Agency's New Jersey Office sent several rookies down there to assist and expedite their recovery. So far, nothing.

Kyle's posture was frozen in a perpetual slouch, with his head cradled in his hand and his elbows resting on the table. He studied the same 60-minute loop for days. With blurred eyes, and a disgruntled expression, he watched the video. Without warning, something caught his eye.

"Hey, wait a minute," Kyle said. He leaned forward and concentrated on the vehicles exiting the tunnel.

"Holy shit Batman! I got it!"

"Huh? What? Tell me something good Kyle. I'm dying here."

"The buses! We've been so preoccupied over the hospital transports, that we've missed it. The buses!" Kyle said almost shouting. His face transformed and he flashed an ear-to-ear grin.

"What about the buses?" asked Moon Dog.

"Why the hell are there so many buses coming out of the tunnel all at the same time we see these ten ambulance transports?" asked Kyle. "And look," Kyle asked as he pointed at the screen. "Why so many buses all taking the exit while the ambulance transports keep on going?"

Moon Dog stared at the buses. With a shrug, he replied, "Okay," in an exacerbated tone. "I see the buses. So?"

"Count them. How many are there?"

They both started counting. Kyle spoke up first. "Twelve."

"Okay twelve. So, what?" asked Moon Dog.

"I know New York is big and all, but why the hell are there twelve buses coming out of the tunnel at the same time? Even for New York, that's too many for a normal route. But these buses all went the same direction.

After a brief pause, Kyle continued. "That's one hell of a busy bus route."

Moon Dog rubbed his unshaven chin as he thought it through. On a hunch, he rewound the tape until he saw all the buses entering the tunnel. He started tracking the time it took the buses to go from the entrance until they reappeared out the other side a mile and a half away.

"The speed limit is 25 mph. But the tunnel speed is much faster than the posted limit. At the time when the buses and ambulance transports come through the tunnel, the traffic was very light. It's basically clear sailing," explained Moon Dog.

"Based on the amount of time to get from one end and appear out the other side, it was like they must have slowed way down," interjected Kyle in a confused manner. "That's too much time that's passed. Those buses should have been flying through the tunnel. Why slow down so much?"

"I have a theory," offered Moon Dog. With a confident smile, he continued. "The ambulances are in the buses. They're hidden inside the buses. As they go through the tunnel, they slow down so the buses can somehow off load the ambulance transports. Maybe they slide out the back?"

"That won't work."

"Why?" asked Moon Dog.

"The engines on a typical city bus are located in the back."

Moon Dog paused as he thought through the dilemma and spoke out loud as he thought. "Well, we're only getting a top side view from the satellite images. So, we're only assuming that these large vehicles are buses. Maybe they're a modified multi-vehicle transport?"

"That would work. But what about the bus lane. How could they have gotten into the tunnel? The toll booth operator would have stopped them as they entered," Kyle countered.

"What if the outside of the transports were modified to look like a city bus," offered Moon Dog as he tilted his head toward Kyle. With a twisted expression and raised eyebrows, it was as if they we both thinking "it's possible."

In a skeptical tone and while shrugging, Kyle spoke up. "That would at least explain why they used twelve buses for ten transports."

"How so?" asked Moon Dog.

"They could use two real buses, one in the lead and one trailing behind the convoy. If they staged them this way, if they ran in a tight formation, it would appear to be a huge line of buses heading back to the main station or something. Also, once they get inside the tunnel, the lead and trail buses would cover the first and last modified transport vehicles. In theory, anyway."

Moon Dog nodded in agreement. "That makes sense."

"I sure wish we could get our hands on the surveillance video from inside the tunnel. That would let us know for sure."

*   *   *   *   *

Agents Walters and Chapin were on a conference call with Lt. Kyle Benjamin and Douglas Elliott, transmitting via a secure satellite link from the aircraft carrier *USS George HW Bush*. Kyle had just explained his theory.

"That was very observant Lt. Benjamin," replied Agent Chapin. "I would never have figured that out."

Kyle and Moon Dog could barely suppress their broad grins. They were practically patting themselves on the back. That all changed once Agent Walters spoke.

"So, which ambulance transport is carrying our John Doe?"

Their confident grins disappeared.

"That's another issue," explained Moon Dog. "We just figured the shell-game out when we got a call from our boss Director Valdez in Korea. She's instructed us to brief you two in on the satellite surveillance tapes. Given what we've uncovered to date, it's enough to conclude that your John Doe had some assistance with some unknown co-conspirators and warrants utilizing more stateside resources if needed.

"The only issue we have is to isolate our search criteria to this situation involving your John Doe. If we see anything else, something unrelated to our investigation, we're to keep it to ourselves. At the conclusion of our research, the data is to be deleted and no other copies are to be made. With this understanding, we've uploaded the looped surveillance file for your review. It's a huge, encrypted file. You should have already received it by now."

"Yes" replied Chapin. "We've got it."

"We're waiting for something from local law enforcement and the New York-New Jersey Harbor Authority. They're trying to track down archived video tapes from inside the Lincoln Tunnel. Apparently, Hurricane Sandy caused some tapes to be misfiled," explained Moon Dog.

"Unfortunately, that's not accurate Moon Dog," explained Walters.

"What do you mean?" asked Moon Dog as he folded his arms across his chest.

"I had the distinct pleasure of working with those guys. My last post was in the New Jersey Office, just outside Newark," explained Walters. "Hurricane Sandy took place back in October 2012. It made landfall just outside Atlantic City on October 29. That was a long time ago."

"So, what are you saying?" Moon Dog pressed.

"Well, when I worked there, that was the Authority's response to most of our requests. It came to be known as their SOP (Standard Operating Procedures) for those guys. Bottom-line, those older records are all stuffed in an underground storage facility. They know where it is. But no one wants to dredge down there and sift through all that moldy damp storage area. It's all FUBAR and smells something fierce. If you really want to rush those tapes, I can push some sensitive buttons with those guys. I know some of their people down in their admin office," offered Agent Walters. As she spoke, a slight grin appeared as If she was looking forward to the opportunity to get involved.

"I'll need the date you made the request, Moon Dog, and the name of the person you spoke to," she explained.

"I don't have that information at my fingertips. I'll email it to you later today," said Moon Dog with a knowing grin. He could sense a little fun may be on the horizon.

"Lt. Elliott, do I have your permission to use your name?" asked Agent Walters.

"You most certainly do Walters!" said Moon Dog.

"We need some shut eye. You two can continue with the surveillance loop review. Moon Dog and I have been locked up tracking your John Doe for the last few weeks. There's an eleven-hour difference between us. So, tag, you guys are it," joked Kyle.

"You bet," Walters and Chapin replied in unison as their voices seemed to echo inside the small secure communications room deep inside the San Jose Agency Office.

"See you tomorrow ladies," said Moon Dog before they terminated the conference call.

Agent Chapin turned toward Agent Walters. She seemed eager to share something with Walters. With a sideways glance, in almost a whisper, Chapin spoke.

"Do you know the scoop on those two?"

"No." Walters replied leaning forward with a curious expression on her face.

With raised eyebrows, Chapin was restricted from elaborating. "Someday, when you're cleared, I'll share their story." Even though she was excluded from hearing it, Walters felt like she was becoming more accepted into her new team. "If the rumors about the Korean mission were even close to reality, both Kyle and Moon Dog are some very serious VIPs."

Walters smiled and turned away as she lifted the encrypted phone. "Let's start shaking some trees in New Jersey. I bet they get the tapes before the end of the day." With an excited expression, she jammed her index finger down as she depressed the key pad. Cradling the receiver between her shoulder and her ear, Walters spoke up in a loud aggressive manner, as if she were psyching herself up to make the call.

"In one of my prior cases, I dealt with those guys. It seemed like I was on the phone with those idiots every other day. I'm not surprised I still remember their number."

Agent Chapin watched this quiet, soft spoken computer analyst transform in front of her eyes. Chapin found herself excited waiting for Agent Walters to get into this guy's grill. With anticipation, Chapin leaned forward to listen in. Walters caught her meaning and put the call on speaker phone.

"This is Kenneth. Can I help you?" The voice sounded slow and lethargic, with no sense of urgency whatsoever. Just hearing his voice and cadence, one got the impression that he was not listening and could have cared less.

"Holy shit Kenneth! I can't believe you're still alive!" said Agent Walters. She had both of her hands spread on the conference room table and was bent forward almost yelling into the speaker phone. After a brief pause, the man's voice, broke the awkward silence. In almost a whisper, Kenneth spoke up.

"Agent Walters? Is that you?" he asked with an incredulous manner, as if it were impossible for him to be speaking to her.

In a sarcastic condescending manner, with a hint of a feigned Ozark drawl, she replied.

"Well, I'll be God damned Kenneth! I'm so damn impressed you remember my voice." Walters said as she winked at Agent Chapin. With a smile that stretched across her face, she could not hide her enjoyment. But poor Kenneth, not so much. Chapin covered her mouth to keep from laughing. Kenneth fell silent on the other end of the call. It was as if crickets began chirping.

"But then again," continued Walters, "how could you forget about the person that went to extraordinary measures to secure a tape from your department and had to wait six months, SIX MONTHS!" practically screaming into the phone.

"Do you remember what I finally had to do Kenneth?" she asked with pure sarcasm. Like a person asking a question, when they already know the answer, but are hoping the other person cannot recall the answer.

In a quiet dejected voice, projected at a volume just above a whisper, they heard his reply.

"Yes, Agent Walters."

"And what did I do?"

"You sent a letter to my supervisor."

"That's right. A letter. Do you remember how many pages Kenneth?"

"Yes."

"How many pages?"

"Six."

"That's right. Six pages. One page for each month. And what was detailed on the letter Kenneth?"

Agent Chapin could feel Kenneth's pain. He was getting a full-court treatment as Walters recounted what was most likely Kenneth's worst day. Walters was enjoying the harassment she inflicted on him. It was for a good reason.

Because good old Kenneth's lackadaisical, bureaucratic attitude, got a field agent killed. Although many factors go into the success and failure of any complicated situation, Agent Walters knew if she received the data sooner, his death could have been prevented. She would never forget or forgive good old Kenneth. And based on what she was hearing, she sensed, even now, Kenneth was still making excuses blaming everything on Hurricane Sandy.

"You documented each call you placed to request the tapes," Kenneth offered.

"And, by the way Kenneth, like I did before, I'm taping this conversation, just like before. But you probably guessed that. Right? Otherwise, like before, you would have hung up the phone. Then, later claimed that you never spoke to me."

This comment went unanswered. The other end of the phone remained silent.

"Kenneth, this time, it's different. This time, a higher-ranking agent, a Lt. Douglas Elliott, asked me to follow up with your department. Given I worked in the New Jersey office before, he figured I would have better success at getting what's needed."

Agent Walters paused. Over the phone, they heard paper shuffling. Walters could almost imagine Kenneth's desk covered with message notes. She saw it all before. They heard the shuffling sounds abruptly stop. Guessing he had found Moon Dog's messages, Walters pressed on.

"There you go. You must be staring at a stack of his messages now, am I right?"

The silence on the other end told it all. Like the famous prognosticator Nostradamus, Agent Walters could see in her mind's eye, the lazy good for nothing Kenneth staring at the stack of unanswered messages from Lt. Elliott.

"This time Kenneth…this time is going to be different, right? You know me. I definitely know you. You know I never bullshit. So, this is what you're gonna do. You're gonna get off your lazy butt, walk down the corridor and into that damp, stinky storage room next to the vending machine. The same machine where I'm sure you spend most of your time. You're going to pull the surveillance tapes from the Lincoln Tunnel, for the dates Lt. Elliott has specified. And don't give me some BS story that they weren't archived, because we both know that since 911, that all changed, right? Remember my six-page letter, all the details, all my investigation into you and all those inaccurate and false stories you told your supervisor. All your lies. We're not going down that path again, right?"

This time, Agent Walters waited for his reply. The awkward silence was deafening. Finally, Kenneth's voice cut through the silence.

"Right...there's no need for that."

"So, when are you going to go get the tape?"

"As soon as I hang up the phone with you."

"You're sure?"

"Yes."

"Positive?"

"Positive."

"Kenneth, you understand what happens if we don't get it right? You realize that if you lie again, and tell Lt. Elliott that there's no tapes available, and you don't even look, things end much differently for you right?"

"Yes. I understand."

"There are no second chances. This is the only chance you get." After a brief pause, Agent Walters lifted the receiver and took the call off speaker. This time, she spoke in a menacing voice of clear hatred, "You still live on Orange Street, don't you?" There was no response. In a soft whisper, Walters spoke her final words, "Last chance," before hanging up the phone.

Chapin was taken aback. Walters sounded like anything but a computer forensic analyst. Walters leaned back in her chair and stared back at the phone.

"That bastard cost my friend his life. If I can help it, nothing like that will ever happen again. I promise."

*   *   *   *   *

A high-pitched electronic tone echoed inside the retiree's parked car. He had dozed off. After waking up, he faced the mini-drone's controller and studied the monitor. Coming from the living room, illuminated as he turned the light on. The miniature drone was small enough to be hidden in plain view sitting on the coffee table. The retiree waited for John to cross the living room before activating the drone.

Careful to stay well behind and out of John's earshot, the retiree maneuvered the drone down the hallway. He paused and hovered the drone and magnified the camera aiming it over John's shoulder. He watched him enter the code and disarm the system and scribbled the access code number down on a piece of paper. The retiree glanced at the dashboard clock. It was 7:04pm. Their plane did not leave until 12:35am. It was the red-eye and non-stop. His suitcase was in the trunk. He had plenty of time.

He watched John walk away from the alarm pad heading toward the master bedroom. He waited for John to walk through the doorway before maneuvering the drone down the hallway. He made sure to fly as close to the ceiling as possible. He pivoted the drone and angled the camera inside the room. From his point of view, the camera focused on an area just above John's head. The retiree continued to hover the drone while John stripped off his clothes and walked across the room wearing only boxer shorts.

He maneuvered the drone into the master bedroom and positioned it facing the open bathroom door before landing on the carpet. After John entered the shower, he made his move. He grabbed the controller and strapped on his hip-pack. He double checked confirming that the syringes were inside.

He glanced up and down the street. It was clear. He scurried across the street. He was not worried about being seen. He looked like a typical tourist vacationing in the San Francisco Bay Area. No one would have guessed he had over 100 confirmed kills on his resume. So much for being semi-retired.

He glanced at the other surrounding houses. Ducking inside the front porch, the retiree put on a pair of latex gloves and opened his tumbler lock pick tools. Within seconds, he opened the lock and entered.

He went straight to the kitchen and opened the refrigerator door. He was happy to find only two cans of beer sitting on the clear see-through top shelf. On the other side of the shelf, there was a half-filled plastic bottle of 100 percent organic lemonade. The retiree glanced at the drone monitor. John was still showering behind the frosted glass door.

Turning his attention back to the refrigerator, the retiree removed the beer cans and the plastic lemonade bottle. He took an exaggerated deep inhale holding his breath, before removing the first syringe and a small wax stick. Holding each can firmly against the countertop, the retiree inserted the oversized thick needle through the top of the aluminum can. He injected the concoction through the top section of the can. He wanted to make sure that the poison stayed in the top section to increase the likelihood that the poison would get swallowed as opposed to settling in the bottom of the can.

As the retiree removed the now empty syringe needle from the can, he pressed the soft wax stick over the hole in the aluminum. For several seconds, he held the wax stick in place. He waited a few seconds before inspecting his work. He needed to make sure it did not leak. Certain it would hold he double-checked the drone monitor. John was still showering. He started on the second can.

In quick succession, the retiree continued the same process two more times; once for the second can of beer, followed by the plastic lemonade bottle. With his work complete, he returned the beverage containers back into the refrigerator only after emptying the last few drops from the syringes, leaving dime-sized drops, on the top shelf just behind the beer cans.

The retiree shut the refrigerator door, recapped the syringes with their plastic caps and placed them inside a sandwich sized zip-lock bag. Certain that the syringes were secure, he placed them inside his hip pack and zipped them inside the front compartment. Finally, he leaned forward and used his shirt sleeve to wipe away the condensation rings in the shape of the bottom of the beer cans and plastic bottle. He took one final glance at the drone's monitor before slipping back out the front door.

As he exited, the distance between the entryway and the street prevented him from being seen. The retiree pulled out his tumbler lock tool and re-locked the door from the outside. As he crossed the street, he checked his watch. Only four minutes and forty-eight seconds had passed since he exited the car. He opened the car door and slid inside.

He glanced at the reflection from the rear-view and side mirrors. With a deep sigh of relief, he re-checked the drone's monitor. He could just make out John's back with his head facing down letting the hot shower water cover his head and shoulders.

Wasting no time, the retiree reactivated the drone maneuvering it back out the bedroom door and into the kitchen. He flew it toward the opposite counter-top before landing it on top of the portable microwave. After several repositioning maneuvers, he was able to angle the camera at the refrigerator door.

As the minutes passed, the retiree continued glancing up checking the time displayed on the dashboard mounted clock. He hoped the target would cooperate. As each minute passed, the retiree became agitated and impatient worrying whether the target had stopped after work and visited a bar. With his mind churning through countless possible variables considering things that could jeopardize the outcome of this assignment. The retiree watched the images streaming from the drone and waited.

*   *   *   *   *

All day, Agent Walters and Chapin fast forwarded the surveillance tapes. They tracked the transport ambulance around the city. It appeared the drivers suspected they were being tracked. The first transport truck drove across the bridge into New Jersey then back into Manhattan, looped around Central Park, then into Queens. After a 30-minute food-break at a corner restaurant, it back tracked the same loop and repeated its exact same route twice. Finally, after another eight-hours driving around metropolitan New Jersey and New York City areas, it drove back to a non-descript industrial park and disappeared into an unmarked abandoned building.

The second ambulance, although taking a different circuitous route, with a similar 30-minute food break, ended up at the same unmarked abandoned building. By now, they learned there was an underground parking garage there. Agent Walters and Chapin exchanged knowing looks.

In a pained and confused expression, Chapin broke the silence first. "Are you kidding me? Did that second transport just go into the exact same building as the first one? Really?"

Pulling off her glasses, Agent Walters massaged her tired dry eyes before replying. "Yup. I bet you a dollar to a donut the other eight ambulance transfers end up here too."

"Wow, crazy. We followed those two ambulance transports an entire day." After a brief pause, Chapin added in an elevated voice, "Those bastards knew we'd be watching them with our satellites. Why else would they be doing this?"

"Well, ever since *Desert Storm*, our overhead satellite and smart bombs received a lot of television coverage. More than we really wanted." With a wry smile, and a tilt of her head, Walters continued, "But I'm in agreement. Those guys are messing with us."

Chapin glanced up at the wall clock. It was almost 9:00p.m. They were about to call it quits when the teleconference satellite call light started flashing.

"What time is it back on the *USS George HW Bush*?" asked Chapin.

"They're docked outside of Italy in the Med, so that's..." Walters paused as she figured it out. "...a nine-hour difference. So, it's six in the morning there."

"Damn, those guys get up early," joked Chapin as she punched the receiver. Within seconds, an image of Kyle and Moon Dog flashed on the monitor.

"Good morning, ladies," smiled Kyle with an ear-to-ear grin.

"You mean good evening, at least for us," corrected Agent Walters. "Boy, you two sure start your day early."

"Well, we literally sleep where we work," Moon Dog explained, as he pointed across the room. Their sleeping quarters were next door. It was large and had twelve bunks and a separate attached room for a C.O. It was only Kyle and Moon Dog. Neither feeling comfortable taking the C.O.'s room, they slept in opposite corners giving each other some privacy.

"Last night, by email, we received the surveillance tape. Walters carries some weight," smiled Moon Dog. "It was delivered to the New Jersey agency. They uploaded it to us, and we just reviewed it." Moon Dog and Kyle exchanged smiles. "We thought you two would get a kick out of what we found. We just sent you a video clip," explained Moon Dog.

On cue, a loud electronic tone sounded.

"We just got it," said Chapin.

"Boot it up!" yelled Kyle. "You won't believe what you see."

Seeing Moon Dog's and Kyle's faces, Chapin and Walters smiled back. Their excitement was contagious. As Kyle and Moon Dog waited, they did their best to control their emotions and flashed ear to ear grins but suppressed their laughter. Kyle covered his mouth with his hand.

Chapin and Walters watched the grainy black and white surveillance tape. Moon Dog edited the clip so they could see the first bus in the convoy pass in front of the wall-mounted camera inside the Lincoln Tunnel.

"At the beginning, you'll notice that the first vehicle to appear on the tape is a New York City bus. The neon sign displayed an out of service notice. As the first bus driver comes into view, pause your tape," instructed Moon Dog.

Walters and Chapin leaned forward in their chairs. As a set of head lights appeared in the tunnel, Walters noticed something.

"Weird. The bus is driving down the middle of both lanes. The dotted line runs right between the two front wheels. He's taking up both lanes?" said Walters.

"We're guessing that the first and last vehicles were used to block the other vehicles from seeing what was happening between the buses," offered Kyle.

"Okay. Here comes the first transportation vehicle," said Agent Chapin. "You wanted us to pause the tape as this vehicle comes into full view?"

"Correct," replied Moon Dog.

As the tape continued playing, Walters held her finger over the dial. As soon as the driver passed in front of the tunnel camera, she paused the tape. They leaned forward and studied the frozen image. Sitting in the driver's seat was a very old Caucasian man. He wore a beret cap and thick framed prescription glasses. He was an ex-Stasi KGB liaison and grew up in the same town as Van Aelst. The driver and Van Aelst worked together for many years. They were childhood friends.

After World War II, the driver slipped out of the country along with other Nazi VIPs escaping Berlin through an underground train system. From there, he made his way to the coast and then on board a submarine. Eventually, the submarine full of high-ranking Nazi members were taken to Argentina. Over time, as more and more submarines bused other officials to South America, the Nazi's dispersed to other countries, Brazil, Chile, Paraguay, and Uruguay. Over the decades, the driver moved to Brazil and then to New York.

Although high profile scientists were actively recruited and protected by the United States government, there existed another not so well-known group that were given privileges. A small group of trusted men, the custodians over the ill-gotten gold, diamonds and other items taken by Germany during the war. In the early years following the war, Switzerland converted a lot of the gold into useable currencies. Their assistance helped with all the expenses required for the displaced Nazi officials.

Van Aelst was part of that secret group of custodians. Unlike ODESSA (Organization of Former SS Members), this group originated from another secret Nazi affiliate; *Die Spinne* (the German word for "The Spider"). There were many *Die Spinne* groups that offered unique skills and knowledge. Van Aelst's affiliates dealt with the transportation, conversion, and disbursement of precious metals. There were others, fine arts, diamonds, life insurance and industrial patents. Like most international conflicts, if one digs deeper, if they search long enough, they will discover a more basic motivation. In most wars, the common denominator was greed and power. Germany was no different. After conquering each nation, plans were devised to extract the wealth from the defeated nation.

These *Die Spinne* groups were held together by a common thread beyond their specialized assigned booty. The commonality was much simpler and created the strongest bond. Each *Die Spinne* group was organized based on pre-existing deep friendships. Like college fraternities, an existing member recommended a childhood friend. Every existing member voted. Only unanimous candidates were accepted into the *Die Spinne*. These small cliques consisted of no more than 40 persons. Each member was given the rank of Captain, with the top four positions held for Generals. Those with lessor responsibilities, were granted the German rank of Commandant (equivalent to Major) and Colonel. These 40 individuals made up the mind trust within each *Die Spinne* group and oversaw disbursing some of the wealth procured by the Third Reich.

The common soldier was unaware that the labor performed was orchestrated by these young *Die Spinne* members and had no idea the organization existed. When a soldier completed a mission related to *Die Spinne*, they were re-assigned. To keep their existence a secret, entire groups of common soldiers were shuffled about. Only the mind trust, the core *Die Spinne* members remained intact as single cohesive units.

Walters stared at the frozen image and studied the old man's face. His features.

"He looks too old to be involved. Look at his face. He has to be in his seventies or eighties, added Chapin as she scrunched her face in confusion.

"Okay, let the tape roll," explained Moon Dog. As the tape restarted, Moon Dog narrated. "We only copied the cameras that showed the interesting stuff. The full tapes will be uploaded later."

Walters and Chapin watched as the tape showed the convoy of ten large transport vehicles between the lead and tailing buses. As each transport truck passed, they paused the tape to get a look at each driver. In each case, they discovered one common denominator; the driver was an old Caucasian male, with receding white hair, thick glasses and wore some type of headwear; a baseball cap, knit beanie or beret. This driver wore a fedora.

"They're all a bunch of old white guys. What's up with that?" asked Agent Chapin.

The next images came from a camera located further inside the tunnel. Walters and Chapin watched the transports, in unison, slowly increasing the distance between each other. Another part showed images from a long straight section of the tunnel. The camera angle was just right capturing the full profiles of two buses. To their astonishment, they saw the back end of these disguised transport trucks miraculously open. Without warning, each transport truck appeared to off-load identical ambulance transports. Once the ambulance transport was clear with all its wheels touching the ground, the transport truck sped ahead. The drivers of the ambulance transport vehicles were different. These drivers were much younger and from different races, not just old Caucasians.

Agents Walters and Chapin watched the tape until the twelfth vehicle, an actual bus not a transport truck, passed by the last camera. To their surprise, the final driver, a geriatric 80-something year old Caucasian, while passing by the wall mounted camera, stuck his hand up in the direction of the camera and raised his middle finger and shook his hand. In a sense of satisfaction, the old man's face lit up flashing a defiant grin displaying his crooked and stained teeth. With a tilt of his head, he bowed as if peeking into the future when, someday, somebody would be looking at this very image.

"Did he just flip us off?" asked Agent Walters.

With chuckles from Moon Dog and Kyle, both Walters and Chapin turned away from the camera images and stared at the satellite feed.

"I think so. It sure looks like the old man gave us 'the bird'," offered Kyle.

After a brief pause, all four agents laughed.

"Crazy old bastards," said Walters.

"Tag, you're it," said Chapin. "We're checking out until tomorrow at eight in the morning our time. Let us know what you find out."

"Sounds good. Good night," said Moon Dog.

"Good night," replied Chapin and Walters.

Chapin terminated the satellite feed and rubbed the back of her neck. It was a long day.

"I'm gonna swing by the hospital on my way home. I need to see if Agent Gall heard anything else. I'll see you tomorrow, Julie," said Chapin.

"Sounds good. I'll see you tomorrow."

8

In an oversized first-class chair, Winstead sat next to Van Aelst. He just finished his first vodka tonic. The plane was still at the gate waiting for passengers to board. Winstead set his second drink down on the retractable tray. Without thinking, he reached under his shirt and rubbed his sternum. He massaged his pectoral muscles imagining the bruise that would appear.

Winstead thought back recalling the pain caused by the projectile. *Van Aelst explained later that it was an oversized thin-shelled membrane filled with blood taken from a San Francisco morgue corpse. As the projectile hit his chest, the red mixture of fluids splattered across his chest. If he was not so surprised, he might have noticed the cold temperature from the refrigerated blood.*

They watched the unedited tape making certain everything looked real. It was perfect. While watching the tape, Winstead learned that he was shot from behind with a tranquilizer dart. The shooter hid out of the camera's view. The dart hit him in the right shoulder blade. Within seconds, the sedative went to work. The shock and momentum of the blood splatter round forced Winstead backwards. He fell onto his back and passed out.

Van Aelst wanted one continuous uninterrupted shot. The camera man intended the camera to flop about filming the floor, wall and ceiling giving the viewer the impression that the entire process, including the filming of the murder, was unrehearsed and spontaneous. When, in fact, much effort and thought went into each maneuver. Part of the planned choreography included several men timing their descent upon Winstead and grabbing his shoulders. Then dragging him down the hallway, while the camera filmed the ceiling and walls. At that same moment, another set of men dragged the dressed corpse forward and staged it in the same spot Winstead fell. To add to the confusion, the photographer adjusted the camera angle bouncing the camera around, while other team members shouted in broken choppy hangul mal (Korean language) yelling random instructions.

In the hallway, the corpse was positioned sprawled out on its back, with blood splattered across its chest and face. The photographer lowered the camera and directed the lens at the carnage. The still camera showed another team member's hand holding a silenced Chinese QS7-92 pistol. Shown in clear view, the camera documented everything. On cue the Korean depressed the trigger twice. The film showed the gun's recoil force rock the wrist backward as the bullets entering the forehead a few inches from the nose.

They used hollow point bullets to maximize the visual damage accomplishing their intended results. The corpse's face was rendered unrecognizable smeared with blood before the bullet impacts completed the charade.

The photographer's still camera showed gruesome close-ups. In the background, the other team members spoke Korean. While the mutilated corpse was dragged into the bathroom, the photographer kept the camera aimed down making certain none of the Koreans' faces were captured. Placed outside in the hallway, the camera focused on the empty bathtub. In the background, he heard the distinct sound. After a few pulls, the chainsaw started with its distinct revving sound blaring in the background.

After a few moments, the camera was mounted onto a tripod. Once the view was fixed into place, the film showed disturbing images as body pieces were flung through the air before landing in the bathtub. The camera continued filming and documented their work. Several team members' hands and arms came into view as diluted acid was poured onto the heap of flesh stacked inside the tub.

Off camera, two Koreans waited as the chemicals sizzled as the acid disintegrated the flesh and bone. The camera followed another set of hands removing a detachable shower head showing a man spraying water on top washing away the decomposing soupy remains down the drain. Off camera, samples of Winstead's hair clippings and blood were strewn about the outside of the tub making certain that this physical evidence could be collected by the crime scene investigation team. From their efficient orchestration, it was obvious that these men did this type of thing many times before. It was disturbing to watch them go about their business.

When complete, the corpse was gone. The sludge and bone fragments were washed down the drain. Any remaining corpse residue was sanitized by the caustic acid, and when tested would provide no useable DNA. However, the hair and blood samples purposely placed outside the tub were sure to return a positive match against Winstead's FBI and personal medical records.

After reviewing the video, everyone agreed; it was perfect. Having achieved their objective, the team gathered all their tools and weapons and stuffed them inside the discarded plastic San Francisco Morgue body bag. Then, the stuffed bag was placed inside an oversized rolling suitcase. With a final act of thoroughness, the lowest ranking team member wiped down every fixture: especially the faucets, door knobs, even the toilet seat and handle.

After everyone exited the apartment, this same team member, using gloved hands, pulled the vacuum cleaner out and vacuumed the entire fourteen-hundred square feet of floor space. The hallway carpet, with the distinct impact splatter, was left untouched. After cleaning the outside of the flash-drive that contained the choreographed video clip, he placed it on the center of the coffee table. Finally, he back peddled toward the front door, vacuuming his tracks behind him, before unplugging the machine, and carrying it with him out the front door.

By the time he reached the street, the other team members were all packed waiting inside the van. As he approached, the side door slid open. Before stepping inside and closing the door, the man tossed the vacuum inside. While the van drove away, the driver glanced up and down the street. No one saw them drive away.

The stewardess's voice booming from the loud speaker interrupted Winstead's thoughts. He blinked awake and flashed a forced smile as she recited her announcement through a hand-held microphone.

Winstead glanced to his right and noticed the same retiree sitting with a drink in his hand. Distracted in thought, he never saw him board the plane. With a tired face, the retiree nodded and raised his drink, a straight vodka over ice. In a mock toast, Winstead raised his glass toward the retiree seated across the aisles.

"It's Slovakian vodka. I asked the stewardess" explained the retiree. "How fitting," he added.

"How so?" asked Winstead.

"The brand name is *Double Cross*," he clarified. After flashing an ear-to-ear grin, he laughed out loud and raised his glass even higher. "Accurate, no?"

With a quick smile, Winstead replied. "Yes. Very fitting."

"I like your new hair cut too. Nice and short. The way a real man should wear it," the retiree said.

Winstead glanced to his left. Herr Van Aelst was staring back, waiting for Winstead's reactions.

"He made it in time to catch our flight," smiled Winstead.

"Yes, I figured he would. He couldn't resist flying out together one last time," replied Herr Van Aelst. With a slight tilt of his head, he continued. "It is First-Class after all." After an awkward pause,

Van Aelst leaned closer and spoke into Winstead's ear. In almost a whisper, "You thought I was going to leave you behind and betray you?"

To avoid eye-contact, he faced forward and nodded. "I did."

"You've proven yourself Winstead. You've remained loyal all these years. You're part of our team now, no longer isolated in a foreign land waiting for orders from abroad. You'll need time to adjust to your new name, Martin," said Van Aelst as he leaned back stretching his legs out as he rested his head on the plush head rest. With closed eyes, he continued speaking. "You are also the youngest member of our team. Welcome aboard Martin, ...Herr Schmid to *Spinne* (German for Spider)."

*   *   *   *   *

Agent Chapin exited the elevator and approached the police officer standing guard outside Gall's hospital room.

"How has she been?" Chapin asked as she flashed her Agency badge. He only glanced at the ID as he recognized her from earlier in the day.

"Much better ma'am. She's been sleeping most of the day. It seems like she's been awake for a while now though," the policeman replied with a caring friendly smile.

Agent Chapin stood on her tip toes and peered through the small glass window in the door. She saw Agent Gall aiming the remote at the television.

"She's definitely awake," smiled Agent Chapin and pushed open the door. "Hey you. How are you feeling?

Agent Gall turned away from the television and smiled. "Much better. I'm starting to go stir crazy though. They want to keep me here through tomorrow. Head trauma protocol because of the concussion."

"Makes sense. Better safe than sorry with head injuries," Chapin said. She pulled up a chair and sat down next to the bed before leaning back in the chair. With an inquisitive stare, she asked "Why'd you join the Bureau?"

Gall's smile faded as she became lost in thought. Her eyes glazed over. It was years since she thought about it. Unlike other agents, she knew the exact moment. She had just turned eight years old, a second grader at Lincoln Street School. There was a small playground located close to the main street. Back in those days there were no high chain linked fences protecting the children, keeping the kids safe inside and others out.

Still gazing across the room, in a soft quiet voice, Gall began speaking. Chapin could barely hear her voice and leaned forward, craning her head forward to listen.

"She was my friend. If she hadn't been taken, I imagine we could have become the best of friends." Theresa said as she glanced down at the IV stuck into the crook of her arm. She scrunched her face, as if she felt guilty for having complained about the discomfort the little needle caused. With a slow blink, she returned her vacant gaze across the room. Without thinking, she fidgeted with the television remote control muting the volume and flipped from channel to channel unconcerned with the shows that flashed by on the screen. The only sound inside the room was the soft electronic chirp from the life support monitor.

"It could have been me. We were climbing up and down playing on the slide. The little kindergarteners and first-graders had already gone back inside. But we were older. We always went back into our classes last.

Theresa paused. After a heavy sigh, she continued. "I told her I was thirsty and needed a drink." As if she remembered being questioned, she jerked her head toward Agent Chapin. With her eyes open in an exaggerated manner, she clarified, "If I'd known what was going to happen, I would have waited for her. We should have gone together."

From her expression, she seemed to be lost in thought. A deep sense of sadness washed across her face. It was as if her memories still caused her pain. Theresa paused and looked back across the room. "I was only a child. How could I have known? We were both the same age. We'd just turned eight years old. Our birthdays were in the same month…December. We were looking forward to the upcoming Christmas break."

In a calm emotionless manner, as if she were reading a grocery list, Theresa continued her story.

"They came to my house. That's when I found out. I ran over to get a drink from the drinking fountain. I didn't want to be late. The other older kids were running back, lining up before heading back inside. After drinking some water, I forgot about her and ran to the line too. I never looked back. I thought she was coming. It was the last recess before we went home.

"The teacher told the police that they hadn't noticed her missing. Everyone was busy. There was a school assembly following recess. We never went back into the classroom. We lined up and were led to the cafeteria for an assembly. There was a little Christmas concert that the older kids were putting on. With all the excitement and confusion caused by the assembly, the teacher must have been distracted. Even the teacher missed it."

In a quiet soft voice, almost a whisper, Theresa repeated herself. "Even the teacher missed it." After a pause, she continued. "That night, the police came to my house. They told me that my friend was missing. She never came home. They interviewed all my classmates. The next day, two FBI agents came to our house. There was a man and a woman. I told them everything I knew."

In a monotone voice, her cadence changed. "They asked me if I'd seen anyone walking by. I had to think about it. And...there was. I hadn't thought about it until then. It was the way she'd asked that question. For some reason, I recalled seeing an old man. He had a small dog on a leash. He had stopped on the sidewalk and was watching the kids playing."

Theresa took a deep breath. She turned and stared into Chapin's eyes. In a determined steely voice, "They never found her. She never surfaced. I never saw the old man with the small dog again either. Later, I learned that the FBI investigated kidnappings. That evening, during the midnight Christmas Mass, that's when I knew I wanted to join the FBI."

Agent Chapin covered her mouth and nodded. Both women were tough as nails. Surrounded by men, they learned to bury their feelings. Only later, when they were alone, hidden from prying eyes and the scrutiny of others, they let it out. Neither one dared to shed a tear. That's just what professionals did.

Being around ex-military high testosterone co-workers, Agent Chapin replied the only way she knew how. It was just something law enforcement people did. A common trait shared by this fraternity the world over. "FUBAR (fouled up beyond all recognition)."

Theresa turned and stared back at Chapin. With a nod, she replied. "Yeah, it was all FUBAR."

Theresa grabbed the remote control. Using her index finger, she stabbed the mute button. The ESPN announcer's voice cut through the silence and began rehashing the weekend NFL scores.

*   *   *   *   *

Director Gamboa tapped his pen against his legal pad of paper.

"So, Chapin, what has the Bureau got?"

"It was *'definitely'* staged. I had our guys take a peek. Her brakes were tampered with. Somebody went to a lot of effort to make it look like an accident."

"Does someone stand to gain from the payout on her life insurance?"

"She's single; just her parents."

"What type of cases has she been working?"

"Prior to our closed 'Director-Only Closed' file, she was just getting started on some kiting scheme run by some Russians in Sacramento. It's still too soon for them to retaliate. No subpoenas or arrests have been made. The other associates are doing the surveillance and sleeping in their cars. Gall isn't even the lead agent on that case either. Other than that, it doesn't look to be related to any of her cases. But you know criminals. It could be something she was involved with years ago," Chapin added while shrugging.

Chapin glanced up from her file and stared back waiting for Gamboa's response. With raised eyebrows, Chapin's body language suggested that maybe the accident was related to their John Doe case. They sat in silence thinking things through when a voice from the Director's intercom came through.

"Sir, an urgent call is waiting for Agent Chapin."

"Who is it?" the Director asked.

"An Agent Gall from the Bureau."

"Her ears must have been burning," said the Director. "Send the call through. Chapin will take it from my phone."

"Right away Director."

While his secretary transferred the call, the Director had a plan.

"Put her on speaker phone. Don't let her know I'm listening. Are you ready?" Chapin nodded and leaned forward as the call came through.

"Chapin."

"Hey, it's Gall."

"What are you doing? Still in the hospital?"

"No. They gave me the green light this morning. I got the hell out of there before they changed their minds," Agent Gall explained.

243

"Good for you. What's up?"

"One of the research analysts is AWOL (absent without leave). He never came in this morning." There was a brief pause as Chapin thought it through.

"What are you thinking Gall?"

"With someone hacking my computer, and now a research analyst going missing, seems a little too coincidental."

"Was he a computer forensic guy?"

"Yup."

Chapin glanced at the Director before continuing.

"How long has he been in the Bureau?"

"Going on nine years, almost ten."

"Never promoted?"

"Nope. He never tested."

"Is anyone on your end going to his place?"

"Not yet. It's still too early. But if he doesn't show up by tomorrow, they'll start looking into it."

After hearing everything, Director Gamboa nodded. Chapin got the message.

"Let me swing by his place. What's his name?"

"Winstead. James Winstead."

*   *   *   *   *

Agent Walters waited outside of the Director's office. She was scheduled to give him an update on the surveillance progress. She had just had a satellite conference with Moon Dog and Kyle. Agent Chapin was inside with the Director on another matter. As usual, Walters arrived early and waited in the Director's lobby.

The double doors pushed open. Agent Chapin leaned out and waived Walters inside. Just as Walters walked through the doors, the Director started speaking, not waiting for her to take a seat.

"Walters," boomed the Director's voice. "I need you to look into a few more things for me."

Agent Walters plopped down in the chair next to Chapin. Without missing a step, she opened her folder, pulled out a pen and was ready to take notes.

"Yes sir. What do you need?"

"I need you to get me everything you can on two guys. First, James Winstead, a computer forensics analyst from the San Francisco Bureau. I need his IP location, his bio and current home address. Also, all of his known associates and close friends. Finally, a quick cursory snoop around to see if he's been looking around anything he shouldn't be."

"A mole?" asked Walters.

"Maybe. And I need that ASAP. As in ten minutes ago. Email it to me and copy Chapin. This new assignment is your number one priority. So, our little satellite review will have to take a back seat for now."

"Okay. And the second guy?"

"U.S. Senator Anthony. This assignment is a secondary issue that may run parallel to the John Doe investigation."

With a slight tilt of her head, Walters asked, "What am I looking for?" She knew that a U.S. Senator's biography, current business addresses, and staff information were all public knowledge available on his website.

"Other stuff," offered the Director.

"Can you be more specific?"

"Like most people, especially politicians, I'd guess that we should start with financial issues. Take a look at these dates in particular," explained the Director as he slid a piece of paper across his desk. Prior to their meeting, he pulled the knock-list (real names of people set to be murdered) that was copied by Curt Anderson. Based on what Director Valdez shared, he had a gut feeling that something may turn up there. Walters grabbed the list and nodded her head as she reviewed the dates.

"You can work on the Senator issue after you brief us on this Winstead guy."

The Director stood. Walters understood their meeting was over. Walters gathered her things and left. The Director waited for Walters to leave before turning toward Chapin. Chapin raised her eyebrows and widened her eyes as if to ask, "What's with Senator Anthony?"

"There might be a problem with the Senator," explained Gamboa.

*   *   *   *   *

Agent Gall was still dressed in the wrinkled clothes she wore to the office the day of the car accident. Her face was pock marked by scabs, wounds healing from the flying metal shards projected from the airbags, and cracked ribs and clavicle. Other than her concussion, she avoided serious injuries. Gall sat at her desk inside the FBI office staring at the plant. As she wondered which co-worker delivered it, a voice interrupted her thoughts.

"Welcome back," one of the analysts said as he stuck his head inside her open door.

"Thanks," she smiled back. "What's up with the flowers?" she asked out of curiosity.

"The IT guys brought it up," he said with a sideways glance as he contemplated the protocol of the situation. He was deciding if his unit should follow suit as well. Feeling guilty, he avoided eye-contact.

"That's weird," Agent Gall offered. She turned her attention to the potted flower and shrugged her shoulders.

As the analyst turned to leave, he added, "It was Winstead's idea. He thought it was the least they should do."

Gall watched him walk away and wondered "*Why would Winstead be the instigator? We hardly knew each other.*" The ring from her desk phone broke her concentration.

"Gall," said Theresa as she spoke into the phone receiver.

"Are you alone?" asked Agent Chapin over her encrypted cell phone. Recognizing her voice, Gall replied.

"Yes."

"I'm inside Winstead's apartment. Something's wrong. I smell a distinct sweet coppery odor in the hallway and the bathtub looks all wrong. There's a greasy shine all over the place. I already ran it by Director Gamboa. Since it might be your ass on the line, he wanted to give you an option."

"What option?"

"If somebody's snooping around your computer, and one of your IT guys has just gone AWOL, and now I discover the MIA's apartment beyond suspicious, we thought it might be nice to get us...my Agency team involved. If Winstead is involved in this, there may be others."

"What about my boss? Cutting him out of the loop like this, there will be hell to pay for keeping him in the dark. What about my chain of command?"

"Don't worry about that. Nobody will know that you were involved. Believe me, this may very well end up on my desk anyway."

"Why ask for my opinion?"

"That's the way we do things over here. Small things could lead to big things. Our 'brain-trust' means a lot. You'd be surprised how many times trust is all that we have over here."

Gall paused as she processed everything. Then it hit her, "Do you think someone is targeting me?"

"You are involved somehow. Your brakes, the computer, now Winstead going AWOL."

"And there's something else."

"What?" asked Chapin.

"I've been staring at this oversized plant all morning. There was an oversized plant delivered to my hospital room as well."

"So, are you loved by your family and co-workers? I don't get it."

"An analyst just told me that Winstead pushed for the plant." After a brief pause, she continued. "And I barely know the guy."

"Bring the plant," instructed Chapin. She had a hunch. "Tell your secretary that you were overly optimistic about coming back to work so soon. Say, 'You're not feeling well' and decided to go home."

"That's not too far from the truth," Gall replied.

Prior to calling Gall, Chapin had briefed Director Gamboa. Winstead's apartment was being processed, photographed and dusted for finger prints. The only thing remaining was the bathtub. One of the crime scene investigators found a flash drive on the coffee table. After it was checked for prints, and its contents copied, it was given to Agent Chapin. While the investigation continued, Chapin went to her car. Using the computer inside the trunk, she copied the flash drive and uploaded an encrypted copy to the Director. She got

Director Gamboa on a secure line. They watched the video clip together.

It appeared to be taken from inside Winstead's apartment. They guessed it documents his abduction. It did not take long for them to realize it was more than an abduction. It seemed clear that Winstead was killed by a group of Asians. The audio was sent to one of their Agency linguists who confirmed that the perpetrators were speaking Korean. Their dialect was from north of the DMZ. There was no doubt that something bigger was happening. They were certain that this was an international matter, outside the FBI's jurisdiction.

Gamboa wondered if all of this, in some twisted way, had anything to do with the Anderson file. Or was it something altogether different? Gamboa decided it was time to put Agent Gall under a microscope. He needed to know whether her being placed in the center of this situation was a random happenstance event. Or, if Gall was involved in another way.

"I need you to meet me at Winstead's place. I've already asked our Agency Investigative Unit to come. I want you on the ground when this goes down. Oh, and bring your laptop," explained Chapin.

"Why?"

"I found a flash drive on the coffee table."

"Will do," replied Gall.

*   *   *   *   *

"Director, it's Chapin."

"What did she say?"

"She's coming down now."

"I want you to record her face while she watches the tape. I want to see her reactions. We need to know if Gall just got sucked into this or if she's involved in something, we are not yet aware of."

"Everything is set. The investigation team is waiting until I finish with Gall before they start working on the bathroom." Chapin needed to catch her breath before continuing. "The cameras are set up. I'll make sure her laptop is placed on the coffee table before she plays it."

"By the way, we may have another problem."

"What's that? The Lincoln Tunnel Tapes?"

"No. John didn't show up this morning." The phone line went silent. Chapin was processing this new information. "I've already called his place and run a GPS confirmation on his car, laptop and cell phone. They're all still at his residence and haven't moved since last night."

"It has to be because of the Anderson file. That's the common thread," offered Chapin.

"The Korean element bothers me though. It could be something else. Something unrelated, just a coincidence. We need to be certain," countered Director Gamboa.

"Did you want me to go there next?"

"I've already got another team heading over there now. I've also asked Nena to reposition a satellite before we go inside. I want to make sure everything is clear before we walk inside there. For now, you stay focused on Agent Gall."

"Yes sir!"

"Things are starting to heat up around here, Chapin."

"You can say that again boss."

*   *   *   *   *

Agent Walters was locked away in her office busy hacking into the Senator's computer. She pulled all his emails, going back a few months before he left his law firm Neebling, Blair & Kerr. Walters was having a difficult time understanding why the Senator altered his path and chose a completely new and unexpected different career in politics. From her research, she could not find any indications that he aspired to become a politician. It was as if he made the decision overnight.

Walters discovered that the Senator was still close to his prior law partners. He was also a constant figure at their annual golf tournament. On occasion, he even vacationed with them. Walters guessed that the Senator was laying the ground work for his exit strategy with plans of returning to the law firm as a lobbyist. She had a gut feeling that the Senator was up to something. If he was, he would certainly involve some of his ex-law firm buddies.

Being a computer forensics analyst, Walters grew to expect and understand, regardless of a person's perceived intelligence, for some unknown reason, almost everyone failed to appreciate the dangers and pitfalls surrounding the use of email. Emails have a way of being an Achilles Heel and the undoing of the unscrupulous.

The senator was no exception. Long forgotten emails, messages that the sender assumed were permanently deleted, still left an electronic trail, capable of being resurrected from the waste basket from the abyss and reproduced in all its unedited glory; date and time stamped with the sender's and recipient's email and IP locations all for the world to see.

With little effort, any computer analyst worth their salt could cross reference those emails against their IP locations. In turn, depending on the sophistication of the sender, pinpoint a real physical address. After tracking the emails using a vast array of surveillance videos, even ones from neighboring ATM machines, parking lot cameras and office building security systems, it never took long for an accused to be staring at a grainy surveillance photo of him or herself, contradicting their previous sworn statements and ruining what was otherwise, a solid alibi. The accused is forced to listen to their obvious lies, given under sworn testimony that now, considering the forensic evidence, are clearly untrue. Many celebrities, corporate figures, and even a few Democratic Presidential candidates, learned this lesson the hard way.

Walters predicted finding a few personal emails disbursed among the firm's electronic communication system. It was inevitable. In relatively short order, Walters accumulated at least two personal emails for every partner. She ran a search through the sent and received folders and uncovered an avalanche of personal emails.

Over time most senior partners became less willing to update their computers, frustrated at having to learn new software. Their inflexibility made them resistant to change, even when forced to adapt to changes implemented for the good of the firm. Due to huge and inexpensive hard drives, computer systems evolved from gigabytes to terabytes, many senior partners instructed their IT department to devise work-around solutions allowing them to continue to use their antiquated operating systems. These customized work-around systems were designed to accommodate these senior partners with the misguided belief that only the staff needed the "real" current computer systems. The firm justified the decision based on the belief that the senior partners only used their computers for emails and internet searches anyway.

After a few hours, Walters learned that the most frequent searches and sites visited involved golf, vacations, on-line gambling and porn. Another common site visit related to their personal investment portfolios with bookmarks to their brokerage accounts and investments. Walters' research centered around the days preceding and following the dates listed on the Director's list. Here, she found many personal emails. Although many of the emails were initiated by the senior partners company email, there were also a lot of emails forwarded or copied to their personal accounts. Walters found it interesting that in every instance, had they avoided using the company computer and isolated these emails to encrypted personal computers and emails, it would have made her job much more difficult. Using other systems, would have forced her to locate each partner's personal computer and perform individual investigations that could have, at least, delayed the inevitable. As in most cases, the only excuse they would be able to offer up, was simple, laziness. It was human nature.

Over the years, Walters learned that older people resorted to familiar features. Trying to use the miniature screens on a smart phone was much more difficult than using a standard key board and mouse. With aging eyes and fat arthritic fingers with swollen joints, pecking out a message from their cell phones became too cumbersome.

With little effort, Walters found the smoking gun. The damning evidence was found inside emails sent several days preceding and following the dates listed on Gamboa's list. Had Walters been briefed on the entire case, she would have recognized the significance of that day. She would have understood that day set everything in motion. That was the day Mr. Drakeson died at the New Bay Meadows Race Track from an apparent sudden heart attack while watching the races. She would have understood why so many emails were exchanged questioning the wisdom in purchasing so much stock in a little unknown company that, until then, had been only a minor peripheral player in the development of a particular missile defense program.

However, that information was on a need-to-know basis. Walters had no need to know. Her involvement centered on the email communications surrounding that particular list of dates. Her focus centered on whether Senator Anthony was linked to any financial improprieties.

Based on what Walters uncovered, she was certain what she found was exactly what the Director was looking for. The most incriminating evidence was a single email string that the Senator sent to each recipients' personal emails. Unlike a majority of the other cryptic and abbreviated messages, this one was blatant. It left no room for misinterpretation. A scanned image was attached. The sender inscribed a message over the top portion of the document. It appeared to be a stock purchase confirmation. The document was dated three days following the date listed on the Director's list. The sender, the most senior partner, circled the number of stocks purchased; one hundred thousand shares. Next to that number, a crude smiley face was sketched followed by four exclamation points.

The senator replied to all the recipients a semi-colon followed by a right parenthesis. The modern sign for a winking smiley face. Several other partners replied actual messages; "You're the man!" and "I knew we could count on you."

Out of curiosity, Walters isolated the senior partner's emails focusing on emails sent after that date. It did not take long for her to locate another outgoing email sent to every senior partner. There was no message. Just a single attachment. A scan of an investment portfolio sheet. This time, nothing was circled. There were two differences. The stock price and the total value of the portfolio. The stock price rose from thirty-five dollars per share to five-hundred-ten dollars. The current stock value was listed at fifty-one million dollars.

* * * * *

Agent Gall stood in the hallway outside Winstead's bathroom. Agent Chapin met her at the door. Gall slid paper slippers over her shoes to prevent contaminating the scene while Chapin held out a small bottle of Vick's menthol cream. Being familiar with this process, Gall inserted her index finger inside then coated it with the gel before applying a thin layer of the ointment on her upper lip under her nostrils. The menthol vapor kept the pungent odor from activating a natural gag reflex. Gall followed Chapin inside and waited outside the hallway bath. Looking over Chapin's shoulder, Gall studied what looked like a filmy residue on the bathtub walls.

There were distinct pinkish residue lines that stood in contrast to the white bathtub lining.

It reminded Gall of her childhood. The ring around the tub, left by the receding residue mark, where the water pooled waiting to exit through the drain. Chapin's voice broke Gall's train of thought.

"Did you bring your laptop?"

Without looking away from the bathtub, Gall tapped the outside of the black leather carrying case. "Right here."

"I've got the flash drive," Chapin said as she raised the small plastic device for Gall to see. "The flash drive has already been processed," Chapin said as she walked back to the living room area and sat on the sofa. "Let's take a look," she said over her shoulder.

Gall made her way to the sofa and coffee table, Chapin glanced up making certain that the small pen-camera placed on the television was in line certain to catch what would follow. Before Gall turned around, Chapin redirected her attention away from the hidden camera. Gall sat next to Chapin, grabbed the flash drive and set up her laptop. After sliding the flash drive into the side port, she started the computer before accessing the file. With a quick flick of her wrist, she clicked the built-in mouse pad and played the video clip. She maximized the screen and turned up the volume. As the video began playing, all the crime scene technicians stood behind the sofa to watch. Having already previewed the clip, Chapin was the only one present that knew what to expect.

Gall's eyes dilated as she leaned forward. The clip started from outside Winstead's front door. Based on the lighting, the clip was filmed at night; presumably, the night before. As the door opened, the camera view zoomed in for a magnified close-up. A man was standing inside the doorway.

"It looks like Winstead," offered Gall.

As the camera operator appeared to be walking toward the man, the camera view tilted out of focus. The view swayed from side to side. At this point, there was no volume. In a sudden jerking motion, the camera aimed at the man's face. Without doubt, it was Winstead. The angle pulled back at the precise moment when the volume on the tape activated. The volume from the video clip caught voices of several people in the background speaking. It sounded like an Asian language. A language no one in the room was familiar with. Without warning, a distinct metallic spit sound echoed from the video clip.

At the same moment, Winstead's chest and lower face were covered with blood splatter that dripped down his body. Everyone assumed that a silencer was used, and a projectile must have entered his chest. The only explanation for so much blood to be flowing was a damaged heart. Everyone watched mesmerized by the images.

Winstead's body fell away as he collapsed onto his back. Several male voices, speaking that foreign language, blared in the background. Gall tilted her head trying to listen more closely.

"It sounds Asian," Gall whispered without looking away from the laptop monitor. Chapin watched Gall the entire time. Three live feeds, intended to capture her reaction, streamed back to the Agency. Director Gamboa sat alone in his office watching the scene unfold. From what Chapin could tell, Gall was surprised. Her expressions were authentic. All her attention was focused on the video unable to turn away. She never exhibited any suggestion of being self-conscious, as if she felt she were being watched. Like the others, she assumed that their attention was focused on the clip, nothing else. Chapin continued watching Gall as the tape rolled.

The camera view bounced around following the men as they proceeded with their grizzly tasks. More harsh loud voices conversed back and forth. As the camera operator moved down the hallway, he stepped forward and the camera view tilted upward toward the ceiling before bouncing downward, blurring as the view zoomed in with a close-up of Winstead's chest then tilted up toward his blood-spattered face. As soon as his face came into view, a hand holding a silenced pistol came into view obscuring Winstead's face. Moments later, the video clip showed the finger on the trigger pull back and the wrist recoil twice as two loud metallic spitting sounds echoed in the hallway.

As the hand holding the pistol pulled away, the camera focused on Winstead's face. An oversized entry wound through the center of the forehead and another entry wound through the maxillary bone (the area between his front incisors and his nasal cavity that covered his nose). The entire face was fractured held together by a piece of skin and cranium bone. The point of the video was clear; to document his death. After a brief pause, more loud verbal exchanges were heard as they dragged the corpse into the bathroom.

The camera man dropped the camera to his side while he struggled setting up a small tripod. The sway and tilting camera view stopped replaced by a rigid still view, suggesting that the camera was now locked into place and attached to the tripod. After an apparent adjustment, the video clip rotated upward showing the floor from outside the hallway peering into the bathroom focusing on the bathtub rim.

To the investigative team and Agent Gall's dismay, the audio picked up a muffled motorized sound. More loud conversations took place in the background. Those huddling around the laptop viewing the clip groaned as the unmistakable sound of a chainsaw motor being cranked up blared through the speakers.

"Holy shit," whispered one of the investigators.

The distinct sound of cutting and ripping away of clothes from the corpse echoed in the living room followed by the distinct high-pitched revving sound as the chainsaw's motor strained cutting through what most people associated with the falling of a tree, not dismembering a body. As the revving subsided, the camera documented what appeared to be body parts being flung into the tub. The combination of the sounds and images was too much. In disbelief, almost everyone turned away and covered their mouths.

Chapin reached across the coffee table and paused the tape and then closed the laptop.

"We get the idea. We can analyze it in more detail later," added Chapin. As Chapin glanced around the room, it was obvious that the horrific scene on the tape affected everyone. Winstead was one of theirs. Chapin regretted even considering the possibility that Winstead was a traitor. With a deep sigh, everyone stepped away from the coffee table trying to regain their composure. Several men walked away out of the view of the others to wipe away tears.

"Okay people," said the lead investigator. "Let's go over the bathroom with a fine-toothed comb. Maybe one of those bastards cut themselves or left some hair. I want every square inch swabbed for DNA."

The lead investigator stared into the bathtub, then the bathroom floor. "There's a lot of blood and hair in there. I'm hoping something can be tied to the perps."

"Bastards," replied another investigator.

As the scene investigators restarted processing the bathroom, Chapin stood.

While leading Agent Gall outside, Chapin said, "Let's move out to my car and give these guys some room." They walked in silence out of the apartment building and paused outside of Chapin's car. They stared up at the night sky.

"This is some crazy shit Chapin. I've never seen anything like that before. It felt like Cartel stuff," Agent Gall said as she rubbed her chin. "This has been one hell of a week. What the hell is going on?" she said while shaking her head.

"Were you guys at the Bureau working on something that could be tied to your accident and now Winstead?" asked Chapin.

"Not that I can think of."

"How about with prior older cases? Did you work on any high-profile stuff? Anything that could remotely link back to anything to do with an Asian gang? Like China Town?"

"Everything I handled was corporate fraud. The closest thing I had was a peripheral role in a Russian counterfeiting scam in

Sacramento. That's it," continued Gall with a confused and frustrated look.

"What's different? Anything? Or is this just random crazy stuff?" asked Chapin.

"The only thing different is this John Doe case I've been working. It seems like everything hit the fan since I caught that case," Agent Gall said with a blank confused stare.

Chapin studied Gall's face. There was no sign of dishonesty. She did not appear to be hiding anything. She spoke clear, candid, and direct. If she were feeling vulnerable, Gall would act defensive and evasive. Chapin was certain Agent Gall was being forthright. As if on cue, Chapin's cell phone rang. It was Director Gamboa.

"Chapin."

"I think she's telling the truth," said the Director.

"Me too," replied Chapin.

"Bring her down. It's time to brief her into the Anderson file," Gamboa ordered.

"We'll be right there," replied Chapin before hanging up. Chapin looked up at Agent Gall. "It's time for you to meet my boss." Chapin opened the door to her black agency SUV and stared over at Gall. "Climb in. I'll drive you over. We need to talk on the way over."

Gall pointed at her car.

"I'll have someone pick it up later," explained Chapin.

9

Agent Walters waited for the Director to pick up her call. Walters was certain she found more than just incriminating evidence. She was briefed years before that dealing with the Agency was different. There was no need for subpoenas, no search warrants, or trials; life and death decisions were based on limited evidence. The Agency dealt with the big picture. It was tasked with protecting the national security of the United States. There would be no second guessing their decisions. There were no Monday morning quarterbacks to be concerned with.

Agency decisions were autonomous and independent. Other than broad stroke philosophical directions that start at the top, the very nature and design of the Agency's framework prevented any one person to control all decisions. In most cases, unless an issue had global consequences, the regional Agency Director had the ultimate authority over the situation.

For that reason, only the toughest, most level headed administrators were elevated to the rank of Director. Without the intervention of Congress to declassify a case, not even POTUS had the authority to forcibly be briefed on any Agency case. It was a fact that every past President took exception with. It was an affront to their fragile egos to be told by some civil servant holding the title of Director that they could determine which cases, if any, POTUS should be involved in. The classified and sensitive nature of what the Agency was involved in extended well beyond the maximum eight-year term of a re-elected President. In the Agency's eyes, POTUS was just a temporary employee with VIP status. One who rarely warranted or justified being briefed in on any of their cases. Most of the time, other than curiosity, POTUS had no need to know.

Knowing the Agency's authority, Agent Walters, for the first time, contemplated the impact of what she uncovered. She appreciated that the subject in question was a seated U.S. Senator. The information she uncovered was obtained without due process and could never be presented in a court of law. These constitutional requirements were the precise intent to keep the powerful Agency directed at persons and entities outside the U.S. jurisdiction. It was intended to avoid gathering evidence and prying into the lives of its citizens. What she learned and how she obtained it was a conflict of interest. She could now prove, without any ambiguity that Senator Anthony continued to abuse his legislative authority. He continued to misdirect resources and base decisions that financially benefited himself and his close friends.

While waiting for the Director, Walters proofed her single-paged bullet-pointed briefing paper. She grappled with the power she had over the Senator's fate. She recognized that another computer analyst, with similar skills, could uncover the same findings. But that happening was unlikely. Throughout her career, she received exemplary performance evaluations. Her findings were thorough and included balanced conclusions and recommendations. If she chose to bury what she uncovered, the Senator could be saved. A corrupt computer forensic analyst could choose to confront the Senator. For the right amount of money, for access to the better things in life, up until now, because one's financial limitations were unattainable. Such a person could choose not only to bury it from the eyes of others but take it so far as to coach this wayward Senator on ways to destroy certain electronic communications and records. By assisting the Senator, a corrupt agent could opt to switch sides; offering to work as the Senator's and his corrupt colleagues' consultant.

To start down that trail of lies and deceit, was a futile exercise. Everyone in the Agency was subject to annual polygraph examinations. These interviews were designed to detect any and all personal indiscretions. Even if a person had the mental capacity, to consistently game the exam was futile. Eventually, sometime in every agency employee's career, regardless of one's tenure and rank, each agent faced background vetting aimed at uncovering a person's hidden life. Every evil, selfish, dishonest act that the Agency deemed inappropriate would be sought out.

The biggest difference with the Agency was the endgame, the resolution to such findings. Unlike in the private sector, being found out resulted in a dramatic and permanent solution. In most cases, contemplating a long jail sentence, was not a sufficient deterrent. The Agency had the authority, means and motivation to make such persons disappear.

The sound of Director Gamboa's voice coming through the telephone receiver interrupted Agent Walters thoughts. She was a straight shooter. There was absolutely nothing Walters could be offered where she would cooperate and jeopardize her career. She had an unquestioned loyalty to the Agency, her superiors, and her position. This assignment was an opportunity to defend the United States. Not even the inalienable rights and means available to a crooked U.S. Senator could make that happen.

"This is Director Gamboa," he said as he answered the call.

"Director, it's Agent Walters. I finished analyzing the Senator."

"And?" he replied.

"Dirtier than dirt, sir. Should I brief you on the phone?"

"No. Something like this needs to be done face to face. Come straight to my office. I want everything you got on him Walters. Don't hold any punches."

"Yes sir."

*   *   *   *   *

Agents Chapin and Gall waited outside the Director's office. He was in a meeting. From the look on his secretary's face, everyone was showing the stress of the situation. Too many rods in the fire. After waiting almost an hour, they were called inside.

"Ladies, the Director will see you now," said Sandy, the Director's secretary.

As they passed her desk, Gall looked up at the wall clock.

"A long day," said Agent Chapin.

Sandy avoided eye-contact and nodded. As the agents entered his office, Gall and Chapin glanced around surprised to find the Director's desk unoccupied and his room empty. From the side wall, they noticed a partition that opened into an adjacent conference room. It was the first time Chapin noticed it. She did not even know it existed.

"Over here you two," said the Director in an elevated voice. "We're in the big room."

As they walked inside, Chapin made introductions. "Director, this is Agent Gall. Theresa Gall," she explained. Gall smiled and waved.

"Nice to meet you Director Gamboa."

"I've heard a lot about you," he smiled back.

Looking across the table, he pointed to another female agent sitting at the far end of the large conference table. "This is Agent Walters. I've asked her to stay to brief you two on a new wrinkle."

"Hello," smiled Agent Walters.

Before sitting, Agents Gall and Chapin exchanged nods with Walters. The Director jammed his index finger activating the intercom and instructed his secretary to hold all calls.

"Agent Gall, I hate to put you on the spot like this, but we don't have time to do this through normal procedures. I have your supervisor on speaker." Turning his attention to the speaker sitting on the table, he spoke. "Supervisor Sweet."

"Yes Director," replied Martin Sweet. He was Gall's FBI supervisor. "Can you hear me Gall?"

"Yes sir. I hear you fine. What's going on boss?"

"Well, it looks like the Agency wants you to be on their side of the fence on a permanent basis Theresa," explained her supervisor. She looked around the table and then at the Director.

"What's the rush? Why now?" Gall asked.

"Given your involvement in our John Doe matter, combined with recent developments, we find it necessary to get you in line with our non-disclosure mandates. In order to fully brief you in on the case, you can't be an outsider. With what we do, there cannot be any other loyalties or conflicting obligations of authority."

"I feel stupid for asking, but what about the benefits and salary," agent Gall asked somewhat embarrassed as she dropped her gaze feeling self-conscious for asking.

"Same insurance benefits, with a different retirement. As for salaries, I cannot go into specifics with you here. But a word of advice, don't make this decision based on financial motivations. Don't make the switch for money."

"What's the biggest difference between the Bureau and here?" she asked.

"The Bureau deals with issues specific to U.S. jurisdiction only. Technically, the Agency doesn't," explained the director. With a tilt of his head and an expression that suggested that the lines between these entities were sometimes blurred, given the case he was about to brief Gall into; a case that should appear to be under the Bureau's jurisdiction.

Agent Gall nodded as the Director continued. "We have offices located across the globe and inside the U.S. Within terms of authority, we are the last authority. We never recruit power mongers or ego-centric agents. Those exhibiting confidence, yes. Egos, no."

"No one outside of our Agency structure has authority over our actions." With a brief pause, the Director elaborated, a clarification that left Gall feeling uncomfortable. "Unless specifically ordered by your Director not even POTUS can compel you to divulge what you know."

Realizing that the needs of the case created this situation, feeling he needed to keep moving forward, the Director sighed as he recognized he was rushing Agent Gall into deciding.

"Agent Gall, as I hear my own words, I realize that asking you in this manner is probably unfair. I'm asking you to make a lifetime career decision. Maybe I should let you think on it."

"It's still law enforcement, right? I would still be working for the U.S. Instead of domestic issues, it would be international ones, global ones, right?"

"Essentially," agreed Gamboa.

After a slow nod of her head, Agent Gall made her decision. "I'm in. I'm not going anywhere, I was planning on retiring in the FBI. So, here's to a change," Gall said as she raised an invisible wine glass to make a ceremonial toast. "Will I be assigned to this office in San Jose?"

"For now, yes. You will be under my direct supervision."

For a moment, no one spoke. There was an awkward silence in the room.

"Are you sure Theresa? There's no turning back? This isn't some temporary assignment. Once we brief you into this case, you will not be able to go back to the Bureau. That will no longer be an option. It's us or nowhere, literally."

With a deep sigh, Gall clarified. "I'm not married. No ties. I'm all about the job. I won't regret it. I'm all in."

"You're sure?" asked the Director.

"Positive."

After one final pause, the Director nodded. "Okay. Supervisor Sweet, please delete Agent Gall's FBI email and deactivate her clearances over there. I'll have the paperwork over to you tomorrow along with her formal written resignation.

"Understood. Theresa," said her now ex-supervisor Sweet.

"Yes Marty."

"Good luck." With a sudden click through the speaker phone, the call ended. Just like that, Agent Gall was working for the Agency.

"We'll finalize the paperwork tomorrow. By the way, how much did you make at the Bureau?" the Director asked.

"I'm a GS-14, step three. Just under a hundred and twenty grand a year," Gall replied with a calm matter of fact voice.

The Director already knew she made $119,489 a year and earned points for not exaggerating her pay.

"Well, you'll be a field agent over here. You just got a raise," smiled the Director. Gall looked around the table. Everyone smiled. For just having made the biggest career decision in her life, she felt relaxed and welcomed, like she was adopted into an extended family.

"It goes without saying Gall, nothing said between us is ever discussed outside of closed doors and only among those here now. And don't be taking notes outside in any format. We take all security breaches seriously," explained the Director.

"Of course. Absolutely," replied Gall.

"Without further adieu, Agent Walters."

"Yes Director."

"I need you to brief us all on Senator Anthony. I'm wondering if he has any connections with this John Doe matter."

*   *   *   *   *

After multiple unanswered calls to his land and cell phone, an investigative team was dispatched to John's house. As the team arrived, John's Agency assigned SUV was parked in his driveway. After several attempts at ringing and then pounding on his front door, no one answered. Everyone present was concerned. Finally, the lead investigator made the decision.

"Jox, do it," ordered the lead investigator. Jox extracted his Agency issued tumbler lock picks. In no time, the Supervisor's front door swung open.

"John! Hey John, are you home?" asked Jox.

The entire Team followed him inside. The lead investigator turned on the living room lights. Sitting on the sofa, John appeared to be asleep. He was wearing a tank-top and sweat pants. His eyes were closed, and his arms splayed out to his side. If there was not a large quantity of dried spittle dripping from the sides of his mouth, he would have looked asleep. On cue, the scene investigation Supervisor took control and began issuing orders.

"Ok gentlemen let's get our feet covered before we contaminate the scene further. It very well could be natural causes. But until that is confirmed, we proceed as if it's a homicide investigation."

The lead investigator pointed at the open beer can sitting on the coffee table. "I want that can and its contents analyzed. Jox, I want your guys in the front half of the house and the other half in the back. SOP (Standard Operating Procedures). I want every room, including the kitchen cabinets and refrigerator and freezer photo-documented," he continued feeling John's neck searching for a pulse. Nothing.

Without delay, he snapped photographs from different angles documenting the position of the body, before he extracted a swab and took a sample of saliva dripping on his chin. He placed the soaked cotton swab into the tube, he smelled an unusual odor.

"Pay attention people. I'm getting a strong pungent odor off the spittle sample."

"Someone at headquarters is getting psychic," said Jox.

"How so?" asked one of the other investigators.

"Why send us down here in the first place? Somebody must have had a strong hunch something was up," Jox replied.

"Right," replied another investigator nodding in agreement.

"Boss! We've got something in the refrigerator."

The sound of his covered shoes shuffling across the flooring announced his arrival. "What 'cha got?"

Pointing his latex covered finger inside the refrigerator, the investigator explained "There's a clear puddle near the beer cans." With his head stuck inside the open refrigerator, he glanced around the other contents stored inside. A smudge on the top section of the otherwise pristine lemonade container caught his attention. "Something about the lemonade container looks hinky too."

Yelling back toward the living room area, the lead investigator shouted, "Hey Jox! Let's get a field test done on the Supervisor. I've already secured a sample for the lab later."

Jox slid a long cotton swab into the corner of the Supervisor's mouth. He extracted the liquid-soaked cotton swab into a small test tube. Using his other hand, he grabbed a vial from his field kit and used a dropper to extract some hydrogen sulfide. He knew if it turned yellow, it could mean he had ingested arsenic or a similar poison.

"Any reaction?" asked the lead investigator.

"Nothing yet boss."

On a hunch, the lead investigator returned to the kitchen and opened the utensil drawer. He glanced at the silverware and grabbed one of the tablespoons. He held the spoon up close to his face to read the manufacturer, *Gorham*. Taking the spoon, he walked back to the living room and held the spoon out and studied the Supervisor's prone body lying on the sofa.

"Get another sample," he directed Jox.

Jox inserted another long cotton swab into the supervisor's mouth. As Jox extracted the sample, the lead investigator held out the spoon. Confused as to how to proceed, Jox looked back up into the lead investigator's face.

"What? I don't understand what you want me to do."

"Hold the sample over the spoon."

As Jox held the cotton swab sample, the lead investigator dripped saline solution saturating the cotton swab until the liquid overflowed into the spoon underneath.

"Okay, rub the end of the cotton swab around inside the spoon."

The house was silent as the other investigators gathered around to watch. None of them saw this procedure before. Jox stirred the sample and swirled it around in the saline solution, while the lead investigator held the spoon with a firm grip. Then he placed the spoon on the coffee table next to the sofa.

"We'll let it sit there for a few minutes and then check for any reaction," the lead investigator explained.

Jox and the other team members returned to their work. Jox removed a thermometer from his field kit and slid it into the Supervisor's mouth and began speaking into his hand-held recorder documenting his findings. "The current room temperature is sixty-five degrees and will affect his body temperature."

"It will at least give us a ball park guess," replied the lead investigator. After several moments, the lead investigator read the thermometer reading. "His temperature is sixty-eight point six degrees. Not quite room temperature, but almost. My guess is he's been dead about twenty hours," explained Jox. As he stood up, he tilted his eyes up as if trying to mentally calculate the estimated time of death. Looking at his wrist watch, it's almost three o'clock in the afternoon, so I'd put his death around 7:00pm last night."

Listening to Jox's best guess, the lead investigator leaned down and studied the spoon. The spoon's head had tarnished. He was certain that there was some sulfur or form of arsenic poisoning. With raised eyebrows, and a quick nod, the lead investigator gestured to Jox, pointing at the spoon.

"Was it made of silver?" Jox asked.

"Yeah, the liquid from the Supervisor's mouth is reacting to the silver on the spoon."

"How'd you know the Supervisor had real silverware as opposed to just normal stainless steel?" Jox asked.

"It was just a hunch really. I've known the Supervisor for a while. I figured he's got at least fifteen years with the Agency."

"So? I don't understand."

"Well, I know he doesn't golf. You see, on certain work anniversaries, following your tenth year, every employee gets to pick a gift." Jox nodded as he continued listening. "There are some other items to choose from, but most guys either get either the golf clubs or the silverware. Since I know he doesn't golf, I figured he probably got the silverware."

With a shrug, "What did you get?" Jox asked.

"Same thing- the silverware."

*   *   *   *   *

Senator Anthony was on a roll. Since he hit it big with his stock purchase several years prior, combined with the unfortunate plane crash eliminating his biggest rival for re-election, he seemed to be on easy street. The Senator's influence and importance to his old law firm buddies continued to grow.

When a person sustains a windfall, it usually comes with a price. Until now, the Senator had the misguided belief that he was just special. He believed that the superstitious laws of Karma did not apply to him. The Senator's good fortune was about to change. He was blinded by the power, prestige, and his celebrity status. He felt untouchable. He believed his past had gone unnoticed. In his twisted mind, his actions were minute; circumstances he manipulated to his advantage, nothing more. If the Senator's actions had resulted in only the accumulation of unscrupulous wealth, the Agency may have been able to look the other way. That was not the case.

The Agency uncovered the depth of his depravity, and proved he pursued his personal agenda at any cost. The Agency never looked kindly at being used and manipulated. Anthony treated the Agency like his own personal assassins for hire. The Senator stepped well over the line of decency and permissibility. His manipulation of the "knock list" sealed his fate.

Agent Gall stared at the documents that Agent Walters presented. It was clear that they were investigating a seated U.S. Senator. She was shocked. Her senses were only trumped when she understood that no standard rules of legal procedures applied to the Agency. They did not worry about search warrants, probable cause, nor face the prospect of building a case. In every practical sense, this small committee inside Director Gamboa's conference room may represent the Senator's judge, jury, and executioners.

She sat dumbstruck listening to the Senator's actions. Only then, did she begin to appreciate the Agency's far-reaching power. Gall continued sitting on her hands and biting her tongue. Until she learned more about her Agency role, she knew she should keep her mouth shut and remain an observer. She found it difficult to ignore everything she learned at the Bureau. The Agency had no such restrictions and felt uncomfortable. How could the Agency be investigating a U.S. citizen and a sitting Senator?

"Based on the emails, it's clear that not only did the Senator have insider information, but an argument can also be made that he overstated the importance of getting Drakeson to sign off on the project. From the information I have access to, it looks like the urgency and necessity of that sign-off request was weak. It looks like Drakeson was targeted purely for financial reasons," explained Agent Walters.

Director Gamboa shook his head in disbelief knowing it had proceeded with his authority. He had signed off on it. The silence of the room was broken by his deep sigh of frustration. Agent Walters glanced at Chapin. Chapin was the most senior agent in the room. It was her place to speak up. Catching the glance from Walters, Chapin looked at the Director.

"Sir, he is a seated U.S. Senator. No one knew what he was up to. He was the committee Chair and had been vetted. Who would have guessed what he was up to? You couldn't have known," Chapin added.

Director Gamboa looked up and glanced around the table. "I'm in agreement. Even still, in hindsight, part of me wishes things were different. Balancing what we do, with the national security of the country..." He stopped short with no further elaboration. There was no need for a philosophical conversation about the powers bestowed upon the Agency. Besides, he was the only one present with the grade level to discuss the matter. This was not the time nor the place.

"Okay people let's condense the matter. Chapin, bullet points only, like a high-flying pass-over at 40,000 feet, what are we looking at?"

"Well sir, based on Walter's findings, the Senator misused his authority. He abused the Agency's trust, manipulated the importance of signing off on the defense contractor's interim findings by exaggerating its importance. All of these actions placed

Mr. Drakeson under our scrutiny and within our three strikes protocol," explained Chapin.

"Furthermore, it appears that the Senator spearheaded the plane scenario. Most likely, motivated more by a desire to eliminate his political rival than to keep a lid on the Curt Anderson situation." Chapin glanced around the table taking a deep breath before continuing. "The worst part, both decisions benefited the Senator financially and politically. It stands to reason that, although it may be a mathematical possibility for these events to coincidentally occur as independent random events, the odds are very improbable and unlikely. Agent Walters, any guess?"

After Walters mentally calculated some probabilities, she responded. "I'd guess 1 in 9,000,000," Walters explained.

"How do you figure?" asked the Director.

"I'm assuming it would be the same odds of being struck by lightning twice during a person's lifetime. Although it happens, it's extremely rare." With a nod, as if she were contemplating some esoteric mathematical equation then added, "That would be about right."

"Recommendations?" asked the Director.

Everyone was taken aback. The person in question was a Senator. It was no surprise that no one responded. Before breaking the silence, the Director waited and glanced around the room.

"Agent Gall? You're the newest member of our team. Your thoughts?"

"Sir. I wouldn't have the slightest idea where to start. I don't even know what's possible. What are our options? Right now, I don't even understand what the term three strikes refers to."

"I get that. But, hypothetically, if you had the ear of a person, who had the authority, resources, and responsibility to handle the Senator, what would you do? What would you say to such a person?" asked the Director.

Agent Gall paused. She felt trapped, put on the spot. She also considered the possibility that all of this was just some huge charade. She wondered if everything she was subjected to was just some elaborate field test; an attempt to determine how she would respond in a real situation. Gall glanced around the room and rationalized that no matter the circumstances, a test of some sort or the "real-McCoy", she owed it to herself and her new colleagues, a response. Her best guess.

"Well sir, under that set of circumstances, and based on what I've heard today, I would ask this hypothetical person to do everything in their power to remove the Senator. He has obviously been compromised and is not capable of upholding his proper allegiances to his duties and responsibility as a committee chair. For that matter, nor to his constituents from the State. Quite frankly, he's an embarrassment to this country and acts in complete contrast to its ideals. He has become an addict to the access of money, fame, and power. He cannot be trusted with the secrets necessary to protect and defend the U.S. Constitution and is in danger of tainting all future dealings through the misuse of his position as a Senator, let alone a chair liaison in the Agency.

The room was deathly quiet. Everyone held their breath. Not even the sound of their breathing was heard. Director Gamboa maintained eye contact throughout her statement and listened to every word. He wanted to hear her opinion, clear from years of field work doing unthinkable things. He came to appreciate the clarity of a new agent's opinion, untainted by the Agency's all powerful, all encompassing, ruthless ability to take immediate lethal action. Gall had not filtered her response to skirt the issue avoiding making a recommendation. Agent Gall was still held captive, psychologically limited by the Bureau's rules and regulations; those prior limiting circumstances; those rules represented rigid inflexible constitutional boundaries. Inside the Agency, none of those restraining factors existed. Nothing was out of bounds. Nothing was impossible. Nothing.

The Director reached across the conference table and stabbed his index finger onto the speaker phone. Within in seconds, his secretary's voice rang through.

"Yes Director."

"Sandy, I need you to schedule me a priority one meeting with Senator Anthony. Please set up a luncheon at the *Bonaventure Hotel* in Los Angeles at 1:00pm two days from now."

The Director paused and released the toggle switch to momentarily take the call off speaker.

"Chapin. I want the A-team, with a full complement of options, even a "Snap Shot", do you have enough time to make that happen?"

With a quick mental calculation, Chapin thought through her response before she nodded. "Yes sir. I can make that happen."

Director Gamboa placed the call back on speaker.

"Sandy, set the appointment. It's urgent. Let his PR team know that there are no exceptions. Unless he's out of the country on official work for the government, he's to be there. We will fly him in. Make sure he understands to come alone. It's a Top-Secret Agency matter."

"Yes sir."

"Thanks Sandy," said the Director before he disconnected the call.

Just as the Director was about to continue with the briefing, the speaker phone tone blared as his secretary called through.

"Director. I'm sorry to interrupt the meeting, but a message just came in from the field. I think you need to see it now. Director's eye only clearance."

Gamboa looked up and stood.

"I'll be right back," he said to the room before stepping outside. Chapin and Walters exchanged serious glances. Agent Gall was confused and spoke up.

"What's a 'Snap Shot'?"

"It's a pre-determined plan that can be initiated at a moment's notice," replied Chapin. The manner and cadence of her voice lead Gall to wonder if that explanation held something back.

"What kind of plan Chapin?"

Walters and Chapin exchanged a quick glance.

"She's part of the agency now. She's gonna learn soon enough," said Walters as she tilted her head toward Chapin. After a deep sigh, Chapin stared straight into Gall's eyes.

"It's an assassination plan."

The room went quiet. Nothing more needed to be said. All Gall could do was nod confirming her understanding. It was clear and unambiguous. Everything was moving too quick. They had just uncovered the Senator's misdealings. And now, only minutes later, plans were being set in motion.

The sound of the double doors closing from the Director's main office echoed into the adjacent conference room where they were sitting. Seconds later, the Director stepped back into the conference room. He had a concerned look on his face. After a brief pause, he made an announcement.

"Supervisor John was just found dead at his house. The initial signs are that he was poisoned."

Everyone in the room froze. Agent Gall subconsciously rubbed her injured shoulder blade. Everyone's attention remained focused on the Director.

"It's unclear if this relates to a case he was working on now, or something else. The lab will expedite their analysis working through the night. We should have something by tomorrow morning. Chapin?"

"Yes sir."

"Sometimes, things are out of our control. When this time came, I was hoping to give a big speech and recognize your rise through the ranks. Unfortunately, I can't have the A-Team without a supervisor. We've got too many irons in the fire for that. It was inevitable, but the circumstances have moved up your timeline. Congratulations Chapin. I'm promoting you to Supervisor effective tonight. Sandy's pushing through the paperwork as we speak. You'll see the pay bump in your next check. We'll go over that in private later."

"Yes sir. Although I appreciate the promotion, I'm shocked to hear about John. He was my friend."

"Mine as well. A good man," replied the Director.

"Let's end the meeting. Chapin, I'll see you in my office tomorrow 7:00am sharp. I need to get you up to speed," explained the Director. "It's been a long night. Longer than expected. Everyone get some sleep. It may be our last chance for a while. I can feel the storm brewing."

Everyone stood and exited his office. As the two heavy doors snapped closed, Agent Gall turned toward Agents Walters and Chapin.

"Things move pretty damn fast around here."

Walters and Chapin nodded without replying and turned away making their way back to their offices. Gall stood there alone not sure where to go. She did not even have her personal car and wondered if it was still parked at Winstead's apartment. She started for the exit sign hanging from the ceiling. If nothing else, she could call *UBER*. She considered leaving and coming back in the morning. As she turned down the hallway, a woman approached.

"Are you Theresa. Agent Theresa Gall?"

"Yes."

"I'm your new secretary. If you'd follow me, I'll show you to your team area and cubicle."

The woman flashed a confident smile and extended her right hand to exchange a welcoming hand shake. She was carrying a clear plastic bag. While she led Gall to her new office space, she saw her car keys inside the bag. As the woman turned the corner, Gall saw a thick file with her name stamped on the front, tucked under her arm. She assumed it was her personnel records. She followed the woman through the building as she pointed out the restrooms and break room locations.

Finally, they entered an open expansive area. An "A-Team" sign hung from the ceiling. One of the front cubicles had her name plate already secured in place.

They shook hands before she entered her cubicle and adjusted the chair.

"Here are your office keys and assigned vehicle. Chapin had your car brought over. It's parked out back," she explained. "Now let me explain how your biometric safe works."

Gall opened the top drawer of the floor safe. "What's this metallic coin looking thing?"

"That's for your thumb print. I'll explain everything,"

Gall looked up and knew her evening was far from over.

*　*　*　*　*

"Kyle! Dude! I'm going crazy over here," said Moon Dog in an exhausted manner.

"Any Luck?" Kyle asked. With his cheek cradled in the palm of his hand, Moon Dog slumped in his chair. He squinted out through his blood shot eyes.

"Moon Dog, you look terrible," smiled Kyle as he stared over the top of another tall ice filled glass of soda. The caffeine and sugar high kept his foot tapping on the metal aircraft carrier flooring. They resorted to rotating back and forth every six hours trying to figure out where the ambulance transport disappeared.

For the last 48 hours, Kyle and Moon Dog studied the satellite surveillance tapes as well as the ones taken from inside the Lincoln Tunnel. Non-stop, they watched the ten transport vehicles unload identical ambulances. They learned that each ambulance drove around crisscrossing back and forth around the city area before returning through the tunnel toward New Jersey. It was obvious that someday they expected someone to watch their movements. Without exception, when each silver haired geriatric Caucasian driver passed by the last tunnel camera, each driver smiled and waved into the camera.

Moon Dog watched another driver flash a crooked tooth grin. In frustration, Moon Dog dropped his head on the wooden table. With a loud thud, his forehead slammed against the wood. He remained bent at the waist. He had reached the breaking point.

"Ugh! I can't continue to watch these old geezers anymore," Moon Dog explained in a tired raspy voice. Kyle could barely understand what he was saying.

"Are you not entertained?" yelled Kyle in an exaggerated theatrical voice, mimicking Russell Crowe's famous line from the movie *Gladiator*.

"Kyle," replied Moon Dog as he raised his head off the table. His forehead had a distinct flat reddened impression created from resting his head on the table. "Enough with the movie quotes."

In his best Arnold Schwarzenegger impersonation, "Okay Moon Dog, but I'll be back!" said Kyle with a wide toothed grin. He grabbed his ice filled soda and took a large drink. Within seconds, Kyle rubbed his temples and pinched the bridge of his nose. "Oh no, brain freeze."

"I hate those," mumbled Moon Dog refusing to look away from the monitor as he watched another ambulance driver pass the camera and wave. Moon Dog could not help himself. In a sappy tourist grin, he waved back to the screen. With a twisted face, under his breath, he snarled back at the screen "You old bastards."

Kyle stepped up and patted Moon Dog's back. "You're done buddy. I'm up. Go get some grub and hit the sack. I'll take the next six hours," smiled Kyle as he set his digital watch alarm.

"Thank God! I thought my shift would never end," replied Moon Dog. "It wouldn't be so bad if those geezers weren't so blatant about it. It's like they're laughing at us, knowing that eventually some poor fool would be watching these damn tapes. It's like they'd done it themselves and knew how painful it was. And all they do is go around and around, crisscrossing the surface streets then back through the tunnel...like a carnival ride."

"If I knew somebody would be watching I'd do the exact same thing," laughed Kyle. "Come on. Get out of here. My turn to be tortured." Kyle playfully pulled on Moon Dog's ear before helping him out of the chair. Kyle settled down, using the same comfortable chair still warm from Moon Dog.

Kyle reviewed Moon Dog's tracking sheet. All ten transports had traveled through the tunnel six times. There were notes scribbled in the margin with calculations estimating each ambulance had a 20-gallon gas tank capacity. At twelve miles per gallon, traveling an average of 40mph, each vehicle could drive around without refueling for six straight hours. If they followed each ambulance, they needed to spend 60 hours of real viewing time.

Before Moon Dog left the room, Kyle asked "They didn't fill their tanks, yet did they?"

"Nope," replied Moon Dog as he shuffled across the room heading to his bunk.

"That's good."

"They won't. I think I figured it out. They're going to make their next move before nightfall," explained Moon Dog in a tired voice. As he walked into the adjacent sleeping quarters, his voice became faint. Kyle yelled back through the open doorway.

"Why do you say that?"

"They want to make sure we can see what they're doing!" Moon Dog yelled back before he flopped down into his cot. He would eat later after he got some sleep. Turning his head back to the computer monitor, Kyle restarted the film, picking up from where Moon Dog left off. As the next old geezer driver passed by the camera, he did the same thing. Leaning forward toward the wall mounted camera, he flashed a toothless smirk and waved.

With a twisted snarl in his voice, Kyle spoke out to an otherwise empty room. "Old bastard. This is gonna be a long six hours."

*   *   *   *   *

Diane watched the newest 20 something year-old *PGA* golfer balance the white golf ball on the small wooden tee. It was the first tee shot at the old course in St. Andrews. She purchased a new set of binoculars and decided to follow the Americans for their entire round.

She spent so much time engrossing herself in the world of golf, that she almost forgotten why she was there. Only after a young couple passed by did she remember. The woman's appearance reminded her of her niece. The eyes, her hair color, the way she walked. The distinct sharp sound from the golf club impacting the ball followed by the "oohs and aahs" from the adoring fans, snapped Diane from her thoughts. The façade of being a golf fan melted away.

She created this entire golf enthusiast charade as a cover story, justifying why, after all these years, she would travel to Europe. She was there to meet Curt's grandfather Cornelius Van Aelst. As the crowd disbursed following the golfers, she remembered her first and only face-to-face meeting with Mr. Van Aelst.

"Excuse me. I was told there was a message for me?" Diane said before glancing about tilting her head from side to side. Only her friend Glenn, knew of her whereabouts. She wondered if Glenn had left the message.

The duty nurse smiled and pointed at a tall basket of flowers. There was no card. Unsure what to do, she smiled and picked up the basket and carried it back to Curt's hospital room. From inside the base of the plant, she was surprised to hear a cell phone ringing. Before retrieving the phone, Diane glanced up and down the hallway making sure no one was around. She ducked inside the stairwell and searched inside the base of the plant. After some effort, wrapped inside a plastic bag, she located and answered the vibrating cell phone.

"Hello," said Diane She heard a man's voice. It was clear and strong with a slight accent, speaking in rapid bursts.

"Diane, I know you've been taking a great risk to help Curt. I know everything. He contacted me before the explosion. If you hadn't intervened on his behalf, your Agency would have gotten him. I'm in the restaurant on the first floor. Please come down. We can discuss your next move."

Diane froze in fear. How could this person know so much? "Who is this?" she asked.

"I am Curt's Grandfather. My name is Cornelius. I'm eager to finally meet you."

Sensing her fear, he did his best to ease her anxiety. "I understand how vulnerable you must feel. Given what I've already told you, it should be clear that if I wanted to eliminate you, I could *have done so well before now. Maybe in Las Vegas, Salt Lake City or Chicago?" In a calm soothing voice, he continued speaking. "I promise you. You will not be harmed or compromised in any way. I am grateful and wish to express my sincere gratitude for your efforts and intervention."*

From the way he spoke, even with his slight yet now familiar foreign accent, she knew that Cornelius was a professional. Her years as a covert operative awoke its long hibernation. Her senses thawed, tapping into the experiences she acquired over the years. Until now, her only outside contact involved the health professionals caring for Curt. She had no choice. This request was a courtesy, a gesture. Under the circumstances, she had no choice but to comply.

"I'll be right down. We've only spoken on the phone. How will I recognize you?"

"I'm in a booth. When I see you, I'll stand up and waive you over."

"How will you recognize me?"

"You'll be the person carrying my plant, no?"

With a slow nod, she closed her eyes and replied, "Right."

To avoid the duty nurse, Diane walked down a floor, before catching the elevator the rest of the way. After locating the first-floor restaurant, she approached the receptionist area. Peering over the plant still holding the cellphone in her other hand, she informed the waitress that she was meeting someone. As promised, a thin elderly gentleman stood up and waived her over. The first thing she noticed was his blue eyes. He was sharply dressed in a long-sleeve white shirt, a thin black tie, and a tailored black wool suit. Based on his appearance, he could have been a technician, manager, salesman or investment advisor. For some reason, his appearance demanded respect.

As Diane approached, she glanced around. The booth was strategically located so he could see all 360 degrees. Other than a couple of old men wearing golfing attire, sitting at the opposite end of the dining room, the area was vacant.

"I'm glad we finally meet," smiled Cornelius Van Aelst. Still standing, with his arm, he motioned her forward inviting her to sit down. "Please, have a seat."

Diane again glanced around the room, then back toward Cornelius. She studied his waistline and upper chest area and concluded that he was not packing a gun. With a gentle smile, Van Aelst sat down. Avoiding eye-contact, he explained "Diane, you may relax. I am not carrying a gun."

Raising her eyebrows, she seemed to be caught off-guard before finally speaking.

"Mr. Van Aelst, you have me at a serious disadvantage." To offer any sort of plausible explanation was useless. Up until this point, he was 100-percent accurate and forthright.

"At first, we assumed you were working with your colleagues trying to confuse and trick Curt. Make him believe you were helping him, simply to flush out what he knew; ascertain who he worked for."

"Who does he work for?" asked Diane.

Van Aelst paused. With a slight nod, he continued. "I can understand why you and your government may believe that he has some formal affiliation. It is the only thing that makes sense, yes?"

After a brief pause, Van Aelst leaned forward and placed both palms flat on the table and stared into Diane's eyes. "As incredible as this may sound, he doesn't. I do not dispute the fact that he went to great effort to infiltrate your workplace. I also concede that the only motivation he had in pursuing a job with the copy service was to gain access.

"As I'm sure you know, he even copied one of your field agent's files. And in doing so, uncovered a sensitive list of people." After a deep sigh, he continued. "That was unfortunate."

"For what purpose? Why would he go to all the trouble?" asked Diane.

"That's the dilemma, isn't it? I understand how it looks. But I propose we look at this situation from another point of view."

Diane raised her eyebrows as if to suggest "and what other point of view could that be?"

"Had Curt gone inside that building, if he were ordered to do so, one would assume that there would have been much simpler means to accomplish copying that file, no?"

Diane returned his gaze. After some contemplation, she nodded in agreement.

"It was a random opportunistic event. Had he been inside prior?"

"No," answered Diane. "It was his first and only visit inside the building. At least from what we could ascertain."

"I was never given the exact names on the list, nor do I care. I've never seen any reproduction of anything he uncovered. It is my understanding that all the data, his paper file and his laptop computer, every piece of tangible evidence was destroyed in the explosion and subsequent fire. However, let's assume that he was after something in that folder. Which one? Which person? As I understand it, each person was a U.S. citizen. If he were affiliated, what would another international agency have to gain from knowing the names from that list?"

A waitress walked up to the table to take their orders. To both their surprises, each had developed a strong appetite. This distraction in the conversation gave Diane time to think things through. It made sense. But then again, why did he do it in the first place? Why take the risk at all?" After taking their orders, the waitress left.

"What you say makes sense. But why? What did he stand to gain?"

"As difficult as this may sound, it was inevitable. Not necessarily that he'd have selected your office, but something like this was bound to happen. It was his misfortune to focus on those particular people."

"I don't understand. Why was it inevitable?"

"When people become bored and complacent, especially when they no longer face normal daily challenges of survival, it's like Pavlov's hierarchy of needs. People begin pursuing activities in search of an adrenaline high. Some argue that it was this very reason, complacency, which started the downfall of Rome."

"You mean to suggest he was just bored?" Diane asked in an incredulous manner.

"As absurd as it sounds, yes." With a quick tilt of his head, Van Aelst explained further. "You probably weren't aware of Curt's past. You see, both of his adoptive parents passed away, at different times. Their passing occurred years apart. His adoptive mother lived until just after Curt graduated high school. As a result of their passing, Curt inherited a large sum of money. He wasn't rich, but more than comfortable."

"I didn't know that."

"Even though he remained intellectually engaged while pursuing his degrees from Berkeley, the idea of a career wasn't motivating. As a student, he pursued things that interested him. School fed his intellectual curiosity."

"Was Curt's mother your daughter?"

"Excuse me?"

"On the phone, you said you were his grandfather."

"No, she was not my daughter. My daughter was his biological mother. My daughter, his mother, died while giving birth to Curt. He was adopted, and I am Curt's biological grandfather."

"Yet you are involved with Curt?" Diane said out loud as if she were trying to understand their current connection.

"I was the one that orchestrated his adoption. There were no other living relatives. My occupation and lifestyle were not conducive to raising a child. I was a widower. My daughter was my only relative. There was no father. She was unwed."

"Where did the adoption take place?"

"Berlin. Curt's parents were stationed abroad. His mother and father, for medical reasons, were unable to have children."

Van Aelst offered these facts freely. He appeared to be truthful. But to what end? "Why are you telling me all of this?" she asked.

"Diane, after next week, I will be taking over his transportation and well-being. I realize you must be in need for some answers. I'm guessing this yearning motivated you to help him. Unfortunately, it is time for me to step in."

A sense of panic set in. She had so little time, with too many unanswered questions. She still felt overwhelmed with grief from the loss of her only living relative. She feared losing contact with Curt. Without Curt, she would never hear the details surrounding the events that led up to losing her niece. This connection was their common bond. The plane crash was something they shared, a mutual understanding. Due to her situation, she appreciated Van Aelst's motivation, his unyielding commitment toward Curt. Then it hit her.

"You thought he'd died in the plane crash?"

"You're partially correct. I thought he'd died, but not from the plane crash. He contacted me after making it back to his house. Discovering it vacant, and being sold, he knew it had to be your Agency. Sitting alone in his closet, he realized he'd made a huge mistake. That's when he contacted me. He never got back in touch with me. Concerned, I made my own inquiries and learned that his *house was destroyed in a gas explosion. Until I was able to piece everything together, yes, I thought he'd been killed. Based on the belief he died in the plane crash, his attorney began the process of transferring his estate to me just last week. Like you, I'm his only living relative. He listed me as his sole beneficiary for everything he owned. After receiving his call, and then hearing about the explosion, I thought the Agency finally caught up to him. My sense of loss drove me to keep looking, keep searching for what really happened to him."*

The waitress returned to deliver their food. As she set down their meals, Diane studied Van Aelst trying to interpret his hidden emotions. She sensed his desperation and need to protect Curt before something else happened to him. Diane could relate having similar feeling for her niece. Unlike Van Aelst, she was grasping at straws to protect the one person who could shed light on why and how she lost her niece. For a different reason, she did not want to lose Curt either.

They ate in silence. Like group therapy, by sharing similar experiences, an emotional connection developed. Diane understood. She could see it in Cornelius' eyes. An unspoken bond was created.

"I need to keep in contact with Curt. He is my only means of learning the truth. I'm certain you understand my need to know."

"I do."

"You can trust me, Cornelius. I have no other ulterior motives. As crazy as that seems. I have to understand what happened. You see, I lost my niece on that plane. She was my last living relative."

"I didn't know."

"She was working with the government. We both worked for the same agency. I even recruited her. Like Curt is to you, she was my last living relative. She was my responsibility. I feel like this was all my fault. I should have known something like this would happen. I should have been able to prevent it."

"I see," responded Cornelius. His piercing blue eyes seemed to soften. The intense detachment melted. "Now, I understand why you helped Curt." He leaned forward and touched Diane's hand. "I'm sorry for your loss."

10

A group of golf fans bumped into Diane as they scurried across the asphalt golf cart path.

"Excuse me ma'am," said a young adolescent boy wearing a bright neon orange shirt with matching pants and hat mimicking his favorite American golfer.

"Sorry about that. He gets a little excited," his parents said as they shuffled behind trying to keep up.

"No. It's fine. I completely understand," replied Diane. She smiled back and watched the little boy's parents chase after him. Diane fell in-line behind the other fans following the golfers in the nearby fairway. She checked her brochure for the golfers' names. She needed to appear more interested. She was distracted thinking about her trip to Germany in four days. She glanced around the other spectators and wondered if she were being followed.

*   *   *   *   *

Director Gamboa sat in the Agency limousine. His driver was part of the A-team. Unlike Directors stationed overseas, Stateside Directors did not require around the clock 24/7/365 protection. When a Director's identity was compromised, or traffic analysis uncovered credible threats, the National Director would act and assign around the clock protection. Providing this type of protection on a normal basis was not something done for Stateside Directors.

Directors' identities were only known by Agency upper management and that Director's subordinates. No public organizational charts existed. Utilizing any form of Internet search engine, no office directories with titles would be found. Each Director learned the names of their counterparts. Everything inside the Agency was on a need-to-know basis. No one in the Agency, regardless of rank, carried a business card providing their name, position and direct contact numbers. Such a thing just did not exist. The absolute identifying markers for a Director was their finger prints, cornea scans and DNA. Other forms of identification were helpful but not always reliable.

Director Gamboa's neighbors had no clue what he did. He never mentioned it and purposely avoided idle chit-chat with others. He had no *Facebook, Instagram,* or *Twitter* accounts. Others knew he worked for the government, but thought he worked with computer programs. He was one of the few Directors that chose to marry and have children. He had no aspirations of further advancements and was adamant that, unless forced to retire, this would be his last position.

In his younger years, Gamboa paid his dues. Been there, done that. As an Agency Director his title was the only recognition he stood to gain. The days of receiving a star on the wall were long past. Such anonymous indirect recognition was for covert field agents, not Directors. The eight stateside Directors were like islands unto themselves, out-ranked only by the National Director. No one else, not even POTUS, a committee, or member of Congress out-ranked a Director. The Agency was self-governed and self-regulated. The only offense an Agency member could be reprimanded for was an act of treason. It was no surprise that the agency had a way of classifying their whistle blowers as traitors. It was a term that everyone understood. A term that was used to discredit and throw a fellow agency member under the proverbial bus; to publicly humiliate and a process used to remove certain people while sending others a message. Everyone inside the agency knew that "real traitors" where handled much differently; they simply disappeared.

Such unpleasantness was rare. The agency did a good job of recruiting certain types of people. Candidates that required external praise, validation or wealth were weeded out. Agents that showed such tendencies, depending on their skill sets, were let go but retained as independent contractors- guns for hire, a common landing zone for covert agents exhibiting such incompatible behaviors. Others, those with fewer skill sets had one option. Suck it up, keep quiet, and bide their time until retirement.

Not everyone had options. For most, there was no turning back. To leave the agency under questionable terms made them a liability. All too often, liabilities found a way of disappearing altogether.

"Are we all set with the Senator?" asked Director Gamboa.

The driver replied through his microphone. "All set, boss. The lead and chase cars are in my sight. We've got the restaurant set. B-team is working the inside."

"Scenarios?"

"All after the meal. Either as we exit the hotel or enroute to the airport on the 405. Our standard procedure at this location," explained the driver.

"Where's Chapin?"

"She's in the chase car. She's supervising the second scenario."

"Has the media been sufficiently distracted?"

"We're ready to go. Four separate events, north, south, east and west. If something goes wrong, we're prepared to block the adjacent streets. We'll also send out a localized electronic burst to fry all local phone towers reducing the likelihood of anything being captured on those dreaded mobile phones. We're using two dedicated satellites ready to target those electronic devices, sure to isolate the damage to areas near our target. We'll send the burst right down the cell towers and bounce the pulse right down to all those connected. We're guessing about 2,000 phones will be affected."

"We have the Senator flying into Long Beach," continued the driver. "Not as many cars or people there as opposed to *LAX*. We've kept him in the dark about you being there. He just knows it's an Agency visit. We've been monitoring his cell, home, office, and emails. For once in his life, he's actually kept his mouth shut. I'm sure he feels pretty special flying in on our Gulfstream. He should be relaxed. We've led him to believe that he'll be back in DC later today."

"How far are we from Long Beach?"

"About 15 minutes. The carpool lane helps a lot. Otherwise, we'd be crawling on the 405," replied the driver.

"Go straight to the hanger. We'll pick him up as the jet pulls in to park. I don't want anyone outside seeing us picking him up," instructed the Director. "He didn't bring any unexpected guests, did he?"

"No sir. He's by himself."

*   *   *   *   *

Senator Anthony stared out the window of the Agency Gulf Stream G650. It was better than flying first class on a commercial airliner. He felt more important having the jet all to himself. The senator began wondering how the President must feel having Air Force One at his disposal.

Since hearing about the meeting, the Senator looked forward to the trip. It would give him a chance to swing by his old law firm and remind them of his value. If it were not for him, the partners would have missed out on the stock purchases. Anthony knew his time as a Senator was winding down. He felt like a temporary employee begging and pleading with special interest groups and his constituents every six years to earn the right to keep his job.

The truth was he was tired playing Senator. He looked forward to the day he could walk away. Anthony failed to appreciate the reluctance of his biggest contributor, several large weapons, and systems manufacturers, to see him leave. He willingly supported and pushed the benefits of upgrading any and all military weaponry, rockets, jets, bullets, vests, missiles, satellites, tanks, air craft carriers and battleships. The list was endless. Each international conflict, each terrorist attack was music to their ears. Given what seemed to be a never-ending stream of global conflicts, the Senator wondered if some of the conflicts were purposely manufactured to keep the gravy train going.

The collective greed spread like a contagious disease. Each area of production and manufacturing took turns as if waiting in line as each sector upgraded their areas of the defense. The collective military industrial complex learned to take turns, like an enormous mechanical albatross that required re-fitting, changes and enhancements while remaining in flight. Protecting the national security of the U.S. was a never-ending, guaranteed stream of future income.

Since World War II, the defense industry embraced each civil unrest. The bloodier the better. Each terrorist attack was like a Godsend to them. The more media coverage of the conflict, the better. Anything that struck fear into the American public was proof that their newest designs of war and defense were a necessary evil. It was more than a good thing reaping unfathomable riches, stashing exorbitant profits into their coffers, paid from secret budgets hidden from public scrutiny, without being subject to normal checks and balances. It was an orgy of greed chasing profits at the expense of the third world and U.S. taxpayers.

If anything, Senator Anthony was the poster child for his special interest group. Over the years, the Senator mastered their game. He capitalized on the information. Why not? In the Senator's mind, he discovered riches available to anyone smart enough to seize the opportunity. In his mind, he was part of a system that helped build and streamline projects, create patents, provide the environment for scientists to test their ideas, where industrialists created machines sold abroad enhanced commerce between nations. He thought he should be rewarded for his efforts and contributions?

Besides, what he did was important. Much more important than simply entertaining the masses. He played a much more vital role to society. Over the years, the Senator convinced himself that what he did was more important than providing transportation to the masses. It was more important than the *PGA, NHL, NFL, MBL* and even *NASCAR*. The atrocities of World War II proved what humans were capable of; the Holocaust; the Japanese conquest; and the killing fields of Cambodia.

Although the special interest groups preyed on the public's fears, real and imagined, it was an inevitable fact that weak countries suffered at the hands of those in power. He never embraced his role as a steward to his constituents. It was always an orgy of greed and power.

Perpetuating this charade required many willing participants. In the big scheme of things, the Senator was only one of those players, just another cog inside the huge war machine. Something past President Eisenhower warned about.

As the jet cruised over *Davis-Monthan Air Force Base* located outside of Tucson, Arizona, Senator Anthony looked down from the Agency Gulf Stream window. It was a restricted dumpsite that stored over 4,400 aircraft, spread out over 2,600 acres of land. It is only one of the many such military aircraft dumping grounds. Others were in Abilene, Texas; Kingman, Arizona; Maxton, North Carolina; Mojave, California; Oscoda, Michigan; Goodyear, Arizona; Marana, Arizona; Victorville, California; and Roswell, New Mexico.

The Senator admired the rows of abandoned planes stretching miles, as far as the eye could see. The planes were parked wing to wing, lined up in nice, neat rows. While others saw these abandoned airplanes as waste, just sitting idle and unused. The Senator saw dollar signs. Each plane below, represented proof that at least one newer, more advanced plane, one that generated additional revenue and profit, had taken its place.

Senator Anthony imagined the $350 million-dollar price tag of a modern fighter jet F-22 Raptor, or the V-22 Osprey at $118 million and the F-35 Lightning at $122 million a copy. His mind reeled as he tallied the profits gained from replacing those mothballed ones below. The E-2D Advanced Hawkeyed Radar plane at $232 Million each, the P-8A Poseidon Navy plane at $290 million each, the C-17A Globemaster III at $328 million each and of course the "jewel" of them all, the B-2 Spirit Stealth Bomber at $737 million apiece.

Imagining the profits, the Senator rubbed his hands together. It was simple. All they needed to do was replace the supposed obsolete weaponry with newer ones yet to be created. Without trying, he had memorized the names of all the new modern planes. He did not know or care what specialized purpose each plane served. What did interest him was their cost. The bigger the better. His biggest reward came from *Northrop*. The order to build 21 B-2 Stealth bombers at $737 Million each, had a total purchase order of

$15.4 billion. When factoring in research and development, that single project cost the tax payers $44.75 billion. As the mothballed planes below drifted out of view, Anthony found himself trying to get one final peek at the boneyard below.

As the planes disappeared from view, he turned forward, adjusted his sitting position, and settled into the leather chair. He checked the time on his *Rolex* wrist watch and figured he had about 30 minutes before touching down in Long Beach. With a smirk, he wondered why the Agency wanted him to land there. They knew he preferred *LAX*. Then, a possibility came to mind. Maybe they were taking him to the Long Beach Naval shipyard. Although that base was technically closed, on rare occasions, it was known to hide a secret experimental vessel. Maybe they wanted to show him something?

*   *   *   *   *

Diane was on the second week of her "golf" vacation. After attending the Men's *Open*, she flew to Germany planning to attend all three days of the women's *Solheim Cup*: a competition between the United States and several European Countries. It took place every two years and rotated venues, once in a U.S. location, followed by an event held somewhere in Europe.

She was unpacked and sat on her bed. Staring at the blank television screen, her thoughts wondered. She had no plans for the day. Curt's grandfather told her he would reach out to make contact. Mr. Van Aelst suggested this hotel, while Diane made all the travel arrangements. The Ringhotel Uinzerhof was nice enough without being too far out of her budget. She reasoned that since this was her first personal vacation to Europe, it made sense that she spent a little extra. It was a special occasion.

The bedside phone rang. She was not expecting a call and proceeded with caution.

"Hello," she said cradling the phone with both hands.

"Ms. Klein? This is the front desk."

"Yes. Can I help you?"

"I wanted to make sure you were in your room. I'm sending a bellman to bring you an envelope."

Diane was taken aback and tried to control her voice, replying as casually as possible. "Okay. Thank you."

"Good bye."

"Good bye."

She paused uncertain what to think. "It has to be from Van Aelst. Who else could it be?" she thought.

While waiting, she reflected on her situation. Since her niece's death, her perspective and priorities changed. Before, her life was dedicated to the Agency. Everything else took a back seat. That all changed. She felt betrayed. Worse yet, she now believed that her feelings, and the safety of people important to her were of no consequence. None of it had any influence over agency decision.

Every day since, a feeling of betrayal was the single reason she helped Curt. She was not naïve and recognized that the world and security of the U.S. took precedence over her personal life. But at the same time, she expected her years of service and unwavering loyalty to warrant some consideration. What purpose did her niece's death serve? Could she have been saved? All those years, all the sacrifices she made, did they account for anything? The Agency owed her that much?

Again, Diane became lost in her thoughts, stuck on the fact that it all came down to one simple truth. The Agency did not care. To be more accurate, it did not care about her. Her sacrifices did not warrant any form of special consideration. It was a one-way street. The Agency only cared about achieving its goals, at all costs. With minimal effort, the Agency could have saved her niece. None of it made sense. For no justifiable reason, she was discarded as if she were worthless.

Her role was not an integral part of the operation. Nor was it a mistake. She was in the wrong place at the wrong time. Her death was senseless. Or was it? A thought flashed through her mind. A simple notion that, with her years of experience, she should have considered long before now. Diane was so devastated by her loss, and so preoccupied chasing the truth, she missed something. In a narrow-minded pursuit to get clarity, she threw caution to the wind. In a panic, she helped Curt elude the Agency in exchange for information.

From her years of training, Diane went into autopilot and zeroed in gathering facts and verifying leads. She became so distracted piecing together everything, trying to make sense of it all, her tunnel vision blinded her. In her rush, she failed to consider another possibility. Like a heat seeking missile, her mind was just unable to unlock its laser-guided radar. Her thoughts focused on uncovering current concerns and proceeding forward without contemplating other options, other targets of interest. As her mind was about to scurry down this unexplored rabbit-hole, a knock on her door interrupted her train of thought. She heard a male's voice coming from behind the closed door.

"Miss Klein?"

She did not respond still frozen in thought. An envelope slid under the door. Diane approached the door. Bending down, she studied the envelope. "Fraulein Klein" was written on the front. The handwriting was in a flowing cursive script. A style taught long ago, during a time when penmanship was important. Unlike the modern forms of communication, through emails and texts, this handwriting took years of practice to master. Without opening it, she was certain it was from Van Aelst.

The delivery time was prophetic. If it was delivered a minute later, Diane would have completed her thought. For the first time in years, Diane's mind was in a relaxed and undistracted state. The air travel, vacation-like environment, walking miles as a spectator at golf tournaments, enjoying England, and now her journey to Germany. Finally, her mind could consider other options. It was just the mental break she needed to begin to see and think more clearly. Until that moment, just before the envelope slid under the door, her mind was no longer pre-occupied with the present demands of the situation. Her mind was at peace; in stand-by waiting until the next intellectual puzzle-piece arrived requiring her attention. But now, it was too late. Since the envelope's arrival, a new mystery was created. Something else for her mind to focus on. Like that, her mind cycled back focusing on its newest concern- the envelope.

Out of habit, she grabbed her cell phone and took several photos documenting its original condition. Then, using a hand towel from the bathroom, she picked it up and held it up to the light. The envelope paper was too thick making it impossible to peer inside. Based on its weight, she guessed there were a few pieces of paper, or a thin object inside. She carried it to the desk next to the television.

With the letter laying on the hand towel, she rummaged through the top desk drawer and found a letter opener. Carefully, she opened the envelope and watched two pieces of paper fall out.

She stood above and studied the documents. Written in the same stylistic cursive handwriting, she read the note. By now, the distraction was complete. She forgot all about that "thought". It represented the most obvious and rationale answer. One that made the most sense. But now, the distraction, the envelope, with its countless possibilities and concerns, dominated her curiosity and disrupted her prior analysis.

And just like that, it was gone. The synchronicity of life is peculiar. The randomness of events. Timing determines many outcomes; it dictates how life plays out. The irony of timing is where those cliché statements are hatched. Where the statements like "it was just a bad time," or "had I only known" were born.

Had she followed her train of thought, she could have altered her course, changed her destiny. Diane still had options. If she turned away now, disclosed everything she did, the Agency might have understood. She could have walked away; left the Agency, taken an early retirement. She might just be allowed to walk away.

It would take some effort. A thorough investigation into the last three years of her life would be required. But it was still possible.

But that did not happen. Her brain was already focused on its next task. She was too engrossed in the next thing. Much later, when it was too late to alter her future, she would learn the truth. By then, it was too late. All she could do was chastise herself for missing the obvious. It was staring her in the face the entire time. Her training was to blame. It was her Achilles heel. Her ability to over-analyze each obstacle, evaluate each piece of evidence. It all prevented her from working it all the way out. That's one of the reasons the Agency worked in teams. Team dynamics reduced the likelihood of maintaining too narrow of a focus. Teams allowed input from others. In theory, it reduced this exact thing from happening. It avoided situational blindness.

For the last three years, in her isolated scenario, she was working alone. Using the tip of the letter opener, she maneuvered the papers around and read. Her earlier thoughts had disappeared. It just was not meant to be. Had she only known.

*   *   *   *   *

Director Valdez reviewed Director Gamboa's file. Loaning two agents to review classified and restricted satellite surveillance tapes was her only involvement. It was limited to exchanging a few electronic communications with Lieutenants Benjamin and Elliott, scouring through tapes chasing the whereabouts of an ambulance transporting a suspect. The use of a large-scale vehicle "shell-game" of hide and seek, reminded Valdez about a case involving the Germans. The only place she heard of such elaborate use of motor vehicles occurred inside the old Iron Curtain inside the now defunct USSR. This tactic was unique. She could not help but think that old habits die hard. The Eastern Bloc countries stuck to the tried and true.

*   *   *   *   *

"Moon Dog, I need a break," said Kyle as he pushed away from the oversized map table they were using as a desk, giving Moon Dog a clear view of the computer monitor.

"What did you find? Anything?"

"I was able to track two transport vehicles back to an abandoned refinery on the outskirts of New Jersey's industrial coastline. The trucks pulled up and parked," explained Kyle.

Moon Dog stared over Kyle's shoulder. "Have the drivers stepped out of the trucks yet?"

"That's the weird part, not yet. They haven't done anything so far. They're just sitting in the parked trucks," Kyle replied.

Moon Dog focused on the trucks. He noticed that each driving cabin included an extended cab. "I wonder if they're sleeping in the back section."

Moon Dog scrunched his forehead as Kyle glanced back toward the screen.

"Maybe."

*   *   *   *   *

Senator Anthony glanced out the port window. Long Beach did not present such a dramatic view from above. Even still, flying over

Southern California reminded him of its dense population. Staring out from the *Gulf Stream* jet, it looked like a concrete sea of roads, streets, boulevards, and freeways. In between these lines, stood a never-ending row of roof tops with countless cars moving about like ants. The horizon was the Pacific Ocean. As the jet descended, the Senator leaned back into the oversized leather chair and tightened his safety belt. The solo stewardess flashed an attractive smile before she returned to her jump seat and strapped in preparing to land.

Waiting in the hanger, Director Gamboa peered through the SUV's dark tinted windows. Agent Chapin was in the lead vehicle and Agent Gall followed in the tail vehicle. Like a convoy, the three vehicles sat in a straight line. The remainder of the A-team were positioned at the *Bonaventure Hotel* in downtown Los Angeles. Anticipating their arrival, the Director spoke through a shared encrypted wireless intercom set inside the armrest. It was synchronized and coded so no outside devices could de-code their transmissions and listen in.

"Are we set Chapin?"

"Yes Director," replied Chapin. "Everything's in place. The Senator's jet just landed and is taxiing over to our location now. ETA three minutes."

"Copy that," replied the Director.

With a deep sigh, Gamboa directed his attention toward the hanger's open entrance doors. In the distance, he could just see the white *Gulf Stream* jet rolling across the asphalt.

"Gall, double check your reception on all of the remote cameras, especially from my lapel pin," ordered the Director.

"We're go on all devices," replied Agent Gall. She sat in the tail vehicle, an oversized van full of electronic surveillance and communication gear along with three Agency technicians. She glanced about making eye-contact with the senior technician. With a quick nod, they started recording. During the Senator's trip aboard the *Gulf Stream*, another group of agency technicians were doing the same thing.

*　　*　　*　　*　　*

Curt sat at the computer terminal nursing a tall American style coffee. To access their computers, he showed the Internet café clerk his new ID and paid the fee. The last time he was there was more than six months ago. No one recognized him.

The Germans had acquired the taste for strong American coffee. Curt, aka Pfeffen, no longer stood out in a crowd. He worked hard at not flashing unsolicited smiles. It was an unconscious habit that he noticed Americans did. His habits were changing. Now, he wrote the date like a European; the day first, then the month, followed by the year. No longer surrounded by Americans made his transition easier. It took time, but he felt less American no longer compelled to discuss *NFL* football or music. Two subjects that Europeans complain about American tourists doing.

Living in Germany helped Curt aka Pfeffen, notice certain American peculiarities. Things that Americans did that attracted attention; like speaking in loud voices and listing all the differences that made America so great. With his life on the line, Pfeffen did his best to appear European.

Pfeffin's scars had healed. By preference only, he now wore his hair cropped close to his skull. Living in Germany, he made a point learning the geographical layout. Over time, he memorized the bordering countries, Denmark, Netherlands, Czech Republic, Poland, Austria, Switzerland, France, Luxemburg, and Belgium. Like most Americans, he had little in-depth knowledge about other countries and perceived it as unimportant. Being trapped indoors for so many months, Pfeffin watched the daily weather forecast. It helped bring him up to speed. Van Aelst was in the U.S. to tighten things up. It was weeks since they saw each other in person. Other than a few of Van Aelst's retiree buddies, Pfeffen went about his routine hidden from view.

Pfeffen turned off the computer and retrieved his ID from the clerk. Without much effort, he now spoke excellent German. In an unhurried purposeful manner, without flashing a smile, he walked through the café. As he strolled down the street, he formulated which transportation transfer he would take. Today, would it be taxis, trains, and buses or some other combination? While walking, he stuck to a routine. One designed to shake any would-be follower. As he approached the train station, he cringed hearing a tourist, in a loud obnoxious voice, telling an off-color Hitler joke. Pfeffen glanced back. His suspicions were confirmed. The ruckus came from a heavy-set man, wearing a tight fitting short sleeved t-shirt with the American Flag image plastered on the front. Without thinking and embarrassed Pfeffin rolled his eyes.

* * * * *

Diane grabbed her purse. Following Van Aelst's instructions, she hurried down to the hotel bar. She assumed he would be waiting. Making her way there, she recalled the last time they met.

Without warning, Mr. Van Aelst tapped her shoulder. She was distracted watching Curt being loaded onto another ambulance transport leaving Pennsylvania.

In a confident clear voice, Mr. Van Aelst said, "I can't thank you enough for what you've done."

Diane was surprised to see him. Turning toward the voice, she found herself standing next to Curt's grandfather. He reached out and extended his right hand.

"I will be in contact," is all he said. With a sincere smile, he turned and climbed into the back door of the ambulance. Before the door shut, Curt stuck his head out and waved good bye.

Diane entered the downstairs bar and found Van Aelst. He was alone. She studied his appearance. With crisp side burn lines, he wore a black pin-striped two-piece suit, undoubtedly made from 100 percent wool, tailored to fit his trim athletic frame. She had no idea of his age. From her years of experience in such things, she guessed he was affiliated, a professional spook. Although they shared similar occupations, Mr. Van Aelst was in a league all his own.

Avoiding eye-contact, Diane sat at the bar leaving several chairs between them. She waited a few seconds before glancing into the mirror behind the bar. From the reflection, they made eye-contact. Mr. Van Aelst flashed a slight smile.

"May I get you a drink, ma'am?" asked the bartender.

"A *Coke*," she replied. She needed to keep her wits about her. As the bartender turned to prepare her drink, Van Aelst stood, slid a napkin across the bar, then left. Diane glanced about. Other than an older gentleman sitting in the corner table peering through his thick glasses reading the menu, the bar was empty.

Diane opened the napkin. A handwritten note read: "At the curb, I'll be waiting inside the yellow cab."

Diane grabbed the glass from the bartender and downed the drink. Setting the glass down and looked up.

"Will five euros be enough?" she asked.

The bartender nodded. She placed the bill on the bar, stood, and walked outside. After pushing the heavy wood doors open, she peered into the street. She saw a yellow cab. Its sign was turned off waiting curbside. The driver appeared too old to still be working. Looking at the back seat, the dark tinted windows prevented her from seeing inside. Unfazed, Diane opened the back door and peered inside and found Van Aelst staring back. In a clear confident voice, he spoke.

"It's nice to see you again Ms. Klein."

Diane paused before sliding inside and closed the door.

* * * * *

Senator Anthony was disappointed. He hoped that this meeting involved a "secret trip" to the Long Beach naval port. His dreams of another round of military contracts to exploit for his personal financial advantage would have to wait. Over the years, he learned to be patient. New contracts would come. It was inevitable. Other than idle chit-chat, the Director appeared to be stalling, waiting until lunch to get into the real purpose for this meeting.

The drive to Los Angeles was uneventful. Flying into nearby Long Beach had served its purpose. No one from the general public or media saw the Senator. The three Agency vehicles maneuvered along the 405 until they reached Figueroa Street, before arriving at the *Westin Bonaventure Hotel*. The Senator tilted his head and looked up admired the three cylindrical shaped mirrored exterior high rise building that reached into the sky. The SUV pulled up to the curb sandwiched between the lead and trailing vehicles. They waited until the Director and Senator entered the building, before continuing to the underground parking structure.

The Director and Senator crossed the lobby heading for the elevator. Gamboa noticed a middle-aged Asian man sitting on a sofa talking on his cell phone. They entered the elevator and pushed the button for the top restaurant floor. For some reason, staring into the lobby, the Director's antennae were raised. Something did not feel right. Unfazed, the Senator assumed since no other Agency personnel or any of his team were included, it must involve something top-secret.

"So, Director what's on your mind? Why all the cloak and dagger stuff? I couldn't help but notice that no one else is in attendance. Just you and me. What gives?" For a politician, Senator Anthony was even more direct and cunning than others. Holding a committee chair position and participating in numerous A-team situations, the Senator felt at ease. The Senator had grown too confident, bordering on a reckless arrogance.

"Senator, the Agency has some concerns over something we thought, until recently, was a closed matter. However, in the last few weeks, our sources reveal that something is definitely coming into play. We need to get your clarification."

"Me?"

"Yes Senator, you," replied the Director in a firm voice. During the pause, the electronic ding from the elevator broke the silence.

Senator Anthony's mind went into overdrive. Like the guilty person he was, he considered the list of his many misdealings that the Agency uncovered. Flipping through his mental *Rolodex*, the Senator fixated on his most recent inappropriate deal. Had the Agency connected him to the contractor and exclusive agreement? Most of his laundry-list of "special" arrangements were finalized. One deal in the Middle East was open as he was still trying to milk a few more projects. He wondered if his go between had flipped.

As each elevator tone announced the arrival of another floor, Senator Anthony was grateful that his law firm buddies decided to delay the purchase of that supplier's stock. Maybe this meeting was good news after all?

Senator Anthony continued flashing his plastic politician's smile suppressing his nervousness. It was all second nature as he shrugged it off, practically yawning.

"I can't image what I may add to your inquiry. I'm an open book," replied the Senator as he glanced around the elevator with a wry smile, grateful there were no mirrors on the elevator doors reflecting his image. Preparing for this lunch meeting, he knew he needed all his wits about him.

By the time the elevator arrived at the top floor, Senator Anthony considered another recent situation where he manipulated the contract negotiations involving 12 mine countermeasure vessels for $5.5 billion. Is that what they had uncovered? Through his global connections, he brokered a deal with India and South Korea. As far as he knew, no one knew of his involvement. He already received the first installment payment for steering the contract to certain players. As far as he could tell, his offshore accounts were safe and out of the purview of probing eyes.

As the elevator doors slid open, Anthony flashed his insincere politician's smile. Without missing a beat, he sauntered out the door toward the receptionist and then followed her out onto the unique rotating floor. No matter how many times he visited this place, although most considered it to be a novelty, something for tourists, it still mesmerized most patrons, even the VIP's. A smile formed on the Director's face as he stepped onto the slow-moving floor heading toward their reserved seats. Their table plus two empty tables in each direction were roped off preventing anyone from sitting nearby and listening to their conversation.

Before sitting, the Senator stared out the huge floor to ceiling windows and admired the panoramic city view. Like an engineering wonder, the entire floor rotated counter clockwise as if floating in the air. Gamboa studied the other patrons and noticed two older men. As one of the older men snapped his dated flip phone shut, based on their t-shirts and baseball caps, the Director and Senator assumed they were tourists.

Their orders were already called in. To the envy of the other patrons, their order was delivered within seconds from their arrival. This VIP section included a button when pressed got immediate attention. After closing the area with a red velvet rope, the waitress returned to assist the other patrons.

The Senator tried remaining calm. The Director leaned down, removed a thin folder from his brief case and placed it next to the Senator's plate of fish and chips. The Senator's eyes bugged as he read the outside: "TOP SECRET- Senator Anthony and Drakeson Corporation"

Eating his side salad, the Senator's mind went into overdrive. He felt like a duck paddling on a pond appearing calm on top, while its legs pumped away under the water line. Drakeson was the last thing he expected to see. He could never forget that name. It represented his first big score. One of the many side deals allowing him to maximize being the Special Operations Covert Services Committee Chairman. Preparing for what was ahead, he refused to look at the folder pretending to be uninterested and considered what the Agency had uncovered.

Did the Agency discover that he added Drakeson's name to the knock list? Or was it the fact that Drakeson's decision not to sign off on the interim progress, really was insignificant to the outcome of the project? Or maybe the Agency connected the large stock purchases made just before Drakeson's death? Or worse yet, what if the Agency uncovered the "real" reason he placed that nosey photocopy technician and his girlfriend on that commercial flight?

There were so many potential misdealings to worry about that the Senator paused, unconscious he was over-chewing his food. Realizing his mistake, he tried flashing his insincere politician's smile. As if breaking out of trance, the Senator almost choked on his salad.

"When...wow, TOP SECRET? Did you want me to open the folder?" asked the Senator as he rubbed his hands together and waited for a reply. With raised eyebrows, the Senator redirected his attention from the folder to the Director's eyes.

Gall and Walters exchanged smiles as they watched the images being piped in through the Director's lapel pin camera. In a whispered voice, Walters smiled as she purposely misquoted a line from the movie *Apollo Thirteen*. "Houston, we have a deer caught in the headlights."

Knowing the others could not hear their comments from inside the van, Gall added, "Busted."

Without flinching, the Director in a calm expressionless face replied to the Senator's comments, "If you would Senator."

The Senator set his fork down on his cloth napkin and reached for the folder. In a smooth purposeful motion, as if inspecting a priceless document, using only his thumb and index finger, the Senator pinched the corner. As if afraid of mishandling the paper, the Senator held his breath. Reading the first few lines was worse than he had imagined.

Agent Walters' 82-page report was condensed to a single sheet with clear, single-sentenced bullet points. He read each one. The Agency had uncovered every dirty aspect of that case. As the Senator read, the pressure inside his arteries increased. He was certain the Director could see his shirt collar quiver with each beat of his over stimulated heart. The last bullet point was the most damning. The Agency connected him to the stock purchases. The report included the *New York Stock Exchange* acronym DRKE (Drakeson Enterprises) quoting the original purchase and selling prices. It was more than a needle in the haystack, or a smoking gun. It was a bull's eye. Like a laser guided cruise missile that obliterated the target's center. Senator Anthony reeled as he read each partner's name followed by their stock values with a running total; their original purchase price followed by the sold realized values. The report showed individual and group totals.

At the bottom, a small asterisk referred to a potential connection between the downed commercial airline questioning its timing as too coincidental given everything else. What were the odds that the Senator's biggest challenger for his senate seat, an upstart State Congressman and his family also died in the crash?

Ever the statesman, the consummate communicator, without flinching, Senator Anthony looked away from the report. In an unwavering confident voice, he looked the Director straight in the eye and did what came naturally. He lied.

"I have no recollection about any of this." With only a brief pause, he added, "Do I need a lawyer?"

11

Mr. Van Aelst instructed the cab driver to take them into Berlin. From the look of the buildings, the red brick construction dated back to World War II. The area had a post-apocalyptic feel, hidden and tucked away from the new modernized Germany. The cab driver maneuvered the vehicle through these abandoned streets and past dilapidated structures with ease. As the taxi careened down a narrow alleyway, Diane held onto the backseat door armrest as the cab descended a road leading to rusty railroad tracks.

To Diane's shock, the driver, rather than avoiding the tracks, positioned the vehicle so the tires straddled the iron rails. Proceeding down the abandoned rail-line, they continued through an archway and descended further underground. In a casual controlled manner, the driver turned on the headlights. She noticed that there were no large platforms or turn gates suggesting a mass transportation system.

"Where are we?" she asked Van Aelst.

In an authoritative dismissive tone, he replied. "We're in one of the Feurer's secret railway tunnels. These tracks crisscross under most of Berlin." With the taxi's interior darkened from the loss of sunlight, Van Aelst turned his attention away from the note he was reading and directed his gaze at Diane. "As a youth, I worked here. Many of my current colleagues did as well."

From the front seat, the driver shouted "Blut und ehre!"

Startled, Diane looked up and saw the reflection in the rearview mirror. The driver's eyes sparkled above his jagged toothed grin. Mr. Van Aelst waited for Diane to return her gaze toward him before speaking.

"That was our youth organization motto: Blood and Honor," replied Van Aelst. He's one of my oldest and dearest friends."

"Ja, mein freund." (Yes, my friend) the driver replied.

To the right side of the cab, Diane could see the underground tunnel expand into a larger area. There was a bright light illuminating the otherwise pitch-black underground area. Other than the light reflecting off the iron track, the area appeared vacant. The driver slowed the cab, creeping forward before coming to an abrupt stop. Van Aelst turned toward Diane.

"We're here. Let me introduce you to some of my team," explained Van Aelst. With a calm friendly smile, he reached over and opened the taxi's back door. At that moment, her pulse raced.

Her mind reeled as she watched Van Aelst reach inside his jacket. To her relief, he extracted and activated a flashlight creating a bright light beam to pierce through the blackness. In a caring manner, Van Aelst held Diane's elbow and lead her through the tunnel. After turning a corner, she found herself face to face with several older white-haired men.

Each man wore a different service uniform. She guessed that, like the cab driver, these men worked in strategic locations around Berlin. Based on the diverse mixture of uniforms, she deduced that Van Aelst's little organization had access to a reliable network of eyes keeping tabs throughout the city. Behind their homely and disheveled appearances, she detected a wealth of experience hidden by their geriatric façade. She was awestruck. Unlike most of the western world who forgot and ignored their contributions; here they were valued. With mandatory retirement ages, most of the West's cold war assets had been lost.

"Diane, I'd like to introduce you to more of my colleagues," announced Van Aelst. Stepping aside, with an outstretched arm, he turned toward his men. It almost looked like a curtain call at the end of a Broadway musical. As Diane turned toward the men, out of habit, they removed their hats and extended a slight bow, bending at the waist.

Van Aelst chuckled almost laughing. His deep crystal blue eyes cut through the darkness. "Old habits die hard," Van Aelst explained.

*   *   *   *   *

Agent Chapin waited inside the vehicle for the Director's signal. It was a simple cue. If the Director ordered dessert, the Senator would be eliminated. Two scenarios were in play. Everyone was in place. Through their conversation, the Director would communicate his decision. If he brought up the *Chargers* moving from San Diego to Los Angeles, they would take the Senator to the Salton Sea. If the Director mentioned the Olympics, they would stage his suicide combined with the leaking of some of his misdealing's to the media.

Chapin leaned forward watching the images transmitting from the Director's lapel pin camera. The audio and visuals were both loud and clear.

During this lunch, few words were exchanged. A first for the Senator. Anthony knew that the Agency had him cold. What was their next move? In his arrogance, the Senator never contemplated the possibility that he could be placed on a "knock list". He never considered the possibility that even Presidents, were not immune from retribution and assassinations. Although the justification for that type of a call was much different than the decision surrounding the Senator. The Director made his decision and pushed back away from the table. Without recognizing the danger, Senator Anthony broke his silence.

"What about some cake?"

For a moment, the Director wondered if it was destiny. This buffoon deserved everything that awaited him. For all the secrets he held, and for all his failures as a Senator, let alone as a decent human, the Senator, on both accounts was a lost cause. Being a U.S. Senator and the Chairman of several Congressional Oversight Committees, were missed opportunities. Anthony's existence, his years and the time invested were in vain. One way or another, regardless of today's decision, the Senator's future as a trusted civil servant were over.

Before the meeting, the Director had already revoked his TOP SECRET security clearance. The Senator was being removed as Chairman and member of the oversight committee. A call was already placed to the National Agency Director in Washington DC. On the drive over to lunch, the Director decided to delay the "Snap Shot" (an agency term to initiate an immediate kill on the target).

Although his authority and power as an Agency Director allowed him to make the call, Gamboa did not feel justified. There were no contracts or on-going situations giving the Senator future opportunities to manipulate. On the other hand, the Senator still had two years remaining in his term.

Other than Director Gamboa's internal disgust toward Senator Anthony, and his yearning to rid the world of this parasite, there was no real justifiable reason to take him out now. He realized his decision to make plans to eliminate Anthony was a mistake, a knee jerk reaction. Given all the unusual activity his team had experienced, the reopening of a closed file, the Director decided to let the National Agency Director make the call. He imagined that, given the circumstances, the National Director, through undocumented means, would seek input and direction from POTUS.

Unable to hide his disgust, the Director's eyes flashed back to the Senator. The Director reached down, grabbed his briefcase, and stood.

"Senator, eating desserts are bad for you." Cracking a screwed smile, like a grimace formed at the corners of his mouth. "Eating that shit will kill you...literally. Let's go."

The Senator, disappointed at not getting a cake and coffee, stood and followed the director out from behind the roped off section of the restaurant. Increasing his pace to catch up with the director, the Senator noticed one of the older tourists reaching for his flip-phone. As they passed that table, out of habit, the Senator flashed the old man a wide-toothed politician's smile. Caught off guard, the old man looked away. With a puzzled look on his face, somewhat hurt that he did not recognize him, the Senator continued walking by thinking "they must not be from California."

The Senator continued forward to the elevator. The Director had already pushed the elevator buttons and was waiting for the doors to open.

*   *   *   *   *

Agent Gall removed her headset. Still waiting inside the parked van in the underground hotel parking structure, she scanned the technicians' faces.

"What's happening? The Director didn't use any of the code words. What's going on?" Gall asked.

The Senior Technician knew it was not his place to speak. He looked up at Agent Gall and tapped the right ear cover of his head set. Catching his meaning, she returned it back on her head and listened as newly appointed supervisor Chapin spoke to the entire team.

"It looks like the Director has aborted the 'Snap-Shot'. Let's wait until I speak to the Director. For now, everything's on hold. Each team leader, confirm your understanding."

"Team Alpha, confirm. Everything is on hold. Copy that."

"Team Bravo, Ditto. Everything's on hold. Copy that."

As Agent Gall processed the instructions shared over the encrypted communication link, she nodded at the Senior Technician inside the van. She knew she had a lot to learn as she leaned forward listening to the chatter on her head set.

"Team Hotel. I want a body in the lobby and one outside waiting. Standard EVAC maneuvers."

"Copy that. Two members moving now."

From the other lead vehicle, Supervisor Chapin studied the images coming from the Director's lapel pin camera. Inwardly, she was grateful he delayed the hit. She knew the "Snap-shot" would be viewed with a lot of criticism. It was not exactly the first choice for her inaugural supervising detail.

Through the Director's lapel pin camera, they watched the elevator doors arrive and open, the Agency team members waited.

*   *   *   *   *

The DPRK (North Korean) agent had lived in LA's Koreatown for over a decade. Other than glorified message drops and an occasional stake-out, his team was left to their own daily routines. Hiding out in plain sight, his team grew agitated from boredom. Until the last few weeks, for the most part, he felt forgotten and unappreciated.

With the arrival of an old ally, one whose ties went back to the Cold War days, everything changed. Until then, he was under the impression that "The Lone Wolf" had long since retired. The Northern California mission was a welcomed change. Given the large number of Asians living in the San Francisco Bay Area and in Los Angeles, it made sense why his team was chosen. He recognized that it was time for "The Lone Wolf" to use others, more youthful contacts, for the heavy lifting. After checking with his handler, they assured him that Van Aelst was legitimate. The DPRK agent was ordered to assist him any way he could.

Waiting in the *Westin Bonaventure Hotel* lobby, the Korean agent ended his call and slid his cell phone into his back pocket. With a quick glance around the area, he checked on the two team members. They were ready. Seeing their leader's reactions, they understood it was almost time. Their target must be coming down in the elevator. As they waited, they repositioned themselves around the elevator area. While they waited, the senior agent wondered why that old man was used as their lookout. Seeing the old man's flip phone, and his decision to call rather than text, was a shock. But what could he do? The lookout was assigned to him, part of the "Lone Wolf's" team, he could not refuse the assistance. It just struck him as strange.

With a shrug, he glanced about at each DPRK agent confident that their strategically placed positions were good; spread about the lobby. The team leader reached inside his oversized black bomber jacket pocket. Inside, he flipped the safety off his Russian made gun and stared at the elevator doors.

* * * * *

Inside the elevator, the electronic tone rang out as each floor passed.

"What now?" asked the Senator. For the first time, he began to appreciate his situation. In his arrogance, he had grown complacent. Having special status as a U.S. Senator, let alone the Chairman of one of the most elite Oversight Committees on Capitol Hill, he felt invincible. Contemplating this meeting, he realized that they knew everything. What were they going to do to him? His thoughts about being untouchable were melting away. For the first time in his career, he wondered if losing his bid for re-election was better than the "other" potential alternatives.

"Have I been placed on one of your little lists?" asked the Senator. In a sad sincere voice, the Senator continued. "No three chances?"

"Believe me Senator, if that were 'still' on my agenda, we would not be having this conversation."

With a sigh of relief, the Senator returned his gaze toward the elevator doors. He knew that his days as a Senator were numbered. Accepting the Director at his word, he appreciated this meeting. It was the Director's way of communicating that the game was over. With a sense of finality, the Senator sighed. It had been a great run.

"It will be up to the National Director. He'll decide what to do with you. Your clearance has been revoked and a new Committee Chair person is in the works." Before continuing, the Director turned and faced the Senator. "I'm guessing, for now anyway, you're out of the woods with your neck still intact. And a full pension. Not that you deserve it," explained the Director ending his sentence with a scoff. He could not hide his disgust and disappointment.

Without turning to look the Director in the face, the Senator did what he always did. He spent so many years pandering to special interest groups and his constituents, it just came naturally. Without thinking, he flashed his wide ear-to-ear politician's smile. It was effortless. It was something he did countless times prior. Something he had mastered, the ability to appear sincere. He seemed to adjust the angle of his jaw and crinkle his brow line just enough to suggest that he was digesting everything the Director was saying. When, in fact, as he stepped out of the elevator, the Senator's thoughts were on something else. He was thinking ahead, finding the words to explain his sudden change of heart, conjuring up some seemingly justifiable reason why he would choose to retire mid-term.

Distracted by conversation, the Senator did not feel the bullet rip through his $2,000 *Armani* suit. The shortest Korean attacker was close enough to the elevator door that the Senator smelled the distinct gun powder odor as a loud percussion echoed throughout the lobby. The Senator's body was peppered by a spray of hollow point bullets shot in rapid succession as the projectiles emptied from a compact *Uzi* sub-machine gun. The Senator's plastic smile melted into a stunned expression before he collapsed forward, falling onto his face dead before his lifeless corpse hit the floor.

From inside the parked Agency vehicles, as the unmistakable sound of multiple gun shots transmitted from the Director's lapel pin camera's microphone, everyone's head snapped up.

"Shots fired!" yelled Supervisor Chapin. "All teams to the lobby. I want all cell phone towers within a mile jammed, now!" Chapin swallowed hard trying her best to control her emotions. Her body's natural responses to the sudden attack sent adrenaline flooding into her blood stream. With a deep sigh, she remained calm and continued to think through the situation. Her years of experience, all her training, kicked into action.

"I'm on it!" replied the Senior Surveillance Technician Marty Sweet.

Supervisor Chapin took one last look at the camera feed from the Director's lapel pin camera. She was grateful that he appeared to still be inside the elevator and watched the Director's hand reach for the elevator button to close the door. As she watched the elevator doors close, her elation was dashed. The view from the Director's camera took a sudden abrupt angle change. Chapin knew it could mean only one thing. The Director was down.

"On the move now!" yelled Supervisor Chapin. Dashing out of the parked surveillance van, she heard the other agents' voices through her ear piece over the encrypted communication. Chapin sprinted across the parking garage floor toward the back-lobby entrance while barking more instructions to her team.

"The Director is in the elevator. He's down. I repeat, the Director is down!"

*   *   *   *   *

The three DPRK agents glanced around the lobby. There was no question he was dead. For good measure, the senior agent walked up to the lifeless body and shot the Senator in the back of his skull. The three men tucked their guns away and casually walked toward the far hallway.

Like most large hotels, the lobby held other tenant businesses that catered to their hotel guests. The first space near that hallway was an Asian restaurant. As they pushed open the double glass doors, other patrons peered out to investigate the loud noise. The large open space of the lobby distorted the gunshots. Not hearing any screams, the first people to arrive would tell the authorities they thought something had collapsed, while others explained they thought it was an earthquake.

Making their way to a back-storage room, the three DPRK agents walked through the restaurant. The senior agent glanced around before holding open the door. Once they were inside, he locked the door and scanned about until he located the garment bags hanging from a shelf. An accomplice stowed clothes inside. Opening the bags, they changed from street clothes into dark wool suits, white long-sleeve shirts, and neckties. From much practice tying silk neckties into a double-Windsor knots, they wasted no time and exchanged smiles. After sliding their dark black socked feet inside black winged-tipped shoes, the senior agent inspected their appearances. With a confident nod, he was confident they looked the part and would pass as business men eating lunch.

Before exiting the storage room, the senior agent stuffed their street clothes, tennis shoes, and guns inside a duffle bag along with two stacks of hundred-dollar bills.

Inside the hotel's security room, one of the surveillance employees adjusted the lobby cameras, aiming them away from the restaurant entrance. The charade required seeing the DPRK agents shooting the Senator. With that part of their mission complete, all their efforts focused on avoiding capture. Their assignment did not include being sacrificed. Their handler was specific. They could use all means to escape. Although the DPRK was not immune from sacrificing its own, this was not one of those times.

Exiting the storage room, their restaurant contact, a waiter, stood outside the storage room door. With a nervous smile, the waiter bowed and pointed to a corner table. The table was already set, their food, ordered well in advance, sitting on the table. A set of wire-framed non-prescription glasses, and expensive black *Montblanc* classic ballpoint pens were placed in front of each plate. After sitting, each agent adjusted their glasses and inserted their pen into the breast pocket.

Without speaking, the men ate their lunch trying their best not to stare outside through the restaurant's glass door. It was well past the normal lunch rush. The only other patrons were a couple of college students too engrossed and distracted with the loss of their cell phone connections to have noticed anything unusual.

The senior DPRK agent paused. Tilting his chopsticks, frozen mid-air, he watched the first government agents run down the hallway past the glass restaurant doors.

"It won't be long now," whispered the Senior DPRK agent.

* * * * *

At the top floor inside the rotating restaurant, a young couple waited for the elevator to arrive. The restaurant receptionist's head jerked up as she heard a scream. Scurrying out toward the commotion, she raised her hand to her mouth in shock. The man she had just served in the reserved roped off area was lying on the ground. After struggling out of the elevator, he collapsed. By the red puddle underneath his prone body, she knew he had been shot or stabbed. There was too much blood. She feared the worst. He was not moving. Running back to the restaurant kiosk, she grabbed the phone and dialed the operator.

"We have a problem. There's a man passed out on the floor bleeding everywhere. Send an ambulance now!" she screamed into the phone.

The other elevator doors opened. Supervisor Chapin bolted out and knelt checking the Director's pulse. Without thinking, she unholstered her 9mm pistol and scoured the area for any potential threats. Speaking into her wireless microphone, "I'm with the Director. He's breathing but unconscious," she explained. Turning him over, she noticed the blood stain on his shirt. The only good news was the bullet missed his heart. Otherwise, he was drowning from the blood entering his lung. From the distinct wheezing sound, she knew his lung had collapsed. Supervisor Chapin tilted the Director on his side, with the bullet injury side down. She knew she had to find a way to keep the lung open. With her free hand, Chapin pressed down on the wound keeping the opening closed.

"He took a bullet in his lung! Hurry up. He'll bleed out!"

From down in the lobby, Agent Gall replied, "An ambulance just pulled up in front of the hotel. They'll be up in two minutes."

The restaurant was as silent as a museum. All the patrons migrated nearby staring down at the injured Director. As Supervisor Chapin surveyed the room, she was grateful no one was filming everything with their cell phone cameras. There was an older white-haired tourist wearing a baseball cap staring down. She hoped the surveillance technician had already cut the cell phone towers.

*   *   *   *   *

Van Aelst read the number displayed on his cell phone. He was expecting the call. With an eight-hour time difference between Germany and Los Angeles, he knew that it must be around two o'clock there.

"Hello."

"Boss, we have a problem."

"What is it? What happened?" asked Van Aelst.

"They got the Agency Director Gamboa too. He was hit in the crossfire."

Van Aelst froze. His attempt to create a distraction, to preoccupy the agency may have backfired. *What was the Director doing with the Senator?* Their Korean contacts had only confirmed the lunch meeting. No one took the time to figure out who his lunch companion was. Without warning the call ended.

"Hello? Boss, are you there?"

The agency had just cut the local cell phone service. Van Aelst was now in the dark. He would have to wait to find out what happened. Diane studied Van Aelst's expression. By his reaction, she could tell something was wrong. With a concerned look, Diane broke the silence.

"Is everything okay?"

Van Aelst set his global boxy cell phone down.

"Everything's changed. Your director Gamboa has just been shot."

*   *   *   *   *

From outside the lobby, Agent Gall and Supervisor Chapin watched the ambulance pull away. The Director was stabilized, but in critical condition. He was being taken to *Cedars-Sinai* heading directly into surgery. Given his injury, the Agency was not taking any chances. The National Agency Director was notified. Plans were already in play for a temporary stand in while Gamboa recovered.

Under these circumstances, operating procedures required another Director to stand in. With the possibility that Gamboa would be unable to return for some time, a more permanent replacement would be sought. Supervisor Chapin was informed that because Director Valdez was currently working on a joint assignment with Gamboa's team, and since she had personnel working on a case with them, she was the most likely candidate. The National Director would get back to her later that afternoon. While an Agency crime scene team was in route from San Jose, Chapin was anxious to confirm who would be temporarily in charge.

The blood spatter from the Senator's head shot enhanced the already gruesome scene. As Agent Gall followed Chapin into the lobby, she thought the decision to quadrant off the body with tall accordion dividers was wise. People were lining up near the yellow tape to get a closer look. Those taking pictures and videos were frustrated unable to upload images to *Facebook, Twitter,* or *Instagram*. Most assumed the large concrete building was interfering with their cell phone receptions.

With a dazed expression, Agent Gall followed Chapin to the building's security surveillance room. During their walk over, several Alpha Team Members approached.

"Supervisor Chapin, ma'am."

"What have you found out?" she asked.

"Not much. We scoured the hallways and each downstairs tenant location. Nothing out of the ordinary. Until we walked in, most had no clue anything took place. Only the novelty shop heard anything. Their doors are always kept open. They heard the commotion but assumed part of the building caved in from an earthquake." With a puzzled expression, he continued. "I'm guessing the acoustics distorted the gunfire."

"I'm hoping the surveillance cameras will give us more information," Chapin offered as she glanced up searching for cameras mounted on the walls.

"Let's do a perimeter search of the entire building. Try to identify all the merchant cameras and ATM machines. There has to be some footage of someone leaving. If not, the attackers may still be in the building. Guard the exits. No one leaves until we can confirm what the shooters looked like."

"Copy that boss," the Alpha Team Member replied before leaving to inform the others.

Agent Gall listened to every word. As they continued walking across the lobby floor, Gall pointed at the security room sign above a simple clear glass door. Neither were surprised to see several local law enforcement officers peering through the door and waving them inside.

"You two will definitely want to see this," explained one of the officers. Chapin stared down at the row of hotel security surveillance operators staring at a bank of wall mounted monitors. None were armed. They wore baggy uniforms and had youthful appearances; none appearing over 24 years old. With Gall at her side, Chapin walked up behind the counter.

There was no audio only grainy black and white images. They were replaying three camera views inside the lobby surrounding the elevator area. There was also an overhead view from inside the elevator angled downward tilting toward the doors looking outward. Each video clip was frozen queued up waiting to show someone of authority. In an unexpected and surprised manner, Chapin asked, "Who cued the tapes?"

"I did," replied the skinnier and youngest looking of the bunch. "I figured you would be asking to see them."

His eyes had been surgically altered and his skin chemically lightened. He spoke perfect English. His hair was dyed a dark brown and he wore contact lenses to alter the color of his eyes. No one had any idea he was Asian. He looked much younger than he was. His slight build helped. Agents Chapin and Gall would have been shocked to know he was 43 years old.

"Can you copy all these tapes for us?" Gall asked.

"Yes ma'am," the other security officer replied. "Would a flash drive be okay?" he asked holding up a small plastic covered drive.

"Sure," responded Chapin.

The room became quiet as they ran the tapes.

*   *   *   *   *

Agency Director-Korea, Nena Valdez, was shocked. She stared down at her desk phone, thinking about what the National Agency Director just told her. The U.S. West Coast Director Jose Gamboa was in critical condition but expected to recover. In the interim, given she was sharing resources on another matter, it made sense that she step in as his temporary replacement. But the apparent race of the assailants had something to do with it. Hearing her male secretary's voice on the intercom broke her concentration.

"Director. X.O. Newland is here."

"Send him in."

As X.O. Newland entered her room, from the look on her face, he knew something serious had happened. With a quick salute, Newland sat in the center chair facing her large wooden desk.

"What's up boss?" Newland inquired.

"We have a situation in California. A U.S. Senator has been assassinated execution style in broad daylight. The West Coast Agency Director was hit during the mayhem. He's critical, in surgery as we speak, but expected to recover."

Newland leaned forward. He could not remember the last time he heard of a U.S. Senator being murdered. He guessed that it was sometime in the 1800's in some duel of honor. Director Valdez continued.

343

"There's another twist, which is probably why I've been tapped for this assignment. The assassins were Korean," she said. Hearing this last part, they exchanged knowing expressions, both considering the possible other explanation; retaliation for what they did along the DMZ.

"Are you thinking this is some form of retaliation?" asked the X.O.

"It might be. The National Director reminded me that back in 1983, when a domestic *Korean Air Lines* flight 007, was shot down by the Soviets. There was some concern that the domestic flight was purposely sent into Soviet airspace to test their early-warning detection capabilities."

"Was it?" asked the X.O.

"Above my pay grade and on a need-to-know basis X.O.," replied Nena. There was something in her voice and the way she tilted her head that suggested she had an opinion.

"But?" interjected X.O. Newland.

"It took place during the high point of the cold war, over an area considered to be the most highly militarized area in the world. Plus..." she paused and looked up leaning forward. "There were very little human remains ever recovered."

"How many total fatalities, passengers and crew members were supposedly inside?"

"269."

"That's unusual," offered the X.O. "You'd guess that many more remains would have been recovered for that many on board?"

"It was attributed to crabs," explained Nena in an incredulous voice.

"Really...crabs?" asked the X.O.

"It gets better. Three weeks later, the North Koreans attempted to kill the S. Korea President. There was speculation that it was initiated by the Soviets for the public relations nightmare over the Airline incident."

"Did the National Director mention all this past stuff too?" asked the X.O.

"It's required reading for all incoming Directors in Korea. Knowing the past is important," she explained.

With a nod, the X.O. understood what the Director was thinking. Many times, retaliatory responses could be expected. Even inside governments, decisions were still made by humans. And humans tend to be consistent and somewhat predictable. The DPRK was modeled after their sponsoring countries China and the USSR. During the most recent incident following Nena's team's direct involvement in destroying the DPRK's tunnel under the DMZ, they made an apparent knee jerk reaction and sent troops across the DMZ to try and take out an American school teacher. It was a crude and immediate message. They wanted to send a direct unquestioning response. But this? To openly murder a sitting U.S. Senator, that took planning.

"Do you think this assassination is related to what we did to their tunnel?"

"It might be. With Lt. Benjamin and Lt. Elliott in the Mediterranean aboard the *USS George HW Bush*, we're a little light staffed. Let's bring in Gibby. Are Carla Jo and Mr. Kim still in Los Angeles?"

"They came back last month. The babysitting job was passed on to Gamboa's team. Unless they've been tapped for another assignment by another Director, they should be available. Do you want me to reach out to them both?"

"Yes. And contact the Supervising Agent on duty where the Director was shot. What was Gamboa doing with the Senator? He had to be there on business. It can't' be a coincidence that both, Agency Director and a U.S. Senator just happened to be having lunch together when this all went down. What were they talking about? If they were working a case, I need to know what that was all about and why."

"Yes ma'am," replied X.O. Newland as he left the room. There was something bugging her. Something just out of her reach. She had a gut feeling that she was missing something.

* * * * *

The three DPRK agents flew non-stop from Los Angeles' *LAX* to *Inchon Airport* in South Korea. Their tickets were arranged and printed as they checked in. After meeting their handler in the airport parking structure, they were given fresh new I.D.'s and passports. After waiting in the *Korean Air* VIP lounge, they boarded the last daily non-stop flight across the Pacific. With the stress from their mission complete, they relaxed and drank several soju (rice wine) shots and slept for most of the twelve hours.

When they exited the airport in South Korea, they were met by another DPRK contact. He picked them up in his bright yellow cab and drove them straight to their handler Halmeoni (Korean for grandmother). The cab pulled up in front of a Kimchi Market and parked down the street away from its large plate glass front doors. The DPRK agents exited the cab and glanced up and down the street in both directions before walking to the front door. The cabbie turned his radio on and waited for their return.

The senior agent pushed against the heavy door. As it opened, the door brushed up against a metallic door chime hanging from the ceiling and sent out a metallic music like echo through the store. As he led his small team inside, he wondered if Halmeoni really sold kimchi to the public. "Probably," he thought.

Approaching the oversized glass counter area, he glanced up at the ceiling mounted mirror. As he came to expect, he saw his handler. An old, skinny, extremely short woman staring back at this reflection. She saw him countless times before. The last time being several years prior, before he left for the U.S. Even still, her routine was the same. She stared back at him, holding the same pistol from his last visit. Without flinching, he stepped forward. In a loud clear voice, he looked at the potted plant sitting on the glass counter top.

"That's a Country Jasmin flower. I have one at home." If anything was wrong, if he was followed or under any duress, protocol dictated that he would change his introduction. Any deviation, and she would take appropriate measures. In the back, there were other DPRK agents capable of improvising if necessary.

After hearing the correct response, she returned the pistol to a small desk table against the inner wall. After gathering herself, she stepped out into view from behind the wall.

"Anyong haesayo (hello). Tashi manaso pongapsumnida (It's nice to see you again)" said Halmeoni.

"Ne (yes)", Anyong haesayo (hello)."

"We have a problem," she explained. "Come with me." She turned and led the three DPRK agents to the back of the store. She paused at the double doors, before pushing it open. She stepped aside and held the door open, allowing the three men to step through. Still wearing their suits and black winged tipped shoes, they were surprised to find themselves standing on plastic tarps. Before they could react, a thick necked DPRK agent stepped out from the alcove. With a silenced pistol, he depressed the trigger. With a whispered spit of air, the first bullet entered the forehead of one man. It happened so quick the other two had no time to react. Their comrade fell in a heap collapsing onto the tarp.

"We found out he was talking to the Americans. His girlfriend told us," Halmeoni explained.

"Is this the problem?" Asked the lead agent.

"No," replied the old woman as she leaned down and retrieved the dead agent's passport and documents from his jacket pocket. She stepped over his lifeless body and directed the thick necked agent to remove the clothes and shoes. They would be reused by someone else later. They all watched and waited for the thick necked man to finish his work. When he finally wrapped the body inside the plastic tarp, the old woman stared at the lead agent. After an awkward pause, she spoke.

"There was someone with the Senator. He was also injured," she explained.

"We weren't told to avoid collateral damage. The only instructions were to make it public. We did that. Besides, two dead imperialists for the price of one. Whose complaining?" the lead agent explained in a confident jovial manner.

"Normally, I would agree. Thankfully, the other person was only injured and not killed. He is apparently a government VIP," Halmeoni explained.

The lead agent glanced at his remaining team member, then back to the old woman before speaking. His smirk had vanished.

"There were no additional guards or protective detail present. It wasn't obvious that the other man was someone important. Who is he?"

"An Agency Director stationed inside the U.S."

After a brief pause, the lead agent gazed down and watched the thick necked agent drag his friend's body across the floor.

"I hope there will be no more need for plastic tarps today," he asked half joking. From the tone of his voice, it was a serious question.

"Lucky for you this isn't a DPRK mission. It was only a favor for one of my Cold War contacts. Otherwise, you would not be here to have this conversation," replied Halmeoni. With a bright smile, she held up a brown paper bag and handed it to the lead agent. He bowed and extended both of his hands to accept the bag. Before he raised from his bent position, the old woman was already walking back through the double doors. Their meeting was apparently over.

Without waiting, the lead agent followed her out and scurried across the store front and out the door grateful to hear the metallic chimes sound as the it closed behind him. The men shuffled across the sidewalk back to the waiting cab and climbed into the back seat. As soon as the door closed, the cabbie drove away. The lead agent reached inside the bag and found ten bundles of fresh uncirculated $100 bills still wrapped with the bank's yellow and white $10,000 band. He stared down at Benjamin Franklin's face and wondered why the U.S. used his image on the currency. Benjamin Franklin was not even a past president.

* * * * *

Supervisor Chapin waited in her office. Since being contacted by and introduced to her new temporary boss via a secure satellite, she was preparing to meet an independent contractor agent driving up from northern San Diego County. This contractor came with high recommendations from Director Valdez. The contractor was ex-military with skills typical of her background. She was also computer and satellite proficient. Her security clearance was above hers. From what Chapin could gather, this contractor was like an international detective with moxie. A knock came on her door.

"Yes. Come in," replied Chapin.

As the door opened, Agent Gall stuck her head into Chapin's office.

"What do you make of Director Valdez," Gall asked as she stepped inside and closed the door behind her.

"Smart, straight forward, and by the book. Just like I like 'em," smiled Chapin.

"Me too. I got a good vibe from the satellite meet and greet. When will she be here?"

"Next week. It'll give us time to get our arms around the hit on Senator Anthony. We need to decide how to proceed on that Director's -Only file also."

"Right. It's hard to believe that it all started with that Sentinel Event follow up from detective Katzmark. A lot has happened since then," added Gall. "By the way, how's Director Gamboa doing?"

"Fine. He'll be out for several months. He's off duty until then. Everything goes through Director Valdez for now," replied Chapin. She glanced down at her watch and stood.

"It's almost time for our meeting. Let's head over now. The contractors Carla Jo Hutchison and a Michael Gibson will be joining us. Agent Walters will get us up to speed on the open Director's-Only file. It makes sense they're involved given we're borrowing two of their guys to review the satellite images," continued Chapin.

As they walked over to the conference room, they saw a middle-aged man with long shoulder length hair in an older 80's style haircut feathered back look. As Chapin approached him, his appearance reminded her of a local rock band legend's original lead singer, Steve Perry. He held a thick binder and adorned a visitor's badge hanging from an Agency issued lanyard. Glancing down at the plastic covered temporary ID picture, she noticed the man bore an identical image as his photograph; an exaggerated smile, like a politician riding a car in a parade waving to the crowd during a re-election year. As she glanced up, the man flashed the identical whimsical smile and stretched out his right hand.

"Nice to meet you. My name is Mike Gibson, but everyone calls me Gibby. You must be Supervisor Chapin. I've heard a lot of good things about you," said Gibby.

With a solid firm handshake, Supervisor Chapin smiled back. His warm disarming smile had a way of breaking the ice and setting a good first impression.

"Nice to meet you Gibby," said Agent Gall.

"Likewise," replied Gibby. "Is C.J. here yet?"

"C.J.?" asked Chapin.

"I mean Carla Jo." Clarified Gibby.

"She should be here any moment. Would you follow us Gibby? We were just heading to the conference room to get acquainted and bring everyone up to speed," announced Chapin.

Gibby followed them through the building. He could not help but notice the stark difference from Korea. Here, there seemed to be an air of casualness. Unlike the DMZ, this California location was sprawling. Each section seemed to stretch out for acres and acres. He also noticed that the entire operation resembled a typical office building. It stood in great contrast to the Agency location tucked inside Camp Bonifas. Then again, this West Coast location was not hidden inside a military base that separated the warring and divided Korea's still deadlocked in a de facto state of war.

"Right this way," said Agent Gall, as she led the way. She was adjusting to her new environment. Gibby flashed his politician's smile again and replied, "Nice digs you guys have here."

As they came to the center of the building, Chapin pointed to the basket on the desk in front of the door. There were already two cell phones laying inside.

"All cell phones are to be left here. The room has a jamming device to prevent the recording or transmission of data from any portable devices. Even still, habits die hard here," Chapin said as she tossed her cell phone in the basket. Following suit, everyone deposited their cell phones in the basket as they followed Chapin into the room. Waiting inside, they found Carla Jo and Agent Walters.

"So, look what the cat's dug up," bellowed Moon Dog as his voice echoed out from the satellite feed speakers.

Carla Jo stopped speaking with Agent Walters and looked up. With a big smile, she spoke.

"Hey Gibby. How's it hangin?"

"Short, shriveled and to the right," replied Gibby either forgetting or not caring about his current status as the new recruit that should be trying to build upon his good first impression. Recognizing his potential misstep, he was grateful to hear the room fill with suppressed laughter. The commotion was interrupted by Chapin's serious voice.

"Let's get started people. We have a lot to cover. I know most of you know each other, but for the benefit of us locals, if everyone could introduce themselves; name and position. I'll start."

After clearing her throat, she started the introductions.

"I'm Cathy Chapin, Supervising Agent assigned to the U.S. West Coast location." Nodding, she directed Agent Gall to go next.

"My name is Theresa Gall. Newly assigned from the FBI from the San Francisco Office."

Continuing around the table, Agent Walters was next. "I'm Julie Walters. I.T. (Information Technology) Communications and Forensic Specialist, also stationed here in the U.S. West Coast location." Walters turned and faced Carla Jo to her immediate right.

"Hello everyone. I'm Carla Jo Hutchison. Gibby calls me C.J. I'm ex-military and am now an independent contractor agent. Many of my assignments come from the Korea Agency." Gibby followed.

With a quick nod, he subconsciously tossed his shoulder length hair from side to side. Every once and awhile, Gibby would transform from the carefree jokester to a dead pan serious professional, with the facial expression and eyes of a cold-stone killer for hire. This was one of those times.

"My name is Michael Gibson, ex-US military intelligence, software satellite specialist and sharp shooter. I am stationed outside Camp Bonifas along the DMZ in South Korea."

Without a pause, voices began blaring from the live satellite feed. "My name is Lt. Douglas Elliott. My friends call me Moon Dog.

I'm a communications and satellite Surveillance specialist, and UAV (Unmanned Aerial Vehicle) pilot, stationed in South Korea."

"My name is Kyle Benjamin, ex-USMC, foot soldier, recently added to the Korea Agency location."

"It's a pleasure to meet you all. As you are aware, with our Director's injury, your Director Valdez will be stepping in until he recovers. We have two specific cases to address," explained Chapin.

"First, who assassinated Senator Anthony? We need to know why. Also, was the Director also a target? The other case involves the cat and mouse game of chase we've been playing trying to unravel the Director's-Only file. And speaking of the cat and mouse game, gentlemen," staring at Kyle and Moon Dog as she turned her attention to the wall mounted monitor. "How has your satellite surveillance hunt been going?" asked Chapin.

"We've been able to track down all the trucks. They all ended up at the same location. And you'll get a kick out of this. We isolated one shot and blew it up for your viewing pleasure," explained Moon Dog. "It's as if they knew, someday, someone would be watching from above."

Reaching into the folder on the table, Moon Dog pulled out a still print out of the image and held it up in front of the satellite camera. Everyone in the conference room back in California tilted their heads and squinted. It was difficult to understand what they were seeing. It appeared to be a group of men staring upward and extending their arms to the sky.

"I can't tell what it is. Can you scan it and send it over?" asked Chapin.

After a few minutes, the group in California received the scanned image.

"Do you have it? Can you see it yet?" asked Kyle.

As everyone saw the scanned image appear on Walter's secure laptop screen, an eruption of laughter filled the room. In a clear photo extracted from the surveillance video, a still image showed a group of old men, all wearing corrective eye glasses, each with a raised arm displaying their extended middle fingers, an apparent group sign of defiance toward the sky.

"Are they flipping us off?" asked Agent Gall in disbelief.

"Yup!" laughed Gibby, who exchanged a look with C.J. who was suppressing a smile.

"Okay, okay," chuckled Chapin. "Why the hell would they be doing that?"

'They knew that someday, someone would be interested in what they were doing," offered Agent Walters.

While the others spoke, Agent Gall leaned down and studied the image. She raised her eyes and thought she recognized one of the men. She stood and approached computer forensic specialist Walters. after a brief verbal exchange, they both stood.

'Hey boss, I need Agent Walters for something. We'll be right back."

Chapin nodded and continued listening to the others speaking. Agents Gall and Walters slipped out of the conference room.

"Those guys are all old as dust," laughed Gibby. "How could they have known?"

"Obviously, they were helping with the shell game," replied Moon Dog from the satellite transmitting on the *USS George HW Bush* carrier from the Mediterranean Sea.

"But were they intimately involved in the matter or just hired guns?" offered Kyle. "For all we know, they're all from a local Moose Lodge or Kiwanis group paid to drive the oversized vehicles."

As the group nodded contemplating everything, agents Gall and Walters returned. Seeing them back inside, they approached Chapin. Holding up a flash drive, Agent Gall interrupted the ongoing conversation.

"On a hunch, I asked Agent Walters to copy a video clip from my phone. From my days at the Bureau, I had a habit of filming my field interviews. It helped me recall the conversations. I never admitted the clips into evidence and deleted them when I was done. It made it easier to write it all up and helped me get all the facts straight. Anyway, after the shooting, we locked down the place and took statements from everyone.

"I was most interested in what people in the restaurant saw. I was curious. While the Director and Senator were eating, I wanted to know if there were any Asians in the restaurants. I assumed that the assassins were getting intel from someone," Gall continued. "So, I started interviewing the patrons."

"Wait a minute. I thought we were talking about these old guys in the photo?" asked Gibby.

"We are," interrupted Chapin, as she pointed to the monitor. She had inserted the drive and played the interview tape while Gall was speaking. After seeing the interviewee's face, Chapin paused the video clip. Sliding the mouse over both images, the satellite still photo and the still from Gall's interview. Everyone stopped speaking and compared the side-by-side images. For a moment, the room fell quiet. They each contemplated its obvious meaning. Agent Walters was the first one to break the silence.

"It's the same guy. Before coming back, we ran a facial recognition program on the faces. It's a 98.7 percent match."

"What the hell?" whispered Moon Dog.

12

Director Valdez rolled her oversized luggage through the back-elevator doors. Her office was over-built, capable of handling a direct hit from a standard artillery round. Mr. Davies, her dedicated pilot had the Air Wolf helicopter warmed up and ready for a short hop to Osan Air Base in Japan. Unlike her prior excursion state side, this trip would be more mundane. They would not be utilizing the Agency's modified *Concorde* jet for another triple hop across the Pacific. This time, she would go the conventional military route; from Osan to *Seattle-Tacoma International Airport* on the mainland U.S., known by those frequenting this route as the "Pacific Express."

Given the recent attack on Senator Anthony and Director Gamboa, until it was proved beyond any reasonable doubt that some international effort was being made to kill or otherwise injure Agency Directors, all Agency Directors were required to maintain 24/7 protective details. Being assigned to the DMZ,

Director Valdez was used to this type of security. The stateside Directors would have to adjust.

Director Valdez's four security member detail escorted her from the elevator to the awaiting helicopter. Their modest luggage was already stowed inside. Given their ultimate destination was California, her security team did their best to dress accordingly. Even still, the presence of four large, physically fit men, all with short, cropped crew cuts, would attract attention. With two men in front and two following behind, they escorted Nena across the back protected helipad. In an orchestrated fashion, the back door was opened, the Director practically lifted inside with a fluid smooth grace that developed through experience. With little effort, her oversized luggage was placed inside before the back door closed.

As Nena adjusted her headset and plugged into the communication system, she tried to suppress her smile. She was secretly amused watching the four men squeeze into the mid-section. With tilted shoulders, they each slipped into place, like a jigsaw puzzle piece settling into its appropriate location. As the mid-section door closed, the pilot's voice cut through the speakers.

"Good morning, ma'am," said pilot Mr. Davies. With a big smile, he turned back to face the Director.

"Morning Mr. Davies. Are we all set?" replied Nena.

"Yes ma'am. There's a 747 waiting for us at Osan. They've saved us an isolated upper-level area," replied Mr. Davies. Everyone seemed excited. It was the first time, as a group, they were going to the U.S. Despite the unusual high global alert status, everyone seemed curious about spending an extended visit in California.

"And from Seattle?" asked the Director.

"An Agency *Gulfstream* will be waiting," answered Mr. Davies. "And yes, I will be piloting that leg as well," he added. With a satisfied expression, Nena nodded.

Mr. Davies checked his co-pilot navigator WSO (pronounced Wizzo), scoured his radar and activated his cloaking programs, before giving the okay. Mr. Davies raised the helicopter only a few feet off the ground before pushing the Airwolf forward. He wanted to keep the bird below the horizon and hidden. Given the recent issues along the DMZ, there was no need to encourage an unplanned retaliation. After travelling south several miles, Mr. Davies climbed into the South Korean airspace. The maneuver was standard operating procedures, flying at the nap of the earth. Director Valdez glanced at her wrist watch. It was going to be a long day.

*   *   *   *   *

An isolated office off the main wing serviced the *Lufthansa* German Airlines' maintenance division. The sound of an old-fashioned desk phone ring tone surprised the young janitor. He glanced up trying to locate the source of the sound. He was the newest addition to this small rag tag bunch of employees wondering why he was assigned here. He detested working with the other two very old German nationals. He was told they were in their 60's. Based on what he saw, he had serious doubts about the accuracy of that information, and guessed their age was more into their late 70's or early 80's. But his opinion mattered very little. The one fact that mattered was that they both had seniority and rank. They represented the final say in how things were run in this isolated maintenance section at *Lufthansa.* What they said ruled. Although theoretically they shared the duties, there was no misunderstanding who did most of the manual labor.

"I didn't know there was a phone back here!" announced the young janitor. He paused and glanced about waiting for a response. With puzzled expressions, his co-workers stared over their matching thick black plastic framed prescription reading glasses and exchanged knowing looks.

Hearing the phone ring, the senior member stood and approached the abandoned desk and glanced at his name plate, Klaus, Nicholas Klaus. It was an inside joke he perpetuated on the unsuspecting Americans. To appear more legitimate, and after several stern recommendations from his handler, they started accepting legitimate workers, people who knew nothing about, nor cared about the forgotten Cold War conflict and its issues. His Stasi handler found it humorous when he learned his cover name- Klaus (a short version of Nicholas). It was his little way to remain hidden in plain sight while still giving the arrogant American capitalists an unsuspecting jab.

"Kid," replied Klaus. "Why don't you go on a break? And here," tossing a crumpled $20 bill in his direction. "Get us all some pastries and coffee from that overpriced green beverage dispensary," ordered Klaus.

The young janitor stared back, glancing back and forth between his two co-workers. With his hand on his hip, he wondered if either one would explain the unmistakable muffled telephone ring coming from inside the desk. The kid knew better than to ask questions. Klaus tilted his head and tried to control his obvious displeasure that "the kid" heard the muffled sound coming from inside the desk. Years ago, Klaus hid the phone in the bottom desk drawer. His handler insisted they maintain monthly calls from that line to verify it was still worked. Otherwise, he would have forgotten that it even existed.

"Hey, hurry up! I'm not asking again," shouted Klaus. His voice was amplified by the metal enclosed walls.

The kid bent down, picked up the crumpled bill and hurried out the door. The men waited until the sound from the kid's padding feet disappeared in the distance. Stepping forward, Klaus jerked open the rusty bottom desk-drawer, while his partner bent forward and stared at the old thick plastic hand-held phone with its long winding chord and clear plastic rotating dialer. As Klaus raised the thick hand receiver, the spiral chord stretched out like an accordion.

"Hello?" whispered Klaus. He had not taken an inbound call from this line. In all prior occasions, he only made outbound calls to local establishments to verify the connection. He did not even know the number.

"My old friend," replied Herr Van Aelst. "Do you recognize my voice?"

"I do," replied Klaus. He could never forget the unique sound of the Lone Wolf's voice.

"Where did we first meet?"

"At the rally," Klaus replied without a moment's hesitation.

"What were we wearing?" Van Aelst probed.

Klaus tilted his head to one side trying to remember. He closed his eyes and envisioned the scene. As his mind retrieved the memory, a smile broke out on his face. "Our brown parade uniforms."

"I have an assignment for you Klaus. It will be your last one. Afterward, you'll be coming home."

Klaus wondered if he would ever get another assignment. Although his spirit was eager, he had no delusions about his limitations.

"What do you need of me?" he replied with as much bravado and confidence he could muster. Standing tall with a sharp mental focus, he listened as Van Aelst explained everything. After a few moments, he ended the call then turned to face his waiting comrade.

"What is it?"

"It's our final mission. Tonight! Afterwards, we leave for the Homeland," replied Klaus. "Get your passport and we'll dress in our suits."

"Our suits?" questioned his partner.

"Hurry up. Our tickets are waiting at the counter. We need to meet our contact there. There is a package to pick up," urged Klaus as he walked toward their locker room. "Take anything you want; we won't be coming back."

Hearing this, the partner stopped in his tracks, dazed from the news. It was happening too fast. It was the moment he dreamed about, yearned for. Yet, now, when it finally arrived, he found himself unprepared, blindsided. Noticing his partner's reaction, Klaus placed his hand on his partner's shoulder.

"It's true my friend. We'll be fine. Come on. I'll explain everything later," said Klaus.

*   *   *   *   *

The customer service representative was nervous. It was a long time since he heard from his contact and assumed he died. He was never a high priority asset and understood his assignment was the safety valve. There was a high likelihood that his assistance would never be required and was only a thing to be used in an emergency. His only signal would be the removal of a specific tree located on his commute route to work. For most commuters, a missing tree would not be noticed. It was a specific tree, part of a group placed along the city park boarder. For years, each day he drove to work, he wondered if the tree would ever be gone. But this day, to his surprise, it was missing.

After recognizing the sign, he maneuvered his car around the park's perimeter and parked. After glancing around, certain no one was watching, he exited the car and walked through the park toward a designated bench. As he approached, he saw an old man reading a newspaper. The man folded the newspaper, tucked it under his arm, stood, and started walking. As they approached each other, the old man-made eye-contact nodding as he passed. With a forced smile, he spoke.

"Auf wiedersehen."

"Hello," he replied. Nervous he avoided glancing about before proceeding to the same bench and sitting down. As he scanned the area, he grabbed and lit a cigarette. Certain he was alone, he leaned forward, bent down feigning to tie his shoelace. Before standing, he inhaled taking a large drag from the cigarette. In a dramatic flick of his finger, he catapulted the burning stub to the ground while exhaling a huge smoke plume. Using his other hand, he reached under the bench and located the paper taped underneath. With a quick snap of his wrist, he crumpled it inside his fist. It happened so quick that even if someone were watching it would require a super slow-motion camera, held at just the correct angle to catch his sleight of hand.

Before returning to his car, he stood and walked around the entire park yearning for the safety of the men's restroom back inside the airport. Once there, he found the courage to read his orders. As instructed, he retrieved a small vial that was hidden inside his locker. Using extreme caution, he was to hand deliver the vial along with a pair of first-class tickets. Perplexed, he wondered why they needed a set of airline maintenance coveralls. The ticket information was sent to his personal email address.

After retrieving the vial, he wrapped it inside several layers of paper towels, then sealed it in a plain envelope and slid it into his jacket breast pocket. With the tickets printed, he tried his best to remain calm. From the relative safety behind the customer service counter, he scanned the terminal area looking for the man. His nerves were shot, anxious to complete his first mission. As he waited, he wiped his sweaty palms on his pants.

From the far side of the terminal, he saw two well-dressed elderly gentlemen walking across the marble floor. Without veering off course, they made a direct beeline to his customer service station. With each step, the heels from their wing tip shoes snapped against the floor sending sharp reports echoing across the area. As they neared, the sound created from their shoes increased. He almost lost his nerve, and found it almost impossible to remain calm. He was certain someone, somewhere was watching him. Fearing detection, he forced himself to remain seated, ignoring his instinct to run for his life.

"Excuse me," said one of the elderly men. "I was instructed to pick up a package and set of airline tickets here."

The customer service representative (CSR) was taken aback. These men. Their demeanor. They seemed so innocent, relaxed, and unrushed. Looking them up and down, he sensed they were also uncomfortable, as if dressed up for prom, unaccustomed to formal attire. With their thick prescription glasses, he sensed they needed his assistance. He..., they, were not what he expected. Their sincere smiles and soft foggy eyes disarmed him. All apprehension he felt, evaporated.

"Yes sir," the CSR replied. Reaching into his jacket pocket, he removed the wrapped vial with one hand, while handing over the airline tickets with his other. As the old man reached across the countertop for the items, the CSR noticed the man's shirt sleeve crept up his arm, exposing the old man's skinny forearm.

"You'll need to be careful with this," explained the CSR handling the wrapped vial using only his fingertips.

With wide eyes, the old man concentrated as he reached into his pocket and extracted a tattered handkerchief. Without speaking, he held out his hand, and nodded toward the CSR. Without delay, while the old man glanced around searching the area, the CSR dropped the vial into the handkerchief. The old man wrapped the vile tight before depositing it back into his pocket.

While reading the tickets, the old man broke the awkward silence. "Where are the tickets going?"

The CSR tilted his head. In a confused expression, he glanced between the men and realized they had no idea where they were heading.

"The tickets are non-stop from Seattle to Tokyo. First class," replied the CSR. They glanced at each other and nodded. After a brief pause, they stared back at the CSR.

"And the coveralls?" the other old man asked. With a quick nod, the CSR pointing his chin toward the opposite wall. A matching set of worn airline maintenance coveralls and caps hung from the upper cabinet drawer handle. Still concerned about being seen, the old men searched the terminal area. Arriving at 2:00am, reduced the likelihood of being seen by passengers and other airline personnel. The area was otherwise empty.

"Thank you," they replied. Without delay, the men turned and shuffled over to the wall and retrieved their uniforms. Without looking back, they hurried back across the marble floor returning in the direction they came from. They had four hours to complete their mission before catching their flight to Tokyo.

*   *   *   *   *

The kid concentrated balancing three cups of coffee stuffed inside the cardboard cup holder plus a bag of pastries perched on top. As he entered the maintenance room, he called out.

"Hey guys! I'm back!"

His voice echoed off the walls. There was no response. He walked up to the desk that hid the telephone, set the stuff down on top, and searched for his co-workers. After pushing open the locker room door, he felt heavy moist air splash against his face. He was certain that someone had just showered. Curious, he checked their lockers and discovered they were emptied.

With a tilt of his head and his hand on his hip, the kid stared at the desk. After glancing about, making sure no one was around, he opened the desk drawers. To his surprise, it was empty. It looked like it was just wiped clean. He detected a subtle lemon furniture polish and recognized the scent. It was the same kind the airlines used.

Resolved that the old coots forgot he was bringing them a snack, he grabbed a coffee, picked a donut, and walked back onto the floor. He never saw them again. All their items, including the dated telephone were ditched inside an over-sized garbage receptacle. One they knew was emptied daily by the sanitation collectors. No one from the airport would find a trace. Only their landlord noticed their absence. After waiting two months, the landlord placed their items in storage. They had been great tenants, never late on rent, and had never received a single complaint from the other tenants. He hoped that they would return believing that one of them had gotten sick. After a year, their landlord donated their things to the *Salvation Army*. He never heard from them again.

*　　*　　*　　*　　*

Director Valdez, Mr. Davies, and her security detail waited near an enclosed tram car. Their luggage was stacked on the back rack. As the men escorted the Director to the tram, the guards were all smiles. They had worked together for years. Providing her protection was second nature. Unlike the U.S. Directors, the Korean detail was always 24/7/365. With the increased risk level, all Agency locations were now on this same uninterrupted protective detail.

"Boss," said Mr. Davies, "we're heading straight to the hanger. Gamboa's team flew their spare *Gulfstream* up. It's ready to take us the rest of the way and should be going through pre-flight and refueling now," he explained.

"Sounds good. Will we have some eats on board?" Director Valdez asked.

"Yes ma'am. It's been stocked," replied Mr. Davies.

"Any tea? I'm coffee'd out," she inquired.

"I always include that. I'll double check when we get there," smiled Mr. Davies.

*   *   *   *   *

The sleek *Gulfstream* G650 was an upgrade from their G550. It was wider, with a more flexible cabin design. It had a longer flight range and could carry eight passengers 7,000 nautical miles. The fuel was topped off and parked inside a secure hanger waiting for pilot Davies and his passengers to arrive.

The Agency contracted maintenance crew was groggy having to adjust to a last-minute flight schedule. Coming into *SEATAC* this early to service the Agency bird was out of the ordinary. The senior maintenance supervisor glanced around the hanger. As he was locking the hanger, he thought he heard something. Tilting his head, he closed his eyes concentrating to hear any unfamiliar sounds. For good measure, he stepped back inside and yelled.

"Is anyone there?"

With no response, he shrugged and locked the hanger door. Knowing a crew from Korea was coming, he decided not to set the alarm. It was just one more thing that could create a delay. If they had trouble accessing the hanger, he did not want to waste time to double-back here again for that. Besides, what could happen anyway? Checking his wrist watch, he hurried back to his electric cart. He had to get back to the other side of the terminal and prep another jet heading to Paris later that day.

The two old men remained frozen in place, with their backs pressed up against the far wall. They wore airline coveralls with matching caps. If they were discovered, they would claim to have fallen asleep inside the hanger. Given their obvious age, it was all they had. They hoped it would not come to that. Hiding in the dark, the senior agent kept the vial of poison wrapped in his handkerchief and counted down the minutes. Their orders were to enter the Agency jet and lace the tea with the poison. Tea was the Director's favorite beverage.

As they waited, the senior agent's mind wondered. He imagined their mission complete having already exited the hanger, ditched their coveralls, and retrieved their airline tickets. His mind ran wild envisioning them scurrying through the international terminal to catch their flight, carrying new wallets and passports and leaving with new identities. Having sat in the crouched position for so long, his spindly legs shook from the exertion and rattled against the thick fabric of the coverall leggings. Sensing his partner crouched next to him in the darkness, he could not help himself. With a broad smile, he whispered, "Kon-ich-iwa," a Japanese greeting similar to "good day".

His co-worker suppressed his laughter. It would not be much longer. In the darkness, they exchanged knowing smiles and continued to wait.

*   *   *   *   *

The enclosed tram made its way through the vacant terminal area. It was surreal, like a post apocalypse B-movie. The area was vacant void of the normal pedestrian traffic during normal peak flying times. This section of the airport was off the beaten path. The hanger was placed there by design, just for these types of occasions. As they approached the isolated hanger, the tram made an abrupt swerve to avoid two well-dressed elderly gentlemen walking down the center of the terminal floor. Mr. Davies flashed an apologetic smile as one of the men shook his arm and extended his middle finger in anger as the tram sped by closer to the pedestrians than the driver would have liked. As they sped by, Director Valdez pressed her lips together suppressing her displeasure at almost hitting the old men.

"Let's slow down before we hit someone," ordered Nena.

"Yes ma'am," replied the tram driver as he reduced his speed. "We're almost there."

*   *   *   *   *

Mr. Davies completed his flight check. Before the handlers gathered pillows and blankets for the passengers, the pre-flight security team searched the jet. The Seattle Agency dogs ran through the cabin sniffing for bombs then cleared the plane of listening devices. Finding the jet as expected, the "all clear" sign was given, and the Director and her team boarded. Nena maneuvered down the aisle and slid into one of the oversized leather chairs. She was accustomed to the ritual and was busying herself preparing to taxi out of the hanger toward the runway. With priority clearance, they would go straight to the runway without stopping. Nena leaned into the aisle and glanced inside the cockpit. She saw Mr. Davies was busy with his pre-flight routine. Taking the initiative, she made her way to the galley and got herself a drink. She was not the type that needed to be served. Unlike other Directors, she never let her position go to her head. She was very capable of getting it herself.

Within minutes, Mr. Davies finalized his flight plan with the tower and ordered the jet hatches closed. The ground crew opened the hanger doors and watched as the $65 million-dollar jet began its long taxi to the runway. One of Gamboa's pilots was onboard to assist with the flight.

"Before we take off, I'm gonna step back to check on the passengers. Please take the controls," Mr. Davies instructed the co-pilot.

"Roger that."

As Mr. Davies stepped out of the cockpit area, out of habit, he planned on making the Director her cup of tea. He walked over to the water pot and noticed it was already steaming with almost a full pot. Opening the mid-cupboard, he noticed the tea box was already opened. The plastic wrapping was gone, and the top appeared to have been pulled back and reclosed. After dropping a tea bag into an Agency stocked silver lined ceramic mugs, he poured the hot water inside. These cups were standard operating procedure and required items for every flight that transported a Director. It was protocol. An old-school procedure but provided an immediate means of detecting poisons.

Mr. Davies steadied the silver lined cup. Using a spoon, he immersed the water-soaked baggy up and down into the hot water. As he watched the clear liquid change to a dark-brown color, his mind wondered off. He glanced back at the cockpit thinking about the eventual take off and mid-flight checks to come. Using the spoon, he removed the soaked tea bag and tossed it into the garbage receptacle. He concentrated trying to balance the hot cup of tea making sure not to spill any. From his movement, the liquid inside jostled about. Staring inside, Mr. Davies noticed the interior silver coated lining had changed colors. He paused and examined the silver lining. Tilting the cup backward he examined it more clearly. There was no doubt. The silver lining was tarnishing and continued fading to a dark black spotted hue. Taken aback, Mr. Davies leaned down and peered inside the metal cup.

His instincts took over. He stepped toward the galley table and set the full cup down careful not to spill any of the liquid. Without turning, he yelled over his shoulder.

"Let's pause here. We need to check something out," Mr. Davies said in an authoritative manner. The co-pilot complied. Just outside of the hanger, the co-pilot brought the jet to a full stop. Mr. Davies turned down the aisle and walked toward the Director to inform her what he found. He approached her down the center aisle. Her eyes were closed and appeared to be sleeping. Stepping closer, he recoiled seeing a *Styrofoam* cup sitting inside the chair's cupholder. Standing in front of her chair, Mr. Davies looked down. He was sickened to see the cup was only half-full of a dark brownish liquid inside. He reached down and touched Director Valdez's resting arm.

"Director."

Her eyes remained closed. There was no response. This time, with a greater force, he shook her arm. In an elevated voice, he practically yelled. "Director!"

*   *   *   *   *

Klaus, the senior agent, glanced at his partner sitting with a relaxed expressionless face, eyes closed, using the padded leather earphones provided to all first-class passengers. This was their first time to fly in such luxury. It was decades before since they last flew and were surprised how much things had changed. The seats were more like self-contained survival pods, with numerous gadgets to appease the elite catering to their demand for comfort, entertainment, and privacy. Before take-off, they visited the VIP Area taken aback at the separate meeting areas and even stairways. The *Boeing* 747-8 looked more like a high-end business hotel than a flying commercial jet.

They were exhausted from their impromptu mission and the emotional roller coaster, grateful to be heading back home. They wanted to enjoy the flight and tried soaking up all the fringe benefits that their return journey home had to offer. As Klaus read through the available movies, he felt a tap on his forearm.

"Excuse me. Nicholas Klaus?"

E.A. PADILLA

He turned to meet the gaze of a male Korean Steward. His blue, white, and red airline uniform was impeccable. He spoke perfect English without a hint of an accent.

"I'm sorry to interrupt your movie, but I need to give you a message." The male steward handed Klaus a sealed envelope and walked away. Klaus never saw him again. Before opening the note, he scanned the compartment. There were several passengers still standing. He decided to wait until all the other passengers were settled in their own cubed area. He was unfazed by this unexpected visitor. Once the other first-class passengers were seated and preoccupied preparing for the 12-hour non-stop flight to Tokyo, Klaus opened the envelope.

He recognized the old fashioned stylized cursive writing. It was from his handler Mr. Van Aelst, aka "The Lone Wolf". Herr Van Aelst wanted them to remain inside the *Korean Air* VIP lounge at the international terminal. Their next contact would arrange their final leg of their journey home.

After finishing most of his drink, certain he left enough liquid in the glass, Klaus crumpled the note into a small, wadded ball and dropped it inside his glass. Certain no one was watching, he swirled the glass and watched the paper dissolve. To expedite the process, he tilted the glass back and forth, and swirled the remaining liquid and ice cubes about until the note disappeared. Wasting no time, he flagged down another first-class stewardess and handed her the seemingly empty glass with the dissolved paper disintegrated at the bottom.

"Could you bring me a bloody Mary please?"

"Certainly," she replied as she carried the glass away.

For a moment, Klaus thought about the person that drank the poison. It had been decades since he did something like that. He glanced around the cabin, seeing all the happy couples and other travelers. He surprised himself for feeling a sense of remorse. He had nothing against the person and did not even know who it was. He shook his head trying to rid himself of these thoughts. "*It must be my old-age*", thought Klaus. With a large sigh, he closed his eyes and scrunched down in his oversized leather reclining chair. By the time the stewardess returned, he was already asleep. She turned off his overhead light and lowered the recliner to almost a flat position before draping a periwinkle blue blanket over his now sleeping body. As she walked back to the galley to discard the untouched drink, she glanced back and heard one of her first-class passengers snoring. It was Klaus.

*   *   *   *   *

"What was the purpose for taking out the Senator anyway?" asked Diane. She was shocked and knew that if the Director was there for a face-to-face meeting with the Senator, her team members had to be there. Something was up. She wondered if a "SNAP-Shot" call was in the works.

"If it weren't for the Senator, your niece and my grandson would never have gotten so tangled up in this mess. It turns out the Senator was manipulating the Agency to do some of his dirty work, not to mention utilizing proprietary information to financially benefit himself and his friends. From my perspective, the Senator was a loose cannon, and a variable that needed to be eliminated," explained Mr. Van Aelst.

"His elimination also provides us with a means of redirecting your people, steering them away from us to the Koreans. Given the recent fall-out over their invasion tunnel being destroyed, such a scenario wouldn't be out of the realm of possibilities," continued Van Aelst.

"You guys know about that?" asked Diane.

"Everyone knows about that."

The room fell still giving them time to think things through.

"And the Director?" pried Diane.

"Which one?" replied Van Aelst.

"Gamboa of course. Who else?" asked Diane. As she studied Van Aelst's face, she realized she was missing something and pressed Van Aelst. Because of Curt, they were in the strangest set of circumstances. For a very narrow and specific reason, at least for the time being, they were on the same team.

"Do you have something in the works with another Director? Is it related to me and Curt?"

After a brief pause, Van Aelst set his steely blue eyes on Diane.

"We needed to sell the idea that everything points to the DPRK, the North Koreans." Glancing away, in somewhat of an apologetic manner, he explained. "The Director assigned to Korea. She is on her way to temporarily stand-in for your Director Gamboa."

"So, he's okay, right?" she urged.

"Yes, Director GAMBOA," emphasizing his name, "is fine." Catching his meaning, she could not leave it alone. She needed clarification.

"What about the other Director?"

Without delay, Van Aelst replied. "We're trying to take her out." His response was cold, direct, and spoken in a matter-of-fact tone void of any emotion.

"Another Director?" Diane responded in a whispered incredulous manner. Turning away, she said "I don't want or need to know any of this. Tell me my involvement had nothing to do with any of this business. Van Aelst tell me you would have gone forward with these plans anyway! It had nothing to do with me, right?" Diane asked in a pleading tone.

"That's correct Diane. None of this had anything to do with you. Your involvement was to help my grandson. Albeit, motivated by your loss. For your intervention and assistance, we are in your debt. This is the reason we've arranged this meeting and brought you to Germany. Diane, although our countries are political enemies, we are still trying to keep you safe. Unfortunately, I think things have changed."

Diane waited for Van Aelst to explain. Curt sat still, unaware of what his grandfather meant.

"Your people are looking at you now."

"For what? Helping Curt evade their detection?" Diane asked.

"I wish it were just for that reason," Van Aelst replied.

13

Gibby and Carla Jo waited inside the hanger. The Agency *Gulfstream* G650 was landing at Moffett Naval Air Station. The San Jose West Coast Agency had special privileges there. Supervisor Chapin and Agent Gall pulled their Agency issued black *GMC Yukon* inside the hanger. In the backseat, a chemist on special assignment from *Stanford* held her field kit. Today would be the first time it would be used. There would be no record of her chemical analysis nor her involvement. So far, as the rest of the world was concerned, none of what took place in SEATAC ever happened. As supervisor Chapin exited the SUV, Gibby and Carla Jo approached.

"The *Gulfstream* jet just landed," Chapin explained.

With their heads facing down, Gibby and Carla Jo stepped up to the double white line painted on the asphalt tarmac. With their hands stuffed in their front pockets, they waited. Before they saw the jet approaching, they heard the high-pitched whine and could smell the pungent spent fuel. The deafening noise reached a feverish scream as the two *Rolls-Royce* BR725 engines pushed the plane through the open hanger doors. With tight lips, Gibby's head jerked up. His face was crimson red flushed from rage.

The state-of-the-art jet maneuvered inside the open hanger door and glided to a stop. The main cabin door swung down, and the retractable step ladder came into view before it stopped snugly against the asphalt floor. Two of Director Valdez's security detail exited first. With grim faces, they scanned the hanger with their hands resting on their *Barretta M-9* pistols. Only after they were certain all was clear; did they turn back toward the open jet door and summon the occupants forward. The first person that came into view was Director Valdez.

With a deep exhale, Gibby stepped up to the ramp stairs and extended his right hand.

"That was a close call boss," offered Gibby. As the Director stepped off the metal rung ladder, she shook Gibby's outstretched hand.

"I'm fine really," Nena explained. "I never drank the tea. I was tired from the first flight. I just poured myself some apple juice."

"Mr. Davies thought you drank the tea," explained Carla Jo as she shook the Director's hand next. "Everyone on board was a little scared when you didn't wake up."

With a shrug, the Director explained, "I never get used to that 12-hour flight." Nena glanced out into the hanger and saw someone she did not recognize. The person appeared nervous and waited to be introduced. Making the connection, Nena stepped forward. "And you must be Professor Kaiser," said the Director.

With exaggerated opened eyes, as if bulging out from the stress of the situation, the woman stepped forward. "Yes. That's correct. How can I be of assistance?" she asked. It was clear that she wanted to get her job done and be on her way. This was Kaiser's first assignment and she regretted accepting the position as an on-call assistant for unknown special assignments. It all sounded exciting until the images in her mind transformed into real world experiences that lead to dark mysterious places. She was warned several times that everything she saw was top-secret and could not be discussed under any circumstances, ever.

As if on cue, Mr. Davies stepped through the jet doorway carrying a clear ziplocked baggy. Inside, the silver cup along with the liquid were sealed inside several layers of plastic bags. In his other hand, all the tea and the carton they came from nearly full of unused bags where neatly wrapped in a similar layer of plastic zip locked bags. Not waiting to reach the bottom of the metal steps, Mr. Davies spoke.

"Professor Kaiser. We need all of these items tested for all known poisons," explained Mr. Davies. "We're pulling all the drinks, ice and food," he added as he held up the plastic baggies for the Professor's inspection. Only after the Professor had a firm grip on the bags, did Mr. Davies release his grip.

"What can I say Mr. Davies? You literally saved my life," said Nena while encircling his outstretched right hand with her hands.

"Just doing my job boss."

"You went above and beyond. I'm serious."

Mr. Davies nodded and appeared embarrassed from all the attention.

Professor Kaiser carried the plastic ziplocked bags upright making sure the seals had not opened. Upon a close examination, she noticed that the samples were double bagged. Mr. Davies followed the Professor, while Carla Jo carried the Professor's chemical field kit. In the corner of the hanger, Kaiser set the bags on top of a small folding table as Mr. Davies stepped up beside her.

"And remember, Professor Kaiser," he started. But the Professor cut him off.

"I know. I know. This entire event never took place, and I won't tell anyone about any of this," she said with a half-smile, on the verge of being annoyed.

"Right...exactly," said Mr. Davies.

*   *   *   *   *

Diane sat in a catatonic pose, with a blank stare with her mouth gaping open. Curt did not know what to say. He had listened to his grandfather explain her new reality. She had some serious thinking to do. It was becoming quite clear that returning to the Agency was no longer an option. Curt's Grandfather's contacts were well informed. Either there was a mole inside the San Jose Agency location, or there was a serious loose end that their surveillance specialists were infiltrating.

"So, my colleagues are taking a hard look at me right now?"

"They are," replied Herr Van Aelst. "And they've discovered the money inside your safety deposit box."

"I told you! I never asked for or wanted the money." Diane replied in an angry hurt manner. Her eyes were down cast. Based on her expression, Curt felt like she was blaming his grandfather for her current predicament.

In a soft non-accusatorial reply, Herr Van Aelst replied. "Yet Diane, you never returned the money."

In a soft defeated reply, she said "I thought about it. I just couldn't figure out how to return it without raising even more red flags. I haven't touched any of it."

"Really?" Curt asked.

"Nothing. The bank bill bands are still intact. I'm sure the sequential bills are still in order."

Curt glanced at his grandfather. With a slight shrug, and a tilt of his head, Herr Van Aelst had nothing to add. He appreciated Diane's anger over the money, he knew that, with very little effort, he could find out if she were telling the truth. He recognized that she was just reacting to these new circumstances, a natural human response. He did not blame her or judge her too harshly. The fact that she was willing to show her emotions confirmed that she had become more comfortable and more trusting of him. Expressing her emotions spoke volumes. Being able to be transparent was a sign that deep down, she did trust them.

"I'm surprised you've been able to pass your annual polygraphs," stated Herr Van Aelst.

Diane directed her gaze at Van Aelst. After some contemplation, she would not be surprised if he knew her test results. Turning away, she thought to herself, *"of course he knows"*. Van Aelst seemed to know everything.

"Up until recently, I was an Agency recruiter. As you're aware, all questions can only be responded with either a yes or no. There are no multiple word responses allowed. Besides, given my area of expertise and recruitment duties, every question was directed toward that end." Diane paused and glanced back and forth between Curt and Van Aelst. "In my mind, I never did receive any payments or money from a foreign agency. Rather, from an individual...you," Diane explained as she raised her hand and pointed her index finger at Van Aelst.

Herr Van Aelst nodded. She had answered his question. Over the years, he was present during countless such interviews. He understood that if a person truly believes his response to be accurate, from the respondent's point of view, there would be no physiological response, no heightened temperature, raised heart beat, or increased perspiration. Diane did not need to beat the machine. She just needed to believe, truly believe, that what she said was truthful. The flaw was in the questions. She had answered the questions honestly.

"Three years," added Van Aelst with a hint of admiration.

"This year, I was transferred to the field. The next polygraph exam, I'm certain would pose questions in such a way that I couldn't side step. I would have failed. It was only a matter of time," she explained before letting out a deep futile sigh. After a brief silence, Curt interjected.

"What are you going to do Diane?"

She looked up and stared at Van Aelst before responding. "What do you think Van Aelst? What's my next move?"

"I have an idea," he said.

*   *   *   *   *

Director Valdez stood at the podium. She felt awkward addressing such a large group of people she was tasked to supervise yet did not know. Until Gamboa recovered and was released back to duty, she would be responsible for the Korea and San Jose offices. Staring out across the large conference room table and the secure satellite feed from the *USS George HW Bush* projecting on the wall, Nena flashed a tight-lipped smile while glancing around the room.

"People, I understand the unusual nature of our current situation. First and foremost, for the agents stationed here in San Jose I, along with my colleagues from Korea wish to express our gratitude for you opening your office and extending us all the professional courtesies. Your Director, Jose Gamboa is doing well and sends his regards.

"Until we get a handle on the recent attacks, Director Gamboa will have a protective detail assigned to his location 24/7. All personal visits are still on hold. We both wish that weren't the case, but it's SOP (Standard Operating Procedures)," Nena explained.

"I've met the San Jose personnel one-on-one. As discussed, we needed to make sure that we did our due diligence and checked for any moles. It's nothing personal, just an unpleasant necessity that we had to check off."

Nena paused, averted her eyes, and looked at Carla Jo. With a nod, she continued to speak.

"To avoid any miscommunications, any information that becomes distorted by human embellishments, I wanted everyone, from both locations to hear it directly from me, first hand." Nena paused with a deep sigh, as if mustering up the nerve to break bad news.

"Unfortunately, one inconsistency was found. I want it to be clear, until all the facts are uncovered, this person is considered innocent. However, going forward, everyone present will be under strict surveillance. At all times, each one of us will be wearing a secure mobile video device recording our every move. It is no time to concentrate on the obvious infringements of our personal privacy. All emails, telephone calls and texts will be monitored."

Nena scanned the room. Everyone's faces were blank, frozen in shock and disbelief. She knew that no one would object, but from the incredulous expressions, she knew this protocol was a first. After a scan of the room, Nena continued.

"Once Carla Jo briefs us on her findings, you'll all understand the unusual guidelines going forward, Carla Jo." The Director stepped away from the podium.

Carla Jo stood, carrying her thick manila folder, strode forward and exchanged a quick OMG glance with Gibby. For one of the few moments in Gibby's professional career, he was speechless; no wise crack remark to toss out as a comic relief for the group. He was all ears. His expression mirrored all those present and equaled the seriousness of the situation.

Carla Jo stepped up to the podium. Without delay, she cut straight to the point.

"The only person we're looking at is not here. She is away on leave, out of the country taking an extended personal vacation."

At hearing the words, Supervisor Chapin and the other members of the Alpha Team began glancing around in disbelief. No one spoke. Everyone wanted to hear what Carla Jo had to say.

"I realize she's been a long-time member of the San Jose operation. We need to look long and hard at Diane Klein."

"Wait a minute," interrupted Supervisor Chapin. "That's impossible. She's done the whole enchilada, from the foreign field assignments, recruitment and now as an analyst in the Alpha Team." Chapin could not suppress her outburst. Diane represented the epitome of an all-American professional. Her involvement seemed out of the realm of possibilities.

"I get that," replied Carla Jo knowing that her words fell on deaf ears. Carla Jo empathized with Diane's co-workers. If an outsider suggested something similar about one of her team members, she knew that she would feel the same way. Reaching down, Carla Jo grabbed and raised the remote control activating the overhead projection display. As everyone read the list of concerns, the San Jose agents searched the room trying to make eye-contact with their colleagues. In a soft whisper, with her lips moving, Supervisor Chapin read the list.

"Safety deposit box with $500,000 cash; satellite surveillance documenting daily visits to random Internet cafes." The list went on and on.

*   *   *   *   *

Kyle and Moon Dog gave up trying to isolate the transport vehicle. After weeks of non-stop tape viewing, nothing. However, on one of the tapes, Kyle discovered an anomaly. From the overhead satellite tapes, it was as if the painted lines along the asphalt road would randomly disappear. At first, Kyle thought the computer was dropping the painted lines during the digital image translation. But then, if that was the case, why would the computer show the dotted lines in most of the tapes, and then only on rare occasions, drop the lines? It was inconsistent and random one that did not make sense.

During the end of one late-night session, Kyle began joking that the ambulance had a cloaking device that caused the painted street lines to disappear. He went on to speculate that as the cloaked vehicle traveled over the dividing lines painted on the road, the satellite was not able to see down through to the hidden ambulance and this was causing the lines to disappear from view by the satellite above. Moon Dog laughed. Neither gave any credence to his theory. It was just a joke to pass the time.

If they only knew. Van Aelst and his entire team understood that if the Agency used their overhead satellites, their plans could be unraveled. Using an oversized common magnet sign, Van Aelst displayed the image of a worn dark grayish black asphalt roadway. Knowing that the color and design of the roadway lines would change as they traveled, they opted to exclude the image of any lines. This low-cost solution was ingenious. Except for the inconsistent appearance of the surface roadway lines, the satellite images could not detect the subtle difference between the actual road and the image on the magnetic sign.

It was the Agency's Achilles heel. The satellite images were so accurate, most analysts over-relied on the images. A simple cross-reference with a standard exterior surface security camera would have revealed the true reason for the vanishing street lines. Van Aelst hoped that the hi-tech advantage also created their disadvantage - situational blindness. In reality, the $300 magnetic signs attached to the ambulance's exterior roof and hood duped the $290 million-dollar spy satellite.

"So far, nothing solid from the overhead tapes?" asked Supervisor Chapin.

Staring back looking into the secure camera, Moon Dog and Kyle, nodded in unison.

"We do have an idea," offered Moon Dog. "Let's assume that our guy makes it across the pond." Being temporarily stationed on the aircraft carrier parked in the Mediterranean Sea, he could not help himself and used the European vernacular for the Atlantic Ocean. Moon Dog flashed a wide grin as he continued speaking, while the microphone, off camera, picked up Kyle suppressing a snorted laugh. The others watching shared knowing glances deducing that those two have spent way too much time together.

"Bottom-line, we only care if it's Anderson, right? So, if the ambulance transport game continues across the continental U.S., let's make some assumptions. Why go there?" asked Moon Dog.

"Right! Why go there?" parroted Kyle, sticking his face into the camera view. "The only reason someone went to all of the trouble of hop-scotching across the U.S. was to avoid detection. Otherwise, why not just put our Anderson buddy on a plane and send him home that way?" continued Kyle.

During the pause, Supervisor Chapin watched Kyle's and Moon Dog's tilted heads trying to squeeze into the camera's view. She looked away and tried to suppress a smile. If the situation were not so serious, their conversation would be comical. Controlling her emotions, Chapin countered.

"Well, what if Anderson is still physically unstable? What if he still isn't strong enough to handle a regular commercial flight."

"But if this Anderson guy was affiliated, working for the other guys, to protect the asset, they would have gotten him out on a direct military or private jet, right? This shell game and cross-country ambulance run was small time; an on-the-fly type of mission," explained Moon Dog.

"So," interrupted Kyle. "...who does this Anderson guy know? His girlfriend supposedly died on the plane crash. We're reviewing the logs on all his known associates and Carla Jo did some follow up on those guys. Nothing out of the ordinary. No contacts, weird calls, emails, nothing."

Supervisor Chapin glanced across the conference room table. Carla Jo was nodding in agreement.

"The only one left, the only person that makes sense is his only living relative; his biological grandfather," with a smug look on his face, explained Kyle. "The sole beneficiary of all Anderson's assets."

"That's right. He was adopted," nodded Chapin.

Carla Jo and Gibby were late comers to the party. Initially, the local law enforcement's discovery of the forged documents, was the impetus to re-open this Director's Only Closed file. The only clear direction in the investigation was to find out who was transferred out from *O'Connell Hospital*. No real evidence was found. However, the rash of seemingly coincidental accidents and murders, combined with the discovery of a mole inside the Bureau, with Director Gamboa shot during what appears to be the assassination of Senator Anthony, the temporary stand-in Director Valdez added to the already muddy water.

"As a relative newcomer and outsider, it seems that so much has happened that, at first glance seems random. When you peel back the skin a little, these events may be related," offered Carla Jo.

"Like the hit on the Senator," offered Gibby. "The Senator was definitely a main player in the Closed Director's File. But the Senator was such a scumbag, maybe he had it coming from another direction. It was just his time? Maybe it was a hit initiated by someone else who was seeking retribution."

"And what about the obvious Korean connection?" asked Computer Forensic Specialist Walters. Who, until now, remained quiet absorbing the information. With raised eyebrows, she stared across the table at Gibby and Carla Jo, hoping they would offer some clarity.

After exchanging glances, Gibby spoke up first. "Well, yeah, there might be another reason for some of this chaos. None of us from Korea can go into any details, but it should be acknowledged that the North Koreans may be trying to exact some perceived retribution," said Gibby with a tilted head as if trying to pass this part of the conversation to Carla Jo.

Not missing a beat, Carla Jo continued. "So," with a slight pause, "the Senator deal and poisoning attempt on Director Valdez, they may not necessarily have anything to do with the Closed Director's file."

Chapin and Walters glanced at Moon Dog and Kyle in the satellite teleconference screen. Until then, their eyes were propped wide open. But now, for the first time during this meeting, neither man had anything to add. Sensing the others were looking to them for more information, Moon Dog and Kyle glanced away from the camera. Self-consciously, Kyle started rubbing his chin almost covering his mouth. It was obvious that no one from the Korean Agency was going to say a word.

Recognizing the situation for what it was, Walters broke the awkward silence. "Let's do this. If the ambulance was transporting Anderson, we need to take a hard look at the grandfather. Up until now, the only thing we've done is focus on the satellite images."

"Good idea," agreed Chapin. "Until now, we were just taking a second look at the Closed Director's file. Remember, it's been closed for the last three years."

Chapin scribbled some notes in her folder and looked up. "Moon Dog and Kyle. Don't worry about the satellite images surrounding the ambulance. Start looking at the grandfather. Walters, Gibby and Carla Jo, you three focus on the Senator angle," ordered Chapin.

"What about Diane Klein?" asked Walters. She knew more about Diane than the others. Stand-in Director Valdez instructed her to put Diane under a microscope. After some initial digging, Valdez told Walters that Gibby and Carla Jo would be doing some more in-depth research. As Walters stared across the table, she wondered what else they had uncovered. By the twinkle in Gibby's eyes, she got the feeling he knew a lot more than he was letting on. Still a relatively new comer to the San Jose Office, Walters bit her tongue. If anything, Walters was strategic and patient.

"It's kind of strange though, don't you think?" asked Gibby.

"What's that?" replied Chapin.

With a tilt of his head, "I mean all this going down and Diane just happens to be away in Germany," explained Gibby. Chapin seemed somewhat taken aback.

"I don't understand. What's the connection? Diane's on vacation that's all," Chapin explained.

"But Anderson's biological grandfather, he's from Germany," clarified Gibby. "A little too coincidental don't you think?"

Supervisor Chapin and Agent Gall exchanged concerned looks. Neither Chapin nor Agent Gall were aware of that piece of information.

*   *   *   *   *

Agent Walters waited outside the Director's Office. The Stand-in Director Valdez just arrived from an off-site meeting with Director Gamboa. There were new developments that she wanted Walters to investigate. As instructed, Walters brought her laptop. After checking the programs, making sure that all updates and security profiles were in place, she was ready to "look into" whatever the Director needed. After waiting a few minutes in the lobby, between the large double doors, she saw Gibby's head peek out.

"The Director is ready for you, Agent Walters."

As Walters entered the large office, only Carla Jo was inside. Given that Diane, a local agent was under investigation, she did not expect any San Jose agents to be in attendance. It made sense. It was a natural tendency for the San Jose team members to have a personal relationship with Diane. This potential bias was being avoided from the "get go". Walters sat in the only vacant chair.

"It's nice to see you again Agent Walters," smiled Director Valdez. "While investigating Diane Klein's situation, I have decided to exclude the other local team members to avoid any potential conflicts. Upon reviewing your personnel file, I see you only recently transferred here."

"That's correct. I transferred in from New Jersey," said Walters.

"Going forward, it's all by the book. Director Gamboa has had his input and we agree on how to proceed," clarified Nena.

"I totally agree," added Walters.

"Gibby. Share what you've uncovered," said Nena.

"Right boss. Walters, as you may know, my background is Naval Intelligence. I'm now, technically, acting in an independent contractor capacity, as is C.J., I mean Carla Jo," explained Gibby. "With the authority I've been given, and as a non-direct employee of the U.S. Government, I have a special latitude in terms of investigative resources at my disposal."

Walters nodded. She understood that Gibby and Carla Jo had greater flexibility and were held to a different standard. It made sense given his primary territory was in a foreign country. Seeing the pause, Carla Jo spoke up.

"Our investigation into Diane, so far, is based on circumstantial evidence. First, we were able to track down a huge withdrawal from her retirement account; about $500,000. We've also confirmed that it was converted to cash. This could explain the large sum of cash we uncovered in her oversized safety deposit box."

Walters realized that keeping such a large amount of cash was unusual. Even if Diane could explain where the money came from, the big question is for what purpose? Gibby, Carla Jo and Nena watched Walters as she processed this information.

"We also decided to use our satellite surveillance to double check her extra personal non-agency related activities," explained Nena. Tilting her head Nena signaled to Carla Jo urging her to show Walters the report.

"We back tracked her last year," continued Nena. She noticed Walters flinch at hearing this. "This is my team's specialty, satellite surveillance. It was a simple matter," clarified Nena.

Agent Walters read the multi-page sheet, a running table detailing dates, times, and locations. During the earlier months, about every thirty days, Diane visited a coffee shop. However, over the last few months, the frequency increased to daily visits. Carla Jo waited for Walters to look up from the report.

"The most peculiar thing are the locations. Why does she avoid going to a local shop? Why go all over San Jose, never visiting the same shop in any given six-month period? No one does that," said Carla Jo.

"It's so calculated that it cannot be accidental," offered Gibby.

"How many different locations?" Walters asked.

"82," replied Carla Jo.

"What do you need from me?" Walters asked.

"Can you isolate the Internet traffic and give us some idea as to what she was doing, who she was communicating with?" asked Nena.

"Do you want me to scan the computers in the coffee shops?"

"No. I'm thinking she's too smart to save her emails and passwords on a public computer. That would be a rookie move. And Diane is no rookie. But given we have an accurate window of time when she entered and exited each location, I was hoping you could work backwards. If we could locate and penetrate her email accounts, presumably secret ones, we could see what's been happening," explained Nena.

"I think I can do that Director," explained Walters. "But are you certain she isn't using her normal standard personal email account?"

"We checked," interjected Gibby. "To be honest, we were hoping she had some sort of other explanation, shrugged Gibby. "porn, sexual deviant behavior...nothing."

Nena stood and led the group to the adjacent conference room where Gibby and Carla Jo were already set up.

"We've got the IP addresses of all 82 shops. C.J. and I are pretty good with computers, but not like you. We can provide some assistance. Just let us know what to do," Gibby explained.

Taking a deep breath, Agent Walters set her laptop down and adjusted the ergonomically adjustable chair before sitting.

"It could take a while," said Agent Walters.

"Top priority. We need to know what she was doing Julie," smiled Director Valdez.

"Yes, ma'am Director. We'll find out," replied Walters.

"Call me Nena,"

*   *   *   *   *

"Diane, I want to introduce Winstead. He's been working with me for some time now. Until last week, he was in deep cover inside your San Francisco *FBI* office as a software and computer forensic analyst" explained Van Aelst.

In perfect German, Winstead spoke to Van Aelst. "Boss, should I really be talking to this American? She is still working for the Agency?" Winstead asked.

"She can be trusted. Without her assistance, my grandson would never have made it out of the U.S. She deserves to know the truth."

Diane, Curt, and Van Aelst were sitting around a dusty folding card table hidden away in an underground shelter. Winstead turned his gaze to Diane and looked her in the eye. In a dry, emotionless manner, Winstead explained what he knew.

"One of my ex-Bureau colleagues now works for the Agency. During my assignment there, I planted many re-routing devises inside her home and car. These tracking devices have yet to be detected. I've been able to use this technology to eavesdrop on their communication devices and computers."

Winstead glanced at Van Aelst before pulling out a single sheet of paper. He placed it in front of Diane. She was the only one at the table that had not read it. As she did, the others exchanged knowing glances. Finally, Diane raised her head.

"So, they know," she said. With slumped shoulders, Diane stared off into the distance.

"There's something else," explained Winstead.

With a perplexed expression, Van Aelst returned Winstead's gaze and raised his eyebrows.

"It just came in. I haven't had the opportunity to discuss it with you. Should I proceed, or wait until we've discussed it in private?" Winstead waited for Van Aelst's reply fearing he had overstepped his authority.

"By all means. Under the circumstances, we need to be as transparent as possible. It appears we are Diane's only remaining friends." With a sincere smile, Van Aelst raised his hand toward Winstead urging him to proceed.

"A directive order has been issued by the Substitute."

"Who is it?" asked Diane.

"Nena Valdez from the Korean location inside Camp Bonifas."

"I've heard of her," replied Diane. She felt conflicted still having a sense of loyalty to the Agency, she was unaccustomed being the outsider. She kept what specific information she knew about

Valdez to herself. Winstead continued. "It was easy for the Agency to connect Curt to Herr Van Aelst. He is Curt's only beneficiary."

After a brief pause, Winstead continued speaking. "It was inevitable. I'm uncertain why they're taking another look at you though boss. My guess is the shell game you used to hide Curt's ambulance transport has something to do with it. They must have figured it out."

"Most unfortunate," offered Van Aelst. "What else? What is the directive order?"

"They're contacting their Paris Office. They're sending someone to investigate the matter. They're sending the asset to Germany."

"Who are they sending?" asked Van Aelst.

"A ghost. It's a female," replied Winstead.

"What's a ghost?" asked Curt.

"A field agent with no identity. These agents had their true identities wiped clean. As far as anyone is concerned, these people don't exist," explained Diane.

"Are you a ghost boss?" asked Winstead, and immediately regretted asking the question. Especially, in front of Diane and Curt.

With a sincere smile, and with a twinkle in his piercing blue eyes, Van Aelst rubbed his hand across his opposite forearm dramatically touching his body.

"No, I'm quite real. No ghost," said Van Aelst. Thinking to himself, *but as "The Lone Wolf" I've sent countless unsuspecting agents into the afterlife.* The laughter from the others, interrupted Van Aelst's thoughts. He flashed a quick subtle smile around the table.

"Grandfather, they'll be looking for me," said Curt.

"We've created a solid paper trail. As far as the authorities are concerned, my grandson, Curt Anderson, who was adopted by a family in the U.S., died three years ago from burn complications; septic shock and cardiac arrest if my memory serves me. As a concerned last living relative, motivated by grief, I simply over-stepped and abused my authority by arranging your transportation here to assist in your medical recovery. In the end, my only consolation was being able to provide you a suitable resting place, in my family crypt."

After a pause, Van Aelst continued. "A coroner's report is filed with actual photos of you and your alleged 'corpse", along with your actual blood samples, x-rays, and medical exam notes-all authentic. Except for the little exaggeration relating to you being deceased, of course," smiled Van Aelst, as if pleased with himself.

"We even went to the trouble of placing a headstone next to my daughter's. It goes without saying we chose to cremate your remains. I assure you, it will all check out. This was our plan all along."

After a deep sigh, Van Aelst continued. "I had hoped none of this charade would be necessary. We are very thorough and always play it out to its natural conclusion, just in case."

"Why do you think they're coming?" Curt asked.

"My guess is to tie up any loose ends. And the fact that Diane happens to be in Germany when this all comes out is too coincidental," offered Winstead.

Looking off across the dark room, Diane closed her eyes and redirected her attention to the others. They're coming for me."

Van Aelst studied Diane's expression. "I think she's correct," replied Van Aelst. "But I have a plan."

*   *   *   *   *

Director Valdez sat next to Director Gamboa's bed. Still bed-ridden, the Agency moved him to a non-disclosed safe-house. A full medical staff, trained to handle VIP dignitaries and heads of state, were tasked with his recovery. They were accustomed to this type of duty. With Nena's four-man protective detail standing post outside of Gamboa's room, she got him up to speed on what was happening.

"Jose, it's not looking good for Diane. My satellite guys have documented unexplained visits to coffee houses all over the Bay Area. Although it took some effort back tracking her whereabouts, there is a definite pattern," explained Nena.

"What pattern?" Jose asked.

"Over the last three years, she would visit a different location, waiting at least six months before returning to the same location. It was too strategic, too systematic to be a coincidence," Nena clarified.

"You guys tracked all of her movements over the last three years?" Gamboa asked in disbelief.

"That's what we do. That's our specialty. We get 90 percent of our intel this way. In my neck of the woods, you can't just drive up in a surveillance van and park in front of the DPRK Ministry of Defense."

"Right," said Gamboa nodding.

"We've pulled some recent video surveillance from inside some of these locations. She's good at changing her appearance, but it's 100 percent her. We've analyzed the computers inside. Although some are new, for the older systems, we were able to document that a wipe program was used, probably from a flash drive. She definitely knows what she's doing. No surprise, right. The Agency trained her."

"It's my fault," explained Gamboa.

"What do you mean?"

"Her niece. In fact, it's related to the Director File you've been helping me on. The plane crash."

"What about the plane crash?" Nena asked.

"Her niece was a newbie assigned to my location. She was assigned as protective detail to this Curt Anderson guy."

"I just assumed you used IC's (Imaginary Citizens). Did you actually authorize the downing of a real commercial airliner?" asked Nena with a stunned expression.

Gamboa turned away. He couldn't look her in the eye. They both knew the immense power and authority they had. Each Director hated being scrutinized and second guessed.

"It was a bad situation. This Anderson guy infiltrated my building posing as one of the contracted photocopy techs and somehow copied an active file with a full knock-list. There were some bad cases being worked. You know what goes inside an active file before it is sanitized and filed away. It documented all the Agency practices. And this list was flush with U.S. Citizens. I sure as hell didn't want to be known as the Director that let the cat out of the bag on that one," explained Gamboa while shaking his head in obvious dismay reliving that decision.

"We had to dispose of him and his computer in a way that appeared 100 percent accidental. If he had plans of splashing the list and our activities to the media, we needed to be as far away from his death as possible," continued Gamboa.

Nena nodded as she listened. "But why put Diane's niece on that plane knowing you were going to drop it?"

Gamboa turned back to Nena. Without saying a word, Gamboa tilted his head. Through his body language, she caught his subtle gesture and understood.

"I got it," said Nena. "The niece. She wasn't on the plane, was she?" Not waiting for a reply, Nena continued. "You took the opportunity to turn her into a ghost, right?"

Gamboa raised his eyes. After a brief pause, he nodded. "We made two in fact. Her and another male agent."

Nena nodded and thought it through before continuing. "So, Diane didn't know? She has no clue that her niece is still alive?"

"None," replied Gamboa. "I struggled with letting her know. But you know how this goes Nena. To protect the asset, everyone, no exceptions, must assume the agent died." After a pause, he continued. "I almost told her anyway. She was having such a difficult time. It was her only surviving relative. I really thought she would have figured it out. She was just too close to it all. Her emotions...she lost it. But this?"

"Would she really flip, and help our enemies?" Gamboa said as he turned back to face Nena.

"Well, from her chair, you killed her only surviving family member. That's text book in terms of creating an enemy, right?"

"I should have told her," countered Gamboa.

"Where's the niece now?" asked Nena.

"Where else? Paris."

*   *   *   *   *

Training Supervisor Marie Sinor read the Directive order. It was the worst nightmare for a covert operative. She read the encrypted message twice, before closing the folder. She heard of similar things happening before. But this was the first time she was involved. From her 17th floor view, Marie glanced out her window across the beautiful skyline. The knock on her door broke her from her trance.

"Yes, come in," said Sinor.

In walked the Agency's newest covert field agent Roberta Finchum. Her cosmetic surgery, with only slight changes to her eyes, cheeks, and chin, combined with her new hair color and style made her unrecognizable to her former self.

"You asked for me?"

"Yes, Roberta. Please sit down."

Roberta caught the subtle change in Marie's body language and was convinced she was avoiding eye-contact.

"Is everything okay? Is something wrong?" Roberta asked.

"There's no easy way to put this," replied Marie. Raising her eyes, Marie locked onto Roberta's eyes. "The Agency has credible evidence to suggest that your Aunt, Diane Klein is a double agent."

"What? Impossible. She lives for the Agency."

After a brief awkward pause, Marie continued. "That was before your death." As Roberta processed the information, Marie slid a thick folder in front of Roberta. She opened it and read the cover memo. It was signed off by Director Valdez and Director Gamboa. Marie waited for Roberta to finish reading and close the file.

Roberta looked up. "This is bullshit!"

"I know. But you know the Agency. You know there's no choice."

"First, I find it difficult to imagine any of this about my aunt is true. Even if it is, what does it have to do with me? Why involve me with this matter?" argued Roberta.

"You're her only living relative. We need to know exactly what happened. She'll talk to you," explained Marie.

"She won't even recognize me...now."

"Convince her. You'll know things about each other that no one else does. You'll be able to make her understand and believe who you are."

Roberta sat motionless. She had learned a lot over the last three years. She knew the Agency. She saw how it operated and knew how it tried to maximize every opportunity. She knew the Agency never missed a chance to use one set of circumstances to uncover and prove some other unrelated set of facts.

"There's something else, right?" asked Roberta. "There's another reason the Agency wants me to do it."

Marie Sinor watched Roberta work everything out in her own mind. She could tell that Roberta already knew the answer. Marie did not need to answer. She listened as Roberta spoke as if having a conversation to herself.

"The Agency wants to know if they can trust me. My aunt's fate is sealed. The Agency just needs to know if it can trust me, given these new set of circumstances."

Glancing back at Marie, Roberta locked onto her eyes. In a calm calculating voice, Roberta said "After I find out what happened, why my aunt did what she did, they want me to eliminate her."

Training Supervisor Sinor slid the thick folder across the desk. "Read the folder. It will help you do what you need to do. You're heading to Berlin tonight."

"What's in Germany?" Roberta asked.

"Your Aunt. She's on leave; on vacation watching a women's Professional Golf Tournament.

"The Solheim Cup?"

"That's it," replied Marie as she slid another piece of paper across the desk.

"Here's her hotel information. You have three days."

14

Roberta stood up to stretch her back. She was stiff from sitting at her kitchen table for hours reading through the thick folder. It detailed everything the Agency knew. For several hours, Roberta struggled with the possibility that her Aunt Diane was a double agent. She racked her brain and concluded *"what other explanation could there be?"* The cash, the strategic visits to 82 different coffee shops over the last 3 years, with increased frequencies over the last few months that reached daily apparent random visits off the long-beaten path, as well as the email account. The most damaging evidence was the satellite images.

It took the Agency's Computer Forensics Team, untold hours of non-stop investigating to locate and hack inside. Although two days of emails were found, the most telling fact was that the account was accessed 162 times, yet no emails were ever sent or received. Half of the access points all came from inside Germany. The other from the Western United States. Everyone knew what it meant. Diane was using an old spy technique where drafted messages were accessed, read, edited, and deleted with nothing ever being sent. This maneuver prevented any communications trail.

It had not gone unnoticed that, since her vacation to Europe, the email account remained inactive and unused. Not a single access was found from anywhere. The only explanation was whomever Diane was exchanging daily communications with was no longer necessary. Why? The only logical reason- she was speaking with them in person, face-to-face.

The thing preventing Roberta from feeling remorse were the Director's comments. He believed that Diane had cracked. He was convinced that she believed the Agency, despite dedicating her entire career, her entire life's work inside the Agency, had acted with total disregard and chose to murder her niece.

Turning away from the folder, Roberta shook her head. She thought back, recounting the number of times she considered reaching out to her aunt. Roberta seemed to forget the fact that Diane was still human. How could she have not understood? With a lifetime inside the Agency, how could her aunt have missed the obvious conclusion; that she was turned into a ghost agent?

Being young, Roberta never appreciated the pain and anguish a person felt from losing a younger family member. The older generation holds onto that mental image, a deep-seated belief that each family member will pass away in an orderly fashion. The hope that the younger generation will out-live the older ones, however unrealistic, increased the distress and shock when things happen out of sequence, in an unorderly unpredictable manner. With the sudden loss of her niece, the realization that she was the sole living member of her family pushed Diane into a place she was ill prepared to address. Regardless of her years of experience, her reality was altered to the point that her normal thought processes were no longer at her disposal. The years of experience, the finely tuned intuition, all the skills she acquired as an Agency member, were inaccessible.

Roberta considered how Diane may have reacted had her alleged passing occurred through an honorable death; perhaps killed on assignment, or during an international mission as opposed to baby-sitting some insignificant spy. If that were the case, maybe Diane would have had a different reaction. But to lose her niece as an after-thought, seen as a person unworthy of saving, just an inconsequential nothing sent on a nothing detail while performing a useless mission was a total waste. The sole purpose was to protect the existence of a knock list against U.S. citizens who were performing forbidden tasks. It all seemed like a cruel joke. In the big scope of things, to die for such a cause was the waste of a valuable resource.

Roberta closed the thick folder. The Agency wanted to know all the details surrounding Diane's involvement in the transportation of Curt Anderson. The last satellite images in the file included enlarged images of a person that looked very much like her aunt standing outside each ambulance location. The figure shown in the pictures, although dressed in different attire, wearing a different hair style, donning a different style of glasses, in each case looked like Diane. The images from San Jose, Las Vegs, Colorado, Missouri and Pennsylvania matched up perfectly with the dates of the transportation for another John Doe leaving another medical facility that just so happened to be one of the regions prominent burn centers.

The Agency went so far as to match those dates with the days Diane Klein had the opportunity to be away from the office weekends and holidays without requiring any formal requests for time off. The Agency even provided images of Diane leaving her home and taking convoluted random routes to the airport. It was like clockwork. The same sequence of events took place during each ambulance transportation date. Although everything was circumstantial, when combined in their totality, there was no other logical explanation. Diane was involved somehow and some way.

Regardless whether Roberta could get her aunt to talk, Diane's fate was sealed. These were the cards that were dealt. To prove her loyalty, Roberta was to be the trigger guy. Under the circumstances, Roberta, aka Gina from her long-forgotten past-life, knew she would have to re-prove herself going forward. To advance her career and climb the Agency ladder, her relationship to Diane made the likelihood of further advancement that much more difficult. To make matters worse, the Agency wanted physical proof of the kill. With a deep sigh, Roberta stared at the test tube and syringe lying next to the folder.

*　　*　　*　　*　　*

Kyle and Moon Dog were elated to learn they no longer needed to track down the ambulance. Since arriving to the Mediterranean Sea, they found themselves stuck inside the secure Agency hanger, yet to see any of Europe. Their new orders instructed them to canvass Germany and find out what they could about Curt's grandfather. It was now more than six-months since Kyle's eye-orbit injury back in

Korea. He was now free to fly. Their first stop was to the Agency International Training Center in Paris, France.

"Gentlemen," smiled Training Supervisor Marie Sinor. This location performed low level cases, intended on giving the newest deep cover agents an opportunity to hone their skills before being subjected to the unsupervised realities of covert operations. "How may I be of service?" Sinor asked. Although she was not a Director, she was one of the highest-ranking Agency members in Paris and maintained supreme authority.

"Morning ma'am," replied Moon Dog while Kyle nodded in respect.

"Have a seat. I received the message this morning from Director Valdez. I was expecting you both. I understand you boys need some local 'old school' intel on a," Sinor paused as she adjusted her prescription glasses and read the file. "...a Mr. Cornelius Van Aelst. Born nine November, on or about 1927."

"That's correct," replied Kyle.

Sinor glanced up and tilted her head, as if something clicked into place. She had not made the connection until just then.

"Hey, are you boys from our Korea location?"

"That's correct, ma'am," answered Moon Dog.

"Well, I'll be. That was some piece of work you guys pulled off," said Sinor flashing a big smile. It wasn't everyday one of their own pulled something off in front of the entire world and got away with it.

Suppressing their smiles, Moon Dog, like anyone lucky enough to participate in such a big mission, wanted to elaborate and go into details. But that mission was beyond Top Secret. Grudgingly, he avoided offering any specifics. "We're not at liberty to discuss any of our past operations ma'am. My apologies. I'm sure you understand."

She understood. Nodding, she held a long satisfying smile before continuing. "Absolutely. I know the drill. Off the record, good job!"

Turning her attention back to the folder, she pulled out the last known photograph and slid it in front of Moon Dog and Kyle.

"The last color picture we have came from his passport." From inside the folder, Sinor pulled out two copied abbreviated dossiers. "You'll need to shred the documents before returning to your ship. Inside, there's also a flash drive. That's all we have on him. I've put our Berlin Office on alert. They're expecting your arrival and are working up more current information. They'll also have access to old paper information and put you in contact with some retirees."

"Retirees?" interrupted Kyle. Like most bureaucracies, the current new blood considered the past personnel as relics. This prejudice was held even more so inside the Agency. The fact that past covert operatives worked during World War II and through the Cold War days was of no consequence. This prejudice toward the retirees left a current workforce that lacked the real world "old school" skills. In comparison, this supposed lack of skills left a nasty taste in the current workforces' mouths. It was lost upon them that the retirees held more secrets and had real world experience during an era where literal licenses to kill were issued. In contrast, most of the current agents believed that things had changed too much thereby rendering the retirees obsolete. In fact, many of the new agents concealed a sense of jealousy and garnered a slight inferiority complex.

The new agents were all about technology. The new world of global espionage focused on the tools and data making them dependent on computers and satellites, while the retirees cut their teeth during the renaissance period of international espionage, a time like no other.

"I know what you're thinking, but those old-school guys, they march to a different drummer. Even our guys," clarified Sinor.

"Why didn't they send us directly to Berlin?" asked Moon Dog.

"Whenever we send people there, we need to get them up to speed. Although technically the countries were reunited, many things, especially intelligence issues, remain separated. The East still struggles feeling excluded from the modern advantages available to the West Germans. Hell, even still, they use different colored streetlamps to light up their night skies. The prior communist based companies found it difficult to compete with their western counterparts. Many East Germany companies went bankrupt."

"Is it mostly an economic issue?" asked Kyle.

"Even politically, East Germany tends to be less user friendly toward foreigners. The stunted financial prosperity has left the easterners disillusioned by the benefits of capitalism. Also, the decades of literal physical separation into east and west, has created natural camps within their intelligence agency."

"I thought the Federal Intelligence Services was Germany's counterpart to our Agency," interjected Moon Dog.

"The Germans call it Bundesnachrichtendienst, we call it the BND for short," clarified Sinor. "They have two headquarters, Pullach, which is like Munich. And then, there's Berlin. Plus, we still have issues with Hamburg where they allegedly housed the 9/11 attackers. All that just re-opened old wounds about the supposed bad intel about Iraq's WMD's (Weapons of Mass Destruction)."

"The German Agent Curveball?" asked Moon Dog.

Sinor simply raised her eyebrows. "No comment. With all the things that happened during the Cold War...some habits die hard." Sinor explained.

"When East Germany collapsed, where did all the Stasi Agents go?" asked Kyle.

Shaking her head, she leaned forward. "Gentlemen, where do 85,000 Stasi officers go?" After a brief pause, she continued. "Hell, the *New York Times* Magazine did an article about that very issue. The title said it all, 'Where Have all the Spies Gone?' We've only been able to verify around 10,000 that found employment in the unified Germany."

"Damn, sounds a little like where we come from," said Kyle in an elevated voice of disbelief.

"I had no idea," countered Moon Dog. "So, is there a literal intelligence separation today?"

"We're certain that many agents are still loyal to their Soviet influences. That intelligence group was a highly disciplined covert network of operatives. You just need to remember where you are."

"Any advice?" Kyle asked.

Sinor glanced away. She needed to give it some thought before responding. "Their agents tend to be bald."

"Hair style preference? Like the U.S. Marines and their crew cuts?" asked Moon Dog as he glanced at Kyle's fashionable close-cropped hair cut.

"No, not a preference. Literally, bald. Those poor KGB sponsors train their agents to use cobalt radiation to crack code pads. This technique causes permanent hair loss," Sinor explained.

"Serious?" asked Kyle.

"Yes. Oh, and look for old guys," she added.

Kyle and Moon Dog looked at each other. Sinor noticed their confused expressions. "Remember gentlemen, a lot of those guys have connections to the original Nazi Party. That goes back decades."

In almost a whisper, Kyle leaned toward Moon Dog. "I wonder if they're good with sign language."

Hearing his comment, Moon Dog smiled. Suppressing grins, they nodded in agreement. Kyle and Moon Dog had the distinct impression that they may have already met some of these guys.

* * * * *

Roberta looked out the window of her business class seat. As the bullet train cut across the south corner of Belgium heading into Germany, she was lost in her thoughts. She needed the ten hours it took to travel from Paris to Berlin to think things through. The file Supervisor Sinor provided gave Roberta everything she needed. Having her location was going to be like shooting fish in a barrel. There was no challenge.

The Agency assumed that Diane had no clue she was being targeted. They had photos of her entering the hotel. The Agency had even secured a copy of her passkey. Roberta could not understand how her Aunt's life had come to this.

For the last three years, the Agency had literally transformed her from Gina to Roberta. The surgeries, hair style and color changes, were not the only changes. The selection process continued well past her formal acceptance into the program. Going forward, everything was a test. Like a fighter pilot, every flight was graded. There was no letting up. She was well beyond the times she was forced to use the make-up, wigs, and glasses trying to create characteristics distracting witnesses from focusing on her face. She proved under real life situations that she had what it took to leave a murder scene without attracting the attention of others.

Roberta remembered the mundane tasks designed to bore the trainees, and then to challenge them unexpectedly requiring them to focus on some discreet task while avoiding detection. For those agents that passed, they received more advanced training; driving different types of vehicles learning to safely push another car off the roadway while traveling 80 kph.

Those trainees that excelled were taught to use fiber optics to see around corners, under doorways, and through vents. Each candidate was responsible for preparing, hiding, and stocking their stowaway packs with cash, false papers, and passports. They learned early on that using a cell phone and credit card was a sure way of being discovered. Roberta understood the preferred method of escaping from an area was to steal a car. And the best place to do that was from a Valet parking area. Another essential fact was to never make travel reservations. It created an easy-to-follow paper trail.

Her skills were honed subject to constant scrutiny at every level, during every task. Her training culminated in the Fusion Center; the location where all communication, data, and satellite surveillance data converged. During a live mission, all available intelligence funneled through there to be evaluated and disbursed. As an observer, learning from the mistakes of others advanced their learning curves.

With a deep sigh, Roberta's shoulders sagged. The weight of responsibility was a heavy burden. In her mind, she made the transition from a normal agent to a ghost. She had pushed out of her mind the life she once led. Gina was a person she left behind. That person belonged to another place, another world.

Now, that charade was interrupted. Her new mission required her to deal with her past. Asked to pull the strings of a person whom she no longer held an attachment. Coming from this new point of view, with her new identity as Roberta Finchum, she felt betrayed by a past that no longer existed. She was being judged for the actions of a person she no longer associated as her own flesh and blood. Roberta found herself conflicted for not having empathy

419

for her Aunt. If she were honest with herself, she had no remorse about her unique task to eliminate her. On the contrary, she felt annoyed as if she were being asked to deal with a nuisance before she could get back to her real task at hand.

Roberta contemplated the situation. Even if she felt different, what could she do? If she refused, or was incapable of taking out Diane, likely that would mark the end of her career as a covert operative. It was just another test.

Roberta knew this is how covert operatives, trainees, and to some degree, Directors, think. Their only loyalty was to the Agency. It was understood that human feelings could get in the way. But feelings belonged to civilians, not covert operatives, not to an asset.

Roberta wondered how many other agents were asked to face such a challenge. Regardless, it was the cards she was dealt. Succeeding on this test was critical, a necessary stepping stone in her Agency journey. Failure would mark the end of a short career. It may very well be unfair, a test that only she would have to face, graded by others unworthy to criticize as they themselves had not faced such a challenge. She would have to accept a grade that would follow her forever. Fairness had nothing to do with it. Eventually, everyone lucky enough to live a long life, learned that life was not about being fair or predictable. One could argue that this test was the best way for anyone concerned, even Roberta, to determine if she really had the right stuff.

The overhead announcement echoed throughout the train's broadcasting system. The announcer's monotone voice announced the next stop which broke her from her thoughts. Roberta glanced up at the digital clock above the passageway connection between the train sections. She had five more hours before she reached Berlin.

*   *   *   *   *

Kyle stared out through a small conference room window looking for Moon Dog. It was his first visit to another Agency Office. Unlike his Korean station, which was hidden inside a military base along the DMZ, the Berlin Office sat in the center of the city. The office was tucked away inside a 24-story building that towered over the modern metropolis shared by other businesses. Here, the personnel wore dark suits and designer shoes. A stark difference from the military fatigues and *Kevlar* vests that Kyle was accustomed to.

From the office personnel's' body language, the office was divided into two camps: general analysts and support staff. Beyond that, Kyle detected something deeper than just a division based on job classifications.

Seeing Moon Dog walking through the cubicles, Kyle met him at the door.

"Man, oh man, this place is a piece of work," whispered Moon Dog as he glanced about making certain that the door was closed before continuing. Grabbing Kyle by the arm, he angled them toward the outer window overlooking the Berlin cityscape below. "This place would be one scary place to work."

"What do you mean?" asked Kyle.

"It's like the Cold War never ended. There are two distinct groups; East and West," clarified Moon Dog.

"Still? For real?"

"Every time I asked a question, I received a separate response from each division. Many times, their responses were pretty much the same answer anyway. It was like each Supervisor had to make sure that each side had a say. I could tell that they've been doing it this way for so long, neither of them notices anything strange about it. It took twice as long as it should have to get the information," explained Moon Dog in a pained frustrated expression.

"So, what's our next move?" Kyle asked.

"After dinner, a field agent will drop by our hotel. They've been working up information on Curt's grandfather."

"Why not just punch it up on the computer?"

"Van Aelst goes way back. Nothing in their data base. But get this."

Kyle leaned forward while Moon Dog glanced over his shoulder. Certain no one was approaching the conference room, Moon Dog leaned in toward Kyle and whispered in his ear.

"The grandfather is an ex-Stasi."

"No shit?"

"Straight up. It gets even more weird."

"What's that?"

"Only the Western Division Supervisor said anything about it," explained Moon Dog. "He waited for the Eastern counter-part to leave before he dropped that little piece of information. And when the Eastern guy reappeared, the Western Supervisor clammed up like nothing was being said."

"Weird," relied Kyle.

After glancing back through the thick plate glass window, Moon Dog repositioned himself in front of the exterior window. Kyle stood next to him and stared out admiring the view. The lights began to come on as the sun slid down past the horizon. They stared down at the large U-shaped building that seemed more suited to mid-1800 architecture than a modern 21st century building.

A little further east, there was another tall boxy concrete multi-story structure, with straight rigid lines, reminiscent of a Stalinist architecture. The frieze depicted socialistic propaganda from a communist Utopia, showing images of workers' eyes raised to the flying dove of freedom.

"It's just like Camp Bonifas except here it's East versus West instead of North versus South," added Kyle.

"It's always us and them."

With their hands stuffed in their front pockets, Kyle and Moon Dog stared out over the city wondering what to expect later that night.

*   *   *   *   *

Dinner was uneventful. They ate at the hotel restaurant and ordered typical American meals: steak and potatoes. For some reason, it tasted bland lacking spices and other flavors. They were on their third cup of coffee before Moon Dog decided no one was coming. They paid the check and headed back to their adjoining rooms to wait.

As they turned the hallway corner, they saw a man waiting outside their door. Moon Dog approached the man. "May we help you?"

A thin man, in his early 30's, looked up. With a tight-lipped smile, he spoke.

"Lt. Elliott? Lt. Benjamin?" the man asked.

"Yes," replied Kyle.

"I was sent by a colleague to give you some information."

Kyle reached inside his pocket to extract his room key. "We didn't think you were gonna make it." Just as Kyle extracted the key from the card reader, the man spoke.

"We should go somewhere else," the man offered. It was the expression on his face that got their attention. It was clear that he had no intention of entering the room.

"Did you have a place in mind?" asked Moon Dog.

Without hesitating, the man replied, "Follow me."

The man led them to the hallway and took the stairs. As they approached the parking garage below, the man looked back and tilted his head toward the far corner of the building toward the surface street. They followed him to a half wall separating the walkway from the busy street. After glancing about several times, making certain no one was nearby, he stopped and light a cigarette.

After a brief pause, the man reached inside his jacket. For a split second, Moon Dog considered the possibility of danger. With wide eyes and an elevated pulse, Moon Dog was relieved to see the man extract a thin folder. As he handed the folder to Moon Dog, he glanced around. In a nervous voice, he spoke.

"Be careful. The man you are looking into is still very powerful."

The cold blank stare was unnerving. Moon Dog and Kyle sensed that the man felt vulnerable, reluctant to be involved. Not waiting for a response, the man turned and walked away. Just before he ducked into the underground parking structure, he whispered back to them. "Don't follow me. Go back to your room." With a quick stutter-step, he added, "your room is most certainly bugged," before he disappeared.

Kyle and Moon Dog watched the man's shadow, cast from the parking lights inside as it disappeared around the corner. For a moment, they did not move. Neither had appreciated the seriousness of their predicament. For the first time, they felt exposed and vulnerable. Moon Dog slid the folder inside his jacket. After exchanging glances with Kyle, he released a deep sigh.

"Let's catch a cab and look at the folder somewhere else."

"Good idea," replied Kyle.

Retracing their way up the stairway, they went back through the lobby and then out into the street. They walked past the Valet and waived down a cab that was passing in the street. Moon Dog instructed the driver to take them to a local bar. As soon as they arrived, they walked to the opposite side of the street and caught another cab. This time, Moon Dog instructed the driver to take them to the train station.

As they walked across the train station, Kyle broke the silence. "What are we doing?"

"Making sure we're not being followed."

Nodding, Kyle replied in a sarcastic manner, "Real cloak and dagger stuff, huh?"

With a slight smile, Kyle waited for a response. With a knowing expression, Moon Dog pointed across the boulevard as he continued walking. Kyle wondered what he was pointing at. He waited until Moon Dog purchased the train tickets heading back to the hotel before asking.

"So, what about the building?"

Moon Dog smiled back. "That's the old Stasi Headquarters," Kyle glanced back over his shoulder.

"Really?"

"Yup. They turned it into a museum."

After a brief wait on the platform, their train arrived. After glancing about, certain they were not followed, they entered the train and selected a pair of isolated seats near the exit. From that location, Moon Dog felt comfortable. After the train doors closed and the train began moving, Moon Dog removed the folder from his jacket and began reading. It only took a few moments before he handed it over to Kyle.

Not worrying to read it, Kyle asked, "What does it say?"

"Van Aelst is more than just an ex-Stasi agent. He was part of Hitler's Nazi youth program. As a teenager, he worked on the underground trains used to evacuate the VIP's."

"I've never heard anything about that before," said Kyle.

"Most people don't. It's not common knowledge. The popular disinformation of the time still dominates the narrative and how the war ended for Germany," elaborated Moon Dog.

"So, he didn't shoot himself in the underground bunker with his girlfriend?"

"Think about it. He had everything so well planned out, so systematic. Would he really have waited for the Russians to enter Berlin and choose to hide in a bunker knowing well in advance that there would be no escape? And doesn't it seem too convenient that his remains were burned?"

The train slowed to a stop. Kyle handed the file back to Moon Dog who in turn slid it back inside his jacket.

"We need to speak to the Director about this. It's getting way over my paygrade," said Moon Dog.

*   *   *   *   *

Director Valdez looked across the table at Gibby and Carla Jo. As with most covert cases, once the Agency committed its unlimited resources into uncovering the truth, it usually identified most of the moving pieces.

"So Gibby and C.J., what do your analytical minds think about this case? What happened?" asked Nena.

After exchanging a quick glance, Gibby spoke first. "Well boss, there is no doubt that Van Aelst had a hand in transporting the John Doe to Europe. Kyle and Moon Dog reported back from their little field trip to Berlin. Given Curt's, or the John Doe's condition, we thought it only made sense that he would turn up in a burn center.

Carla Jo nodded in agreement. "Berlin's Trauma hospital has been pioneering a new technique of sprayed on skin," Carla Jo added.

"Really?" asked Nena in disbelief leaning forward to listen to the explanation.

"They culture the patient's skin a few days and then spray it onto the wounded area. Apparently, the skin responds to the cells and heals with much less scarring," explained Carla Jo.

"So, Kyle and Moon Dog did some nosing around the burn center. C.J. helped secure some computer information," Gibby interjected. "And B-I-N-G-O. There's another John Doe matching Anderson's profile. In fact, he showed up eight days after we lost the ambulance transfer in the Lincoln Tunnel shell game."

"What about Van Aelst's last known address?" asked Nena.

Carla Jo pressed the enter key on her lap top. An image of a multi-story rectangle concrete structure popped up on the monitor. It looked more like a government building than an apartment.

"He lived there?" asked Nena.

"I doubt it. They're just screwing with us."

"How so?"

"Well boss, the building is the Stasi's Berlin Office structure," explained Carla Jo.

"What does our local resources say?"

"That's just it. Germany's a different place. It's like the Cold War never ended," said Gibby.

"I know that feeling," replied Nena. Since they worked together through the Korean tunnel issue, nothing else needed to be said.

"Right," smiled Gibby. "But in Berlin, it's like no one wants to give up too much information about Van Aelst. For a supposed ex-Stasi, he sure carries some serious weight."

"The man's a living legend," Carla Jo added. She slid Van Aelst's updated bio sheet to Nena. While Nena read through the report, Carla Jo continued.

"Moon Dog and Kyle have a meeting with a contact inside the burn center. He's gonna spend some Euros to see what they know about the John Doe."

Looking up from the report, Nena shook her head in disbelief. "This Van Aelst gentlemen is a serious player," Nena said. Her tone was that of respect. "This retiree has still got it."

Handing the report back to Carla Jo, Nena added, "The man was an Olympian at the 1952 games in Oslo."

Gibby reached across the table. "What was his event?" asked Gibby.

"The Biathlon. Long distance skiing combined with rifle shooting," confirmed Carla Jo.

Nena smiled. Without speaking it was obvious that she held Van Aelst in high regard. Mutual respect amongst fellow spooks. The fact of the matter, the Cold War ended decades before. Technically Germany was now one of the Unites States' closest allies outside of the European Union.

"Let's keep looking down the rabbit hole and see where it takes us. We still have no confirmation that our John Doe was Curt Anderson or not," explained Nena.

"One thing for certain. Whoever made all the John Doe records and hospital surveillance tapes disappear has a sophisticated network," added Carla Jo. "Assets located throughout the entire U.S."

"If our John Doe wasn't Curt Anderson, he was certainly affiliated," said Gibby.

"What about Diane Klein?" asked Carla Jo.

Nena paused before looking up. "That call has already been made. The National Director signed off on it."

Gibby and Carla Jo exchanged knowing looks.

"You guys know the drill. In our line of business, the perception of being untrustworthy becomes reality. A reality that, under her set of circumstances, can only lead to one outcome."

"We need to focus on securing the Bona Fides (proof of a person's identity). This issue all stems from a reopened Director's Only file. Let's not lose sight of that."

With a quick nod, Nena stood and left the conference room. As she pushed through the door, she let out a deep sigh of frustration.

It was an aspect of her job that she disliked the most. Only Director Gamboa, Training Supervisor Sinor and herself knew who the trigger man was going to be. Or in this case, the trigger woman. Nena walked down the hall shaking her head. Thinking that "a person like Diane, with all of her life's service to the Agency, deserved to go out better." But rules are rules. Diane knew the game better than most. Bottom line, Diane's actions proved she could no longer be trusted. Her emotions, although misplaced and inaccurate, got the best of her. All for nothing. What a waste. Her niece was not even dead. She was a ghost. And now, the Agency needed to make Diane disappear for good.

*   *   *   *   *

"Herr Van Aelst?" one of the retirees said as he stood at attention in front of an oversized wooden table propped up next to the underground building in the labyrinth beneath Berlin. The man held his hat in his hand tilting his head down avoiding eye contact with Van Aelst. Glancing up from the report, Van Aelst flashed a confident smile. The light from a battery-operated lantern reflected off his piercing blue eyes.

"Yes," smiled Van Aelst looking up at the gentlemen. "How is your family?"

"Fine Herr Van Aelst. Thank you for asking," replied the old man. His face lit up happy that Van Aelst remembered him.

"What can I help you with? Did you have a question?"

The old man seemed uncomfortable as if he was about to broach an awkward situation, reluctant to discuss the matter in front of Diane. Not wanting to offend Diane, the old man nodded pointing his chin in her direction. She caught his meaning.

"I'm sorry. Of course, let me give you two some privacy. My apologies," said Diane. As she stood, Van Aelst placed his hand over hers. He knew she felt vulnerable having no one else to trust.

Van Aelst smiled. "She's with us now. It's okay to speak in her presence."

Tilting his head, as if asking for additional confirmation, feeling the need for more reassurances, the old man asked one more time.

"Are you sure? It's about your grandson," said the old man almost apologizing for doubting the wisdom in sharing information in front of Diane.

"It's fine. Please, continue. Tell me what you have," instructed Van Aelst using a firm yet understanding authoritative voice.

"Two Americans are attempting to access his medical records from the Trauma Hospital in Berlin."

Van Aelst nodded. "Thank you for letting me know."

The old man paused and extended a slight bow while backing away several steps before turning and walking out heading back underground. Diane watched the old man leave before glancing back toward Van Aelst. Her face held a firm concerned expression while Van Aelst padded his hand on her wrist.

"It's fine. I already knew," said Van Aelst. He tapped the report with his index finger. "They received the information from one of my people. We planned on this eventuality years ago. Everything is in place. There's nothing to worry about." He still detected concern on Diane's face. "We'd hoped that the Americans would have left it alone. But in our line of business, it's best to plan for the worst-case scenario, yes?"

Diane nodded in a lethargic slow manner, like a person resigned to her fate. What choice did she have? She was in no position to protest and had no resources that would alter the situation.

"Besides," continued Van Aelst. "We have more important matters to deal with." Diane looked up.

"Your Agency, they're coming for you," Van Aelst explained in a calm clear voice. "She's already been dispatched and is enroute now."

Diane averted his eyes. After a pause, she looked back into his piercing blue eyes. "How do you know everything? It seems like you're always one step ahead of everybody," said Diane in an exasperated yet grateful tone.

Almost chuckling, Van Aelst turned away and smiled staring at the long dark corridor that ran away from the main underground train track. "Two traits are needed for people, like me, and those fortunate enough to live long enough. You must be patient and thorough. From what we've seen, all the atrocities, a single mistake is all it takes."

Without speaking, they remained seated at the dusty table. The dark underground railway beyond remained abandoned and unused. The linking stations along the tracks continued to decay from their lack of maintenance and attention. There were no passing cars, buses, or pedestrians. There were no normal outdoor sounds; birds chirping, the roar of passing jets, the blaring horns from frustrated drivers stuck in traffic, no cell phones ringing, or conversations being exchanged. But mixed in with this silence was a subtle unique background noise created from water seepage dripping through the cave openings splashing into accumulated pools.

*   *   *   *   *

Parked outside the Berlin Trauma Center, Kyle and Moon Dog waited inside a van provided by their German counterparts. For this part of the mission, they used other skill-sets. Right on cue, they saw two familiar figures walking along the otherwise deserted sidewalks. With a distinct bounce in his step, and the flowing shoulder-length hair, the man flung his head side to side to keep his hair out of his eyes.

As they approached the van, the man flashed his unmistakable trademark politician's ear-to-ear smile. Kyle and Moon Dog were grateful that he was not waving. From behind his dark sunglasses, the lines around his eyes crinkled. Gibby was always on the verge of laughter. He grabbed the van's back door handle and slung it open. After helping Carla Jo inside, he slammed the door shut behind him.

"Gentlemen!" said Gibby. Holding up both of his arms out to his sides and a slight bow, as if he was waiting for applause.

"Hey Gibby. Hey Carla Jo," replied Kyle.

"We meet again," smiled Carla Jo. She glanced around and surveyed the van. "Where'd you get the wheels?"

"Our Berlin counter-parts were kind enough to help us out," explained Moon Dog.

Wasting no time, Gibby waved Kyle and Moon Dog into the back section of the van. "We've already staked out the Trauma Center's communication cables." Gibby glanced around the interior of the van. "Did you sweep the van?"

"It's clear. We checked it out before driving over," added Moon Dog.

Carla Jo and Gibby exchanged concerned looks. Carla Jo returned Moon Dog's gaze. "Did you use their equipment?" she asked.

Recognizing his mistake, Moon Dog nodded with less enthusiasm than before. "Yes, we did," Moon Dog replied.

Gibby reached into his jacket and removed a small electronic device designed to interfere with all known frequencies. If the van was bugged, both audio and video transmissions were rendered useless. All four of them stared down at the LED light emitting a constant green light.

Gibby extracted one of his burn cell phones. After turning them on, he tried to call his other burn phone. No connection was made. It was as if all communications to and from the wireless devices were cancelled out. After turning the phones off, Gibby opened the burn phones, removed the batteries, and tossed everything on the carpeted floor before crushing them with the heel of his boot.

"We're good to go now," Gibby said smiling at the others.

"So, what's the plan?" asked Carla Jo.

"Kyle and I were hoping one of you two could hack the Trauma Center's communication lines. We'd really like to get a look at the days following the ambulance transport video from the Lincoln Tunnel," explained Moon Dog.

"We're guessing that once we lost the trail, if this John Doe is Anderson, and from what we've learned about his biological grandfather, if this is our guy, he'd bring him to Germany," added Kyle.

Carla Jo and Gibby nodded in agreement. It made sense.

"I can splice into their computers, with C.J.'s help, we should be able to get a look at their surveillance video archives. That's assuming they've been backing them up?" said Gibby.

"We're in Germany. They backed them up," said Moon Dog. "I'd bet a dollar to a donut."

"What about the medical records?" asked Carla Jo.

"We're hoping you guys could worm around their computers for our John Doe too. If not," explained Kyle, "we've made other arrangements to get us inside."

"The main medical records personnel are about to end their normal day. Unlike the rest of the hospital, this part runs a normal nine-to-five schedule. It's not open 24/7," explained Moon Dog as he pointed at the uniforms hanging from above.

"Right," smiled Gibby. "Janitorial services. That makes sense."

* * * * *

Cramped inside one of the Trauma Center's small supply closets, two elderly janitors held earpieces tight against their head.

"What happened?"

"They must be jamming our transmission," the other elderly janitor replied. He glanced down at his wrist watch before he continued. "They should be arriving at the back-service door in about 30 minutes."

"Is everything set?"

"They should have no problem locating the archived videos. My computer guy informs me that he's left enough bread crumbs for them to find it."

"And what about the paper trail?" The medical records?"

"I was part of the original team that created those documents. There are x-rays, blood samples, photographs, even finger prints. We continued to identify him as a John Doe."

The old men paused. Even in the dark confines of the crowded storage closet, the subordinate agent sensed concern.

"Don't worry comrade. I placed the documents in the cabinet myself. Last week, I double checked. They're still there. Right where I left them."

With a quick nod, the senior agent looked into the other man's eyes. "I'll let Herr Van Aelst know we're all set."

*   *   *   *   *

Curt and Diane sat across from each other. The dark underground room was her only sanctuary. She knew the Agency. She had no doubt that she was being tracked by satellite, back tracking her from her last known location. It was only a matter of time.

Curt watched Diane. He felt guilty for being in this predicament. Without Diane's help, he would be dead. And now, the Agency was certain that Diane was somehow involved. At the very least, she was a participant. At the very worst, she was a double agent. Either way, Diane's fate was sealed. Going back was no longer an option.

The echo from approaching footsteps caught Curt's attention. From the sound of the crisp quick pace, they both knew who it was. They turned their attention waiting for Van Aelst to appear.

"I have something to take care of," explained Van Aelst. While I'm away, I've asked Winstead, I mean Herr Schmid, Martin Schmid..." smiled Van Aelst as he continued to adjust to his colleague's new identity, "to show you something."

"What is it?" asked Diane.

Van Aelst paused. It was a ritual that every one of his team members went through. It was a necessary step. It was the way he demonstrated his trust. Trust is a subtle phenomenon. An emotion that is earned and developed over time. She had risked everything to help his grandson. It was time that he returned the favor. The only way he could protect her was to bring her into his organization.

It was risky. Diane was a career Agency member. Van Aelst recognized the potential that Diane could choose death over this option. Her alternatives were limited. She could either embrace

Van Aelst's world and become a full-fledged member of his literal underground society or choose death. Whether she died at the hands of one of her own Capitalist American counterparts or from his, was up to her. It was almost time. The time of reckoning.

"Diane, in the very near future, you will need to make a decision. A decision I know you never expected to face," said Van Aelst. He glanced at his grandson before continuing. "My grandson and I are in your debt. You risked everything to help him. Now, the only way for me to help you, is for you to become part of my team. You are bright and experienced in this crazy underbelly we inhabit. Although the choices are clear, your decision is not. In your eyes, in the eyes of the Agency and your government, even though our countries are not formally at war, we are still considered an enemy.

"I see things differently now. Such things come with experience. They come from being fortunate enough to live a long productive life. A life where you've helped others. Where loyalty is more than just an expected reaction, a decision that is engrained into your psyche and requires no effort to reach," continued Van Aelst.

"As you contemplate this offer, I urge you to re-evaluate your commitments. Consider the actions of others, myself, my network, and yours. Who has shown you kindness, appreciation, understanding, and trust? Which side is offering protection, while another sends an assassin?"

Diane listened. She knew he spoke the truth. Without Van Aelst, she too would be dead. But to voluntarily choose to be a traitor, to turn her back on everything she had loved, to walk away from friends and her country.

"You have time. There is no rush," added Van Aelst. Just then, Martin walked around the corner. With a heavy sigh, Lone Wolf glanced between Diane and his grandson. "We'll talk later."

"Are you ready Diane?" asked Martin. "I need to show you something."

*   *   *   *   *

Gibby and Carla Jo exited the van, then doubled back to the Trauma Center. After waiting for the personnel shift change, they side stepped into the alley near the communication box. With ease, Gibby opened the oversized locked box and found a multitude of cabling and fine wired telephone line connections. Within minutes, Gibby spliced into the Trauma Center's computer system. With Carla Jo as the look out, they exited the area without being noticed.

They meandered back to the waiting van. Certain they were not followed, Gibby and Carla Jo slipped back inside.

"How'd it go?" asked Moon Dog.

"Smooth as silk," smiled Gibby with his ear-to-ear politician's grin.

"Your turn," said Carla Jo.

"You take the wheel," asked Kyle as he and Moon Dog finished buttoning their coveralls and lacing their matching leather boots. Using her laptop, Carla Jo accessed the Trauma Center's medical records. Gibby climbed into the driver's seat and repositioned the van to the back-service entrance. As the van arrived, two elderly men opened the door. Kyle and Moon Dog exchanged knowing glances. As they opened the van door, Kyle recognized one of the men. He was one of the bus drivers they tracked on the Lincoln Tunnel surveillance tapes.

Kyle and Moon Dog stepped onto the asphalt alley. Gibby waited for the van's sliding door to close before driving away. In an awkward silence, both groups were reluctant and uncertain whether the others could be trusted.

In a thick heavy German accent, the senior German agent broke the silence. "Well comrades, let's get to it."

Also dressed as janitors they followed the two elderly agents. While the German agents turned the corner, Kyle leaned forward and whispered.

"Comrades?"

"Relax. We're in Germany," replied Moon Dog.

The two Germans knew their way around walking through the hallways without concern. Having worked here for the last few years they knew the pulse of the Trauma Center. The other Trauma Center employees learned that no amount of complaining about these new janitors, with their aggressive demeanors and privileged attitudes would have any affect. Grudgingly, the other personnel accepted the fact that these guys were here to stay. Everyone else did their best to stay out of their way.

The two Germans showed little concern over being watched and led Kyle and Moon Dog straight to the medical records room. In disbelief, Kyle and Moon Dog watched the senior agent extracted a key and unlocked the door and continued through the open doorway. Without turning on any lights, he punched in the security code. After disarming the alarm, he turned and waived them inside.

"Down that corridor," pointed the senior agent. "You'll find the archived folders. You should find what you're looking for there."

"We'll stay by the door, just in case," added the other German agent. It was the first thing he had said.

"What if someone comes inside?" asked Kyle.

The senior agent looked at the other German agent with a jagged smirk. "We're janitors. We clean the toilets. That's what we do." In a sarcastic tone, he added, "Nothing out of the ordinary here. Except you two obvious Americans, who can't speak German... so hurry up!" snarled the senior German agent in disgust.

After exchanging nervous glances, Kyle and Moon Dog proceeded down the corridor in search of the archived medical records. The Germans watched them scurry down the carpeted hallway and suppressed laughing out loud. Everything was going as planned.

*   *   *   *   *

Martin led Diane and Curt down the main train track. Except for the battery-operated lantern that Martin carried, there was no light. Curt and Diane stayed close. It was a challenge to see and maintain their balance. Martin illuminated the wooden railroad ties and guided them inside. For a second, Diane wondered if this was it. Had Van Aelst ordered her execution? Would her corpse remain hidden deep underground never to be seen or heard from again?

Pushing those thoughts from her mind, Diane concentrated on the railway ties. It was a difficult enough task to keep her balance without being distracted. After a 20-minute walk, the main line split and continued down another tunnel. Martin led them toward the smaller track.

"We're almost there," explained Martin. Several hundred meters further, he raised the lantern above his head and searched the tunnel wall.

"What are you looking for?" asked Curt.

"The Roman Numerals for four (IV)", replied Martin.

"Why four?" asked Diane.

"Germans associate the number four as lucky, like with the four-leaf clover. It's our favorite number," he explained.

The trio stumbled forward. With the lantern light directed upward, the light no longer illuminated the ground. After a few minutes, they saw two rusted metallic Roman numerals nailed onto a wooden beam.

"Here we are," said Martin. Setting the lantern on the ground, he searched his front pants pocket then extracted a thick rusty iron key, something one would associate with a Medieval dungeon castle. Martin handed the key to Diane. She raised the key into the light and studied it. Curt and Diane looked confused while Martin lit a cigarette.

"Do either of you care for a smoke?"

Although neither was a regular smoker, for some reason they nodded. Martin flicked the striker on the cheap plastic lighter. The small flame seemed larger than life as it erupted casting long shadows against the otherwise dark walls. They enjoyed their smoke in silence each one lost in their own thoughts. After a short break, Martin broke the silence.

"Are you ready?" Martin asked.

Without speaking, Curt and Diane nodded.

"Go ahead, unlock it," instructed Martin as he held the lantern. Diane inserted the oversized key into the lock before she leaned against the huge solid metal door. After some effort, she twisted the key and heard the tumbler emit a loud metallic click that echoed through the dark tunnel. Diane turned back to Martin.

"It's okay. The door's heavy, push hard. I'll explain everything later. You have to see for yourself."

Diane's jaw tensed as she leaned her shoulder into the heavy metal door. She felt the large metal rivets dig into her shoulder. Seeing her struggle, Curt stepped forward and helped push. An eerie screech, metal on metal noise sounded as the hinges gave way. Holding up the lantern, Diane and Curt peered inside through the open door.

15

Van Aelst exited the subterranean labyrinth having walked the last several kilometers alone. Staring up through a metal grated drain cover, he paused, making certain that no one was above. He slid the grate along a rolling track and stepped up into the abandoned building. After the war, the building was converted into the Field Station Berlin, occupied by the U.S. and British intelligence agencies. During the entire time, unbeknownst to the capitalists, Van Aelst's crew were hidden below listening.

Van Aelst slid the grate back into place. He walked through the now abandoned dilapidated ruins with a satisfying smile. He glanced through the broken glass window frame and waited for his ride. Right on time, an older model *Mercedes* taxi cab driven by another one of his comrades. Wasting no time, Van Aelst exited the building and jumped into the cab.

"Good morning, Herr Van Aelst."

"Good morning comrade."

Without delay, the driver stomped on the accelerator. "Where to this time Herr Van Aelst?"

"To our Seniorresidenczy near the Spree River."

The cab driver was another retired Stasi and one of the thousand beneficiaries of the social network Van Aelst and other custodians implemented. When it was obvious that Germany would lose World War II, in preparation for the inevitable, plans were made to take care of its loyal citizens. Germany learned a lot from the First World War. They had no illusions about how the victors would react and treat them. All efforts were made to give the survivors a better outcome than before. This time, unlike the first great war, there would be no repeat of the Treaty of Versailles. The humiliations, given the concentration camps, were unavoidable. Saving face was not an option. But facing financial ruin, being required to pay damages, more than $3.3 billion dollars, or $2.3 trillion when factoring for inflation, was to be avoided at all costs.

Van Aelst remembered when he transitioned out of his Hitlerjugend (Hitler Youth Group) to the regular line SS unit. He was one of the many Lebensborn children; it was a plan devised to propagate the Aryan beliefs. With their strict upbringing and high expectations, it was no surprise that only the elite from these Hitlerjugend groups were selected into the underground custodian positions.

Those selected not only orchestrated the transportation of the high officers out of Germany before the fall, but also were tasked to oversee the survival and continuation of Germany after the war. When Germany was divided into East and West, any plans to bring these elite custodians to Argentina were abandoned. To assure the survival of the loyal SS party members, the custodians willingly stayed behind. Part of the system included an informal social service program. Any loyal German person could, through informal word of mouth, seek assistance through the custodians. Over time, Seniorresidenz's were created to house and care for the aged and ill Germans. These benefits extended to their children and grandchildren.

As the cab reached the main boulevard near the Seniorresidenz location, Van Aelst opened his cellphone and scrolled through his photo gallery and studied Diane's pictures. He took several photos days after she arrived at the underground hideout. The cab driver's voice interrupted his train of thought.

"We're almost there, Herr Van Aelst."

*   *   *   *   *

It took a few moments before Diane's eyes adjusted. Stretching forward leaning inside the open doorway, she glanced inside the deep cavern. As the lantern light illuminated the interior, Diane and Curt's mouths gaped open. It was the last thing they expected to see. She turned to face Martin.

"I don't understand. What is this? Why is he showing me this? Where did it all come from?"

Diane and Curt stared back into Martin's calm face. He took another drag from his cigarette, before flicking the burning stub into the darkness leading to the main railway tracks.

"It's been hidden here for decades. Ever since the end of World War II. Let me explain."

As Martin spoke, Curt and Diane stared inside through the open doorway. The lantern, now sitting on the floor inside the doorway, lit the vast interior. The light seemed to multiply, like a single candle held up and reflected off a wall of continuous mirrors. The light bounced and ricocheted off the smooth surface, sending a distinct golden reflection cascading around the interior of the room.

Diane stared from floor to ceiling admiring the neat, stacked rows of gold bars. The room was full.

*   *   *   *   *

Carla Jo stood and stretched. After accessing the Trauma Center's computer records and copying the documents found in the archive room, they returned to their hotel suite and poured over the information. Doing her best to suppress a full-on open-mouthed yawn, Carla Jo broke the silence.

"It looks like their John Doe is our guy all right. Same approximate age, height, weight," she said with a shrug of her shoulders.

Moon Dog rose his head from the coffee table. It was covered with photographs; finger prints; and even a blood sample. "I agree. But look at all this information. It's almost too easy."

"It seems too thorough, too detailed," added Kyle. "Even the autopsy photos seem too clear." Kyle continued studying the photos. Van Aelst went to the trouble to make sure Curt was lying on a heated blanket to prevent the presence of goose bumps, while forcing Curt to practice propping his lower jaw open. Nothing was left to chance.

"I would tend to agree with everyone's skepticism. But these documents were obviously prepared years ago. The video surveillance coincides with the arrival of the male John Doe patient by ambulance transport. Hell, we were even able to back track that same ambulance to the freighter that so happened to have left a New Jersey dock about the same time we lost the transport in the Lincoln Tunnel," said Gibby. "If it walks and talks like a duck?" he added with a shrug.

"But they're always a step ahead," offered Kyle.

"And the images of those old geriatric guys giving us the bird. What's up with that?" asked Moon Dog.

"What about this? Anderson's ex-Stasi agent Grandfather Van Aelst gets word that his grandson gets caught with his hands in the cookie jar and needs help," explained Carla Jo. "Because he's no longer a full-blown active agent, he has to get creative to get the grandson to safety. And after all his efforts, bam, the kid dies?"

Carla Jo watched the others' reactions as they pondered her theory. Some were bobbing their head back and forth batting around the theory. Gibby broke the silence.

"I like everything up until the kid dies part."

"Yeah, pretty damn convenient if you ask me," added Kyle.

"But we're missing the main point," said Moon Dog.

"Which is?" asked Carla Jo.

"Why are we so worried about all this anyway? From my chair, the original reason the San Jose guys wanted to whack Anderson was the fear that an active "knock-list" would find daylight and be released through the media. And now, it's been over three years. Nothing but crickets," explained Moon Dog.

Carla Jo added, "I agree. What's the exposure now? All those cases are long closed. Any allegations to the contrary are after the fact. Even the decision to down the airliner. It sounds more like some conspiracy theory than reality."

The four agents absorbed it all for several moments. After exchanging looks of agreement, a consensus was reached.

"I'll write it up," offered Carla Jo.

"And the kid?" asked Gibby.

"I'll work it in the report, both options. Either dead or alive, there's no downside now," she said.

"Except the fact that potentially a Stasi operation penetrated one of our secure U.S. based offices," countered Moon Dog with a disapproving snarl.

"Tit for tat," countered Carla Jo. "It's all Cold War mentality stuff."

"I still don't like it," added Gibby. "Let's at least run the DNA on this John Doe. This way, we can rule out any question as to whether this guy was even our Anderson guy."

"I agree," said Moon Dog. "I'll ask a favor from our Berlin buddies."

Kyle watched in silence. He was the newest Agent, only recently coming on board. He had nothing to add and knew when to keep his mouth shut. He had no illusions of being the brains of this group and accepted his role as the muscle.

*   *   *   *   *

Diane bent down to pick up one of the gold bars. Using her finger tips, she struggled to get a grip. After muscling up the bar, she guessed it weighed more than the curling bar she used in the gym.

"These things are much heavier than you'd think," she said.

"Each bar weighs about 400 ounces, around 25 pounds," said Martin.

"How much is one bar worth?" asked Curt.

"Depends on the market. Right now, about $500,000 U.S.," explained Martin. He watched Curt and Diane as they glanced around the vault trying to calculate the value of all the gold inside.

"There's roughly 300,000 bars inside this vault. Just short of $400 million."

"This vault? You mean there are more?" asked Curt.

"Yes. Many more."

After a brief pause, Diane set the heavy gold brick down. "Martin, why would Mr. Van Aelst show this to me?

"Everyone knows Diane," Martin replied. "Well, everyone in our group."

Martin paused and directed his remarks toward Curt. "Your grandfather is a great man. He is one of the original custodians responsible for taking care of the loyal Germans after World War II. He is one of the last surviving custodians."

"What's the gold for? Where did it all come from?" Diane asked.

"At the end of First World War, the Treaty of Versailles forced Germany to pay damages. In fact, most Germans blame the treaty as the cause of the second war. The German economy was devastated. Those in power made sure that such a thing would never happen again."

"But where did it come from?" Diane asked.

"Some came from those sent to concentration camps. But most came by conquering other countries. From their banks and vaults. It's nothing new in human history. During most wars, this type of thing happens all the time; it wasn't just with Germany. In fact, during World War II, the Japanese did it on even a much broader scale."

"It's hard to believe that the treasure hasn't been filtered off and spent," said Diane.

"Germany and Italy are unique. Both countries lost both world wars. Germany was divided and reshaped into its sponsoring countries. In the beginning of the cold war, unlike other nations, Germany was in jeopardy of losing its identity. That's why we have a soft spot for Korea."

"This treasure was established to assure Germany survived. The fortune belongs to everyone. These custodians were given charge of protecting and looking out for the well-being of all loyal Germans."

"And when Mr. Van Aelst passes?" asked Diane.

"A replacement is chosen," clarified Martin.

Diane looked around the vault. The gold was stacked 30 bricks high, a 100 bricks wide, and 100 bricks long. The lantern's light reflected off the golden bricks filling the chamber with a soft gold glow.

"We should get back," said Martin. "Herr Van Aelst will be returning shortly."

As they exited the vault, Curt helped Diane shut the heavy solid metal door. She raised the key to hand it back to Martin.

"You keep it. You can give it back to Herr Van Aelst."

As they made their way back toward the main railroad track, Diane could not help but wonder how many other vaults existed. Like this one, were they still full of gold or other treasure? Her thoughts returned to Mr. Van Aelst. *Why did he share this with me? What did he have in mind?*

*   *   *   *   *

Van Aelst waited until all the folders were placed on the desk top. With mixed feelings, he examined each file. As a custodian, one of his duties was to give input and reassure the hospital medical services were paid. The files included only patient profiles for this location. As he scanned their photo, they were all familiar. However, the purpose for this review was something altogether different.

Today, he was looking for a potential match. This situation was unique with its own special set of circumstances. The candidate had to possess a certain height, weight, and most important, similar facial features.

This type of mission was used before. Staring at the stack of folders, it occurred to him. Over the years, the number of terminally ill patients had increased three-fold. He could not decide if it was the food with all the artificial ingredients or the constant exposure to known carcinogens present in most modern cities that were to blame. Regardless of the cause, Van Aelst had more candidates from which to choose.

The Medical Director watched Van Aelst weed through the folders making certain only the terminally ill patients were presented. Given their situation, he imagined that each patient welcomed an early departure from this world compared to an existence dominated by pain and suffering. Even still, the Director felt pangs of guilt for participating. Knowing the selected person's family would receive a fee and never know that their illness was not the final cause of death helped ease his guilt. As a medical doctor his participation was in direct conflict with the German equivalent to a Hippocratic oath- "nil nocere" meaning to do no harm. He could not help but feel guilt and shame.

"Herr Van Aelst, when do you anticipate this to take place?" asked the Director.

Van Aelst studied one particular file. "It could be as soon as this weekend," replied Van Aelst.

"Have you found any matches?"

"I think I've narrowed it down to these two," replied Van Aelst as he patted the top two folders. The Director saw the names and pictured their faces. With a blank expression, he waited for Her Van Aelst to decide.

"I'll need to meet them both. Are they available now?"

"Yes. They've just finished lunch. I can take you to meet them. Just let me know when you're ready."

"Are they aware that this offer is even a possibility?"

"Neither probably remember our conversation, but they each expressed a desire to participate. We always include a set of questions on the entry paperwork that addresses this possibility. In most cases, patients who have already undergone so much treatment rarely recall giving consent," explained the Director. Van Aelst slid the remaining stack of folders back across the table. He placed the remaining two folders on the table and fanned them out allowing the Director to read their names.

"I'm ready now. I'd like to visit this one first", instructed Van Aelst as he tapped his index finger on the name.

"Follow me."

This Seniorresidenzy housed only retirees and their family members. Each patient had a private room, equipped with a large wall-mounted flat screen television, access to 24-hour kitchen staff, nurses and doctors who specialized in the terminally ill. Before entering the room, Van Aelst placed his hand on the Director's shoulder.

"Are these two patients ambulatory? Still capable of walking without any assistance?"

"Yes, they are."

With a nod, Van Aelst stepped forward and opened the door. He was about to close the door behind him but leaned back.

"Thank you for your time, Director. I'll take it from here," said Van Aelst as he closed the door.

The Director walked back down the hallway. Herr Van Aelst was the hospital's sole board member. He met him the day of his interview and monthly thereafter. During that initial meeting, Van Aelst said he knew his grandfather and that his organization funded many social programs designed to provide services for certain loyal citizens and their families. The Director was surprised when he learned about the financial influence his grand-father's organization wielded. Over the decades, it became clear that every employee and patient belonged to this same group of loyal citizens. Although Van Aelst never said, the Director sensed that he was the driving force behind everything.

As the Director turned the corner, he paused admiring a framed oil painting hanging on the hospital wall. He never questioned the origination of the art. The paintings this hospital possessed had similar style to some of the great works that hung at the Louvre and the Germaldegalerie. He had never inquired about the artists' names. The German culture had a "don't ask don't tell" mentality.

The Director continued walking to the elevator. He pressed the button and waited for its arrival pondering the peculiarity that, unlike other hospitals, there was no formal accounting department. They never processed bills or insurance forms. He was never asked about the budget or urged to cut expenses; something his other colleagues from other hospitals were always preoccupied with. Likewise, his compensation. It took some adjusting to. His employer paid him through direct deposit without any formal paper trail. Their process was used long before it had become the standard means to pay employees. Other than the annual tax documents, no other form of proof of employment or compensation was provided.

When the elevator arrived, the Director took it to the top floor. Occasionally, he wondered why, on only rare occasions, he met his Supervisors and almost never had employment evaluations. He would just receive a memo detailing a generous pay increase keeping him well above inflation.

Unlike his colleagues at other hospitals, he never had personnel issues. His focus was on the quality of care provided to the patients. Not on a single occasion had any of the other nurses, doctors, janitors, or food servers ever complained. The only constant was the monthly visitations he received from Herr Van Aelst, who would just showed up. The visits were always unannounced. Van Aelst knew every staff member and most of their families. Van Aelst would browse around making many one-on-one visits that ended with him stopping by the Supervisor's office to check in. It took several months before he made the connection. It seemed like whenever he mentioned even a slight concern with Herr Van Aelst, the issue would somehow resolve itself without the need for him to intervene or become involved.

During later visits, he learned that Herr Van Aelst had a special skill; making sure things got done. Once, in passing, the Director mentioned "wanting" to expand and modernize the hospital, enhancing the radiological and x-ray machines and pharmacy. To his delight, the following week, he saw surveyors outside his window inspecting the adjacent lot. He was taken aback to find an architect and engineer waiting outside his door ready to discuss the expansion and construction of the new hospital wing.

The elevator's electronic tone interrupted his thoughts. The Director stepped through the oversized patient elevator doors. As he approached the double doors to his office, his secretary greeted him.

"Good afternoon Direktor. How was your visit with Herr Van Aelst?"

"Very good."

"He's such a nice gentleman. He is my grandfather's good friend," she added with a bright smile.

"Mine as well Ingrid. Mine as well," the Director replied.

*   *   *   *   *

Director Valdez, Agents Gall, Walters, and newly promoted Supervisor Chapin sat in the San Jose Agency conference room reading the reports sent over the encrypted computer server.

"Based on these autopsy photos, it certainly looks like our guy," said Agent Gall.

"I've double checked the medical records and x-rays against Anderson's original medical file. It looks like a match. Our lab is checking out the blood sample for a DNA match," added Agent Walters.

Director Valdez glanced around the table, stopping at Chapin. "So, what do you think Supervisor? What's your gut say?"

Supervisor Chapin raised her head from the file and stared at the papers strewn about the table. "The evidence is pretty overwhelming. Almost too obvious. Once I hear back from the lab, I'll feel better. But if I were forced to offer a guess, I'd say it's our guy. But I've been doing this for a long time, you just never really know."

A knock came on the conference room door.

"Director Valdez?" said a staff member as he stuck his head through the door.

"Yes?"

"A package from the lab. They asked me to hand deliver it to you," the assistant said as he looked back at one of her security guards breathing down his neck with one hand on his 9mm *Barretta*. Feeling self-conscience about interrupting the meeting, he added, "I've already been searched by your guards."

"Thank you," replied Nena with an apologetic smile. As soon as the assistant handed her the envelope, one of her guards practically pulled him back through the door.

Nena tore open the envelope and read the memo. "It's the lab results," she explained.

The other three waited. Nena flipped through the pages before passing the folder to Chapin.

"The blood work confirms that it is our John Doe. And more importantly, it matches Curt Anderson's DNA," explained Nena.

While glancing through the report, Chapin asked, "How'd we match it up against Anderson's DNA? I thought we only had the John Doe's."

"We pulled a sample from the same hospital. Several years earlier, he'd gone there for an emergency appendectomy. He has a rare blood type AB negative. It's very rare. Because of his surgery, he was advised to be a regular blood donor to make sure there's always an available supply, just in case. It came up handy during our John Doe research," explained Agent Walters but guessed by the blank stares she was getting that more clarification was needed.

"It turns out the local supply of blood for AB negative was well stocked by none other than Curt Anderson. He was apparently concerned about needing blood sometime in the future. He was a regular blood donor. The hospital still had several bags of Curt's blood. Our lab must have pulled that blood to match it against the samples taken from Germany."

Hearing this information, the other three nodded in agreement.

"I guess that's it. It has to be our guy," said Nena.

"If Anderson didn't have so much outside help, I'd suggest we re-close the file. But, to save face and gain some respect with Van Aelst's affiliates, at the very least we should reach out and let him know that we know what happened," explained Nena.

"I agree," added Agent Gall as she exchanged glances with Walters and Chapin.

With this mystery resolved, Nena considered ending the meeting. However, she recognized the need to address the other issue- Diane Klein.

"I know that you all must be, at the very least, curious about the status of your co-worker Diane Klein?" explained Nena.

The three San Jose team members exchanged quick side glances as they waited.

"First, I imagine it's difficult being excluded from this part of the investigation. As much as I'd like to include you all, God knows my team would expect the same treatment, but I can't. Given her actions, combined with the obvious leak inside our Agency, it's not possible. With the loss of sitting U.S. Senator and several other Agency personnel, not to mention Director Gamboa becoming critically injured during the Senator's assassination, we need to isolate everyone previously involved.

"I'm sure you all can appreciate the situation for what it is," added Nena. "I think it's important that this call comes from the National Director himself. It's out of my hands."

"Are we being looked at?" asked Supervisor Chapin. She avoided eye contact focusing on the center of the table.

"It should come as no surprise that you were. Rest assured my people were beyond professional. And for the record, you three are clear. We have communicated our findings to the National Director. Unfortunately, he still asks that, until the Diane issue is resolved, no one from the San Jose location will participate with that part of the investigation."

The three women listened to everything not saying a word. Supervisor Chapin was certain, she would never see Lt. Colonel Diane Klein ever again. Agent Walters was a new transfer to San Jose and had little history with Diane but had her suspicions, while the greenhorn Agent Gall had no clue. She did not even consider the possibility that the Agency would take out one of their own. Coming from the Bureau, Gall was still adjusting to the absolute unquestioning authority the Agency possessed, over not just international affairs, as the jurisdiction was allocated, but also domestic.

Nena detected varying emotions. Remaining stoic, Nena withheld the newest piece of intel. An agent from Paris was dispatched. It was Agency protocol that during such sensitive matters, the Director whose team member was being terminated, was briefed by the Agent doing the dirty work.

This part of the business was the most unpleasant. It was a rarity, but from time to time, it became necessary. Her pilot Mr. Davies and security detail were already preparing for her departure. Director Gamboa had sufficiently recovered and was chomping at the bit to get back in the game.

"Ladies, it's been a privilege to work with each of you," interjected Nena. "And I've got some good news. Next week, Director Gamboa will be returning on a limited basis. There won't be any need for me to be around. It's difficult enough to have one Director around, but two?" joked Nena.

Nena stood. "Should any of you ever need anything from my neck of the woods, by all means, give me a call."

Nena walked around the table and shook their hands.

"Nena are you heading back across the Pacific or the long way home?" asked Chapin. She could not help but ask. Being the most senior one present, Chapin had a suspicion that Nena would be heading through Europe and knew its significance.

Director Valdez considered lying. But why? Her itinerary would be easy to verify. A simple call to Camp Bonifas would verify her absence. Being away from Korea for so long, made it unlikely that she would take R&R before returning. They deserved better. They were cleared and needed to be treated as the trusted personnel they had proved to be.

Returning Chapin's intense stare, Nena exchanged a firm handshake. "I'll be going the long way."

Without any direct verbal confirmation, Nena knew Chapin understood its significance and appreciated her honesty.

The three women watched Director Valdez walk out the conference room. Supervisor Chapin released a heavy sigh. It was difficult enough losing a fellow agent during a mission. It was altogether different to watch one eliminated and removed from within. Diane would be missed. She was one of Chapin's good friends.

*   *   *   *   *

Waiting outside a small café for her contact, Roberta sipped a strong cappuccino. For the longest time, the only other person that entered was an elderly white-haired gentleman. She dismissed him as a tourist. Well after the appointed time passed, she returned her gaze to the old man.

She was taken aback to see him staring back with a wide-eyed intense glare. His solid gray eyebrows were pushed back high on his wrinkled forehead as he tried to get her attention using non-verbal cues. He was grateful that he got her attention and was trying to establish that he was her contact. Having her attention, he removed his cotton red beanie cap and held it in his hand. Until that gesture, Roberta never saw the red cap. Given his age, she disregarded the possibility that he was her contact. Caught off guard, Roberta stood.

"I'm sorry, I didn't..." she paused unsure how to explain her mistake. "I didn't expect someone like you to be my contact."

"It's okay fraulein. It happens with much frequency," replied the old man. His cadence and thick German accent caught her off-guard.

"I need to take you to someone. If you will follow me."

The old man led Roberta to a parked yellow *Mercedes* cab and opened the back door. Sliding into the back seat, she was surprised to see the size of his thick forearms. She expected to see skinny wrinkled ones. She reminded herself not to assume anything. Given the importance of her mission, she expected to meet key players inside the German intelligence. They were allies. She expected full cooperation.

Roberta was on full alert. Just in case, she had her 9 mm *Barretta* and *stiletto* knife. She was not expecting any trouble. But her years of training taught her to remain on her toes. In her line of business, nothing was ever out of the ordinary.

"Your target has moved. She's no longer at the hotel. We're trying to reacquire her whereabouts."

With a heavy sigh, Roberta glanced out the cab windows. As the cab entered the abandoned section of Berlin, she wondered if her aunt had lived her final days hidden inside this strange forgotten wasteland behind the brick walls that divided the city.

Roberta stared out at the horizon. A rusted Ferris wheel rose from an abandoned amusement park. At the height of its popularity, *Spreepark* was bustling with families. Roberta marveled at a large decaying statue of Lenin that was propped up along a heavy treelined road. The bust, although darkened from moss and algae, was void of any spray-painted graffiti.

The old cab driver sped through the abandoned streets. The leaf cluttered roads gave Roberta the impression that this roadway was seldom used. Yet, the driver sped along making precision turns, bounding through alleyways and side roads. It was obvious that he knew his way around. She found herself holding onto the door handle to brace herself. She glanced up into the rearview mirror. The cab driver remained relaxed and in control. They drove at least 30 minutes before anyone spoke.

"We're almost there fraulein. We'll be driving underground," explained the cabbie. With a smirk, he reached down and turned on the headlights. Without warning, the cab cut through a narrow road. With a sudden loss of sunlight, she thought they entered an alleyway. Through the window overhead, she saw a solid brick awning. Without reducing speed, the cab descended still driving on the roadway. The overhead covering transformed into a canopy of large beech tree limbs. Seeing these huge trees, Roberta thought about how much time had passed since the USSR fell. This part of the city was returning to nature. The cab continued its descent into what turned out to be a literal forest.

With the world focusing on the Middle East and Asia, the espionage underworld had forgotten about Eastern Europe. There no longer seemed any urgency to keep tabs on this part of the world. For the most part, the former East Germany, was dominated by vacant areas that belonged to history. Finally, the cab went underground where the remaining slivers of light disappeared altogether.

Once underground, the cabbie reduced his speed and drove through a network of underground tunnels. By the looks of the wooden railroad ties and steel rails, Roberta figured that they were inside an abandoned subway system. Veering off the main line, they passed a large oversized locomotive engine with distinct swastika markings stenciled on its side. The once deep red circle background long since faded and cracked from decay. She imagined what this area must have looked like when those engines barreled along underground carrying God knows what.

Like a sponge, Roberta continued absorbing everything. Trying to maintain her wits, she expected to receive full cooperation from the Germans. The U.S. was interested in one of their own not a German. She had no reason to expect any resistance.

From what Roberta was told, although Diane helped extract an ex-Stasi agent's grandson, given the grandson died from his injuries, why would the grandfather continue to protect her? She was an

American agent. The agency made it clear what needed to be done. Even if the grandfather wanted to protect Diane, what could he do? The full power and reach of the United States outweighed the wants of an individual, especially an ex-Stasi retiree. So, she thought.

*   *   *   *   *

Inside the hospice wing, an intimate celebration was underway. A middle-aged woman diagnosed with an inoperable brain tumor surrounded by a group of other patients. A cake was cut. A piece served to everyone present. The patients were surprised when crystal fluted glasses were filled with champagne. Out of habit, they glanced about making sure no nurses were around to chastise them for drinking alcohol. It had been months since they had smiled.

"What's the celebration about?" asked one of the women.

With a controlled smile, the guest of honor, in a daze, looked at the woman. Just moments before, a senior custodian from the German Relief Society approached her with a unique opportunity. For months, she battled her tumor. Her prognosis was an abrupt and painful ending. She was still adjusting trying her best to accept her unknown future. The only certainty was that her days were numbered.

Contemplating the question, she did her best to be elated. However, she was sworn to secrecy. No one could know. To receive this opportunity, that was the condition. She glanced at the onlookers one last time before answering the question.

"We're celebrating a new opportunity, a new procedure. Later today, I will be taken from here. If everything works out as planned," she explained, "I will be one of the few never to return again," she said as she raised her fluted crystal glass in a toast. "I will miss you all so much," she said as she suppressed her anxiety. The other patients were too busy exchanging cheers and tapping their glasses to notice the small bag sitting on the chair across the room. Hidden inside was a fresh pressed set of khaki shorts and a United States Solheim Cup golf shirt.

*　*　*　*　*

"Hey Pfeffin, (Curt's new given German name)," replied Diane.

"Right. I still find it difficult to respond to my new name."

They stared at their plate. The food barely eaten. Neither were hungry.

"It's all my fault you're in this situation."

"Not really. You may have started the sequence of events, but if my niece was spared, if the people in charge saw it fit, they could have kept her alive. It was their actions that started me down this path," Diane replied.

Pfeffin knew the truth about Diane's niece. His grandfather explained everything and agreed that Diane could not know the truth. It would make it worse. Besides, his grandfather had a plan to help everyone concerned.

"Even still," said Pfeffin. "I'm sorry you got involved."

"Me too," replied Diane.

The distant sound of shuffling feet echoed in the dark room. After a moment, the light from the battery-operated lantern cast a shadow of a person approaching.

"It's time," said Martin.

Diane thought his voice sounded melancholy and detached, like the bearer of bad news.

"Where are we going?" asked Diane. She turned away from the shadowy figure speaking out from the darkness beyond.

"My grandfather needs to explain something to us. He has an idea to resolve your situation," explained Pfeffin.

For decades, Diane's job was to read people. But living like a rodent, hiding underground, forced to rely on artificial lighting without being exposed to natural sun for the last week, dulled her senses. Somewhere deep inside, her intuition screamed at her to wake up, stay alert! Knowing the Agency knew of her involvement, becoming an unofficial member of Van Aelst's group dominated her thoughts. The distractions interfered with her mental sharpness. It was difficult for her to concentrate. Her unknown future kept her emotions on edge.

She followed Pfeffin and Martin out to the main underground track where a yellow cab waited. Diane slid into the back seat. Most of the old men stood on the platform above. They removed their hats and waited for the cab to leave. Diane peered through the darkness staring at the silhouettes created by the battery-operated lanterns. She got the impression they came to pay their respects. For some reason, it reminded her of a funeral procession. As the cab pulled away, Diane found herself waving good-bye to the fading images on the platform.

Even the shaded area above ground stood in deep contrast to the underground she had become accustomed to. Eventually, the canopy created by the overgrown beech trees thinned allowing small amounts of sunlight to cut through the darkness. Seeing sunlight, Diane squinted yearning for its warmth. The cab accelerated along the road for several miles. With each passing moment, the frequency and size of the sun rays increased. As the road leveled out, the leaf canopy was replaced by solid layers of brick. Within no time, the cab emerged out from cover and was engulfed by unobstructed sunlight. Diane closed her eyes and soaked up the natural warmth enjoying a sense of freedom as if she just escaped from an underground tomb.

Diane squinted and blinked adjusting to the environment. She leaned back facing upward through the rear window and enjoyed the warmth. She forgot about being chased by the Agency and enjoyed the ride and change of scenery. Although Pfeffin felt the same sensations, knowing what lay ahead for Diane, his experience was much different. That all changed when Diane saw the objects on the horizon.

"What's that?" she asked. "Where are we going?"

No one replied. As the cab crested the hill, Diane got a clear view. Bright bleached white walls with matching windows on both floors, surrounded a large rectangular doorway centered on the first floor. Diane recognized the building. She saw similar images plastered on many tourist brochures. As they approached the building, the name came to her- Sachsenhausen Concentration

Camp. It was the most centrally located concentration camp of all the European camps, just outside Berlin's city limits. It was converted into a museum.

"Why are we going here? I thought we were meeting your grandfather?" asked Diane. Turning her attention to Pfeffin, Diane's voice raised an octave. Knowing the history of this place, understanding its purpose during World War II, brought images of suffering and death. Driving past the building, she was relieved glad it was not their destination. Just past the building, she saw rows of grave stones and plots. It was the adjacent camp cemetery. The cab slowed and pulled toward the back-parking area.

"Why here? Why a cemetery?" asked Diane.

"Don't worry. It's where Herr Van Aelst's family members are buried," replied the driver.

The driver maneuvered the faded yellow cab around the building and parked near the ambulance service entrance. A driver stood next to a parked ambulance and stared out across the gravestone, tomb, and cross covered landscape. He was smoking an unfiltered cigarette and propped up a foot resting it on the ambulance's back bumper. Diane found it peculiar that, a man of his advanced age, would still be working as an ambulance driver.

The cab driver maneuvered through the lot and parked on the opposite side. Craning his neck in a wide turn, he scanned the entire area before exiting the cab. With their eyes still adjusting to the sunlight, Diane and Pfeffin struggled out of the cab. Diane thought she saw a shadowy figure from inside step away from a tinted-window but she was not sure.

"My eyes are still adjusting," announced Pfeffin as he removed a set of sunglasses from his jacket to cover his eyes.

"Follow me," said the cab driver and led them through the back entrance. The lobby was not modernized. There were no artificial lights only the natural sun light that passed through the windows lit the area. It felt sterile like an administrative building unaccustomed to dealing with visitors. White square ceramic tiles covered the floor. The white-washed plaster walls had an institutionalized feeling, void of framed pictures, colors, or carpeting. The cabbie's heels snapped against the floor and echoed throughout the otherwise vacant lobby. They followed him inside as he marched down the corridor.

At the end of the hallway, a bright light shown under one of the closed doorways. As Diane passed by the closed door, she heard a distinct high-pitched sound, like tennis shoes squeaking on the floor coming from inside. She was certain someone was behind the closed door. Instinctively, she turned toward the noise. Watching the driver continue walking forward, she hurried to catch up.

"Diane, this way," smiled the driver.

The cabbie held the door open waiting for Diane. Stepping through the doorway, she was unprepared for what happened next. Her mind reeled trying to make sense of everything.

"Diane. We've been waiting for you," said a familiar voice.

She turned toward the voice. Her eyes locked onto a pair of clear bright blue eyes. She had grown accustomed to his presence. For a split second, she was relieved. *But why was Mr. Van Aelst wearing a surgical mask?* Without warning, Diane felt a sharp stabbing pain in the side of her neck. Within seconds, her legs failed. As she lost consciousness, she was grateful to feel several sets of latex covered hands reach out and catch her from behind. The only thing she heard was Herr Van Aelst's voice.

"I'm sorry Diane. Please forgive me. There's no other way."

16

Roberta was more than concerned. She was getting the feeling that the Germans were not cooperating. She was restless waiting in an abandoned room. Outside, she heard several conversations, all in German. Her initial concern evaporated, and now felt annoyed.

While waiting, her mind circled. For the last three years, Roberta had achieved the impossible task -forgetting her past. She was no longer conflicted about abandoning everyone. It was part of the job, something every ghost agent did. Those that could not fully commit, unable to let their pasts go, were "washed out" and sent away, relegated to non-essential positions. They would never participate in another Top-Secret mission. Contemplating such a fall from grace, kept most deep cover ghost candidates committed and motivated.

Roberta made the cut having transitioned with a clean back-story. Her career path was not some throw-away, expendable run of the mill agent. She was not some sleeper agent, living in a foreign country waiting to act should the situation arise. To finally be accepted, she was trusted enough to be set loose to do her thing. Others trusted her ability to disappear without a trace. This elusiveness was the goal. And now, forced to interact with a past long forgotten, a sacrifice already made, seemed like a cruel trick of fate.

Her psychological transformation demanded that she literally sever all emotional ties. To accomplish that, to truly cross that line, each ghost candidate somehow, someway, annihilated their past. The sad consequence about crossing that line, is there is no turning back. It was not a switch that can be turned off and on. All those deep feelings of love and attachment, any sense of belonging and affection were destroyed. The boats were burned.

Roberta felt no empathy. Her aunt, regardless of the reason, made bad decisions. Given her background, Roberta could not comprehend how her aunt allowed her emotions to get the best of her. How could she have not figured it all out? Of course, the Agency had moved her to deep cover assignment. It seemed obvious, right?

None of that mattered. Her aunt made her own choices. She knew the consequences. And now this. It made sense that the Agency wanted her to prove her loyalties. Diane's fate was sealed. Involving Roberta in its resolution addressed two issues: the elimination of a mole and avoidance of any future blow back. What if another agent took out Diane? It could create potential repercussions if Roberta learned the truth. This plan was the best solution. It was the most efficient and straight forward plan.

Roberta checked her watch. With a sigh of frustration, she glanced around the underground room eager to get things going. To her, she had reduced the idea of eliminating her aunt to a "task" that needed to be checked off her to-do list, nothing more, nothing less. The sound of the door opening got her attention.

"He'll see you now," said another different old man carrying a battery-operated lantern. The bright light reflected off the man's bifocal glasses and shiny bald head. "Follow me," he instructed.

Roberta followed him up a crumbling concrete staircase. From the top, she watched the old man lean his shoulder and push against the thick concrete wall. Until she heard concrete scraping against concrete, she had no idea that he was trying to open a hidden doorway. Stepping up next to him, Roberta planted both of her hands against the thick concrete barrier and pushed. As the heavy door disappeared into the wall space, Roberta noticed a musty damp smell.

The old man led her through the opening and held out the lantern as he pivoted toward Roberta. As he spoke, she noticed his jagged toothed smile.

"This way fraulein. We're almost there."

As she followed him inside, she saw beams of colored rays of light illuminating the cramped interior. The bright blue and orange colors created by the stained-glass windows, stood out against the white marble walls highlighting rusty bronze name plates with dates going back to the 1800's. Each plate included the same last name- Van Aelst. Then it hit her, she was inside a family crypt.

"We're here," whispered the old man. Roberta could barely hear his quiet voice as she hurried up behind him.

"What next?" she asked.

Following the man's eyes, she stared out through the stained glass. "Wait here."

She heard the crunching sound of someone walking over gravel just outside the crypt. As she watched, her breath fogged the glass. The old man removed his hat and held it in both hands waiting for someone to approach. From his posture, she sensed that the other man was of some importance. The men stood too far away. She was unable to hear what they were saying. After a quick exchange, they turned and stared in her direction. Then, the other man waved encouraging her to come outside. She felt their eyes burning holes through the stained-glass window.

Roberta paused at the crypt's metal entry gate and glanced about. She had to remind herself that the Agency and her German counterparts were allies working together. Even still, she could not ignore her training. *"Why stage this elaborate set up?"* she thought. They could have taken her out long before now. She checked her sidearm and the hidden stiletto knife before emerging.

She assumed this other man was in charge, the one who made all the arrangements. All Roberta knew was that her target, Diane Klein, was in hiding. She was told that her contact knew everything that took place inside Germany. The rumor was he still maintained a long string of contacts.

"Pleased to meet you Gina," smiled Van Aelst extending his right hand.

Roberta froze. Only three people knew her real name. Hearing it now sounded foreign. Through a squinted and suspicious stare, she replied.

"Excuse me? My name is Roberta, Roberta Finchum."

"My apologies Roberta. I must have been mis-informed."

"I hope you weren't mis-informed about the person I'm looking for."

For a moment, they stared at each other. Van Aelst broke the awkward silence.

"Roberta, there's a change in plans."

Before she could respond, the graveled pathway filled with several gray-haired men each wearing prescription glasses. It was obvious they each knew how to handle their *HK USP* 9-millimeter pistols; some with suppressors screwed tight on the barrels. Before she could react, the only man decades younger than the others stepped forward and shoved his pistol into her ribs.

"I'll take that," ordered Martin as he reached inside her jacket and removed her gun.

"The Agency's not gonna like this," said Roberta through clenched teeth.

Van Aelst glanced upward grateful for the foul weather. He was certain that the clouds would obstruct the view from the overhead satellite. Not taking any chances, he shouted orders to his men.

"Take her inside!"

With a deep sigh, Roberta followed. What had she gotten herself into?

*   *   *   *   *

Roberta glanced around the mortuary room. The other retirees had slipped away through a side hallway, leaving Van Aelst alone with Roberta.

"Diane's inside," said Van Aelst. His voice was clear and solemn.

Roberta was taken aback. *Given what just happened, she did not expect their cooperation. If the plans had changed, why deliver her to me now?* Van Aelst stepped up to Roberta and placed a hand on her shoulder. She stared into his clear blue eyes.

"Roberta, you must understand that your aunt saved my grandson. I am in her debt."

"It was not her place. Besides, it looks like she did more than just help your grandson escape to Germany," countered Roberta.

"That's not accurate," explained Van Aelst. Removing his hand from her shoulder and walking across the marble floor. He took his time, choosing his words with care.

"It was the North Koreans. As for the Senator, my guess is he had it coming, probably some form of payback. Regardless, Diane had no hand in what happened."

Skilled in the art of deception, this exchange was effortless. He never wavered, more than capable to deliver his next part. He needed to make sure to time everything perfectly.

"I understand how you find Diane's actions and decisions incomprehensible. You're simply too young to understand. You are beginning your career. You've never married, nor had children. Having only to think of yourself, your career..." making certain to pause, Van Aelst glanced at the closed door. He then changed the cadence of his speech. It had its intended affect. She was distracted. Her human curiosity was peaked, wondering what lay beyond the door. The distraction created the perfect opportunity to proceed.

"Diane finds herself in this predicament because of her love for you. Your loss, combined with the apparent Agency's disregard for her years of service, loyalty, and sacrifice; your staged death caused her a momentary lack in judgement. Fueled by anger and betrayal, she decided to reach out using her own resources, determined to understand your loss, to find meaning in your death."

Van Aelst purposely increased his breathing and raised the volume and speed of his speech. He needed to tap into Roberta's temporal lobe; to literally, get inside her head. Van Aelst needed to bypass her training and over stimulate the center of her emotional control. He knew overloading her amygdala could alter her memory and attention.

"I'm certain, she regrets everything; her decision to help my grandson and for hiding her actions from the Agency. I'm surprised she could pass her polygraph," he continued.

He paused checking to see if he had set the scene. He needed to time everything perfectly. He had performed this subtle song and dance many times before. But it had been a while. He needed to be certain. He stepped forward, purposely invading her personal space; that imaginary boundary a person protects to avoid potential harm, to prevent escalading conflicts into altercations. It was a human reaction. Seeing her expression, Van Aelst knew it was time.

"Regardless, I owe Diane. I am pained having to deal with the demands of your imperialist employer. But what choice do I have?" Van Aelst asked making sure that his voice elevated to almost a yell.

"If I wasn't certain the Americans would retaliate, impacting even more innocent lives, I wouldn't cooperate. But I have too many people that depend on me. I couldn't jeopardize their well-being by placing myself and my team in jeopardy," he added.

With a quiet smooth motion, he pulled out a 9mm *Beretta* pistol. Extending his arm, he pointed the barrel at Roberta's face. He bombarded her with questions.

"Do you understand my dilemma, Roberta?"

Shocked, she recoiled and nodded. Reeling, she contemplated her options.

"Every bone in my body tells me to pull this trigger and deal with the Americans later. You understand I am not a willing participant, yes?" added Van Aelst through clinched teeth.

With wide eyes, Roberta remained still, afraid to say something that would set him off. The last thing she wanted to do was give Van Aelst another reason to pull the trigger.

"So here we are. Before we go inside, you need to understand the situation. At the very least, I owe her a quick, painless death. You will be the one to do it. Collect whatever physical proof you undoubtedly need to bring back. My people will take care of her burial. It will be respectfully done, worthy of a person that has shown so much loyalty to my grandson and ironically even to your Agency."

With much more force than needed, Van Aelst pushed the gun into her chest hitting her sternum. From behind, she heard the distinct sound of several pistol action levers locking into a cocked position. Startled, she glanced around the room and saw several geriatric men all aiming pistols at her head.

"Do we have an understanding?" asked Van Aelst, more as a threat than a question.

"We do," replied Roberta. She rubbed her sternum feeling the tenderness around the area where the metal pistol thumped her earlier. It was sure to bruise. Roberta waited for Van Aelst to make the first move. As he pushed open the door, the bright lights inside forced her to raise her hand to cover her eyes.

The other men pushed her forward through the doorway. There, Roberta saw a woman lying on what appeared to be an autopsy table. A white sheet covered her up to her shoulders. Several IV stands stood next to the table with plastic tubes connected to her outstretched arm. There was a monitor displaying her vital signs. The volume was muted. In a puzzled manner, she looked at Herr Van Aelst.

"What's this all about?"

In a stern voice, Herr Van Aelst replied. "My instructions were to deliver Diane Klein to you. I have no illusions that she won't be eliminated. However, she saved my grandson from the clutches of your employer. What good it did. He died anyway. But then, I'm sure you knew that already. The least I can do is return the favor."

Roberta studied the woman's face. With the uncertainty of the situation, the cloak and dagger charade, for a moment, worried about being unable to interrogate her aunt. What option did she have? She approached the table. With the glare of the lights, distracted by the circumstances, Roberta was not certain if it was her aunt. With a tilt of her head, she leaned down for a closer look.

Still perched over her torso, bent at a 45-degree angle at the waist, Roberta looked up. "I need proof."

"Blood and fingerprints should suffice, yes?" he replied.

Roberta nodded. Van Aelst stepped up and stood next to the sleeping body. With obvious care, he reached under the sheets and held her arm firmly at the elbow.

"Do you want me to do it? Or will you?" he asked.

"I have to do it."

Van Aelst stood next to the table holding her arm, making sure Roberta had clear access to the crook of her arm. Roberta took out the syringe and tube from her jacket pocket and glanced up at Van Aelst.

"I guess you won't need to sanitize her skin with alcohol before you take the sample. She doesn't need to worry about an infection, no?" Van Aelst said with a sarcastic snarl.

Ignoring his comments, Roberta concentrated on her task. She noticed that Diane's skin was warm. Using her index finger, she felt a strong pulse register against her finger tip. She had no doubts that this woman was still alive.

Roberta concentrated as she inserted the large six-millimeter syringe into the vein before extracting the blood filling the test-tube. She was about to extract the needle from the arm but realized without a cotton ball or band-aid to tape onto the hole in the skin, blood was certain to pour out. She had not contemplated this problem and glanced up at Van Aelst.

He watched not missing a thing. With a quick nod, he directed one of the men to intercede. He was prepared for everything. The man taped a cotton ball on the wound. Roberta was taken aback at the gentle care the man exhibited. Out of guilt, Roberta, for the first time studied the woman's face. She seemed at peace. The lighting was dimmer than she expected and was distracted by the presence of so many people in the room. She taped the lid of the blood sample and placed it into a small zip-lock bag before dropping it into her jacket pocket.

"They want fingerprints too," she added.

With a disgusted expression, Herr Van Aelst pulled the same arm further out from under the draped sheet.

"Martin, help Roberta with the fingerprints," ordered Van Aelst. Roberta unfolded a piece of paper and an inkless impression pad used by Notary Publics. Together they began taking fingerprint impressions. Van Aelst repositioned the portable light, directing the lights onto her hand. The light, momentarily blinded Roberta causing her to squint.

With the fingerprints complete, Roberta laid another clean sheet of paper over the ink prints preventing them from smearing. Finished, Roberta slid her arm back under the sheet. She was so focused on securing the physical evidence that, until that moment, she had not noticed the ring. It was Diane's birthstone. A present Roberta gave her the year following her acceptance into the military. Roberta reached out and touched the ring. It moved easily and spun about her finger. Roberta wondered if this ordeal caused her aunt to lose weight.

For a moment, the emotions she buried came flooding back. Until then, she felt nothing. Today was just another mission, just another poor soul being pursued by the Agency. Until that instant, this target, the person behind the paper bio, had no meaning. They were just inconsequential facts. But seeing the ring somehow changed her mental state.

Viewing the ring brought those suppressed memories forward. For the first time, she thought about her real birth name; the name Diane called her during countless conversations. Seeing the loose ring hanging from her finger, undoubtedly from the weight loss caused by the stress of what she endured. For the first time, Roberta allowed her conscious mind to process and begin taking in everything; her exposed arm, the cotton swab taped in the crook of her arm; the human being waiting asleep unaware of what was to come. She paused and noticed her aunt's face appeared much thinner than she remembered. Her hair looked a little different too.

Roberta felt the first pangs of tears start to materialize in her eyes; the bright light still aiming down; a dull pain resonating from the center of her chest. The combination of sensations all stacking up on each other took its toll. Roberta was not prepared for these feelings. Seeing the ring somehow cracked the emotional shield she built. Now, she found herself doing her best to control her emotions, trying to blink back tears and regain control. From the shadows, Herr Van Aelst watched everything as it played out. Sensing it was time, he broke the silence.

"Regardless of my promise, I realize the power and tenacity of your employer. trying to protect Diane is useless. I can only do so much," muttered Van Aelst with closed eyes. After a pause, he opened his eyes.

"If nothing else, I want to give her a dignified burial. I'm certain you've been ordered to eliminate her while no thought was given to what to do afterwards were there?" he asked.

His voice broke her train of thought. With the back of her hand, she wiped away a tear. Hearing his words struck deep. He was right. Until that moment, she had no plans for the corpse. She planned on shooting her in the head and walking away. The blank expression on her face said it all.

Looking away in disgust, Herr Van Aelst glanced around the room acknowledging the presence of his men. With a strong impassioned voice, he pushed on.

"Just as I thought. I'll make sure she gets the send-off she deserves and place her remains inside my family crypt. It's the least I could do." With a deep sigh, Van Aelst studied her calm face. The sedatives were working. In quiet whisper, he spoke.

"She's still in a deep sleep. She won't feel a thing. You have what you need. Let's get this over with." After a pause, he continued. "Make it quick!" and he pointed at her temple.

Roberta paused. It was surreal. Realizing her gun was taken away, she looked up. As if on cue, the youngest German agent in the room stepped forward and handed her gun back.

"There's only one bullet in the chamber," explained Martin. He placed Roberta's 9mm *Barretta* into the palm of her hand. She flipped the chamber open. He was telling the truth. Roberta raised the pistol. She aimed the barrel at her temple and pulled the trigger.

*   *   *   *   *

Director Valdez's *Gulfstream* jet landed. While it was being refueled, Mr. Davies remained with the plane. Later, they picked up Lt's Kyle Benjamin and Doug Elliott (aka Moon Dog) from the Berlin office. But first, she had a couple of impromptu meetings to take care of. She needed to make sure that everything was taken care of. While men from her security detail waited outside the bullet proof door, she checked her Agency emails. The others double checked the credentials of the locals assigned to the detail and reviewed the route they planned to take to meet Van Aelst. Since their little scare in Seattle, they were not taking any chances.

*   *   *   *   *

Roberta rode back in the yellow cab, oblivious of being bounced along another abandoned road deep inside East Berlin's ghost town. She regretted not speaking to her aunt. Did it really matter? She kept thinking it would have been worse having to cross-examine her. Nothing her aunt would have said would have changed anything. Reaching into her pocket, Roberta felt the tape covering the test-tube holding her aunt's blood sample, grateful that it was no longer warm to the touch.

Roberta proved her loyalty. Now, the guilt began to set in. *What if she'd broken protocol?* If she had reached out some way, used a third party, she could have let her aunt know that she went under deep cover. But to make such a decision would be to fail before she even began her new assignment. It was the first rule of a ghost. No one, especially family, could know she was alive. If she did, it would inevitably get out. And what about her annual polygraph exam?

The cabbie reached a paved road and began sharing the roadway with other vehicles. The urban noises brought Roberta back to reality. She had one more stop. Protocol dictated she hand-deliver the evidence to the Director in charge when the decision was made. In this case, Nena Valdez. Afterward, she would be debriefed. The entire interview would be recorded, and the evidence verified. Only then could she return to active status.

With a disappointing sigh, Roberta worried that her career would be sidelined. Regardless that she eliminated Diane, Roberta would be forced to jump through new hoops.

The 45-minute drive back was helpful. It gave her time to clear her mind. Her friends thought she was dead. And now, she was certain she had no living relatives. She was truly alone. As she stepped out of the cab, she felt different. She felt stronger, more focused, ready to attack her career with a new vengeance and vigor.

Her surroundings were new and unfamiliar, just like her future. She was living the life she had signed on for. Stepping out she slammed the cab door shut. With each step, she felt more focused with extra energy and purpose. Her mind was clearer than it was in years. With one final shrug, Roberta pushed through the lobby doors. She presented her Agency ID and passed through security before pressing the elevator button. She had one last thing left to do. She heard good things about Director Valdez and looked forward to meeting her face to face.

*   *   *   *   *

Herr Van Aelst watched the mortician and his assistant remove the body off the oversized metal table. Another assistant attended to the blood splatter covering the tile wall. While cleaning, he noticed an IV still positioned next to the examination table. He was about to dismantle the IV stand when Herr Van Aelst entered the room.

"That will be all, thank you."

The orderly paused mid-stride, with his arm extended reaching for the IV Stand. Realizing he was being dismissed, he pivoted around gathered his cleaning materials and exited the room. Alone, Van Aelst allowed himself a satisfying smile. Everything had gone as planned. He stepped toward the oversized table, when he heard a knock on the outer hallway door and heard Martin's voice.

"Herr Van Aelst, it's Martin. I have an envelope."

Van Aelst opened the door. Martin, aka Winstead, stood outside holding a sealed envelope.

"Perfect, Martin. Please, come inside."

Herr Van Aelst opened the envelope, removed a check, and spoke in a disappointed manner.

"It's difficult for me to accept seeing checks using Euros. They should be in Deutsche Marks," explained Herr Van Aelst. "Martin, I need you to stay in this room until I return. I'll be right back. No one is to come inside. Do you understand?"

"Ya Herr Van Aelst."

With a tight-lipped smile, Van Aelst exited through the side door. Through the crack, Martin saw a group of people outside. Based on their distraught expressions, they must have recently lost a loved one.

Martin walked over to the opposite wall and locked the outer door and waited alone inside the examination room. During that time, no one approached the room. He did notice an IV drip next to the table, and that the fluid inside continued to drip. Later, Martin thought he heard a soft gasp. Curious, he approached the metal examination table just as the back door swung open. Being shut away inside a morgue, where thousands of dead people were examined, was getting to him.

"Herr Van Aelst," Martin said in a startled voice. "Finally," he whispered as he forced a smile, embarrassed for being caught off guard. Unexpectedly, a light tapping sound came from the other side of the now closed door followed by an unfamiliar voice coming from the other side. Van Aelst turned toward the sound and opened the door. Standing outside was a distraught young lady. Staring at the floor, she stepped forward.

"Thank you again Herr Van Aelst, for everything you've done. Will you be at her service?" the young lady asked before finally looking up from the floor to make eye-contact.

"Of course. Me and many of my colleagues. We'll all be there," replied Van Aelst flashing a genuine sincere smile.

Raising an opened envelope, she added, "And thank you for this. It will help so much. I can't express enough gratitude for all you've done."

Martin watched Her Van Aelst's reaction. It was the first time he saw him embarrassed. With a wave of his hand, Van Aelst dismissed her compliment and waited for her to leave. They watched her walk away before shutting the door.

Van Aelst retrieved his cell phone from his jacket pocket and sent a text message. He waited to receive a reply, before looking up.

"Martin, could you lock the side door please?"

After securing the door, Martin wondered, *who was Herr Van Aelst waiting for*? Hearing sounds coming from outside in the graveled back entrance area, Van Aelst turned toward Martin.

"That will be all for now Martin. I have one more thing to attend to. I'll meet you in the lobby," instructed Van Aelst.

It was clear Herr Van Aelst wanted him to leave the room. After an awkward pause, Martin nodded and exited into the hallway. As the door shut, he heard what sounded like squeaky metallic wheels being rolled through the back-gravel area. Martin walked toward the lobby. Looking through the front windows, toward the back section of the building, he saw a parked ambulance. He thought someone was being delivered. Down the hallway, from inside the examination room, he heard the oversized deadbolt slide into place. Martin knew he wanted his privacy and walked farther down the lobby.

Martin was just about to extract a cigarette when he heard the deadbolt unlock and watched Van Aelst exit the examination room. Martin glanced around and did not see anything out of the ordinary. He must have been mistaken thinking that someone was being delivered inside. But he did notice the IV drip stand was gone.

"Now, everything is in order Martin. It's time to head back. Let's go the long way, back through East Berlin," instructed Herr Van Aelst with a smile.

As Martin held the lobby door open for Van Aelst, an ambulance sped away past the museum parking lot.

*   *   *   *   *

Director Valdez looked through the one-way mirror and watched Roberta's polygraph exam. It was standard operating procedure, more so with this type of unusual mission. Regardless of the person's position, every member of the organization underwent an annual exam. After a couple of sessions, the experience became less intimidating. For the senior members, it felt like an annual dental check-up; a necessary procedure that one had to endure.

The Director glanced across the room as the technicians reviewed Roberta's vital signs. Her temperature, heart rate and breathing were normal.

"How's she doing?' asked Director Valdez.

"Truthful on all her answers," replied the senior technicians. "No variations."

Cradling her chin in her hand, Valdez stared through the one-way mirror and continued to watch. Through a speaker, they listened.

"Did you personally see the target?" asked the interrogator.

"Yes."

"Did you personally collect the physical evidence?"

"Yes."

"Did anyone help you?"

Roberta paused as she recreated the scene in her mind before answering. "Yes."

The interrogator paused glancing between the one-way mirror and Roberta. When clarification was needed, getting information through questions that could only be answered with a yes or no, became awkward. Unlike a Hollywood movie, respondents could not engage in a long dialogue. It does not work that way. This answer needed to be clarified.

"Was there one other person assisting you?"

"No."

"Were there two people assisting you?"

"Yes."

"Did either of these persons come into contact with your syringe?"

"No."

"At any time, did either person assisting you touch the transferred fingerprint paper?"

"No."

"Did these two people assist you by holding the target's body secure so you could collect the samples?"

"Yes."

"Was this the only form of assistance either person provided?"

"Yes."

Upon answering the last question, the instruments spiked, suggesting that this answer may be inaccurate. The interrogator circled the question. He needed Roberta to expound on her answer.

"Did you pull the trigger on your gun?"

"Yes."

"Was she alive before you pulled the trigger?"

"Yes."

"Did you touch the target?"

"Yes."

"Was she warm to the touch?"

"Yes."

"Did you feel a pulse?"

"Yes."

"Was she breathing?"

"Yes."

"After you shot her, did she immediately die?"

"Yes."

"Did you shoot her in the chest?"

"No."

"Did you shoot her in the head?"

"Yes."

The interrogator glanced up at the one-way mirror. With a nod, he seemed comfortable with Roberta's responses. Speaking to the interrogator through the headset, the Senior Technician behind the one-way mirror reminded the interrogator to get clarification on the one question.

"Roberta, we need some clarity on one question. Tell me in detail how these two people assisted you." With this type of question, although still hooked up to the polygraph monitor, the answers would not be evaluated based on her physical response. They just needed some clarity.

"What do you mean?" she asked.

"Your response spiked so we're wondering if you're missing something?"

Glancing away, Roberta thought about the question. With a quick nod, she seemed to understand what happened.

"The German contacts took my weapon away. Only after we were inside the room, did they return it to me." She then added, "the man that handed it back said there was only one bullet in the chamber. I guess they didn't want to risk me shooting others in the room.

"I see. Okay, let me ask a few more questions." Turning his attention back to the instruments, he continued.

"Other than holding the body, and giving you back your pistol, did you receive any other assistance eliminating the target?"

"No."

Everyone, including Roberta watched the read out. It remained flat without any movements. From what the Agency could tell, Roberta was being honest. After the Senior Technician received the okay from Director Valdez to conclude the exam, he spoke through the intercom.

"That's good. Thank you, Roberta."

Hearing the voice come through the overhead speakers, Roberta exhaled a sigh of relief; glad that this experience was over. The technician helped remove the electrodes and the spring coil around her chest. Director Valdez continued watching through the one-way mirror. Without looking away from the activity inside the examination room, Nena spoke to the technicians inside the hidden room.

"Have we tested the blood and run the prints?"

"Yes ma'am. It's a perfect match. 100 percent certainty. We cross-referenced them with her personnel records and latest medical exam."

"No doubts?"

"No doubts."

"Thank you, gentlemen. When Roberta's ready, please escort her back to the conference room," instructed Nena before she walked out of the surveillance room. Waiting outside were her four-man security detail. They escorted her through the Berlin Agency building. The extra security requirement was still in place. As she followed her two guards through the hallways, the other two trailed behind. The Berlin personnel made sure to stay clear and gave them a wide path, so the entourage was unobstructed as they walked to the secure conference room.

Accustomed to this type of constant security, Nena found her thoughts drifting. She felt a sense of disgust that their Agency occupations required loyal personnel such as Roberta to be placed under so much scrutiny because of the actions of another relative, that even after years of loyal service, was still required to prove their trust by terminating a blood relative. With a shake of her head, Nena followed behind her security detail. The only justification for such devotion was for love of country.

Director Valdez entered the conference room and waited for Roberta. She sat in an overstuffed leather chair with her guards waiting outside the door.

* * * * *

Curt walked through the lobby. He paused outside the cafeteria looking at the gift shop contemplating whether to buy flowers. Feeling the stares from the cashier, Curt decided to go straight up instead. After finding the elevator empty, he pressed the button and listened to the electronic tone echo inside the otherwise empty car as it announced the arrival of another floor. It was one of the first times since arriving in Europe that he felt relaxed. His grandfather was certain that the Americans gave up their search for him, believing he died.

As the elevator doors opened, Curt walked past the empty receptionist area. Unlike an American hospital, there were only a few nurses on duty. Here, the doctors performed many of the mundane procedures. Curt walked down the hallway, peeked inside the open door, then glanced up and down the corridor before stepping inside.

*　　*　　*　　*　　*

Detective Peter Katzmark's European vacation was almost over. He spent most of his time visiting relatives, traveling by train crisscrossing the continent. He got reacquainted and met new relatives, people he did not know existed. He was so distracted that he did not think about being an ex-homicide detective. Retirement was everything he had imagined and then some. His final European outing was a visit to the resting place for many of his family members.

Katzmark was enjoying a croissant and black American style coffee at the hotel restaurant's first floor outdoor patio. He opened the English version of Germany's premiere newspaper *The Spiegel* when the siren from a passing ambulance got his attention. As the peculiar sounding siren with its flashing lights passed, Peter thought back to his visit to the cemetery.

Katzmark exited the museum. This cemetery was once Berlin's central concentration camp. As he walked toward the cemetery, something caught his attention. Habits of a detective are hard to change. Seeing an ambulance picking up someone from a cemetery, as opposed to delivering a corpse, seemed out of place. Curious, Peter strolled up to a parked ambulance. The back doors were open with the engine still running. Raising up on his tiptoes, he was surprised to see the keys in the ignition. The ambulance was empty.

The sound of crunching gravel caught his attention. Turning toward the sound, Katzmark watched two EMT's pushing a gurney. As they approached, Peter stood back to give them room. Seeing Peter, they assumed he worked with Van Aelst acting as a look out. Not understanding German, Katzmark did not realize that they were saying, "We're fine. We've got it from here."

The EMT's maneuvered the gurney carrying an unconscious woman, with an IV bag laying across the white sheet covering her body. As the two men approached the back open ambulance doors, they rammed the gurney against the bumper and depressed a lever. The gurney started to collapse and fold into an upright position. The sudden jolt seemed to awaken the woman. Katzmark craned his head and watched the woman open her eyes. The EMT's paused, adjusted the gurney, then loaded her inside. All the while, Peter stood by watching everything. He was only a few feet away and watched the woman blink as if waking up. Peter watched the EMT's close the back door and drive away. Not thinking anything more, Katzmark walked back across the gravel road to catch up with his waiting relatives.

As the sound of the peculiar siren faded away, Katzmark scanned the newspaper. He flipped through several pages, and a photograph of an American woman caught his attention. As he glanced between the article and the grainy picture, he thought he recognized her face. Given his lengthy vacation and now being adjusted to his retirement he almost did not recognize the sensation.

Katzmark continued reading the article: *An American tourist visiting Germany to attend the Solheim Cup, was shot, and killed. The victim was identified as Ms. Diane Klein.* The article speculated that a *gun man was preying on wealthy tourists and targeted other vulnerable people. Ms. Klein was apprehended traveling alone and sustained a single fatal gunshot. Her jewelry and wallet were taken, while her passport and purse were later found in a nearby garbage can. No suspects have been identified.*

Turning his attention from the article, Katzmark leaned forward and studied the four by six -inch grainy portrait photo. After several moments, ex-detective Katzmark raised his head and stared down the empty boulevard.

* * * * *

Roberta was escorted from the polygraph exam to one of many secure conference rooms. As she approached the area, she noticed two very large men. Dressed in black fatigues and donning matching black caps, with full body armor and 9mm *Barretta* pistols at the hip, the men glared down the hallway guaranteeing all those foolish enough to approach would receive a thorough shakedown. Unintimidated, Roberta marched up to the doorway and raised her arms above her head without waiting for instructions. With stern expressions, they patted her down and scanned her front and back side for good measure. Once cleared of any listening or recording devices, the senior guard opened the door.

As Roberta entered the large room, she was surprised expecting to find a woman, presumably Director Nena Valdez, but not the two other men: one on each side. There was only one available chair, and it was positioned in front of the large oversized wooden table. Against the back wall were two more guards resembling the two outside. With a deep sigh of frustration, Roberta took her seat. How quickly things had changed.

"Roberta, it's a pleasure to meet you. I've heard a lot of good things," started Director Valdez. "As I'm sure you've deduced, I'm Director Valdez. This is Lt. Benjamin and Lt. Elliott. Neither of these men have been briefed on the 'in-depth' background concerning your mission. The agency has asked a lot from you Roberta."

Uncertain how to respond, Roberta replied, "Thank you ma'am."

"Given what you've just gone through, I wanted you to know that, although things may feel unfair at times, and you may feel like your career is going to be placed under a bigger microscope than it should, I want you to understand that the right people know what happened. They know the whole story." With an intense expression, Nena added, "I promise you."

Nena knew Roberta was exhausted. She was on the go since leaving Paris. Not wanting to prolong the scrutiny, Nena continued.

"You've been completely exonerated. Regardless of your target's shortcomings, nothing will be held against you nor stifle your career."

Empathizing with Roberta's situation, Nena wanted her to get back into the game, to fulfill her potential. She was an asset whose confidence was rocked and needed some time to get her head on straight.

"Thank you, Director. I appreciate it." Roberta stood to leave and appreciated the gesture. Although her mission was sure to remain classified, including the other two agents in on this face-to-face meeting was done for her benefit, sending a disguised message, a show of support. Their presence was unnecessary. They could have easily been left out. Nonetheless, their presence would be documented witnesses to what was said. Witnesses subject to polygraph exams if required.

Unprepared for what followed, Roberta watched lieutenants Benjamin and Elliott stand and extend their right hands. As she exchanged firm handshakes, she suppressed her emotions and tried to project a confident expression. She was heading back to Paris, followed by a mandatory two-week vacation. Her mission was coming to an end, and it was starting to sink in.

After Agent Finchum exited the conference room, Director Valdez shook her head in disbelief. *"That's one hell of a thing to be asked to do,"* she thought.

"Back home boss?" asked Moon Dog.

"Not quite, Lt. Elliott. I've got one final off-site meeting remaining," explained Nena. Seeing Lt. Benjamin's expression, she knew he was eager to get back into the game. His excursion to the Mediterranean Sea was not what he had expected. The good news was he could now fly back to Korea. With his eye-orbit fracture healed, there was no medical reason to avoid the air pressure changes from flying.

Turning her attention to Moon Dog, "Lt. Elliott, did you get any valuable face time with the UCAV's (Unmanned Combat Air Vehicles) on your assignment on the *USS George HW Bush?*" asked Nena.

"I did. We started as soon as we sailed from Korea. I shared my experiences and even got enough SIM time to be trusted with a few live take-offs and landings with those *X-47B* drones," smiled Moon Dog.

"Glad to hear," offered Nena. "We leave tomorrow. We'll all fly together on our *Gulfstream.* Wheels up at 0700 so don't be late."

*   *   *   *   *

Curt sat next to the hospital bed and reflected on how much his life had changed. His injuries were healed, and the skin-graphs were done. He was even getting used to seeing his new reflection in the bathroom mirror. Thankfully, his facial cosmetic surgery was done concurrently with other procedures. Combining them was the only fortunate outcome of his impromptu mission inside a clandestine organization.

Over the last three years, he had contemplated everything and blamed his intellectual curiosity. It was a perfect storm, possessing the financial means to devote so much time and effort to infiltrate the Agency. Without both the time and means, none of it could have become reality.

The sound of a nurse's footsteps padded by as she hurried to check on another patient. Curt watched the nurse pass by the open doorway. With a deep sigh, he stared at the sleeping patient lying on the bed transfixed by the sheet rising and falling in perfect unison with the sound of the patient's breathing. Curt wondered how much longer before she would awake.

*   *   *   *   *

Director Valdez was mesmerized. She stared through the tinted windows from the bullet-proof SUV's back seat. With two of her security-detail in the front seat, one driving and one riding shot-gun, she sat squished in the center row between two other guards. She felt safe. In real time, Gibby and Carla Jo watched from an Agency Surveillance satellite, and monitored the vehicle.

Having been assigned to the Demilitarized Zone between North and South Korea, Nena was surprised to see what she saw. She would have never guessed there were other areas of the globe that looked like Korea. This swath of East Berlin was abandoned a long time ago. It reminded her of a post-apocalyptic movie scene. They drove over roads long since covered by dirt and cut through sections overgrown with beech trees. The canopy of vegetation created an impenetrable blanket of darkness. She felt like she was in a rain forest as opposed to just outside modern-day Berlin.

As they passed a rusted rollercoaster and Ferris wheel with oversized dilapidated animal-themed boats scattered about, an area that used to carry vacationing Berliners inside the *Spreepark Amusement Park*, Nena shook her head in disbelief.

She drummed her fingers across a thin manila folder, unaware of her anxiety. The folder contained what little information the Agency had on Curt Anderson's grandfather-Cornelius Van Aelst. Aside from a few old photographs and basic background information extracted from surviving World War II personnel records, the Agency knew very little. Based on his ability to assist his grandson, the Agency decided it was time to pay this Van Aelst character a formal face-to-face visit.

The fact that Curt Anderson was unable to survive his escape and complete a family reunion to spend the remainder of his life with Van Aelst, was of no consequence. The Agency recognized the importance of demonstrating their global superiority. They needed to keep this renegade agent in check. They needed to demonstrate their ability to reach out anywhere around the globe. Nothing less was expected from a super-power.

The SUV sped along until they escaped from the overhead forest canopy. The gloomy grey images of Berlin's only active concentration camp and functioning cemetery loomed on the horizon. They passed a large building that was converted into an historical museum of some sorts. Nena read the large metal archway with the thick block letters announcing the location-SACHSENHAUSEN. If Van Aelst had not assisted Roberta to deliver Diane Klein, Director Valdez would never have agreed to such a meeting. Despite the Agency's assumed superior technology, the Agency was unable to locate Diane. Given the outcome of that mission, Van Aelst proved his loyalty and demonstrated his relevance. Based on his present-day connections and ability to still, even at his age and with limited resources, pull the right strings, and make difficult things happen, he had proved his worth. Van Aelst was a contact worth nurturing. In this business, one never knows when having such an ally, could come in handy. However, after traveling through the abandoned remote location, Nena now questioned the wisdom of coming here.

To bolster her confidence, she reminded herself that using one of their satellites she was being watched from above, monitored by her two most trusted contractors. For added protection, her pilot Mr. Davies was flying inside a borrowed F-35, one of Berlin's teasers from *Lockheed Martin*. It was donated to the Germans in hopes of receiving the contract to replace their aging *Tornado* fighter jets. With the local air authorities aware of Mr. Davies' "open" priority one flight plan, he was granted an unfettered airspace above that section of abandoned Berlin.

With no desire to hide his presence, Mr. Davies dropped down from above and made a low-level fly-by skimming over the cemetery. The jet's air-disturbance caused the SUV's frame to vibrate. Nena smiled and looked skyward. With a deafening roar, Mr. Davies flew by cutting across the horizon. The jet wash sent a shockwave that engulfed the area.

The SUV pulled into a gravel parking area where they saw a thin elderly gentleman. He was wearing a dark charcoal suit, white shirt, and black silk tie. He looked like the stereotypical old-school secret-agent even down to the dark sunglasses. Unfazed, he waited by a faded yellow cab. The SUV parked a good distance away allowing all four guards to exit the SUV and survey the area before disbursing east, west, north, and south, strategically surrounding Nena. Watching from above, Gibby and Carla Jo radioed down speaking through a shared communication link. The surrounding area was clear. Finally, Director Valdez stepped out of the vehicle.

On cue, Mr. Davies flew by at a slow rumbling velocity reminding Van Aelst and his band of unknown associates of his presence. Nena felt safer knowing that the Germans, an ally, were aware of this meeting with Van Aelst. It seemed less likely that a double-cross was in the works. Regardless, the Agency tried not to take even these informal meetings for granted. The recent injury to Director Gamboa was a recent reminder of such short-sighted considerations. Van Aelst waited for Director Valdez to approach close enough before breaking the silence.

"Director, you should have your pilot's maintenance team check their fuel mixture. The exhaust seems a bit too rich," shouted Van Aelst over the jet engine noise. His voice echoed across the gravel parking lot and bounced about between the brick buildings.

Hearing his remarks, the senior guard waved off Mr. Davies. Their point was made leaving no doubt about the lethal force present. It was not a mere threat. At the sign of any danger, it was a promise of immediate and over whelming retaliation.

Nena continued her approach. She stepped up to Van Aelst and removed her sunglasses before extending her right hand. As they exchanged firm handshakes, Van Aelst returned the gesture and removed his sunglasses. The satellite above was angled to take close-up photos. By the time Nena released Van Aelst's hand, images were being processed through their most sophisticated facial recognition program available. Using multiple computers, Agent Walters and Supervisor Chapin watched the meeting through a live secure satellite feed. Van Aelst's images were churning through the Agency computers. Everyone waited for any hits.

"Mr. Van Aelst, we finally meet. I must say, you and your team gave us a run for our money. We had our work cut out for us tracking your ambulance transport through the Lincoln Tunnel. Ingenious really."

Herr Van Aelst flashed a slight smile. From his contacts, he knew that the Americans relied on other means to pick up his trail. He expected as much and anticipated the Americans would be unwilling to show their hand by admitting any shortcomings. Van Aelst never let on what he knew.

"How could we expect to deceive the Americans?" he countered. "Yet, we gave our best effort, even in a losing effort. It's our nature," shrugged Van Aelst.

Nena studied Van Aelst. His piercing blue eyes and intelligent wit was disarming. She began questioning the accuracy of what they knew about him. She found it difficult to believe that he was as old as they suspected. Aside from his hair color and a few facial wrinkles, he looked to be in his late sixties or early seventies. She was taken aback.

"Given your grandson entered one of our secure locations, and removed sensitive documents, we needed to make certain of his and your intentions," explained Nena.

"Director, this new generation, with their non-stop access to all forms of information, the Internet, the exploitation of social media, your YouTube...today's youth have distorted their personal importance within this world. Their perceived rights and subsequent ignorant views of the world cloud their judgement.

"As difficult as it might be to believe, my grandson's actions were in no way connected with my loose knit retirees nor the German intelligence. As I'm certain you know, for all my efforts, my poor misguided grandson did not survive his journey. At least not arriving in the condition we had hoped. He was fortunate to have been able to survive most of the trip. My only consolation was to see him one last time, alive, before he passed. He's now buried next to his biological mother, my daughter.

Van Aelst paused and stared across the gravel road toward his family crypt. "If you'd like, I could take you inside to view his resting place and the documents proving what I've said is true. But I'm guessing that would be a waste of time. You've undoubtedly had your people verify all this. Otherwise, we would not be having this conversation."

"In all honesty, Mr. Van Aelst, we weren't certain how to proceed. But given your cooperation and assistance resolving the 'other' matter, we've decided to look the other way. Of course, such a dismissal is contingent upon none of those sensitive documents ever seeing the light of day," added Nena.

"Director, if my grandson's motivations involved releasing your internal knock-list to your news media, he would have done so years ago. As you know, not a single piece of evidence pertaining to any of those U.S. citizens has ever surfaced. At least, not in connection with being murdered by its own government. Rather, some otherwise mysterious accidental or natural death was blamed."

Nena gazed at Van Aelst. The entire conversation was being recorded. Inside her jacket, a small device captured everything, audio, and video in high definition. Later, it would be analyzed by her colleagues. After a pause, Van Aelst added, "He is family. What could I do? He paid the ultimate price for his immature curiosity and actions."

With a nod, Director Valdez extended her hand.

"It's been a pleasure Mr. Van Aelst."

"Likewise, Nena, is it? And if I or any of my retiree comrades could be of any future assistance, I encourage you to reach out and contact me. I appreciate the leniency with which you and your government are handling this matter," offered Van Aelst. "We're allies now, on the same side, correct?"

Certain that she had conveyed the message that the Agency was aware of his involvement in the soon to be re-closed Curt Anderson file, destined to be stashed away inside Director Gamboa's Agency safe, Nena felt it was time to conclude their meeting.

"Until we meet again, Mr. Van Aelst."

"Auf weidersehen (good bye)," replied Herr Van Aelst.

Nena's security guards escorted her to the awaiting SUV. She took one final glance through the dark tinted windows at Van Aelst. He remained standing tall, with a confident tight-lipped smile. She almost expected him to wave as they pulled away. He did not.

With the meeting over, Mr. Davies descended to escort the SUV back to the main paved road leading back to the populated well-used streets and boulevards inside modern Berlin. As soon as they reached the first smooth paved roadway, a call came through on Nena's encrypted cell phone.

"Valdez," Nena announced to the caller.

"Boss, it's Moon Dog."

"Yes, Lt. Elliott."

"We have a flash warning from Camp Bonifas."

"What is it?" she inquired.

"Somebody is trying to hack into one of our ICBM's," explained Moon Dog.

"Which ones?"

"From Japan."

"Any idea where the intrusion is originating?"

"Yes. China."

"I see," replied the Director. "We'll meet you at the jet."

"Roger that Boss. Your ETA?"

"Twenty minutes."

"Copy that. Out."

As Nena redirected her driver to the airstrip, she glanced at her watch. With a shake of her head, she thought to herself, "*things move quick at the Agency.*"

Just before Gibby was about to terminate the satellite transmission, he and Carla Jo watched the faded yellow cab pull away leaving Van Aelst standing alone in the cemetery. With the satellite image still magnified, they were caught off-guard when Van Aelst raised his hand into the air and stared back as if he were peering directly into the satellite camera. With a defiant thrust upward, Van Aelst extended his middle finger. For good measure, he added a firm shake of his fist accompanied with a wide toothed grin.

"What the hell," whispered Gibby while Carla Jo suppressed her laughter. "The old bastard," he added.

Gibby shook his head having already started to terminate the satellite connection. As the screen turned to static, Gibby's phone rang. Recognizing the number, he knew it was Agent Walters calling.

"What's up Walters?" answered Gibby.

"We got a hit on Van Aelst."

"What do you mean?"

"The facial recognition program has a 99.9 percent match. It's saying Van Aelst is 'The Lone Wolf,'" she explained.

"The Lone Wolf...who the hell is that?" asked Gibby.

"A cold war agent. He was quite active. After the Berlin wall came down, we lost track of the guy."

"Was he a player in the day?"

"Big time!" replied Walters.

Out of curiosity, Gibby and Carla Jo rebooted the satellite program. The transmission was down for only a few minutes. When it began transmitting new live images over the same location, they could only see the departing taxi cab almost out of the camera's view. They watched it bounce down the dirt covered roadway. To their surprise, they found no trace of Van Aelst. Without speaking, Gibby and Carla Jo mentally calculated the distance from the gravel road to the nearest building. There was not enough time for him to have walked that distance. He would have had to make a full out sprint. Even for a youthful twenty-year-old, it was unlikely that he could have made it there without them seeing.

They redirected the satellite angle and scanned the entire area. *"Where did he go?"* they thought.

* * * * *

Curt was surprised to see his grandfather walk through the open hospital room doorway. He seemed to be in an extremely good mood. With a wide smile, even his eyes seemed bluer than normal.

"How's she doing?" asked Herr Van Aelst.

"She's been sleeping most of the day. She just started mumbling, complaining that her arm hurt. Which was a little surprising given the amount of surgery she's had," replied Curt. "She still hasn't recovered from the affects from the anesthesia."

The sound of their conversation disturbed her from her sleep. The medication from the reconstructive facial surgery; nose job, forehead lift, neck, and cheek augmentation was wearing off. Once healed, she would go through more surgeries to further enhance

513

her appearance. With a new hairstyle, contact lenses and surgeries to alter her finger print patterns, she would become unrecognizable. Peering through the gauze covering her face, Diane cracked a timid confused smile.

As she rubbed the crook of her elbow, Diane mumbled, "What happened? The last thing I remember is a sharp pain in my neck."

Van Aelst's expression softened as he flashed a heartfelt smile. He reached out and held her hand. He wondered if he would ever tell her the truth. For now, he was convinced that the less she knew the better.

"I owe you an apology. Due to the time constraints, and the fact that your Agency was actively searching for you, there wasn't enough time to consult you about my plan. To be honest, I was afraid you would be against the plastic surgery to alter your appearance. But rest assured, the best plastic surgeon in Germany was flown in. I've been promised you'll look decades younger...not to imply that you look old. you don't," back tracked Van Aelst as he explained everything.

Staring down at the crook in her elbow, a deep red bruise stood out in contrast to her otherwise pale skin color. There was a solid straight-line shaped bruise across the top section of her arm above her triceps area.

"The needle must have penetrated too deep during your surgery," observed Herr Van Aelst. He hoped that this explanation would suffice. When in fact, he was certain that the awkward angle her arm was pulled while tucked underneath hidden by the oversized examination table was the real cause of her discomfort and unusual bruise markings. It was all necessary to make sure her body was hidden under the woman who volunteered for this mission. The one diagnosed with an inoperable brain tumor. She had suffered long enough, to the point that she welcomed being put out of her misery. Having the knowledge that her surviving family members would receive financial assistance for this sacrifice, made her decision to volunteer that much easier.

Van Aelst continued examining Diane. He was no longer concerned that Roberta suspected something. He was certain that all the orchestrated distractions were perfectly timed: the varying lighting, bruising of her sternum, and the overwhelming of her senses all while being surrounded by guns. The cumulative effect did the trick. His biggest concern was when Martin helped stabilize Diane's arm allowing Roberta to extract the blood and take her fingerprints. Their physical positioning prevented Roberta from noticing Diane's arm protruding out at an odd angle. But everything went as planned. Herr Van Aelst was certain that, other than the ambulance drivers, no one else had any idea what happened.

The anesthesia was wearing off. Diane looked up into Curt's face. He wanted to wait by her side. The tables were turned. Three years ago, she was the one waiting next to his bed.

Feeling the effect from the medication surge through her veins, Diane closed her eyes and drifted off to sleep contemplating her new future. Decades prior, in another lifetime, she was offered a chance to become a deep-cover-operative. For personal reasons, she turned it down. This time, the decision was made for her. Diane could only imagine what reflection she would see, later, in the bathroom mirror.

THE END

Afterword

Originally, "Sentinel Event" was supposed to be a stand-alone sequel to "Rule One Twenty". However, after finishing my third book "Tunnels" I decided to incorporate many of these same characters going forward and expand their adventures. As a result, this book became a cross-over. Readers can still enjoy each book on its own. My goal was to carry forward the adventure of the main characters introduced in "Tunnels" (Gibby, Moon Dog, Kyle, Nena, X.O. Newland, Mr. Davies, Angelie, and Carla Jo). Extending their stories enhances the entertainment factor and provides a deeper and more fulfilling reading experience. In future books, I wanted to avoid having to constantly introduce a stream of new characters who will be doing the same investigations and dealing with similar things that any global espionage organization requires.

With this goal in mind, fans of the Agency members stationed along Korea's DMZ at Camp Bonifas may now continue the journey in the next three books: "Gamers", "Mission Golden Lily" and "Comrade Down". In future books, we will cross paths with Van Aelst and his group of retirees; Marie Sinor and her trainee agents; Director Gamboa's team; as well as Curt, Diane, and Roberta.

"Until we meet again! Sincerely, I thank you for your continued support." - *E.A. Padilla*